# GEAR HEART

## FREEDOM IS WORTH THE RISK

MICHELLE R YOUNG

# YOUR EXCLUSIVE ART AND STORIES ARE WAITING!

*Gear Heart* received so much praise, there is no way the story could stop there!

New secrets and stories will be available here! Click the link to receive exclusive content such as the official art of the characters, maps, the cities' perspectives and Aspen's inventions. And that's just the beginning!

Click the link for exclusive content or scan the QR code.

www.mypureart.com

# DEDICATION

*Dedicated to my great great great grandfather Lovick Pierce the VI who ministered to slaves on the plantations before, and during the civil war, saving hundreds.*

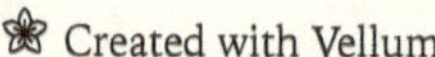 Created with Vellum

# TABLE OF CONTENTS:

CURRLION ENGLAND, 1848

"Hurry up!" I yell at the workers through the communication pipe. *Those slugs are more trouble than they are worth. If they mess up another part of the machine, I swear I'll send them all to bloody Hell. If the plague hadn't wiped out so many of the plebs, we might actually have more men with functioning brains to take care of such a sensitive machine.*

"It's ready, Boss," one of the grease-stained workers calls back into the copper pipe. I look through the glass barrier where the pipe connects, allowing me to talk to the workers safely. I see that the men are signaling me with thumbs up whilst more are running to the makeshift shield barriers to protect themselves.

"All right, boys, make yourselves scarce. I'm turning it on in ten," I call over the projection pipe that runs with the catwalk above the machine and along the sides of the walls. The engineers hastily get behind their own barriers, each a hundred feet away from the massive machine in the centre of the old brick building. The sooner we get this multidimensional machine working, the sooner we can get out of this drafty old warehouse. As if on cue, a steamship calls out into the cold night, announcing its arrival into the harbour. *Let's let this be our chance at a new breakthrough tonight as well.* I flip the ignition switch to full power and pull the levers down individually to start the chemical pumps.

I clench my teeth so tightly my jaw begins to tremble. *Our calculations can't be wrong this time; I refuse to admit defeat.* Holding my breath, I watch as the machine's engines and glass tubes filled with fizzing chemicals, gradually come to life. The engine has barely begun to project its rays through the lens when something catches my eye: there is a small shimmering object between the light beam's angle of projection and the warehouse wall. One of the workers must have noticed the glinting obstruction because they began to run full speed towards the portal machine. Despite the other workers calling out for him and flailing their arms, he doesn't pause for a moment or turn to the nearest protection barrier.

I squint my eyes and see that it's Mr Jay Lane. *That idiot! He was always showing off the new engagement ring for his girl to everyone. He must have been bragging again to one of the workers and left it on the machine whilst he was greasing it.* I grip the lever to turn off the chemical pumps, but it won't budge. *I can't turn off the ignition switch without turning off the chemical pumps first—if I do, it could cause an explosive reverse reaction.*

Jay starts reaching for the ring; he's too close to the machine now to turn back in time to be safe from the blast that's coming. I have to turn the machine off right now or he could be killed. I rush back to the controls, but the bolts are too rusty and won't budge either.

Running to the projection pipe, I yell, "Get out of—"

Too late. The machine emits a concussive blast of energy waves that reverberate throughout the entire building. The sudden blast sends Jay rocketing through the air, with his limbs flailing, until he lands on the concrete ground motionless, five metres from where he was standing by the machine just seconds earlier. Even my glass barrier was shattered from the blast; it now resembled frost flowers on a window in winter. A bright flash across my shattered barrier reverts my attention to its source, the portal generator. Something peculiar is definitely happening not only to the machine itself, but also to its projection on the wall. An image is beginning to form: the foggy view of a strangely coloured landscape of multicoloured trees with deep purple- and blue-hued leaves. It appears that our view is from the top of a rocky hill with copper red stone piling down an embankment. There are other forms down there though; they appear to be huts of some kind—like the natives in the tropics would build.

*Something doesn't seem right though. Some of the forms are moving.* Just as I realise that this isn't a plain picture projection, a small horned bird-like creature with an ornate fanned tail flies right through the fuzzy image before it jolts and flies straight back from whence it came. I realise then that this is a real gateway to another place.

*I've never witnessed a creature like that before. What if we've actually created a window to another dimension? What wonders await us further?* I think as I scramble around the control desk drawers for my workbook or something to write down the details. I look back at the portal every few seconds as I begin to write, eagerly waiting for what might come next from the window. Time ticks on, and a small form comes into view, looking back at us just beyond the veil. From the expression on its face, it appears to be wondering what's going on. This creature is nothing human, though it walks like one, with its tall skinny body covered in purple fur along with a long curved tail. It resembles an otter in body and face; however, its human size, tail, and horns are quite taboo in appearance.

The foggy blur in the projection is starting to diminish slightly, allowing me to see more creatures. Some are pulling stone-filled wheelbarrows, others are building stone huts, and still more are milling around or cutting down trees. There's a large variety of them in all shapes and sizes of different forms of animals, and they are all strong and working hard under what appears to be a tropical climate. I feel my ambition rising as I furiously note every detail down to the fact that we just found a gold mine.

However, the feeling doesn't last long; the clarity of the image is beginning to blur again at an alarming rate. *Maybe it needs more power?* I ponder just before a large zap emits from the machine as its entire frame begins to shake convulsively. It's giving off bursts of energy again in great arrays all over the engine in a way that makes the portal look like a lace parasol opening up again and again.

"What's wrong? It was finally starting to work," I mumble to myself. I take a pair of binoculars from the desk and peer closely at the machine.

The engagement ring is gone, but there are gleaming specks of glitter in the air around the projection lens. *This does not look good.* I pull with all my might on the jammed levers. They begin to moan and creak, but they barely move. The doors to my control room blast open as three workers rush through the door towards me.

"Boss, turn the machine off!"

"Gosh, Charlie, I never thought of that!" I bellow back to

the daft cow. "Get your arses over here and help me with this before the machine explodes!" I yell as the men rush over, and together we finally pull the three stubborn levers down, turning the machine's engines off. We don't dare breathe whilst we wait to hear for the clicks of the gears letting us know the machine is powering down. *Click, click, click.* I release a relieved exhale as I wipe my brow and try to relay all that just occurred within the past few minutes.

I think back to what we did differently this time. Same time frame, same amount of fuel... *The ring, maybe? Could that little jewel really have made the machine work? There must be something about the elements in the gold, diamond, or whatever stone it was that allowed the machine to project a picture of another place or even another dimension.* I turn to my open journal and flip the pages frantically to find a clean space. Once I do, I scribble down my theories and notes of gems combined with the properties and chemicals in the machine.

The key component missing to open the portal wasn't the multi-coloured lenses like we've been using, but rather gemstones or gold. We will have to put different gemstones and precious metals to the test, which is going to put us in *so* much debt. However, if it worked once it'll work again, I'll make sure of that. More of those gems will open up the portal again, and then it's easy pickings for free labour. And Lord knows, we need as many helping hands today as possible. If we strike this gold mine, we will be rich in more ways than one! I turn away from the shattered glass and see the men still standing before me with gobstruck expressions.

"Well, don't just stand there, get to work and collect Mr Lane off the floor! We've got work to do if we are to get that portal to show up again," I order.

With that, they scurry out of the control room to pick up

the unconscious fool on the ground. I take my pipe and inhale a long drag before expelling the smoke. Through the thick grey clouds I can see all the new possibilities: the money and royalties, notoriety of the queen and Parliament's approval, the discoveries this will bring, and new beginnings for our families. What a gold mine I've found.

# CURRLION TRAIN STATION, ENGLAND, 1886

## ASPEN

Smoke puffs out of the train's engine at the screeching sound of the brakes when the train slowly came to a halt. It's still raining it seems, and the late afternoon sun peeking behind the clouds is beginning to set, falling below the tall white mountain in the distance. Rays of yellow and orange light illuminate the open train station, allowing every particle of soot and water droplets to be seen in the final rays of afternoon glow.

People in their latest fur coats and gear-bezeled hats mill about, going to this platform and that with open umbrellas. One lady just lost her new feather chapeau as her aircraft ascended from the ground with a sudden jolt and large gust of wind. As she reaches out to grab it, it is already back on the platform and there is no returning to the station for a measly hat after a train has taken flight, despite her cries.

I pray that Lori and I will enjoy ourselves and have more than enough chances to leave our mark in this new city for its special inhabitants. *It has to work this time; we are running out of family that will house us.* I think as I glance over in Lori's seat. She's still asleep. I reach over and jostle Lori, who would much rather continue to doze off on the window pane whilst she fogged up the glass. As she slowly stretches and wakes up, I begin to take down our luggage from the overhead compartments. In a few moments she helps me take them out of our car and head towards the train's exit steps. I have a much easier time going down in my favourite split skirts than Lori does in her dress; poor thing would have fallen face first if one of the ticket masters hadn't caught her.

"Oh, thank you. Such a gentleman," Lori purrs, expressing her gratitude to the young ticketmaster with her best blushing face whilst her blonde hair shines like the dying sun on the horizon. The young man begins to stammer as he helps her down the stairs and hands us the rest of the luggage.

I swear she loves toying with men's hearts too much. I would have rolled my eyes if my heart was not so heavy after the latest forceful goodbye from our cousins still fresh on my mind. However, the more I look out to the city beyond the station, I find the sour memories beginning to quickly fade. *Currlion is said to be one of the most beautiful and innovative cities in the whole British Empire, after all,* I muse as I catch a glimpse at a man coming out of a shop with a tophat that has a clock on the centre. Just as the hour hand hits five o'clock a cuckoo bird shoots out from a pocket above the clock. I watch in awe before bumping into a lady with a bionic toy monkey on her shoulder.

"Pardon me, m'lady," I apologize before walking on.

I look on beyond the platform to the long bustling street

painted in shades of grey and blue yet illuminated by warm street lamps just now being lit. A bright shock of mauve catches my vision in time to see a purple-feathered birdlike bi-dimensional slave- or *dimie* as everyone has been calling them as of last year-carrying luggage to a horse buggy. The sight sucks all the excitement out of me as his mistress owner scolds him for not opening her door fast enough. It reminds me why we convinced our cousins to send us here in the first place. We will just have to do our best at our job as long as we are still welcome in our new home. I'm not sure if I should even call it that yet to be honest though.

I continue to ponder as we walk towards the departure gate through the thick crowd. What with us leaving – well *escorted forcefully out of* – the last three homes of our family that still reside in England. Yes, I suppose it is far too early to call this place home yet, but perhaps we can soon. Besides Lori and our machine, the one thing I must never lose is hope.

I remember the look on Lori's face as we boarded the train in Kingstown seven hours ago. She was actually quite cheerful, and I admit to myself that I was too. We both have had enough of Uncle Arthur's stories about how he would lay out strategies of war with his fellow generals. However, I will miss the fencing lessons that he implored us to practice in. It was quite wonderful to send dopey Cousin James on his bum during duels more than once.

I recall how even Lori enjoyed beating our cousin in fencing every now and then, though she's made it clear that she much preferred learning poker from Uncle Arthur instead. If only Cousin James didn't have such a tight hold over his old father and his household, maybe we could have stayed and would still be under our uncle's protection.

We walk to the end of the railcar and wait in a line to step onto the platform. Just as we are nearing it, Lori's bustle gets covered from her billowing slitted coat as a gust of steam shoots out before us. I help adjust her skirts between the slits in the back of her coat before we take a look about the station. A flying express air train just landed across from us as the cause for the sudden draft before letting off the few passengers it holds. I couldn't imagine many people wanting to try out such a new innovation that deals with air travel, the whole idea seems terrifying, and yet strangely exciting.

Trying to watch our step whilst carrying our long trunk together proves to be a difficult task – now if we can just make it to the arrival gate without tripping or bumping into five more people. We looked all about, trying to spot the familiar face of Mr Myrack Senior and his son, but after forty-five minutes of standing, pacing, and sitting around the arrival gate, Lori seems to have grown agitated.

"They know we were coming today, right?" she questions worriedly.

"Mr Myrack told us that this was the best day to come, and he was always a punctual person; perhaps there was traffic causing their delay," I reply.

Just then, a man with grey hair poking out of a bowler hat in a black suit, holding a sign, came into view on the platform.

"Look! That man over there – our names are on his sign," I exclaim.

Lori whips around and sees the sign that says: *Miss Aspen and Miss Lori Wolfe.*

"Let's gather our things, Lori, there's no time to waste," I say, standing up.

"Why must you always be in a rush?"

"Why must you always question my actions?"

"I don't question all of them," Lori huffs.

"No, just most of them," I bite back with a teasing tone. We begin waddling towards the old man, with our heavy luggage, through the milling people. The man sees us coming his way, tipping his hat to us as he approaches. With his hat off I recognise him from when we were here over twelve years ago. Once we meet in the middle of the mosh pit of passersby, the man politely asks, "Would you happen to be the Wolfe sisters?"

"Why yes, we are. I'm Lori, and this is my older sister Aspen, but who might you be?" Lori replies.

"Oh, forgive me. My name is Charles. I'm the Myrack's family chauffeur and grounds keeper. Today, I am to drive you to the Myrack estate; if I may take your luggage we can head to the motorcar," he says with a smile.

Lori's amber eyes are full of curiosity about our caretaker, and she begins to ask Charles all sorts of questions about him and the Myracks. I, on the other hand, am currently having trouble passing bags to Charles whilst a few brown locks begin falling out of my bun and into my eyes. I'd much rather lay my eyes on the new steam-powered engine of the motor car we are approaching, than rushing about in the drizzling rain whilst dodging passing horse carriages. Once we have carefully secured all of our luggage in the trunk, we are seated in the car and ready to go. As I attempt to repin my hair, Lori, inquisitive again about seeing the Myracks, asks, "Weren't Mr Myrack and his son supposed to meet us at the station in person?"

"Young Mr Myrack... is in the stages of mourning for the death of his father, Mr Myrack Senior. I'd be careful of what

I'd say to Master Keagan if I were you." Charles' answer is glum and to the point.

Lori and I look at each other, and I know we had the same feeling and thought in mind: He finally gave up on living. As the automobile drives through the long side streets that bypass the city and heads towards the hills, my mind begins to whirl again. We knew how close Papa was to Mr Myrack – they were blood brothers after all. Losing his best and most trusted friend must have been worse than when he lost his wife. I remember when Evelyn Myrack died – seeing Mr Myrack ten years ago at the funeral – the image of death painted on his face as if he were already a ghost. Ever since then he relied on his bond with his son, Keagan, and our papa to keep his spirits alive. But young Mr Myrack, as all the rumours go around, has always been very adventurous and is constantly reported for his frequent travels, many times leaving his father to his own devices for months to a year on end.

I remember Keagan as a child. Lori and I both believed him to be selfish and insincere. I vaguely recall when we used to visit we could only play the games he wanted to play, and whenever we would get in trouble from climbing the book-cases or trying to steal cookies, my sister and I were always blamed if we got caught. He would often get in trouble with us after the first few times of trying to blame us solely, however. This would be the first time we will have seen him since I was six and Lori was five. Keagan should be in his early twenties by now, I suppose. I'm usually full of curiosity; but thinking about the memory of that boy has got my interest tampered down tight, just the thought of seeing him again gives me a slight pain in my arm.

# MYRACK MANOR

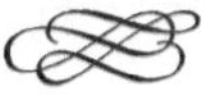

## ASPEN

Perched on the top of a great sloping hill now painted in fresh pastel rain stood the Myrack manor. As we drove up through the forest trail I noticed how the surrounding area was a dense pine and fir forest, except the clearing where the manor overlooks the large city of Currlion.

"Perfect location, wouldn't you say?" I ask in a sly tone only Lori would recognise as we gaze up at the manor. Lori answers with a smile and gives an agreeing nod. A loud grunting sound catches our attention from behind only to find poor Charles trying to unload the large trunk by himself.

"Here, let us help," Lori offers to take a handle before Charles can stop her. I follow Lori's actions and grab the other end, helping her carry the heavy trunk up the stone steps. Clouds of steam accumulate around our mouths as we nervously wait for Charles to catch us up and unlock the doors. *I bet Master Keagan won't even be home to greet his new guests.*

When Charles eventually does open the tall dark oak doors, we stare at a beautiful grand double staircase with mountains painted on each side of the curving walls. Where the stairs join together on the second floor, creating a lovely outlook balcony, a young man appears from the side hall. He is wearing a black day coat and dark trousers. His face, however handsome, has an all-too-obviously painted smile on it as he trots down the stairs. *This couldn't possibly be the Keagan Lori and I knew as kids.* I give a bewildered look to Lori, but she isn't looking in my direction at all. Only his. We knew a scrawny, occasionally stuck-up, rich brat who knew far too well how to get into trouble. *So who is this?*

"Master Keagan, may I present the Wolfe sisters, Miss Aspen and Miss Lori," says Charles.

"No need to be too formal, Charles; after all, we are not complete strangers," Keagan replies, taking a short bow to us. I am taken aback for a second now that I can take him in fully at a few feet away, not only because of his grief he's obviously trying to hide, but also because of his features. Blue eyes that deepen in hue towards his irises – they remind me of rays of light shooting to the bottom of the sea. Short dark brown hair that swoops to one side and a strong physique, which is evident from his fitted day suit. *Oh bugger, I was hoping I would dislike him completely. There's still a chance that he could be a complete jerk though, and that all those rumours were true. Then even his face couldn't cover up his true nature.*

"It's a pleasure to see you girls again," Keagan says in a smooth pleasant voice extending his hand to greet us.

"It is a pleasure to see you as well, Mr Myrack. I hope that soon we all will get reacquainted with each other," I reply in a silky voice that puts a smile on his face as he kisses my hand and then Lori's.

"Once you both settle down in your rooms, I hope you will join me for dinner, and then I can give you a tour of the house.

Oh, and you needn't call me Mr Myrack; Keagan is just fine," he adds with a sincere smile.

"All right, Keagan, I'm sorry, but is it all right if we share a room? We hate being separated," Lori asks.

"That's perfectly fine. If you would follow me, Charles and I will show you to your room," Keagan offers, keeping his attention on me, however, instead of addressing Lori directly. Taking two suitcases, he begins to walk down a long corridor on the east side of the manor with us in tow. The walls are filled with paintings of faraway places and newspaper clippings of charity events the Myracks participated in and managed. *As if they weren't prideful enough, now they have to expose their 'generous' nature on every inch of the walls.* We stop at a small door on the left sidewall right by a tall frosted window at the very end of the hallway. Keagan opens the door and lets us walk in to get a better feel for the room, I took one look at Lori when we set our large trunk down, and she looks just as pleased and grateful as I do with what we see.

Two daybeds, two ornate wooden bureaus, a tiny pocket room with a large desk, a small lounging space with cushioned chairs on a oriental rug near the end of the room with a curved-out seated window.

"This is just wonderful," I breathe out whilst walking closer to the rain-speckled window that stretches all the way to the tall ceiling.

"Agreed. Thank you so much," Lori exclaims as she gazes at the height of the ceiling.

"I'm glad to hear you like it," Keagan replies, setting down the last of the bags.

"Would you like our help unpacking?" Charles offers kindly.

"Oh no, we can handle all of that in a little while. Right

now, however, I think it'd be best for us to rest for a short time after such long travel," I reply with a tired look in my eyes as I sink into the plush chair.

"We will let you both settle in; however, I hope the two of you won't be too tired to join me for dinner at eight o'clock. There is something special being prepared just for your arrival," Keagan says.

"We wouldn't miss it for the world," Lori assures him, enticing Keagan's first authentic-looking smile since we arrived.

"If you need anything at all, don't hesitate to ring," Charles says, pointing to the butler's cord on the wall next to the powder room. And with that, the men bid us adieu and leave us to rest.

Immediately, as they leave the room, I get out of my seat and stroll over to the windows whilst Lori flings herself on a bed and lets out a satisfied "Ahh."

"Any luck?" she asks. She must have noticed me examining the windows for latches and locks.

"No these windows can't be opened, hang on," I reply as I open the door to our powder room.

"Jackpot," I sing out once I hear that faint click and squeaking sound from the windows' hinges. The next sound that comes is Lori scrambling off her bed and walking my way. Taking a few steps back to meet Lori, we size up the windows' opening.

"It's a perfect space for us to squeeze through; four feet by three feet, but it's a little small for the larger ones, don't you think?" I question.

"But we can make this work still as long as we get the machine rebuilt again. We will just have to figure it out as we get used to this house." Lori turns her head to one side as she looks at the windows.

"You sound just like Mum: so optimistic."

"Do you doubt our chances here?" Lori questions.

"Not too much." I giggle. "We still have a problem though. It's not that we can't get out anymore, but who can't come in."

"Maybe we will have to just butter the windows then," Lori jokes, making me laugh a little, thinking of a large bear dimie trying to squeeze through a buttered window.

After we moved the trunk into the study cave area, Lori promptly launched herself back on her new downy bed whilst I started to unpack and sort through our things. *I'm pretty sure these shoes are hers?*

"Lori...?" I call.

But before I can ask my question, Sissy jumps off the bed and exclaims, "Isn't this amazing? I mean the whole deal! The house, the town, it's unbelievable."

"I gotta admit this really does seem like a great opportunity for us, socially and objectively," I agree.

"Yeah, and all the whilst staying close to Mr Rugged and Charming. Talk about a score!" Lori says, batting her lashes as she gives a mock swooning motion with the back of her hand to her forehead.

"Just because he might be attractive does not mean he will be a gentleman other than today. I mean, I bet that this place is filled with the very bi-dimensional slaves that we are trying to get back home. And I bet he treats them like rubbish, just as everyone else does." The words drip from my mouth like acid, causing Lori to stand quietly for a few seconds before crouching down by my side.

Surprising me with a hug, she whispers to me with a reassuring smile, "Our papa wouldn't have been such close friends with a man who would treat dimies cruelly, and his son would likely be raised to the same standards. You know that." This put a smile back on my face till she added, "I'm starting to think you are coming up with excuses because you don't want to admit that he is handsome and charming!"

"What are you, a psychiatrist?" I ask.

Lori just laughs and stands back up though. "Well, we saw part of the manor already and did not see one single dimie."

"Yeah, whilst being here for what ... fifteen minutes? I give it two days – no I bet we will see one tonight before bed," I assure her.

"I'll take that bet. What's on the line?"

"Setting up the hallway alarm system tonight."

"Deal."

And with that, our fourth wager of the day is set.

Charles comes to our room ten minutes till eight to see if we are ready to be escorted to dinner. When he sees that we had changed out of our travel clothes and into more proper dining wear, he immediately begins to lead us to the dining room. On our way out of the room, I give Lori the *'distract, please'* signal on her elbow; I want to examine the walls and lengthy trailing rug along the hallways.

"So how long have the Myrack's lived in this house?" Lori begins her first of many questions, walking in front of me and almost hip to hip with Charles. I quit listening and start taking measurements in my head. Four-metre-tall ceilings, two three-metre-wide hallways. But where is a good opening amongst all these damn vain newspaper clippings and paintings?

"The house is really that big? I can't wait to see the garden!" I hear Lori ramble on. *Ahh, there we are.* A small break between the gold moldings that runs vertically along the wall, and that maroon wall paint is just dark enough to hide the wires. Just far enough from our room to alert us in time and the perfect place to conceal the trick wires. I give Lori a tap on her elbow again, and she begins to add me into the conversation so I don't seem too quiet or aloof.

"Charles was just telling me that this mansion has a large bundle of hidden secrets, like secret rooms for instance," Lori coos.

"Really? Well, do you think there is a chance that we could see a few of these secret rooms, or at least be allowed to find them on our own, Charles?" I reply.

"I don't see why not. However, we won't be able to show you all of the rooms and secret doors."

"Why is that, if I may ask?"

"Well, there are so many that are cleverly hidden, that some have been covered up or forgotten over the years. The first Myrack that built this house left in the deed to the estate the number of rooms and hidden passages that he created. But since he didn't specify where all sixteen secret doors were, we only know of six, sadly. If you find a new one, consider yourself lucky. Master Keagan has been trying to find them all since he was old enough to walk."

This made me want to laugh, thinking of a younger Keagan searching the house for secret doors when he used to be as scrawny as a twig.

"I've always wanted to live in a house with secret doors

and passages. It's so exciting," Lori exclaims as we reach the doors to the dining room.

The dining room is as beautiful as I expected it to be with its long walnut table, two gas-powered medium-sized chandeliers, and red-cushioned seats. Charles promptly pulls out our chairs for each of us, and once we are seated, he excuses himself into the kitchen. As we sit, waiting for Keagan to join us, I begin to observe the ornate chandelier. The top appears to be a brass flower that projects long stamen tubes lined from it's centre with hanging crystal bleeding heart flowers. At the end of each wavy metal tube there are bright Edison bulbs that illuminate the room in a warm glow. What a lovely dining room chandelier; I've only seen two others like it.

"Good evening, ladies, sorry if I kept you waiting long." Keagan strides through the dining room doors, catching my attention. Keagan must have put on cologne – it's kind of nice, actually. I can smell it from where I'm sitting – not too overbearing and smells a lot like vanilla. *Up till now, Keagan has seemed charming, but I'm not about to give in as easily as Lori.* Not a moment less than Keagan comes in, the food starts coming out of the kitchen's swinging doors. The food is being carried out by Charles and a dimie. *Just as I suspected,* I think as I tap Lori's foot with mine as *there's one, I win.*

"Miss Aspen, Miss Lori, I'm glad you were not too tired from your trip to join me for dinner. My apologies that Winona here could not aid you in dressing yourselves for dinner, but she was preoccupied in making tonight's special meal," he says with a soft smile, gesturing to the dimie setting the table as he seats himself. The dimie known as Winona is about a hundred and seventy-five centimetres tall, covered in mint green fur, and has a bear's face, the nose of a bison, very large round ears, and a wide body. However, despite her large appearance, she has a kind face. Winona and Charles quickly finish setting the table; but instead of going back into the kitchen whilst we eat, which is customary, they both sit down on either side of Keagan. After we bow our heads and say Grace, Keagan speaks up and announces, "Ladies, this is Winona, she is our cook, housekeeper, and to me she is family, so I hope you will treat her as such since she regularly dines with us."

I turn and look at Lori who has the biggest look of surprise on her face that could only be matched by the look on my own when I heard these wonderful words. "We don't mind at all. In fact we prefer it, we used to do the same thing back at our home before our dimies retired," I reply, to which Keagan and his household look surprised.

"I didn't think that dimies could or were even allowed to retire?" Charles asks.

"Thanks to our father's political ties in Bath, instead of being slaves till they die, they all have a set time when they are to retire. They can also choose who they work for as servants or in shops for food and lodging in return. At least he made it possible for them back home in Bath," Lori responds.

"What our father wanted most, however, was a way to see them free with rights like us, but he was never able to. 'I would have made too many dangerous enemies' is what he always told us. That is other than those not already made with his retirement law idea," I add.

"I see. If only that law were passed in this city, things could be a lot nicer and more civilized for the dimies," Keagan replied with a half smile straight at me. A sharp pain shoots through my ankle, causing me to flinch a little; Lori kicked me with her foot harder than she should have as way of saying, *I told you so.* I keep my eyes down and hope no one noticed, whilst my silly sister suppresses a giggle for my reaction. For the rest of dinner we joke and inquire about what happens throughout the city.

"In three weeks there will be the annual winter ball at the Governor's manor, and I would be honored if I could serve as your escort to the event," Keagan says with light in his eyes.

"We would love to. We haven't been to a ball in a long time," Lori replies eagerly.

"Aspen, what do you think?" Keagan asks me.

"It sounds wonderful, and I would love to come." I chuckle, with my best bright-eyed look.

"But with a ball like this we will need new dresses," Lori quickly adds.

"That's true," I say. Keagan looks at us with a knowing smile on his face, then turns to Winona and asks, "Well, what do you think? Do these girls deserve new dresses?"

"Well, considering how they view and treat my people, I say get them ten dresses each!" Winona laughs showing her pointed teeth. "You don't find people like them anymore," she adds, making me blush a little.

"So it's settled then; tomorrow we go into town and pick out new party clothes. I'll even treat us to tea whilst we are there," Keagan announces.

"Yes!" Lori and I exclaim before we can catch ourselves, causing our hosts to push back in their seats a bit with surprised faces. *Tea, pastries and getting a good survey of the town? Excellent. Oh yeah, and the dresses – yay, dresses...*

"Sorry for our outburst; Lori has a sweet tooth, and I'm a fool for tea," I apologize after I realise how loudly we actually shouted. It seems to wake our hosts up a little bit as I catch them sharing looks of surprise.

"By jove, if you love tea so much I must fix you some from

my special stash. I have tea from all over the empire, some even come from China," Charles offers enthusiastically with a broad grin under his bushy mustache.

"I would love that very much!" I respond. I remember the only time I had the chance to taste green tea from the orient. Mother said it was the best tea she ever sipped, and of course, I thought the same at the time. I just wish I had not been so young, maybe then I could remember the taste now.

"And I can make the finest of pastries that ever tickled your tastebuds, Lori," Winona states proudly.

"Thank you ever so! And would it be possible for you to teach me how to make some of them as well?" Lori responds gleefully. *Oh No! Not charred pastries again! Last time she tried to bake she nearly burnt the kitchen down. Maybe that was the real reason cousin Briar kicked us out of her house?*

"Why, you only need to ask, m'lady. I've never met a lady who wanted to cook, but I'd be happy to teach ye," Winona replies with surprise. *I know Lori loves goodies, but I wish she would just concern herself only with eating them.*

The rest of dinner is full of catching up, people we must meet, and a few who will talk your ear off if given the offer to afternoon tea and the like.

After a delicious dessert of mulberry cobbler and peach tea, Lori and I insist on serving it after some gentle persuading to Winona until she finally consents.

"Just a forewarning," Lori pipes up with a shy smile. "I can't get enough cobbler; it's my favourite dessert... also, Aspen could drink her weight in tea if given the chance."

"Lori!" I exclaim, a little embarrassed, making me overfill

Keagan's cup a bit. Chuckles and snickers come here and there, causing my face to redden somewhat. *I mean, it's true. I've once had ten large cups of tea in one night out of stress to finish an important project, but she didn't have to say that!*

Once satisfied with the dessert, Keagan takes us on a tour throughout the mansion. I'm immediately in awe when he opens the doors to the vast library two storeys tall and filled to the brim with books. Next is the fireplace room that is slightly larger than our bedroom and has a rustic look to it that only adds to its warmth. Next is the gym, in which mirrors cover the walls and long windows stretch high above to let light in. We are shown the living room that has its own staircase to a small loft similar to the library. The room is wide and filled with small tables and couches. Then a small ballroom that consists of cream marble floors, two giant chandeliers, and a lovely piano in the far corner by the glass doors.

When we came here I looked over at Lori and saw that her hobby still had a hold on her; this room only made Lori fidgety, dancing slightly in place, proving that she desperately wished to dance. Whilst the ornate moldings, mirrors, and paintings covering the walls only added to her energy it seemed.

The last section of the manor we are shown is the west wing; which consists of a small study with large windows, a fireplace, a desk, and head-height bookshelves. The other rooms consist of two more guest rooms and Keagan's room.

Keagan opens the double doors to his room and welcomes us to come in. Inside is quite large for a bedroom. It has a king-sized bed with bed posts that connect to a red cloth canopy. There is a couch area in the right corner near a fireplace and a writing desk. Then there are the long, almost ceiling-high, windows on the farthest wall and doors below them that open up to a covered balcony half covered with moonlight.

"You can see the stars and moon at night here," Keagan tells us.

"How enchanting," I reply, memorizing the space outside that looks out to the thick black fir forest as well as the balcony doors' measurements.

"Has this room always been yours?" Lori questions.

"No, it belonged to my parents. This year, before my father's death and during my travels, my room was converted to a guest room. My belongings were brought here once my father learned of Mr Wolfe's death. Doesn't matter much anyhow."

"Why is that?" Lori asks innocently.

"Ah, my room never really felt like mine that much for the six years I was away at boarding school. My father sent me there till I was sixteen, after my mother died, he had me stay here but allowed me to travel and study abroad when I turned seventeen."

"Well, it was good that your father cared about your education, wasn't it? But he must have been lonely here without you. Was he not? What, in this giant house, the empty expanse, or space can start to get to someone when their only family left is almost always abroad?" I question. I want to see if his temperament has changed at all since we last saw each other. *Who are you now, Keagan Myrack?*

"Indeed, he probably was at times; however, he had his business meetings here four times a week and the rest of his work left him busy. Besides, when I was home, we spent almost every day together," he says, eyeing me down.

I begin to walk around and return his challenging look, replying with, "If I remember correctly from the rumors, you were banned from half of the cities you had traveled to. What on earth could you have been doing, sir?"

"Only if you can explain why the both of you were practically thrown out of the last two homes you stayed at," he retorts coolly.

"So our cousins thought it best for us to travel to different areas of high- and middle-class society to find where we are most comfortable. What's so terrible about that?"

"Oh, nothing except maybe…" he muses walking closer to me slowly in the low light, making him look larger and more intimidating than he did this evening at the base of the stairs. "Maybe the whisperings were that you were performing unsavory acts during the gas-lit hours of the night. Now how does that look for such young women?"

"Oh, I wouldn't doubt that you'd be able to think of all sorts of unsavory acts, what with all the ladies you've been seen running around with," I spit out, unable to hold my tongue or my temper a second longer.

"Is that really what you think of me? Don't be a fool, there are only sparks of truth in that whole bonfire of lies that's spread around. Your trail of gossip, however, sounds just like you, by how you two would act when we were children: Damaging and stealing from the homes of your own family whilst managing to break the law at the same time."

I open my mouth to deny the claims, but he continues his theory.

"Or the fact that they hired people to move you in the night to your next of kin again and again till you're now here, living with an old family friend instead of your own blood. Now that looks quite odd if you ask me."

He is standing three feet away, and all I can do is stare at him with pursed lips and no answer but Lord, would I have paid good money for a sharp retort right now. *He's smarter than I gave him credit for, and his temper seems cool yet quick; it's just non-explosive. He seems to do well under pressure and can turn the tables on a conversation quite easily.*

"You're not the only one who listens to rumours, Aspen," he whispers, with a smug smile, so quietly I'm sure I was the only one to hear.

I just stare at him unable to reply, my mind blank. *This never happens, I've always been able to bite back, but now, nothing. Well, don't just stand there staring at him, say something, anything.* "Now look here –"

"You know, I think we could all use a good night's sleep since we have such a big day tomorrow," Lori interrupts as she nudges me nervously towards the doors.

"Goodnight, Keagan. Thank you for the lovely tour," she says quickly.

"You're welcome. Goodnight, ladies," he replies, standing like a statue with that stupid smug face whilst his eyes follow me towards the door.

I remain silent as we walk out of the room. Lori holds my hand tightly as she walks us so quickly to our chamber that we are almost running. When we get inside our room and shut the door, Lori spins around and blurts out, "What was *that*?" gesturing towards the door dramatically. "Do you want us to be kicked out of this place faster than the last one?"

I take a seat on my bed and play with my green skirts, replying with, "If you ask *me*, he was enjoying it. Did you see that annoying smug face of his?"

Lori pauses a moment, then looks at me with a twinkle in her eyes. "Yeah, and I think your heart melted a bit at dinner though, for how kind he is and how Winona is like an aunt to him," she teases back with a grin on her face.

"Oh yeah, well, I also won the bet, so get your scaling gear on," I say, getting up from the bed and walking across the room.

"Wait, what?"

"Well, we did see a dimie at dinner, did we not?" I sneer with that same teasing look she gave me.

"B–but he's nice to Winona; she's like his family."

"Family yes, but also a dimie. Hope you didn't eat too much dessert tonight, Sis, I'd hate to see that second helping of cobbler run down the walls," I say, blowing a now-nervous Lori a kiss before I pull a trunk into the study-cave area of the room. I hear Lori groan and can't help but smile as I unpack the broken pieces and parts yet to be put together for the multi-dimensional-transporter. We have carried this so far and it's nearly complete. Papa would be proud to see how far we've come on our first tesseract since the incident. I still can't believe our own relatives we stayed with wanted us to throw it away and forget about the whole idea.

*"What if you get caught? You know it's not just your neck that's on the chopping block. Our family name, status, and relationship with our fellow man in society would disintegrate the moment you were found out."* ... *"How could you two be so selfish; what would your mother and father say?"* ... *"Your poor parents must be rolling in their graves due to your reckless nature for a dead cause."* The voices of our aunts, uncles, and cousins ring through my mind.

We know how dangerous the machine is and what laws are being tried and broken; we just don't care. Not just at what it might do but how dangerous it is to be making such a machine, and what would happen if we got caught with it in our possession. No one can find out this time, not Keagan, Charles, or even Winona...for now, that is. At least right now we can build it, and soon we can help the dimies escape; we just need more time. If it was done once to enslave the dimies then we can do it again to free them back home to their own dimension.

# FOOLS' JEWELS

## LORI

I just finished pulling up my split skirts and scaling gear, all the whilst wearing a regretful expression on my sombre face. No doubt my sister is thoroughly enjoying herself since she is showing off her winning smile whilst pulling out the last of the wiring alarm system.

"Whilst you were distracting Charles on our way to dinner, I noticed the perfect placement for the cords to hide," Aspen begins.

"Perfect, do you think it's late enough to do this now, or should we wait another hour?" I ask, trying not to sound too put out. It wasn't so much the task itself that I dreaded, but scaling a very lengthy wall not too long after a large meal that consisted of extra servings of cobbler is not an event I'd enjoy performing.

"I'll go check the halls and the main entrance to see if anyone is mingling about," Aspen responds thoughtfully, answering my question in a way.

As she leaves the room it gives me a chance to put on the most awkward part of the scaling gear: the harness. I start to get annoyed and begin to squirm and wrestle with the infernal thing. Unable to see my footing, I end up tripping on my split skirts, falling face first on the bed. The next thing I hear is Aspen's voice coming in the room, saying, "All right, coast is...again, Lori, really?"

"It's harder than it looks, you know," I say, still trying to untangle myself.

"Yeah, it's hard in split skirts, not trousers." Aspen helps me back up.

"Trousers are just so unladylike, I hate having to wear them already for our night runs, you know."

"Well, do you really think what we do on those rendezvous calls for us to be ladylike?" Aspen rivals back, and she's not wrong even though I hate to admit it; she's rarely ever wrong.

"Why does three metres always feel like six?" I moan as I'm centimeters from the ceiling.

"Hehehe," Aspen giggles.

"Quit laughing at my pain and send up the wire cutters and radio-wave transmitter," I demand.

"Yes, ma'am," Aspen says cheekily as she puts the items in the pull-up sack and gives the rope a slight tug, signalling that I could bring it up. As I connect the trick wires' sensors to the radio-wave–projecting transmitter, Aspen sends the harder line of wire under the lengthy rug with the help of our unfolding stick. It can gradually unfold and then slide easily from one end of a long rug to the next whilst pulling the alarm trick wires with it.

Aspen has explained it to me about five times already like with all her other gadgets. She runs towards the beginning of the hallway and back to our room to hide the wires, placing them in three spots under the rug along the way. *Yet another of her brilliant inventions, kinda like the infernal contraption that I so luckily get to set up right now...on the ceiling.*

Once I finally get the transmitter ready and wrap an opaque maroon cloth over it for good measure, I signal and whistle to Aspen that we are ready for a test. I slide my way down the wall from the ceiling and head back to the bedroom, waiting for the bells to ring. Aspen must have stepped over the first wire since the bells ring softly; a few seconds later she hits the second wire because the bells ring twice and loud.

Perfect, I finally figured out how to put that thing together correctly the first time. Unlike last time when we had to retry everything four times more because I couldn't get the stupid wiring right. *I always hate it when Aspen has to take over and fix my messes. This time I got it right though,* I think to myself as I head back down the hallway to help pick up the rest of the scaling gear and equipment when I hear the two bells ringing again, but it's the next thing I hear that sends my heart racing.

"By the beard of Zeus, what is this!?" I hear someone exclaim from the hallway.

I immediately begin to claw off my scaling gear, tripping again in the process, and straighten up before heading back out into the hallway. It's Winona, and she has her arms on her hips whilst looking sceptically at Aspen who is trying to "explain" what all of our odd mess in the hall is for. When I get closer, to be a part of the conversation, I try to join in.

"Didn't Aspen explain to you what this is all about?" I ask.

"Well, she was trying to, but why don't you enlighten me, Lori?" Winona questions expectantly.

I realise my mistake now. If my sister was already making up a lie then I could easily botch it up with my own. I should have remained silent, but now I don't seem to have a choice with the expectant look that Winona is giving me.

"Well, isn't it obvious?" I say, noticing that Aspen has already taken down my scaling rope, allowing me to give a better excuse.

"Aspen loves to tinker, but it easily gets on my nerves at times, and this was one of those times, so she must have just come out here to play around with her doo-dads," I say whilst wringing my hands. *I hate lying, Aspen is much better at it than I, anyhow.* Winona regains her posture with a sceptical look on her face.

"Aspen, if you need a place to work and tinker, for Pete's sake, use the study or the library. But do *not* use the hallway! Surely you have more decency than that," she scolds my sister who is trying to appear sheepish, but I can still see the slight grin on the edge of her face.

"It's getting to be too late to tinker at this hour; now off to bed," she commands us after a minute of scolding and apologizing. *I think I'm going to like Winona; she's very motherly. I just hope she doesn't scold me or correct me in the kitchen with a wooden spoon.* Even with that grim thought, I can't help but smile as I imagine her teaching me how to bake.

Once we bathed and dressed for bed, the topic about our plans for tomorrow came up.

"So any ideas on how we can ditch Keagan tomorrow to find parts for the machine and...possibly pastries?" I ask. Aspen paused, brushing the knots out of her wavy hair, to ponder.

"Either we will have to get in an accident, one of us faints, or we must fight with someone. We could also insist on going shopping for food and split up then, but one of us will have to stay with Keagan so he will not get suspicious or too worried."

"Hmm… All right, well, if I must stay with the handsome Master Keagan, you won't have to twist my arm. I mean, we want to make this diversion as realistic as possible," I say sleepily in my best overly dramatic voice.

"Actually…" Aspen sighs, closing her eyes, obviously reluctant to finish her thought, arousing my curiosity.

"I think it should be I who should stay with Keagan whilst you get the parts. You know exactly what we need and what the parts look like, and if I go off then he will definitely think something is going on."

"Fair enough, that way you can also apologize for the way you acted towards him tonight," I mutter, too tired to say much more and not even able to catch what Aspen blurts out next as I fall fast asleep.

After a delicious and slightly awkward breakfast, we all prepared to go into town. Aspen gave me the list of things we needed for the machine just before Winona came to help each of us dress into our day clothes. Me in my purple skirts and black leather corset with the hidden knife compartment, not to mention my matching purple wool and fur winter jacket and hat. Aspen however, chose to wear her blue bunched up skirts with hidden pockets; which show her ankles, making it easier for her to walk around. The rest of her outfit consists of her navy ruffle day shirt, dark brown leather corset, white wool winter coat, and favourite feathered side hat with the hidden compartment she likes to hide her brass knuckles in.

We both carry our own specially made switchblade fan that Aspen designed a few months ago after a skirmish with a fresh young man at a party. The first switch unsheathes the blades and the trigger ejects them; which can prove to be quite fatal, we've observed. Because of this, Aspen created a safety switch for everyday use after Cousin Edith nearly killed a maid whilst playing with it without our knowing. *That conversation was quite unpleasant with the hysterical maid screaming across the hall and Edith wailing in our ears.*

We join Keagan at the front door where we all put on our gloves and mufflers before heading for the motor car. Keagan gives each of us a hand into the back seat before closing our door and climbing into the front passenger seat next to Charles. After Charles adjusts his driving goggles we are all ready to go. He revs up the engine and drives around the front of the house where Winona is waving goodbye to us from the front door. Looking quite cold, she hurriedly runs back inside the warm house.

We didn't get to see much of the town the other day since the train and aircraft station is on the corner of the town, and there was a more country-like road that we took to get to the mansion. We only saw the overlook of the town sadly. But today, there are bustling store fronts that display anything from exotic pets, weaponry, the newest in Victorian fashion, or simply a bakery or butcher shop. One that we pass by catches my eye, Cogs and Bogs. It looks like a weapon-and-tinker shop. I'll go there first; hopefully, they will have the parts we need or know someone who will.

As I gaze out the window, I notice the townspeople have the most embellished clothes I've ever seen; detailed with lace, gears, and even gemstones here and there. It's no wonder Currlion finally managed to trump London as the capital for fashion now that they are including the latest high-end inventions. The women here are even allowed to show their knees now, but the style is to still have an asymmetrical skirt that is long in the back so we can still have a ruffled bustle.

It's their shoes, however, that catch my interest; I've never seen leather-heeled boots that have gold embroidery, I notice as a lone woman passes by. I even catch the sight of a small gun handle on the inside of her left boot, mid stride. *Aspen would love her boots to have built-in gun holsters.* I notice that I'm beginning to fog up the glass of Keagan's car as I gawk at the other fashion trends so I sit back upright in my seat once more. It's nice to feel like you are in a small village sometimes when you know very well that this town is anything but small.

Stopping at a shop called Masie Lacy, Keagan, Aspen, and I step out of the car and head towards the shop. Just before heading inside we wave goodbye to Charles who is slowly driving off to spend his half-day today for himself. A bell rings as we open the glass door, and we instantly hear a woman's voice as we pile inside.

"Welcome to — Keagan Myrack!" the woman exclaims when she sees who came through the door and rushes straight up to him.

"Greetings, Miss Masie, it is a pleasure to see you again," Keagan says to the woman as they give each other a light embrace.

"I've not seen ya in town in over a year! I was starting to think that ya left dis town for good," Miss Masie replies in a beautifully exotic accent — Jamaican maybe?

She's just as lovely as her voice, flawless dark skin, striking smile, and chocolate-hued eyes that scream jolliness. Her coal-black hair is piled up in a thickly braided bun and decorated with golden hair combs whilst a few curls poke out every which way. She looks to be in her mid thirties and wears a gold satin dress of the latest designs from Paris like those shown in the illustrated Pearl newspaper.

"I have two ladies staying with me who are old friends of the family, and we need to find them some ball gowns for the dance at the governor's manor that's coming up in a few weeks."

"Well, don't just stand there, introduce me to these lovelies!" she exclaims.

"This is Miss Aspen and Miss Lori Wolfe; they are from Bath, but as of now they will be living with me for as long as they like and as long as I see fit," Keagan boasts rather proudly. Aspen and I look at each other with raised eyebrows that read as: *Prideful much?*

"Ahh," Miss Masie sighs as she suddenly draws very close to each of us. In turn, cupping our faces with her hands and taking a good look at our features a little too close to her own, I dare say. All the while Keagan just looks on like there is nothing in the world out of the ordinary. She turns our heads this way and that, inches away from her own. I swear I see him smirk as he watches Miss Masie play with Aspen's face and hair like a doll. *Could this be his way of getting back at us for last night's little quarrel?*

"Wonderful colour and such beautiful features these two young ladies have! I've got in my shop da perfect dresses and corsets for ya both; some of them even come with their own gadget attachments and holsters!" she exclaims with a knowing look on her face.

"While I am lookin' for the dresses ya be lookin' around ya selves and find something dat ya like," Miss Masie calls back to us as she disappears into the forest of dresses and coats. As we all walk towards the clothes ourselves, I think of the perfect distraction method, and I won't even have to lie about it either. I remember our rule that we try to only use excuses and ruses that are mostly truths so that we can always say we weren't lying or get caught in lies without truth to back us up.

"I never even knew some of these colours existed!" I say, holding up a coral-coloured ball gown, making Keagan's smirk into a full bright smile.

"You know, we used to play a game whenever we would go out and shop for clothes," I begin.

"Really, how's that?" Keagan muses.

"Oh yes, the one where we choose for each other," Aspen says in such a playful tone that I can tell she is aware of the ruse I'm cooking up.

"Choose for each other? As in our clothes?" Keagan echoes curiously.

"Yes, just that, but the rules are to pick out two to three nice-looking articles of clothing and two or more bad pieces of clothing for your selected person, and they have to model it for you as well," Aspen finishes.

"What do you say, Keagan? It'll be a jolly good time," I say as we both look at him with beaming faces.

"Hmm, all right, why not?" he shrugs, allowing me to set the last piece of the plan in place.

"Wonderful. And since there are only three of us, why don't we do it where... Keagan, you pick out for Aspen, Aspen, you pick for me, and I'll pick out for Keagan," I suggest, and before anyone can speak, I burst out, "Great! Let the game begin, let's go, go, go," as I push all of us deeper into the maze of clothing and spread us into different aisles in the process. When I get to a random clothing row for men,

I pause and listen to see if they actually begin to play the game.

"Aspen, is your sister normally that... forceful when it comes to games and clothes?" Keagan chuckles out.

"Well...yes, but not usually at that level, we just haven't been shopping in quite some time. All of our clothing is a bit outdated. So it's no wonder she is so electrified over this special outing for new dresses," Aspen replies in a thoughtful, silky voice.

I hear Keagan clear his throat before replying with, "I see, well, then I'm glad I could bring you here today; it makes me feel better seeing you both so... excited after all you've been through."

"I could say the same about you, sir."

"Please, no sir, I'm still much too young for that. Just Keagan is fine... Aspen. If I may call you that, Miss," Keagan says hesitantly.

"You may, Keagan," Sissy replies.

The plan is working. Now, after a few more minutes of searching, I can run the errand whilst they are modeling for each other. I quickly pick out a few gold- and filigree-detailed vests and coats along with a strapping hat that comes with a spyglass attachment to it. Then I choose some of the baggier and overly colourful day coats that look like they ought to be a part of a circus act, no offense to Miss Masie.

Miss Masie finds me and holds up a stunning peach ball gown with white roses on the bustle and white lace around the scooped neckline and sleeves. She must have noticed the awestruck expression on my face since she begins to beam with her own broad smile.

"I'll begin a changing room for ya along with the others that your sister picked out for ya. Are those for ya or Master

Keagan?" she queries with a questioning look, pointing to the pile of clothes that's draped over my arm.

"Oh, Keagan. I'll be there in a second to try that dress on. I would just like to find a few more articles before then." I reply, handing the pile to her for his room before rummaging through the clothing line further. Miss Masie starts to head back towards where I saw the changing rooms were in the centre of the room, taking the clothes for Keagan with her. I wait for her to be out of sight to begin making my way to the entrance. As I'm walking quietly towards the door, I pass through an opening between dress racks just as Aspen steps out of her dressing room in the most beautiful forest green dress with sheer black lace detailing and hanging shoulders. She walks over to the three angled mirrors to get a better look of herself just as Keagan comes out from behind a row of clothes. The moment he looks in Aspen's direction he stops dead in his tracks. She must have noticed him staring in one of the mirrors, because she turns around and gives him a shy smile.

"Is this a good time for me to apologize about my behaviour last night?" she asks in a sweet voice, making me beam from ear to ear. *This is the perfect distraction for Keagan. She's much more effective than my idea, I dare say. He probably doesn't even recall my existence right now, let alone where I am, as long as he's gaping at her, I think* to myself. I exit the store as quietly as possible and head down the bright and dusty street towards Cogs and Bogs gear shop.

The walk there is uneventful besides men tipping their hats and sharing pleasantries when I walk by, and children playing blasting marbles and hop scotch in the alleyways. They begin chasing each other around whilst the cold breeze and horse-drawn carriages blow up tiny whirlwinds. I know how important it is that I get the supplies, but there is a pastry shop filled with delectable-looking sweets that I would very much like to *observe* closer. *If Aspen knew you stopped to drool in a pastry shop before getting the parts for her machine, she'd throttle you,* I remind myself as I reluctantly say goodbye to the gooey morsels. *Maybe later on today if events permit.*

Cogs and Bogs seemed like a normal mechanics shop on the outside, but once I take my first step inside, I realise how ghastly of a place it is. Now that is to say the clocks, barrels, and shelves filled with gears, cogs, and bolts — those are all run-of-the-mill everyday parts you'd find in a tinker store. But geared pull-string cannon top hats, goggles with multi-coloured magnifying lenses, telescopes with planetariums swirling around their sides, driving goggles with projecting map screens, gyroscopic compass boots, barrels and barrels of toy bugs and spiders that can fly and crawl on walls and ceilings — now that's special. Walking through, I gaze at the walls and ceiling, which are a maze of glass and steel pipes containing multi-coloured liquids that bubble and occasionally fizz.

The store itself had a metallic taste to it, along with its strange smell, kind of like a winter's night. I decide to grab a small bagful of toy flies and two spiders. I'm sure Aspen could do something great with these; possibly make a few *flies on the wall* for us?

"And what are you doing here on your own, young lady?" comes a low stern voice from my left. I spin around and straighten up when I see a thin old man with a skeletal look in his appearance. A shiver runs up my spine at the sight of him.

"Oh, my escort is waiting for me just outside; I wanted to get a few items for my little brother — he just adores tinkering," I lie.

The old man's expression turns from sceptical to pleasant. Well, as pleasant as a living skeleton could get.

"Ah, I see, well then, could I interest you in one of these? It's a build-your-own-pocket-watch kit, perfect for inventive little children. Or how about this mobile mechanical dog? It can walk and even bark," he says with a kind smile.

The small metal Scottie dog does look adorable with its two glowing bulb eyes and wagging watch-band tail, but I'm not here for cute stuff. "Thank you, Mr Gearmaster, but I'm actually looking for a few specific parts he has been needing."

"Name them off. We have most everything here. And please, M'lady, call me Gerald to save time," the old man says tenderly.

"All right, Gerald, let's start with twenty three-centimetre-in-diameter spindle gears," I say.

In ten seconds, the old man makes it up the mobile stairs, reaches into a shelf box, and comes back down with a small parcel containing the twenty spindle gears. *I'm impressed at how fast he is for his age.*

"He also needs a half a dozen clock belts, thirteen washers, two brass sheets of metal – twenty-five by twenty centimeteres please, and ..." I stop short as something twinkling blue catches my eye. A blue crystal heart and a slew of smaller gems around it in its glass display box that's a part of the front counter catches my eye as it glimmers in the light.

"What's this here?" I start before I realise I'm speaking. The skeleton of a man comes down the stairs with most of what I need and sets the pieces on the counter before speaking.

"Ahh, yes," he starts in an enthusiastic tone.

"Those are for people who like to embellish their work with bezeling."

"Oh."

*Aspen and I could bezel the outside of the machine to make it appear to be ornamental; maybe even a Fabergé egg. People won't want to play with it if it's a Fabergé egg.*

"Miss?... Miss!"

"Oh, I'm terribly sorry, what is it?" I say as I'm startled back to reality.

"I was just saying that the sapphire heart was five thousand pounds and the smaller gems all together were three thousand four hundred pounds."

"Oh, thank you... but um let's just get the items that my sis–*brother* needs," I say, a little flustered as I realise that Aspen would kill me if I bought us those gems at that price along with all the other things we need.

"Uh, we need two small faucet handles, a bottle of ink, a thermocouple..."

*Maybe she will think it is a good investment.*

"And a thin coil pipe...umm are there any cheaper stones maybe not as precious?" I ask, still staring at the little lovelies. Gerald removes his gear embellished cap, scratches his bald scalp and heads to the back of the store. I can hear him rummaging around, making quite the ruckus as I gaze at the large heart jewel, thinking of what to do. Gerald comes back to the counter with a small flour sack, and when he reaches the counter he empties a bit of its contents on the table. There are gems of all cuts and sizes – even another sapphire heart, and it looks identical to the one in the glass counter case. He then places the two next to each other.

"This one is just costume jewelry..." Gerald starts explaining, pointing to the gem on the right. "But it's made to look almost identical to the real thing; the only way to tell the difference is by the weight, colour, and–" Gerald's sentence is suddenly cut off by an explosive bang, followed by a sharp hissing noise as if a giant snake burst through a wall in the back of the shop. Gerald and I jolt from the explosion, scattering some of the gems off and around the countertop. As I begin to help pick up the ones on my side of the counter, a young lad comes out of the side back room. He must be the old man's apprentice because he bellows out, "One of the main pipes just burst, and I can't get it to calm down!"

Gerald curses under his breath and charges off to the back room whilst pushing the young boy towards the counter.

"Ring this lady up. I'll take care of this blasted old–" the rest of his sentence is drowned out by the sound of the whistling pipe, the boy now red in the face is trying his best to get everything into a sack for me. He looks to be no more than twelve or thirteen, with short messy brown hair sticking out from his cap, grease smudges all over him, and his bright red face blushing as he sheepishly looks my way. In a word: adorable.

"D–did you want the costume gems also, m'lady?"

"Yes, I–" I stop short as I see that there is only one large blue heart gem amongst the multiple tiny jewels on the counter top; it doesn't look too blue, I guess. *It must be the fake sapphire.*

"Uh, yes, I would like the costume gems as well."

The young boy scoops up what is left on the counter, puts it in a small drawstring sack, hands it to me, and rings me up to pay thirty pounds. I hurriedly pay him thirty-five for his troubles.

"Thomas!" Gerald calls out for help. The young lad named

Thomas takes the money I owe him and dashes to the back of the store, stuffing the notes and coins in his overall pocket as he runs, turning at the last moment to spit out, "Thank you for shopping with us today, m'lady."

Before I can answer back, he disappears around the corner. That's my cue to leave, I guess; I hope I have not been gone too long. *I'm sure Aspen could think of a couple of ways to keep Keagan occupied*, I say to myself with a mischievous grin on my face.

As I am leaving Cogs and Bogs with my parcels, I start speed-walking back to the dress shop and decide to take a quick closer look at the patisserie across the road. The moment my foot touches the cobblestone street, however, I see someone with a boyish grin on his face beginning to exit the exact shop I'm aiming for. *Keagan.* If it weren't for a bouncing buggy going by, I would have been caught for sure. I act fast and dart behind a medium-sized mailbox, holding my parcels tightly to my chest.

I count to ten as my breath puffs out in a great fog around my hiding place, frightened that it might give me away. I hold my breath as a man passing by gives me a bewildered stare. I finally dare to look around the mailbox and can release the breath I was holding in. I see that he is heading back to the dress shop and not my way. *But at the same time… he is out of the dress shop and so am I, but he doesn't know that. This may put a damper on things. What the heck did Aspen do? Or should I say what didn't she do? She was supposed to sidetrack him; it sure worked with the dress the first time.*

I mope to myself and grit my teeth as I dust myself off and slowly head back to the shop. My eyes never leave Keagan; however this makes me bump into a few people once or twice as I stay a safe distance down the road from him. I noticed that, as he makes his way back in the direction to Masie Lacy, two women have stopped him and are openly flirting with him. They are dressed too tastefully to be bed warmers, but still, they sure act like they know him well enough the way they each rushed to him with big eyes. Keagan, though, is somehow able to slip away from them with a few words, a quick turn around, and a tip of his hat. There is one thing for sure, the rumours that follow him around for being popular with the ladies sure becomes him.

After he heads into Masie Lacy, I cross the street once the last buggy passes and crouch down to the base of the tall shop windows. Doing so earns me a few strange and sultry glances from some men passing by, but what am I to do? This is one of the safest ways to see if Keagan is far enough in the store for me to head in undetected. *I can still see him, dash it all; if I were Aspen I would have figured out a way to get back in by now!*

"Just wait right here for me, Geoffrey, I'd like to pick out a few things before we head to Lucinda's for tea," I hear from behind me. Turning my head, I see a very large woman in a fur coat and an even larger frivolously feathered hat, climb down the steps of a horse carriage.

"Yes, m'lady" replies her driver, a small bird-like dimie with a chimp's tail and feet covered with dark purple feathers. Seeing that the woman was eyeing the doors to Masie Lacy before she put her final step on the ground allows me time to stand back up from my odd crouching position and walk backwards a few steps. I stroll slowly towards the shop now so that she may beat me to the door. Her dimie, Geoffrey, opens it for her with a blank face, but then smiles and tips his driver hat to me. I give him a warm smile and nod back to him. I follow his mistress in, falling into step, hiding behind her massive figure without her being the wiser. I'm just a few paces away from the first dress rack when I hear, "Why, Lady Pomley, how wonderful to see you." It's Keagan's voice, and I can hear his footsteps coming this way. I look left and right frantically to find a way out of this possibly awkward situation needing an explanation as to why I am standing so close to a woman I don't know behind her back, let alone the front door.

"Keagan Myrack!" I hear the plump woman exclaim as she rushes over to meet him where he stands. *Thank God,* I say to myself through clenched teeth as I hurl myself in a bent position towards the rack of dresses when we pass them. Rushing inside a rack to get to the other side where he can't see me, I spy a clear shot where I can quickly slip into the changing rooms. I run on my tiptoes towards the changing rooms and find Aspen outside of them in her day clothes, helping herself to a fresh and flaky raspberry danish. Right as I come into the waiting area we meet eyes, causing her to nearly choke on her danish.

"Where have you been? I've almost run out of excuses to where you were hiding in the store. Now get into the dressing room before he's done talking to that lady!" Aspen scolds me in a whisper as she sets the pastry down, wiping crumbs off her hands.

"Can I have a pastry first?" I say, reaching for a glazed tart with sugar sprinkles.

"No, you may not. Dresses first," Aspen hisses out, picking me up and flinging me into the dressing room. She promptly shuts the door two seconds before I hear, "Aspen, I'd like you to meet Lady Pomley..." I stop listening as I frantically unlace my corset and change clothes after rubbing my bum; which I unfortunately landed on quite hard. *Stupid Aspen.* When I am fully clothed in a new ball gown, I step outside and am immediately introduced to Lady Pomley. M'lady then babbles on about my dress, Keagan, and then her precious dogs at home – mostly about her dogs actually. After a compliment or two from everyone on my new dress, I excuse myself to try on the others.

"I've just come for some light shopping before having tea with an old friend. I hope to see you all at the governor's gala in six weeks!" Lady Pomley calls out.

I'm in my new dress and coming back out at this point when Keagan replies, "Oh, don't you worry about that, it would be a crime not to allow these ladies to wear their new beautiful dresses," Keagan calls back to her and then rests his eyes on Aspen with a radiant smile. I don't think she notices it as she watches Lady Pomley walk off, but I sure see it. *Looks like my new personal mission is to get these two closer,* I say to myself.

# LIBRARY SECRETS

## ASPEN

"Are those gems? Those are gems! Why did you buy gems!" I question Lori whilst looking in the sack full of small glittering jewels and then back to her.

"Because I have an idea that will allow us to hide the machine in plain sight, and to do that we need these gemstones."

"How much damage did it do for us?" I ask, anticipating the answer to be monumental as I put on my work goggles at the study cave table. Turning on a gas lamp, I look closely at the large royal blue gemstone.

"Everything all together was only thirty pounds. I know that's a bit more expensive than the last few cities we were in, but you should have seen this place; it was top of the line!"

"Lori, this is a real stone," I say.

"What? No way, the gear master sold me the fake one. How can you tell if it's real?" she questions, coming towards me.

"Look at it through my work goggles." I move so she can sit down by the light whilst she puts on the special multi magnifying lens and colour goggles. I remember when mum and I used to polish and study gems as a little hobby; we were pretty good at it, too. Whilst we would scrutinize the real gems, Lori would play with the fake ones and pretend she was a princess balancing them on her hands and head as jewelry.

When Lori puts the gem down after looking at it, I hold up the jewel and say, "Lori, this is an eighteen-carat sapphire. It's worth thousands of pounds! How could the shopkeeper give this to you for not even thirty pounds? You didn't trade something important for–"

"No, but there could have easily been a mix up," Lori interjects my worried questioning with her own theories.

"How's that?" I say, putting a hand on my hip whilst raising an eyebrow.

"Well, when he was showing me the differences between the real and the fake gems, there was a pipe burst and they could have been mixed up – the young apprentice checked me out instead and... it was stressful chaos. I didn't know what to do but hurry and leave." Seconds of silence follows when she finishes.

I just stare at sissy before adding, "You have the strangest luck, and it somehow always involves men."

*I need to clear my head and think about something else for a little bit. I think I'll go check that library out. I wonder if the Myracks have any books on thermoelectric mechanics?*

"Lori, I'm gonna head to the library for a bit, okay?"

"All right, but hurry back soon; I'm freaking out a little."

"Look, everything is right as rain, we will exchange the gem for the fake one in a day or two. Maybe Winona will need to go into town for food and we can go with her and exchange it."

"All right but what if that little apprentice gets in trouble?"

"Just explain it in a way that makes everyone sound inno-cent and the pipe is to blame. I'm leaving now," I call, walking out the door.

"Wait what if–" *click.* The door is shut, and I'm on my way to that beautiful library. *Now there is a place I'd be happy to get lost in.*

Through those ornate oak double doors I walk in, getting a tingly feeling all over just from the size of the immense book collection, and what's better is that someone kept the fire going. I could read by the fire for a little bit before heading back for bed. *Now how do I possibly find what I'm looking for in this place?* I say to myself as I gaze around at the small tables over-filled with books. Near the doors sits a large pedestal holding the largest book I have ever beheld. Curious, I walk over and look at the open pages.

The book is thinner than I thought, and to my luck, it has the records of the books and where they're placed in the library. *Let's see here, science and mechanics, where are you? Second floor, section three. Wonderful, I wanted to check out the top floor.* I head up to the second floor through one of the small spiral staircases in the corner. The rows of books are illuminated by the warm-but-bright gas lamps, and there is a delicious scent of vanilla in the air mixed with the smell of old books.

"Ah," I breathe out in great content when I find the section three science shelf of books. As I begin to browse closer to the books, the hairs on my neck begin to stick straight up, and I get the sense that there is someone right behind me. I can feel it. Ready for whoever it might be, I whip around into a ready boxing stance. It's Keagan, and he is no more than two metres away from me.

"Hey, I surrender!" Keagan exclaims jokingly, hands raised and a big smile on his face. I quickly return to a normal stance, but with a flushed face this time.

"You gave me a fright," I manage to say.

"My apologies, I didn't mean to frighten you. Are you looking for a distraction?" *What kind of distraction is he talking about? Wait – the books, you dunce!*

"Uh, yes, but there are so many to choose from, I have no idea how you don't go mad from wanting to read them all at once."

He gave a chuckle before continuing.

"Well, if you really want a page turner then you must start with the classics, for example..." Keagan started walking to the shelf on the right, beside the science section, and pulled out a book at knee height.

"Sherlock Holmes – now this is a page turner if ever there was one, I highly recommend this series."

"Oh, thank you, but I've already read the whole series. You are right though, they are great."

"There are over sixty stories in the series."

"Yes, what's your point?"

"...Um nevermind, uh, look, I never got a chance to apologize back to you about last night in my room," Keagan says, rubbing his neck. That's right, Keagan got cut off by Miss Masie before he could respond to me, she was trying to get his measurements for a new suit and compliment me on the dress I found.

"I'm sorry about that, I didn't mean to frustrate you or push you either. I've been under a lot of stress lately, and you know, what with everything else that's transpired in the past month," he apologizes.

This makes me turn away completely from the bookcase where I was searching again and look directly in his eyes. But when I see that his expression is pained and genuine, more of my own stubbornness breaks away, allowing me to reply with, "I'm sorry as well. I like to test people, and I forgot to take into account that you've recently had a great loss. I guess it was because you acted so happy when you talked to us at dinner," I say, glancing at the black mourning band on his shirt sleeve.

"Well, apology accepted, and I wasn't acting; you both are very intriguing ladies and were able to bring me a little happiness, which is something I haven't felt in a long time."

"So then I guess I don't need to apologize after all?" I say in a teasing voice that surprises even me as I walk back to the spiral stairs.

Keagan follows, trying to catch up, saying, "You are by far not off the hook for that. Besides, you already apologized and I forgive you, so what's done is done," he replies playfully. Noticing this, I choose a random book from the nearest shelf as quickly as possible so as to not rile him on and possibly change the subject back to books.

He catches up so close to me that I can feel the heat coming off him. I realise now how shallow my breathing is when he is close. When I turn my head, I see him looking right in my eyes with a boyish curious look, making me worry he might try something fresh. *This guy knows nothing about personal space.*

Reaching for the book in my hands, he asks, "So... what kind of book are you looking for?"

"Anything really. I'm interested in all genres," I lie coolly.

"Then why not try this one?" he says, suddenly leaning towards me, his face even closer than I am comfortable with. When he pulls back he has a book in his hands. "Here, try this one."

"Forget Me Not." I've always been a little interested in this book, but my mother told me once when I was a child that it's only suitable for the eyes of married couples and women who have come of age. I'm eighteen so I suppose I can read it now.

"I managed to read it in three days," Keagan brags.

"I bet you I can read it in two," I spit out before I can stop myself. I place my hand over my lips wishing I could put the words back into my mouth.

Keagan raises his eyebrows for a second, then that mischievous grin returns as he answers, "I didn't take you for the gambling kind, Miss Aspen; who ever taught you such behavior?"

"Ah...my old uncle who was a General actually. He taught us quite a few things that could easily surprise you," I state proudly, looking him in the eye and raising my chin.

"I can't wait to be surprised more often then. So this bet, what's on the line?"

"You will... buy Lori and me a gadget or goodie of our choice the next time we go into town."

"Fine, but if I win..." Keagan begins to inch closer to me as he goes on. "You owe me four dances at the Governor's ball."

My mouth twists as I ponder the stakes. "I accept," I agree as I extend my hand.

"It's a deal then." Keagan shakes my hand with a cocky smile.

"You know, Charles told Lori and me that there are secret rooms and doors everywhere all over this mansion. I was wondering if you could show us a few? We would love to be a part of the hunt to find them all; we're great at puzzles!" I say in an alluring and curious voice.

"It's funny you mention it because there's actually one in here that we know of. What if I give you a hint and you try and find it?" Keagan says with that boyish look on his face, seemingly happy to play along.

"Here's your hint," he begins to whisper in a low voice so I have to lean in closer.

"Life as we knew it, far and deep, prickles and burns on angels' feet," he says with a now deadpan expression, and I just stare straight ahead, thinking, *What a strange hint that was.* But, nonetheless, my mind starts going. *Life as we knew it, could be old history. Far and deep: oceans, caves, hell, maybe? Prickles and burns on angels' feet: fire angels, Lucifer, the devil! It's biblical history – particularly on the devil, how gruesome!*

"Can you show me where the biblical history section is in the library?" I say with a twinkle in my eye.

Keagan just nods and starts walking. "Right this way, past the fireplace."

We descend the stairs and begin walking farther down the grand library to the eleventh section across the warm fireplace where the fire crackles and flares. *What a lovely mantle, wait...* I stop in my tracks as Keagan keeps walking, unaware that I've paused. I stare at the mantel and notice two figures that look like angels. Right in between a stone map of the world that's dated '1742'. The angel's feet are hanging off the mantle and towards the flames. Life as we knew it: the old map from over a hundred and forty years ago, far and deep: this fireplace is far from the doors and is on the bottom floor. Prickles and burns on angel's feet: the little angels are hanging their feet over the flame. *This must be it.* I looked hard at the angels' feet, the mantel itself, and then the map. That's when I saw it. A tiny bump that looks like a moon on the upper right-hand corner of the stone map with a tiny M engraved on it.

"Aspen?" I hear Keagan call, but I don't listen. I press in the moon and immediately the warm fire blows out, causing embers to rush towards me. Keagan grabs me and pulls me far away quickly before I can get charred. As he holds me tightly by my side, we watch the back of the stone fireplace creak open a touch with a clicking sound of old gears working. We stand there a few moments, not saying anything and feeling a dreadfully cold draft coming through the opening.

"Well, I found it," I say in wonder.

"You sure did. You found a new one."

"What? What do you mean? That mantle is made up of the exact clues you gave me."

"Yes, and so is that bookshelf at the farthest corner of the library. It has the painting of the devil in hell below a flat earth." He points to the tiny painting in the bottom corner.

"Oh... well, tada! I found a new one!" I say with enthusiasm as I turn to him and realise how close we are and how tightly he's holding me.

"My apologies," he says abruptly, releasing me with a start. "I just didn't want you to get burnt," he adds, beginning to redden a bit whilst he scratches his head.

"Right, um, thank you. I didn't see that coming," I say, dusting my sleeves off as well.

"It sure is cold in there; do you think it leads outside?"

"I'm not sure. I've never seen an opening on this front side of the house."

"Is there a basement maybe?" I ask as I inch closer to the opening, crouch down in the fireplace, and gently push the door open. The draft blows harder now – a bitterly cold breeze – and it even begins to emit a low whistle.

"I think we should wait till it's light outside to go spelunking, don't you?" Keagan says close to my ear in that low voice again, making my cheeks tingle with heat. He's right though; it'll be warmer in the daylight.

"Good idea, plus no one knows where the door is but us, and we don't have any lanterns either."

"Agreed, so, great puzzler: any idea how to close this door?" Keagan teases. I turn to look at him and see his glowing warm expression. Just like that, there's that little boy I remember who would tease Lori and me with the happiest look on his face. He loved to tease and joke with us, careful not to take things too far after what happened the one time he did. That pain in my arm goes off again as I rub the feeling away and bring my mind back to reality. I begin to feel along the cold soot-covered stones around the rim of the opening until I come across a trick lever to close it on the inside. Once it shuts with a click, I turn back to Keagan with a smug face.

"Bravo. Now I think it's time for bed, don't you?"

"Can you at least show me the other secret passage before I go win our bet – I mean go to bed," I request in the same playful tone as his. He gave me his patented smug look that's just dripping with mischief from his eyes to his mouth.

"I'll show you where it is, but I want to see if you can open it as easily as you did this one, Miss Smarty Britches," he says as he holds out a hand. As much as I dislike playing the damsel in distress, I do need help standing back up in this infernal dress without making a scene. I take his hand, and he helps me out gently, allowing me to pull on his arm to bring myself up straight. But once I'm standing up, he doesn't release me or my hand. He places it in the crook of his arm and leads me across the library as if he were escorting me onto the dance floor. We don't say a word as we go to the now-dark far corner of the library. Keagan releases me, folding his arms across his chest once we are standing right before the Rococo-style painted bookshelf, keeping an expectant look on his face.

"All right, let's see if you can open this one," he says as I crouch down and analyze it for a minute. I try touching the devil horns, pushing the whole painting in, and even trying to pry open the panel to see if it moves. Nothing.

"Do you need a hint?" Keagan asks from his seat he's pulled up right behind me.

"No," I call back; I don't want to admit defeat yet, and I certainly am not going to ask for help from him.

"Heh, well, did you ever think of sliding, instead of pushing and pulling?" He chuckles. I make a pout with my lip when I hear the enjoyment in his voice. *Wait, the last secret door had an M engraved on it; what if... bingo!* I find a small but definable M on the devil's wing and slide it up. When that doesn't work I try downward. It's then that I hear a hiss before a lever pops out of the moulding near my head. I pull it down, causing the wall directly to my right to slide into itself, leaving a small metre-wide doorway that shows off a secret little room holding a pedestal in the centre of it. It's a wooden box with a glass lid on top that holds the deed to the estate atop what I could only guess is their family bible. *Why would Keagan want me to find this?*

"All right, you know about this secret place, but now that I've shown you, I need you to promise that you'll not go near it again so you don't raise suspicion."

"I'll promise when you tell me why you wanted me to find this secret door."

"Heh, well, Charles told me about how eager you and your sister sounded about finding the hidden rooms and doors in the house, and I think I can trust you enough to keep this one hidden now that you know how important it is to *stay* hidden. Understand?"

I nod my head, knowing what would happen if someone outside of the family got the deed to the house and went to court with it *signed* over to them – Keagan, his household, my sister, and I would be out of a home. Lori and I are used to it by now, but Keagan wouldn't be; this is his lineage.

"I promise," I say suddenly, realising that Keagan is just a half-metre away now, I take a step back only to bounce off the bookshelf and towards him. I readjust myself, new book in hand, and begin to walk off a bit before I realise I forgot to say goodnight to Keagan.

"Um, goodnight, Keagan. I think I'll be heading to bed soon, and I want to start reading. I can't wait to find more secrets here though."

"Neither can I. Goodnight," he replies with a knowing smile that only makes me want to walk faster to my room.

"Aspen, I've been worried sick! I know you love books, but it took you nearly an hour! Usually you're very quick."

"Well, you saw the library; it's monstrous. So many books to choose from," I state, but Lori doesn't seem to buy it.

"You ran into *him*, didn't you?"

"Who?"

"You *know* who."

"...How could you tell?"

"There's mischief in your eyes, and it doesn't look like it's from scheming. What happened?" Lori chirps, her eyes twinkling with curiosity.

"We made a bet on a book, if I finish it in forty-eight hours then we get to pick out gifts for ourselves – his treat."

"Oh, I love it! What if he wins?"

"Then we have to dance with him at the ball at least four times."

Lori pauses for a moment with a confused look on her face.

"Where's the downside to that? I love this bet!"

"Lori," I moan, rolling my eyes. Lori just giggles whilst bouncing her way to the bathroom to prepare for bed. I decided to find a comfortable place on the couch to get started on our little bet. *Just you watch, Keagan. You're only going to supply me with more ammunition for my cause with this wager.*

# BLU MAN'S CLIFF

## KEAGAN

"Morning, ladies," I say cheerfully, hoping to hide my own grogginess from how long I was awake due to last night's library tunnel discovery. *I barely slept from searching through all the old relics that were down that forgotten rabbit hole.*

"Morning, Keagan," Lori and Aspen echo in unison, one yawning after the other as they join me at the breakfast table. Winona made quite a spread this morning, as usual – croissants and jam, breakfast tea with honey, and fresh pumpkin bread with butter. The drapes are already drawn allowing the room natural golden light of the morning. I wait for the ladies to have a few sips of tea and bites of croissant so they can wake up before I tell them the plans for the day.

"I've arranged for Lady Pomley to come join us for lunch and a visit. You mentioned something the other day, Lori, about getting acquainted with the people of this town? Well there's no one better to turn to than to Lady Pomley, she knows practically all the elites and middle class families." I explain before taking a sip of tea.

"Oh, how wonderful, thank you for setting it up. It will be

most helpful for us entering into society here, don't you agree, Aspen?" Lori chirps.

"Huh? Oh, um yes, quite invigorating" Aspen mumbles. *She still looks tired. I guess she isn't much of a morning person, or perhaps it had to do with our wager. I'm worried to ask how late she stayed up reading that novel.*

"Aspen, you look rather out of sorts still, would you like a nap after breakfast before Lady Pomley comes to visit us?"

"Oh, could I? That would be most helpful, I'm afraid that I got carried away last night... with a book," Aspen sighs out, looking rather sheepish.

"I can see that, and of course you may. You know, Lori, I'm rather surprised you are looking so much more chipper than your sister; didn't her reading light bother you?" I say with playful humor.

"Ha, actually I've gotten used to it over the past few months; since she stays awake so much at such late hours," Lori replies. Right after she finished speaking I heard a strange *thump* sound that came from under the table causing Lori to jolt. After that, Lori spoke again in a rather rapid tone.

"B-but she doesn't stay awake every night reading, thank goodness, so we won't need to worry about her being tired like this every morning." Aspen gives her sister a sideways glance before finishing the rest of her tea, whilst Lori returns it with her own small sneer.

"Yes, well, good then," I muse. *Whatever these girls are doing at night doesn't sound like it's just reading. Maybe I should give them a late night visit sometime soon to make sure everything is up to par.*

～

Lady Pomley rides up in her new blue phaeton carriage, which is filled to the brim with nearly all of her dimies, one of her dogs, and herself. When I meet her at the doors with Charles, her pooch Minnie gives us the usual greeting: a snarl and shrill bark. However, due to M'Lady's ensemble, I pay no notice to the mutt. I nearly mistook Lady Pomley for a giant fluffy peacock with her feather cape and multi-coloured feather hat; she seemed to strut through our door as if she were one as well.

For a split second, I didn't know whether to greet her or grab my rifle to go hunting. Stifling my snicker, we welcome her in before showing her to our small tea room. Nearing the tea room, I turn around at the sound of Charles chuckling in time to see him strutting around like M'lady with her hat on his head and cape over one shoulder. Two of her dimies are walking briskly to the kitchen, but I know they had to have noticed that rude display. I'll have to throttle him later for insulting our guest in front of her party like that, even if she does act that ridiculous.

I'm relieved to see that she is wearing her usual dark skirts and black-strap corset so there is nothing to laugh about during lunch.

"I've lived here all my life and have seen this city rise from the ground up. I can tell you where all the best patisseries and shops are. And where the most eligible men are to be found as well. Lori, there is a young gentleman your age just a few houses down from here who is currently single and is such a gas." Lady Pomley giggles as she takes a sip of her tea before leaning back again in the lounge chair. Her odd entertaining fashion I can handle, I can even take her annoying lapdog, I just wish she would have the courtesy to talk about anything else besides the possibility of pairing up Aspen and Lori with the single gentlemen in town whilst I'm still here in the room. Though I must admit I'm outnumbered by females at the moment to attempt to govern the conversation. It just gives me a terribly uneasy feeling for some reason just talking about finding the ladies gentleman callers.

"You must have a very thorough knowledge of the sectors in the city then; pray tell us more about the ones we should see and even the ones we should stay away from. Should the event ever turn up that we get separated from Keagan or our party, we want to know where it is safe for us to be in the city," Aspen asks with all the charm in the world.

"Well there are a few places you should certainly stay away from, my slaves Desmond and Lucille are from the bad sector of the city near the Blu Man's Cliff. Before my dear husband departed, he had bought them from The Market. They were practically begging to be bought and to get out of the neighbourhood. Apparently there had been rumours of attacks on dimies over there at night time after their curfew.

My slaves would say that the attackers were metal men, but we've never seen any robots that would just go out and attack people or slaves during the night or daytime for that matter. So it must've been just a fantasized rumour to aid in the horridity of the area's grimness," Pomley babbles out. *Metal men? Wouldn't the police or the governor have warned the town to stay off the streets at night as well if there were such things going on? Must be men in armour or just fantasized stories to keep the dimies in their owners' homes during curfew.*

*I forgot how much she loves to talk.* I lean back into the corner of the couch and pray that I wouldn't fall asleep. If it were not for the sake of the ladies and hiding the secret I found in the library, I would never have asked Lady Pomley to come. I'm beginning to dread my decision even more now as she gabs about the designer of her dresses. *I wonder if divulging what I found in the library was in fact the better alternative?*

"Excuse me, Lady Pomley, but you mentioned something about Blu Man's Cliff?" Aspen asks. My interest in the conversation has suddenly returned. There's supposed to be a horrific story tied to that cliff, but I've never remembered to ask anyone about it, and frankly, there's never been a proper time to ask anyone.

"I don't believe I've ever been given the pleasure of hearing the tale of Blu Man's Cliff," I add, looking from Aspen to Lady Pomley whose expression of growing excitement is a bit overwhelming.

"Oh, my dears, that cliff has a deliciously tragic story tied to it; would you like to hear it?" Pomley beams. I look at the girls, and they both give me a nod and a smile.

"Let's have it, Lady Pomley," I state.

"Oh good, I do love a scary story. Ahem," Lady Pomley announces, clearing her throat before beginning the story. "One winter long ago, when our bustling city was just a small growing village, one of the well-known men in town was a man named Jonathan Blu. He was liked and respected by many and even had a fiancée for a while. But our town back then was even more dangerous than it is now, bless our stars. The town's surrounding forest used to be filled with gypsies, thieves, savage beasts, and Lord knows what else. Well, just days before Blu's wedding with his love there was a horrible raid on our town by a band of garish thieves! They set buildings and homes on fire only to wait for people to come out to meet their deaths by blade whilst the women were to be kidnapped or abused.

"Homes and stores were looted, it was an all-out war between our town and the pillaging thieves. Blu's fiancée was one of the women who were taken during the heat of the battle. When all the thieves had fled, been killed, or imprisoned, and the buildings on fire were being tended to, hordes of men went into the woods to find and save their women and possessions. Two days passed, and the worst blizzard on record hit this area; large parties of men came back – some with women, some with their women and possessions. Some, however, didn't return at all, but a few ladies had even managed to escape on their own and make their way back home.

"Jonathan Blu had been separated from his group during the blizzard, and the last thing his friends heard come from his mouth was his fiancée's name: *Florence*. When the blizzard had ceased the next morning, the town could see something gleaming in the morning sunlight atop of the overhang cliff near the town. Worried, a group of men, many of whom being Blu's friends, went to the cliff to see what it was. As they neared the edge of the cliff they noticed that the glinting form began to look like a human figure." Her tone goes grave and her face becomes stricken as if she's looking straight through us and right at Jonathan Blu himself.

"It was Jonathan, frozen where he stood. His eyes were still open and covered in clear ice. His skin had turned purple and blue. In his hand was a note that the men could still read out. *She was my woman first,* it said, but not in Jonathan's handwriting. They buried him right there on the cliff, and there were rumours that the following year the ghost of his bride could be seen on the cliff still wandering around in the cold, waiting for her groom to save her."

After these cold words, the room seems to feel as icy as it looks outside the frosted windows. All three of us are leaning on the edge of our seats when I look over to see Lori holding her teacup in midair, slightly shaking. Aspen's expression, however, worries me slightly as she looks intrigued, with wide eyes and a slight smile on her face. *This lady can be unpredictably scary herself at times like this.*

"Would anyone like –"

"Ah!" Lori screams, interrupting M'lady's dimie Lucille and spilling her tea all over her skirts in the process. Minnie begins to bark at the sudden outburst; however, her attention isn't on Lori whom everyone else tends to, but Lucille.

"Oh dear," Lady Pomley and Aspen exclaim as they grab at the napkins for Lori's skirts. I dare to side glance at Lucille who is still being barked at to see her body jolt with wide eyes at each yap that escapes the pup's mouth. *She's even scared of small dogs? Could Desmond be the same way?*

"Now, now, Minnie, that is quite enough. Lori and Lucille didn't mean to startle you," M'lady says, stroking the growling Minnie's fluffy fur.

"Lucille, must we ask for help when it is so obviously needed? Go take Lori's skirt to clean the stains out and help dress her again. At least be of some use today." M'lady snaps out at poor Lucille who is still gripping her own skirts with her sleek otter paws. Lucille hops to work as she walks towards Lori despite the growls coming from Minnie.

"I think I should go see if I can help," Aspen says abruptly, beginning to get up from her place on the couch.

"Oh, tish tosh, my dear, no need to worry about your sister's skirts. She and her dress are in professional-stain-cleaning hands. Why, my Lucille once got wine and chocolate icing out of my lace pink blouse. She is truly amazing when it comes to stains, so please, stay and enjoy yourself," Lady Pomley says, waving her hand at Aspen as if she were the guest in M'lady's home instead of the other way around.

Aspen sat right down, brushing her skirts, fiddling with the trimmings as she did.

"Of course, M'lady," Aspen says, looking slightly defeated. *That's strange behaviour. Well, maybe she is actually as bored as I.*

"So tell me, Miss Wolfe, what are things like back home for you? Do you know how long you will be staying with us before you go back?" she asks Aspen out of the blue. Aspen's smile returns, but instead of answering Lady Pomley's questions, she asks her own.

"Actually, I was just about to ask about your dear husband, Ma'am, he must have been someone wonderful."

That did it.

"Oh, my dear Philip! He was such a wonderful man and was always concerned about the good of our children and..." Lady Pomley went on and on about her late husband. She may not have noticed what Aspen did, but I had. And that silver-tongued little minx deliberately avoided her questions about her home. *Does she genuinely not like talking about where she grew up?* The other night when we had that little argument she seemed to shut down at just the mention of where they last stayed. *What secrets do you hide behind those closed doors of yours, Aspen?*

After what feels like forever of listening to what her late husband was like, Lori rejoins us in a fresh new day dress; the violet one that I had purchased for her the other day. Seeing her wearing that dress makes me feel happier since it was a gift. I think I realise now the difference in how I view the girls. For Lori I feel somewhat like an older brother doting on his younger sister with gifts. However, I don't get that same feeling with Aspen even though the girls are only one year apart.

Once the teapot has been thoroughly drained, and only crumbs are left of the biscuits, M'lady announces she must be going. I stand up like a straight pin perhaps too eagerly. We all lead Lady Pomley and her entourage to the door and exchange pleasantries whilst Minnie growls goodbye.

"Oh, we simply must do this again, and the next time it shall be at *my* home. I cannot wait to show you my wardrobe, ladies. Not to mention my private collection of maps of the city like you inquired about, Aspen."

*When did she inquire about that? Maybe I really did fall asleep on that couch.*

"Why, of course M'lady. Call for us as soon as you can; both sound quite intriguing," Aspen chimes in almost before M'lady even finishes her sentence.

I get that strange feeling again about her, she seems too eager to look at maps and/or dresses. But then again, to rise in rank and society one must be ambitious and take opportunities when they come. *Father sure believed that, and I'll be struck dead if I were to say he didn't try to ingrain that into my mind.* The moment the doors shut I felt as though all my energy had been sucked out as well.

"I'm going to lie down awhile. Charles, please wake me up before dinner if I'm not up by then already. And ladies, please don't get into too much trouble whilst I'm out," I say, winking at Charles. Nodding back, he knows to keep them away from the fireplace as he promptly begins to walk off towards the library.

"Us? Why, Keagan, you insult us. When have we ever gotten in trouble?" Lori says playfully.

"Need I remind you of all the schemes and little heists you executed as kids – half of them just for the biscuit jar," I call back to them as I stride towards my bedroom.

"Don't forget, more often than not, *you* had your hand in our grand schemes as well. Lest we forget what happened to the jade vase when you were eight?" Aspen calls back loud enough to where Charles must have heard it because I can hear his footfalls advancing. *Oh, that was a dirty card to play,* I think to myself as I begin to walk faster towards my room whilst I can hear the girls giggling down the hall.

"What was that about the jade vase?" Charles exclaims, sounding a bit peeved. That jade vase was his to inherit in my father's will until I had knocked it over as a kid. I make it to my room and hop towards my bed as I struggle to take off my shoes and get under the sheets before Charles comes in with a load of questions about his one valuable piece of inheritance. I frantically take off my day suit and trousers, and plop under the covers. *I would just hate to show him the broken pieces of that vase. I've been meaning to fix it for years but never got to it.* I begin to make plans on going to the secret door where we three hid it years ago and fix it at night. But in the midst of my planning I soon find myself nodding off completely.

Dinner comes quickly and is rather peaceful, but there is much talk about Lady Pomley's outfit, and how Charles and I agree we've gone shooting for something just like it. Aspen relishes in diving back into the story of Jonathan Blu and discussing how the paper got into his hand before he froze to death, among other theories about the ghost tale. Because of the extra cooking and cleaning that Winona had to do for all our extra guests today, she appears very tired during the whole meal. After some gentle persuasion and help from Lori wishing to tell Winona about what she thinks of her stay thus far, Lori and Charles keep her company whilst Aspen and I clean the table. As we carry our piles of dishes back into the kitchen, Aspen clears her throat, catching my attention.

"I finished the book," Aspen beams with pride.

"It hasn't even been twenty-four hours! There's no possible way you read that novel that quickly...wait a bloody second." I set down my pile of dishes in the sink and take Aspen's pile from her hands to begin cleaning.

"Did you read more of the book instead of taking a nap earlier this morning?" I question her. Aspen's face twists, trying not to smile, but she can't help it and breaks out into a broad grin.

"Perhaps I did. Perhaps not," she says, averting her attention to the bowl she's drying.

"You little... all right, then I guess you won't mind answering some questions, just to make sure you actually read the whole book."

"Go right ahead," she challenges me.

"What was the symbolism of the forget-me-not flower in the Whey family?" I question her.

Without missing a beat she answers with, "It's the women's flower of the family and their emblem of love."

"That's much too easy; what was the name of the clerk's son at the bank?" I question her, handing over the serving utensils.

"Theodore, but everyone calls him Teddy."

"At what time did the lightning strike that William shot his gun, and who did he kill?"

"Ten fifteen, Marian's brother, and it was because he tried to poison him but killed William's sister instead by accident," she blurts out and stares me straight in the eyes, proudly pausing her cleaning. I can clearly see how green her eyes are for once, like a great forest I'd happily get lost in if given the chance.

"Well done," I praise her whilst placing both of my hands on the counter top with her between my arms, trapping her. "Now how shall I reward you?" I purr out.

She puts her arms on my chest, stopping me from coming any closer. "Don't you think you are overstepping a boundary? This is being much more than just forward."

"Most women don't mind when I am; some actually prefer it," I reply boldly as I study the rosy soft skin of her cheeks and lips before looking into those green eyes of hers again. I must be making her uneasy because she seems to have a hard time looking back.

"Well, I am not like most women, and I'm especially not like the women that you probably strut around with in the taverns," Aspen declares proudly as she regains her bearings and turns her back on me as she begins cleaning a silver spoon.

All I can do is gape at the back of her head for such a bold accusation. *It's obvious she thinks very little of me; I'll have to change that.* "No, my dear, you most certainly are not, and for the record I don't fraternize with those types of women in the taverns," I defend myself as I tilt my head closer to her ear.

But Aspen holds her gaze forward whilst she stutters out, "Uhm, s-so I, I guess you owe Lori and I uhm... what was it again?" She slowly regains her composure as I push off the counter, allowing her the freedom to move again.

"I believe it was gadgets and goodies, *regrettably.*" *At least I get to lavish her with a special gift now; maybe that'll change her mind a little about me.*

"Well, those were the terms, and you agreed to them," she states, piling up another plate.

"I did and I'll keep my word, but if I ask to dance with you or your sister, I hope you will still allow me the pleasure at least once."

"Well, we will just have to wait and see how nice of gifts we get, I guess, and if you remain a gentleman during our stay here."

"Even if that's so, if you choose to wear that green dress I bought you the other day, I'm afraid I wouldn't have enough self-control to accept no for an answer at the dance," I say with a smirk on my face.

Aspen goes silent at this but nearly drops the dish she was drying. "Uh, ahem, when would we be able to go shopping for them? W-when would you prefer?" she asks. I detect a light blush rising on her cheeks that gives me a small feeling of victory.

"What say we go into town tomorrow or the next day and have tea time with Miss Masie whilst we are there as well."

"Why, that sounds splendid! She seemed like a stellar lady, I know for sure that Lori would agree with me on that," Aspen says, returning to her calculating normal self again.

"Wonderful. Besides, Charles and Winona have some errands to run in the farmers market anyhow. Your sister was practically begging poor Winona to teach her how to bake a special dessert this morning whilst you slept. It's supposed to be a surprise for tomorrow night."

"Well, we still have to act surprised about it then, and between you and me, this isn't the first time she has tried to bake. So as a forewarning, if it comes out undercooked or a bit well charred....go easy on her," she says, trying to hide a grin.

"They do not come out charred! Oh-" Lori's voice booms against the kitchen door, snapping our attention back at her through the crack in the open door. Lori, mouth covered, quickly dashes away, disappearing from view.

"I'm trying to figure out who will be more of a handful between the two of you: the clever one or the snoop," I chuckle, handing Aspen a teacup.

"I think we balance each other out when it comes to mischief. We've been told many times that there is rarely a dull moment with us around."

"I'll be sure to remember that."

*It will be interesting to see what kinds of trouble these girls are accustomed to,* I think as I observe the curve of Aspen's waist as she reaches for a dry tea towel.

# SUGAR, SPICE, FIRE, AND ICE

## ASPEN

"Oh, but that one looks so scrumptious. Aspen, help me out; I can't decide," Lori drools out whilst looking at the cakes that are kept just beyond the glass. And thank goodness there was something stopping my sissy from getting too close to the goodies or Keagan would have to buy the entire inventory. Keagan has already asked for an apple crumb cake and five mini honeycomb cakes; now we are just waiting on Lori.

This was our third bakery we've been to today; the first had delicious tea, but the cakes didn't look or smell fresh enough for Lori, at the second shop we had berry scones, but the pastries didn't have enough fruit on them according to Lori's expertise. And now here we are at the third bakery, and after having tea time with Miss Masie, we are thoroughly full to the brim. And yet she still demands the perfect goodie.

"This is the last patisserie we are visiting today, Lori; Aspen hasn't even had a chance to find her gift yet," Keagan tells her as we walk together. I feel like such a child when he talks to us like that. He's what, three years older than me and about four more than Lori?

"I know, I know, but how can you choose just one so easily?" she whines.

"Oh, good glory, close your eyes, and I'll choose for you then," I say annoyed.

"What? No!"

"What's your freshest berry pastry?" I ask the clerk.

"Wait," Lori objects, but the clerk and I don't pause for a moment. We've been here for at least twenty minutes without actually paying for anything yet and are overstaying our welcome.

"Here we are, we just pulled it out of the oven five minutes ago. It should have cooled down by now, so it's not too hot to eat," the clerk says, placing a large and gooey mini pie that is nearly overflowing with fresh berries and cream on parchment paper. All Lori can do is stare and gape at the pastry like it asked her to marry it. Personally, I could see her saying yes if it actually could ask her, just before she devours it, of course. Too full from the tea and scones, Lori has her pie boxed with the other goodies. Keagan pays the bakers for their troubles and we are finally off.

Since we were just a block away from where Winona and Charles were for the fresh market, we decided to leave our treats in the car before going to search for my gift. Lori, however, insisted that she held onto her precious pie, in case she got hungry. As we head down to the stores closer to Cogs and Bogs, I attempt to form a plan of returning the sapphire. There has to be a way to exchange that sapphire without a lot of trouble; sadly that also means we will need to get away from Keagan again. The only problem with that is he seems to stick to us like glue today.

So many of the shops here are quite charming. The weaponry, clockmakers, fabric and tailor shops, bakeries, teahouses and the gadgetry stores. One of which we pass by leisurely. As I look in the windows at the display, I see something that stops me in my tracks. There is a lovely cameo of a young woman reclining in a meadow; it's border is made of freshwater pearls and the backing is cogs that embellish the sides perfectly. Mum used to wear one a lot like that; it was her favourite ever since papa gave it to her that one Christmas.

"Keagan?" I ask gently. Lori and Keagan turn around at this to see me looking in the window.

"Yes?"

"Could I have that cameo as my gift?"

Keagan bends down to my level to look at the brooch. "I think we can make that happen." I can hear the gentle smile in his voice.

When we enter the shop we realise this isn't just an accessory store, but a gadgetry shop as well. The owners seem to have a knack for combining common objects and weapons together. There are hats with binoculars, gloves with switchblade knives and retractable guns, recorder bowties and jet-propelling boots to name a few. *I'm in heaven. There are so many things to draw inspiration from I wish I had a pen and sketch pad for this!*

"I definitely want to ask about the brooch, but can we please look around first? This place is quite eclectic," I say with starry eyes.

"By all means, I'd like to see what they have myself," Keagan agrees.

Whilst looking at a pair of the jet-propelling boots, the

store mechanic, who introduced himself as Antonio, comes around the clerk desk to where we are. When he sees the curiosity in our eyes he starts twisting his long handlebar mustache, thinking of what to show us first. The one that catches Lori's eye is a jeweled bracelet. Antonio explains that when the pin is pulled, the smoke-bomb jewels fall off and explode, giving off a cloud of fog. The hat he wears has a telescope attachment that doubles as a dart shooter on the sides of the lenses. After the fourth gadget he shows us, Keagan broaches the subject of the cameo brooch.

"Ah, yes, the pretty little cameo! I can attach many things to it: fog pellets, a camera, voice recorder, you name it and I make," he chirps out in an Italian accent.

"That won't be necessary; she is clever enough on her own without gadgets," Keagan responds, sliding a glance at me.

Antonio's expression looks as if he had been insulted, but he tries to hide it by going to retrieve the brooch from the window display.

I tap Lori on the elbow for the distract signal. She immediately walks straight to the other side of the cluttered store where the cutlery ties are. "Keagan you simply must look at these," she cries.

"Just one moment. Brooch first, ties later," Keagan calls back.

"No, it's fine, actually, I'd like to hear more about the cameo's history. Besides, Lori gets overly curious in places like this; sharing her excitement will lessen the possibility of an accident," I reassure him.

"Say no more; just come and get me when you are ready to buy it. Thank heaven this isn't a pastry shop," Keagan says, walking in Lori's direction. I can't help but giggle; he can be so easy to persuade. At the clerks desk, there is a pad of paper and a pen.

"What can you tell me about the cameo?" I ask as I write down the message:

*Please add a hidden camera and voice recorder into the brooch.*

I slide it to Antonio, and his mustache lifts two inches as a broad smile returns to his face. He motions for me to follow him to his work bench in the far corner of the store.

"Well, this brooch was made by three artisans," he says over the sound of him rummaging for his tools.

I peek over the display of lipstick and tweezer gloves to see Lori and Keagan still enwrapped in conversation. Antonio is quick with his hands and soldering stick. He spouts off random information that may or may not be true about the pin, but I don't question him whilst he is working. He conceals the attachments by placing a detachable, thin metal box with holes over them.

Antonio explains in a whisper that the box must be removed to listen to the recording and to remove the micro-film from the camera. When he is finished with the attachments, he quickly gives me a demonstration of how to use it. When I do a test run to make sure it works, I can hear padded footsteps coming our way. Frantically, I give the pin back to Antonio, who stops the recording and places the brooch in a cotton padded box, but not before stuffing two rolls of micro-film and rolls of recording tape under the cotton.

We take two steps back towards the main counter, and

Keagan emerges from a hat rack, looking around for us. He must have noticed that we are next to the workers table because he gets a suspicious look on his face.

"So what's going on over here?"

"Oh, uh the broach's pin was stuck. Antonio said it was soldered to the clasp, so he had to fix it just now."

"Si, si I-I fix, now it pin on smooth as silk," Antonio stammers.

"You're sure you still want it? There aren't any other problems with it, right?" Keagan looks from me to Antonio who is still holding the box nervously.

"Oh yes, I'm sure about this one, I looked over it and so did Antonio; it's perfect now."

"All right," was all Keagan said as he took the box from Antonio to look at the pin. The cost of the pin was a bit much for what a normal brooch like it would be, but Keagan didn't say a word against it.

"I sure hope you wear this piece around; it's truly lovely," he says as we exit the store.

"Don't worry about that; I think you will see me wearing it around quite a lot actually."

As we leave the shop to continue our stroll, we slip into a street that seems to be almost empty. It's quite strange to see so few people out on a bright morning like this. But still it is refreshing not to be crowded on the sidewalks for once.

We somehow get in a conversation about our most terrible and wonderful food experiences. When it's my turn, I remember when our baby cousin wanted to be a gourmet chef and tried to make us dinner one night.

~

"And that's when our cousin James brings in the main course," I say, cringing already.

"Which was?" Keagan prods.

"Boiled cow tongue!"

"Augh, God!" he exclaims in disgust. We all have a laugh before hitting a lull in the conversation again.

"You know, Keagan, I've been wondering, why is it you have only Winona and Charles to take care of such a large manor on their own?" I ask.

"Well, we used to have many dimies and humans employed to help keep the house in order when I was younger. But each year that I came home we had fewer and fewer housekeepers and workers. My guess is that they became too old and passed away or father gave them to a new family. But Winona and Charles were the ones that were always there no matter what. And to be honest they are a little competitive against each other in who keeps their cleaning skills at peak condition," he adds with a chuckle before continuing.

"But whenever we have a large party coming to the house I employ some of the lower-middle- and poor-class human workers since it's so hard for them to find work. Charles was one of them before my father employed him full time."

"Wow, that's good that you hire humans who need work instead of buying a bunch of dimies," Lori observes. Just then we pass a partly bionic man.

"Afternoon," he greets us, smiling whilst lifting his hat with his extendable robotic wrist.

"Afternoon," we reply, smiling back whilst we bow our heads and Keagan tips his hat. *How wondrous it would be to be partly bionic.*

"Poor chap probably lost his arm from the plague, eh?" Lori mentions when the man is out of earshot.

"Indeed, you will see a few survivors here and there, but you can always tell who was affected physically when they have the bionic parts and the scars to prove it."

I want to ask him, how badly was your family affected? But that kind of question would be too forward, besides I already know the basic answer. Keagan's mother, like ours, died from the plague. It's still hard to believe that fever spread for so many years. I guess Lori and I were lucky to make it out with only a few scars on our legs and backs since we only had a weak strain of it. I count the names of those our family lost from the epidemic, but I don't think that we can share this with Keagan just yet at our current relationship level though.

"How hard was your town hit when it came?" Lori asks.

"Well, I can't give an exact headcount since it came to our town a good two years after it first came about in Ireland. But a few medical friends of mine have told me that from the year 1848 to 1875, about eighty percent of our working class died and a third of the middle and upper class were taken away from the disease as well. Everyone lost somebody to the plague, we three sure did," he answers sombrely, which takes the conversation to a heavier feeling than it was just a few minutes ago.

No wonder the Slave-Trade Organization began here; this city seems to be the worst hit of any town we've been in. They needed cheap labor fast and the dimies were the way to go once they opened the gateway. *But I wonder what they were looking for at first? A cure, help, money, or actually cheap labor?*

My thoughts are ground to a halt at the sound of loud voices and bashing rubbish cans coming from the alley way that we are approaching. Keagan begins to walk in front of us protectively with a hand extended backward to slow us down. I look at Lori and give her a nod to prepare for anything. I take my pocket size pistol out and brass knuckles from the hidden pocket in my hat whilst Lori takes her blade-projecting fan out.

I glance around us, and the street is completely bare; no pedestrians, no carriages, no children playing. Only a few stray dogs roam around, and I get an uneasy feeling at what might be waiting in the shadows. I peek around the hole opening between the wall and Keagan's neck to see what's going on. It's an old dimie; his clothes are in tatters, and his eye appears to be swelling. The cause appears in front of him in the form of two roguish men.

"Please, leave me be!" the dimie whimpers.

"Shut up, you bastard!" yells the dirt-covered man wearing a black jacket and a full red beard. He grabs the brown otter dimie by the collar of his yellowed shirt and raises his fist as if to punch him again.

"Stay here and hide," Keagan whispers in a low rumble whilst keeping his eyes on the men.

"He asked you to leave him alone," Keagan says to the men as he walks into their view.

"Bug off, pretty boy. You should leave whilst you're still able to," the other man with a smug, pudgy face growls. He wears a bowler hat and an old pea-coat jacket that has tears here and there; he doesn't seem like a merciful man.

"Leave. Him. Be," Keagan says, pausing after each word.

"Oi, we could, boy, we could," the pudgy man muses in a southern cockney accent as he smiles at his accomplice. "What of a trade?" He steps closer and nods his head in our direction. "The slave for the two little women you have over there?"

Keagan turns his head sharply to where the man is looking to see that there is a view of us on the other side of the wall through two filthy windows. We are in trouble now; if he can't fight these men off himself we will have to intervene.

"What do you say, boy?" The man takes one step around Keagan with his eyes on us through the windows. Before the man can move again, Keagan raises his cane and swings it at the man's head. The man catches it inches from his head and swings a fist at Keagan. Keagan twists the bottom of his cane, catching and trapping the man's arm on the wall adjacent to him, giving Keagan the window to left hook the man square in the jaw.

This causes the man to hit his head on the wall hard before stumbling to the ground. His accomplice throws the old dimie to the side of the rubbish heap and brandishes a large jagged knife. Keagan takes his cane's handle and unsheaths a long thin sword; he points it directly at the now-nervous-looking man.

I see in my peripheral vision a large hand clap onto Lori's shoulder; my eyes widen as we both spin around. Lori jabs the man in the gut with the butt of her fan. When he hunches over I punch him in the face with my brass-knuckled fist. He falls to the ground before we see two more men coming our way and they appear to be just as ragged and desperate looking as the ones Keagan is fighting.

"Oi, calm down, ladies, we just want to help you get away from the danger. Don't we, Dredger?" He scratches his whiskery face, looking back at his mate who must be Dredger.

"I think that we will be just fine, take one more step towards us and you'll end up like your mate here," I warn, gesturing to the fallen man on the ground with my fist.

"Hey-" the man says, taking a step forward. I immediately raise my hidden gun to him and Lori unfolds her fan, showing it's blades. The men's eyes widen and their hands begin to raise. I fire two warning shots at their feet, causing them to tuck their tails and run.

"No!" I hear a distressed call from the alley, causing me to spin, looking straight through the dirty windows. It was Keagan; he looks at us with a terrified disheveled face before turning into bewilderment. *He must have thought someone shot us.* But whilst he was looking at us, the mangy man that he hit first is now off the ground and coming towards him. I zip around the corner and point my gun at the angry man as he raises a knife in his hand. When Keagan turns to face me, he jolts as he catches a glimpse of the man right before he tries to stab him. Keagan raises his sword in time to catch the knife, but the man still manages to slash him near his shoulder.

"Augh!" Keagan calls out in pain.

"You should leave now whilst you're still able to," I say in a mocking tone as I slowly walk towards them. I can hear the faint sound of horse carriages barreling our way; hopefully it's the constables. The man pinning Keagan to the wall turns his face to me but holds Keagan still with his knife in his arm.

"Oh, come now, poppet, you're not gonna shoot me. You couldn't shoot a-"

His words are drowned out by the sound of a gunshot. The rat flinches and reels backwards, checking his body for a bullet wound, releasing the knife that pinned down Keagan. He takes his hat off to touch his balding head when he sees the hole that is still smoking through his bowler cap.

"You're a crazy broad, that's what you are!" he shouts at me.

I just snicker with a large grin and recock my pistol. The rat makes a mad dash to the other end of the alley and disappears, leaving his comrade in the dust. I put my gun away as Keagan grips at his arm for a second staring at me with a concerned look. I signal Lori to put her weapons away before moving towards the bruised dimie.

Keagan sheaths his cane-sword before helping me put the old otter dimie on a crate. His fur has lost its luster, and his eyes are a little cloudy; he's probably partly blind from cataracts. He appears to belong to a poor or stingy master by the looks of his clothing. I quickly hide my brass knuckles in my skirts, forgetting that I still had them on.

"All right now, easy, what's your name?" Keagan asks, holding his own shoulder still now with a handkerchief.

"Jasper," the dimie wheezes out.

"Okay, Jasper, can you explain what happened?" I ask him.

"I was running errands for my master, and this alley is a shortcut home; unfortunately for me that gang of men was here as well. They were angry and it looked like they had been drinking. When they saw me coming with my parcels they started running and throwing their bottles at me." Jasper says, pausing to breathe again. I glance back at Lori who appears to be messing with her pastry. Then I see the wall next to her has remnants of liquid and shattered glass on it, so his alibi is feasible.

"When I tried to turn and run they were too close and caught me. They began to beat me till you came. Thank you, thank you ever so for helping me!" Jasper says gratefully.

"I only wish we could have prevented it," Keagan says.

Lori comes over to Jasper now and extends her hand to him. In it is a handkerchief holding half of her gooey mini pie.

"It looks delicious," Jasper says, eyeing it and not understanding that she is giving it to him.

"She wants you to have it," I whisper to him.

His eyes widen as he slowly takes the pastry; he also takes the hand that Lori has extended and bows his head down to it until his forehead lays flat on the back of her hand. Lori and I learned from our aunt's dimie Delilah that this gesture is a sign of thanks and great respect in their native culture.

The constables have finally arrived on our street; Keagan flags them down with his good arm when they get close. He starts talking with a few of the policemen who seem to know him well by their body language. Jasper finishes off the last crumb on the handkerchief when the men come to talk to us and collect the unconscious rat that lays on the ground, his knife still in his hand. They drag him away to the buggy as he begins to regain consciousness.

After everything is taken care of. Keagan assures us that one of his friends in the force will personally escort Jasper home safely and make sure that he is properly cared for. We decided that we should get going out of this neighborhood to somewhere safe. We begin to walk back to the area where Winona and Charles are shopping but as we turn the corner, we see that they are coming our way on the carriage.

"Well, speak of the little devils," Charles calls out as he pulls the horse's reins back.

"We just finished our errands and were on our way to come and collect you if you needed us. And it looks like you do," he states as Winona haughtily stands up from her seat next to Charles.

"Keagan, what in Queen Victoria's name happened to you?" Winona exclaims as she dismounts the driver's seat.

"Someone was in trouble and–"

"Not another word, into the carriage. Let's get you bandaged," she orders, pulling Keagan by his good arm inside the carriage.

"How do you know if he needs bandaging?" Lori asks as

Winona makes her hold open the medical box when we sit down.

"I practically raised him. I know exactly when he's trying to be tough and hide his wounds. Like the ones on his shoulder and those busted knuckles of his."

I look down at his hands, and she's right; his knuckles on his left hand are bloody and busted, and his cut on his right shoulder is beginning to soak through his coat.

"Aspen, go help him," Lori nudges me, handing me a roll of gauze. I can't just say no with our host wounded, though I'd sure like to. I move over to his side begrudgingly as the carriage bounces, and I help Winona take Keagan's coat and suit off, leaving his vest and blood-stained white undershirt.

I watch his chest rise and fall under his shirt as I begin to wrap his arm; he seems so... stiff as I address his wounds. Though with every wrapping motion I make, I can feel the muscle in his arm staying rigid. Is he trying to act tough and show off still, or is he trying to hold back pain? I glance up at his face and catch his eyes staring at me from the side before they quickly dart back to the floor. Looking past Keagan, I can see the sly grin on Lori's face. *Traitor! Trying to pair me up with Keagan. I see what you're doing, sissy; it's not gonna work,* I think to myself as a hot blush begins to creep over my face, betraying me.

"He was quite brave to stand up for the dimie, Winona. He risked his own safety for Jasper," Lori explains.

"Yes, it was," she agrees with a proud smile on her face, as she ties the knot on his bandaged hand. "That was stupid too though! You risked these young ladies' safety as well as your own," Winona adds, thumping Keagan on the head with her paw.

"Ow! I wasn't the only one fighting," he snaps. "Who

taught you to shoot a gun anyway?" he questions me in an expectant-looking way as he rubs the back of his head.

"Our uncle taught us how to protect ourselves and shoot since he knew that we would be travelling alone for some time. I guess it came in handy today to protect someone other than ourselves, huh?" Lori answers for me as I tie off the bandage on his arm.

"Where did *you* learn to fight like that?" I question him.

"You pick up a few things when you travel the world. I learned boxing and fencing at boarding school."

"As well as making friends with policemen," I add.

"Yes, you tend to do that when your father's cousin is the retired captain of the guard. The man you saw me talking to is my old school mate Nicholas Finley. You will actually be meeting his old captain, my second cousin, soon. We have been invited to what will be your first formal dinner party in Currlion at the retired captain's home," Keagan explains.

"Well, can this day get any more exciting?" Lori beams as Winona and I replace the leftover bandages in the box.

She really hit the nail on the head with that one. I just pray there won't be any terrible surprises on our first run tonight. I want to map out the city as much as possible and find any secrets there might be that we could use. It seems that in every town we've been, there is a secret path or alleyway that leads to possibly incriminating locations. Let's pray everything goes smoothly.

# FIGHT BY LAMP LIGHT

## KEAGAN

I pace the floor of my room whilst my mind swims in a sea of great frustration and anxiety.

"They have a right to know," I say to myself. *It concerns their father and mine, so would I be to blame if I were the one to tell them? No. We all would have figured it out together if I had just waited for the girls to go down the fireplace with me. Would they already know? I highly doubt it, they never gave any indication to it whenever we all talk about them. I need to sleep on this,* I think as I pull off my dinner vest and unlace my shoes.

I take one glance at my bed and can't even stand to look at it. They need to know, and I can't bear to waste one more second pondering over it. I don't bother with putting my vest or shoes back on and head straight down the hall to their room. As I pass the main foyer, I glance at the grandfather clock before continuing on my way. The hands read eleven forty-five. Quite late, but I'll be tossing and turning all night if I don't get this off my chest. I knock on their door and wait for an answer. Silence follows.

"Aspen? Lori? There's something important I found out in

the library that you have a right to know," I say. Still no answer. I run out of patience and open the door slowly.

"Ladies? Please forgive me for intruding-"

I see the mounds of their resting bodies under the covers, but I just can't wait any longer to tell them.

"Aspen, wake up," I say, lightly pushing on Aspen's shoulder. I light the lamp and move to Lori's bed to wake her up next. Something is wrong. My hand touches where her shoulder should be, but there isn't one. A quick spin of the gas knob, and the lights are on in a flash. I do not see a head on her pillow but a sleeping bonnet filled with cloth stuffing and a blonde wig. The same thing is on Aspen's pillow, but with a brunette wig. Upon further inspection I find that their beds are just stuffed clothes and blankets. I search the room but there is no one here; not in the study, and the bathroom is empty as well. *Where are they?*

Winona, Charles, and I search the house and the grounds in a frenzy, looking for any sign of the girls. No luck, none at all! *What happened to them? Did they sneak out or were they kidnapped? When I thought of all the trouble that they could get themselves into, disappearing into the night was not one of them,* I think, raking my shaking hands through my hair. I walk slowly back to the girls' room as my body aches to go to sleep in my soft warm bed. I open the door, ignoring my exhaustion as my mind swarms with the horrid possibilities that are the only thing keeping me awake at the moment.

Two in the morning. What an ungodly hour. No one in their right mind would be up this late. No one should be out this late at night for that matter. I take a seat on one of the couches in the dark room and stare out the windows, my mind beginning to draw a blank. It finally stopped raining for the night, but the moon is still covered by the clouds, making it slightly harder to see in the dark. But only slightly.

Two small hooded figures walking across the grounds catch my attention as they hike closer to the lavatory. *What kidnappers would come back to the scene of the crime so soon? They appear to be men by their physique, but their height is all too familiar.* The moon's light begins to project its cool glow upon the grounds just as a large gust of wind ripples through the long grass, causing the hoods of the intruders to billow back, exposing both dark and golden pinned-back hair.

Sitting in the dark, I wait for them to come in, my chair turned towards the bathroom door, the lamp switch chain in my hand at the ready. *Come to your unexpected surprise, girls. It's time for the truth to come to light,* I think to myself as one at a time I hear the ladies slip through the bathroom window and into the bathtub.

"We need to check that tunnel further in the morning – careful," Aspen whispers so quietly, I have to strain my ears from where I am sitting to hear. Once I hear that they are both inside, they sound like they are taking their squeaky shoes off. Next thing I see are two dark figures coming into the open door frame of the bathroom.

At this sight I pull the switch on the lamp beside me, causing everyone to be illuminated in the faint light. Lori lets out a scream before covering her mouth. Aspen's eyes bulge as she reaches for something near her waist that's hidden in the shadows of her cloak but stops as realisation returns to her eyes that it's me. Deeply distraught, and on the verge of fury from their little adventurous behaviour, I glower at them.

"Welcome back, ladies. Mind telling me where you were, and at such an hour alone?" I press on, leaning back, arms propped up on both sides of the chair and hands together in front of my mouth as I await their answer. However, they remain silent, their cheeks flushed, whether from the cold or their astonishment to see me I know not. Seconds tick by and I lose my patience.

"I asked you a question," I say, deepening my voice.

"We went on a stroll," Lori blurts out.

"Yes, my sister and I had some pressing things to think over, and we were feeling so stuffy inside that we decided to go on a walk about the grounds," Aspen adds.

"And the best way to leave was through the window?" I reply sceptically.

"Well, haven't you ever wanted to do something normal a little differently?" Lori says, obviously trying to lighten the mood, which was currently feeling a little cutthroat.

I stand up and begin to pace the room. "I come to visit you girls with important news, and I find the room empty, as well as the library and the kitchen. I wake up Winona and Charles, fearing for the worst," I start, beginning to sound more and more heated.

"We search the entire house from top to bottom, even the secret passages and doors, calling out your name quite frantically, to say the least. I finally come here to think what possibly could have happened and begin contemplating if I should call the constables about you missing girls. When, from the window..." I pause, pointing out into the night. "I see two little figures on the grounds, coming back to their room late at night. And here we are. Now I will not ask again; where were you?" I demand, standing right before them both, glaring down.

"We told you we were outside," Aspen replies, trying to meet my gaze with a seemingly innocent one. Usually just one look like that from her would be able to subdue me, but they crossed a line tonight.

"Don't try to lie or swindle your way out of this one. You were gone for two hours – that I know about, at least. A walk in the snow at night for two hours in those cloth...what are you wearing?" The girls look down at their attire that was all black under their capes. They appear to be fitting men's clothing along with buckles, leather holsters, and pockets that are filled with God knows what.

"Are you trying to traipse around as men whilst you talk about your so-called pressing subject?" I mockingly say straight in Aspen's face.

"We believe that men's clothing is so much more liberating to wear, especially when trekking through the snow."

"Yes, in the snow and straight from the direction of town as well," I snap back, causing them to have a look of alarm on their reddening faces.

"That's right, I saw you both long before you were on the grounds of the manor. Do you know what dangers lurk in the dark along those roads? You could have been robbed, taken advantage of by a swarthy man, or even killed! There are no excuses for this; and right now there are some people in the hall that you need to apologize to so they can go to bed again finally with ease," I growl, pointing at the door. The girls begin to move towards it with me behind them. When we head into the hall we see Winona and Charles at its end; we all can hear the conversation that's boiling over between the two; they're obviously thinking the worst has happened.

"Winona! Charles!" I call out down the corridor. One glimpse in our direction is all it takes for Winona to exclaim and come running towards us, bunching up her night dress as she does.

"Oh my gracious, where have you girls been?" she exclaims as they meet her halfway down the hallway for an embrace.

"What the bloody hell happened to you two? Where did you go?" Winona blasts out before fretting about their appearance and their whereabouts until Charles and I catch up to them.

"Yes, why don't you tell all of us what happened, ladies?" I press on, trying to sound less annoyed than I really am. I know those girls' twisted minds are trying to think of a way or excuse out of this. Hopefully, with Charles and Winona around, they won't lie so easily. I thought they would've twisted the story up a bit, but the little minxes quoted the story, word for word, as they had said it to me. When I explain that I saw where they had come from and how they got in, that's when the real questions begin to pour in.

"Blimey, you climbed in the window? What are you trying to come off as, cat burglars?" Charles exclaims.

"What if you were attacked on the road? We wouldn't have known where to look or what to do!" Winona cries.

"We are so sorry to cause all of you grief and worry; we just really needed to clear our heads," Lori apologizes pathetically.

"Well, with all due respect to whatever you had to talk about that was so important, couldn't it have waited till morning when conditions were better and safer? That way we would have known you were leaving," I go on.

"You know, there are a few holes in your story as well. What was so important to try and wake us up at such a late hour anyway?" Aspen interjects, trying to change the subject.

"Well, I thought you personally might like to be awake to hear some very important news, and I guess I was right, except you were awake somewhere else," I challenge back.

This statement obviously piques their curiosity when their expressions and composure go from closed off and sunken to open and inquisitive.

"Well, what was-"

"Not so fast." I cut Lori off quickly.

"I'll tell you when you tell me everything that you two are up to. You are hiding more than what you lead on. I can feel it. And of course, when we were searching for you, you left a certain strange elaborate gizmo on your desk; can you tell us what that's for?" I calmly demand, making the air go rigid with tension once again, something that seems to be the theme for tonight.

"Aspen," Lori mutters, looking at her older sister helplessly whilst holding onto her arm for comfort. We all hold our breath whilst Aspen gives a sombre knowing look and nod to her sister, making her let out a small gasp and only tighten her grip on Aspen's arm. Aspen turns her head and looks at me with those sad beautiful green eyes whilst opening her mouth to speak.

"We're showgirls!" Lori blurts out dramatically.

"Lori!" Aspen and Winona exclaim in unison.

"Oh, my heart," Winona goes on, clutching her chest and beginning to lean backwards whilst fanning herself with her other paw. As Charles and I rush to steady her and attempt to calm her down, Aspen bickers with Lori.

"Oh, tell me it's not true! Not you poor sweet girls," Winona cries out, clutching Aspen's hand now.

"No, Winona," Aspen replies, seemingly flustered by her sister and the whole situation. Aspen gives a quick glare to

Lori before speaking. "My sister and I are *not* showgirls. We are trying to save the bi-dimensional slaves, and the machine you found is the transporter we are – well, I'm – building to get them back home."

Everyone is stone silent and can't seem to come to terms with what she just confessed. Lori looks scared, I'm dumbfounded myself, and Winona and Charles are gaping and shocked.

"Of all the lies that you could have told, I think that is the worst possible one, especially with Winona present," I call Aspen out, beginning to raise my voice.

*How could she just simply throw that out like it means nothing? It's illegal for one thing, and insensitive for her to tease about with a dimie herself here who's already having a bad night!*

"It's not a lie," Aspen says cooly. Her face looks so determined and stoic it's almost too hard to argue with... almost.

"Prove it then," I say, leaning down to her face level and staring her straight in the eye.

With gritted teeth and a peeved demeanor, Aspen grabs hold of my forearm and practically drags me back to her room with everyone else tailing us. Once inside, she pulls out a trunk that was hiding under her bed. She flips the latches, and it opens up to show maps of cities, including Currlion, with circled areas in red. In the trunk lay weapons of all types, some of them I have never even seen before. There is also a large journal that Aspen takes out and begins flipping through furiously. Apparently I had struck a tender nerve; serves her right, though, with all the panic we had tonight.

"Aspen created half of those weapons herself, you know," Lori pipes up proudly.

"You created these? By jove, you are quite the tinkerer aren't you?" Charles exclaims, making Aspen grin for a split second whilst Charles bends down to examine the weapons closer. With the intricacy and oddness of the gadgets in the trunk, she should be called an inventor regardless of being a woman. I bet she hates how women are only seen as tinkerers and hobbyists instead of real inventors.

"Please don't applaud her just yet. We still don't know what the use of these things are-" Aspen forcefully thrusts the book into my hands and stomach, catching me off guard. I guess she found the right page. "-for," I finish breathlessly.

On the page is a small letter and scribbles dated from five years ago by both Aspen and her father.

Enough with the mistreatment and suffering—we have tried to be lawful about it. No one will truly listen or even seem to care—not even my brothers and sister will come to reason. They are too greedy to be waited on hand and foot than to help the bi-dimensional slaves. Ever since the plague that wiped out nearly all of the working class and even took my dear Charlotte, those who can take advantage of free labor will take it anywhere and in any way. The poor and working class have begun growing again slowly, and soon we will not need the slaves as much as we once did. The poor will need to find real work again somewhere. Call me an extremist, a mad man, a dreamer. But with Aspen's help we can send them home.

Yours Truly,

Asher Wolfe

Under Mr Wolfe's entry there was a preliminary sketch of a machine titled Gear Heart. All around the sketch were Aspen's notes and comments on what to change, how to connect things, chemical compounds, measurements, and the like.

My expression has changed completely from put out to speechless. How do I start to come to terms with this at this time of night? Aspen just then pulls away the curtain that hid the study area from the rest of the room and begins placing bits and pieces on her bed. She describes the pieces of the machine and even shows us the blueprints.

"Keagan, what do you say now?" Lori asks nervously whilst Winona holds her tight in a hug.

"I-I uh." *My head is swimming with all this new information; I can't think straight. I've been used and deceived yet again, but it's not anger that I feel right now. It's betrayal and pain. Am I just some large target with an easy-to-deceive sign on my forehead?* I make my way to the door, and just as I am about to leave, I hear Aspen's voice clear as a bell.

"So is this goodbye then?"

I stop in my tracks and turn my head slightly; I can't look at her fully right now. The funny thing is, what I can see in her eyes looks as if she is in just as much pain as I am.

"I need to sleep on all the events that have happened tonight; we will discuss it later. I'd advise you to stay inside for the rest of the night and get some rest yourself, Miss Wolfe." And with that I am out of the door, trudging my way back to my room and the bed that I so desperately wish I had stayed in now.

As I undress again, I ponder why she looked so disappointed. *What did she think was going to happen? Even though I'm kind to dimies like Winona and Jasper, I would risk my life, my legacy, my family name, and their lives as well, just to send them back home?* I say to myself as I throw my undershirt to the ground in frustration. *It's a suicide mission doomed to fail; they must know that...and yet they continue to risk their lives, family name, and legacy. Just like their father said he would,* I think as I'm pulling off my trousers before reaching for my bedclothes. *And what am I doing? I'm doing exactly what my father would do, that's what!*

I look up after pulling over my night shirt and find myself staring back into the eyes of my dead father. I feel the air in my lungs being sucked out as I stumble backwards in fear and hit the bureau hard with my back. When I look up again quickly, I see now that I'm looking back at myself in the mirror. I clutch the side of the bureau as I try to get my frantic breathing under control.

"Just like my father," I mutter to myself as I slide to the ground. I don't know how long I am there staring at myself in the mirror that sits on the opposite side of the room, looking as small as I feel, but I have to make sure my father's ghost doesn't reappear.

"I can't let this happen," I mutter to myself.

# CONCERNING DINNER PLANS

## ASPEN

"You know, I'm surprised you let us come at all tonight, to be honest," I whisper as we climb up the snow-dusted stairs to the front doors. Keagan was so quiet towards us these past two days, especially on the carriage ride here; it's almost chilling how sombre he's become compared to his general euphoric energy when we first arrived.

"Well, I did say that it would be a crime not to let you wear the dresses I bought for you, and I meant it...I still do," Keagan replies, watching a twinge of guilt and blush sweep over my face. I look down at my navy blue satin and cream lace evening gown that has pearls sewn into the hanging neckline. *I will not argue with him on the matter*, I think as I look past Keagan to Lori in her peach gown with the white roses on the bustle and ruches with embroidered petals spread around here and there.

I pinned my recorder cameo brooch on tonight, but Keagan hadn't so much as looked at it since the dimie butlers took our coats. The only weapons that we carry tonight are our blade-projecting fans just in case. Luckily, I've been able to modify them enough that they appear to look like any other fancy feather fan. Once we are inside the foyer, we are introduced to the hosts who are two old elites: the veteran captain of the police force and his kind-looking wife, Elisabeth.

"Mr and Mrs Captain Reighleh, I'd like to introduce you to Miss Aspen and Miss Lori Wolfe. The Wolfe sisters are staying at my home for the time being," Keagan introduces us.

"It's a pleasure to meet you, Captain and Mrs Reighleh. Thank you for choosing to include us in your dinner party tonight," I say.

"Yes, it will give us a chance to become more acquainted with the community." Lori adds sweetly.

"My word, what lovely young ladies you have there, young Myrack, be careful of the other men tonight; they may try and steal them away," Elisabeth jests.

"Oh, Lisa!" Mr Reighleh scoffs at his wife as she giggles.

"I think you and the captain's wife are going to get along swimmingly," I whisper to Lori, making her chuckle as we walk away and into the dining parlor.

Keagan whispers to me the names of the couples at the table that we are about to sit with. We sit next to the Pembrooks, a rather tired-looking couple, and across from us are the Flanigans and the Cinderbottoms, both around their thirties and quite chipper to sit near us. Keagan chooses to sit between Lori and me however; whether it's to separate us so we don't get into mischief, or simply because he seems a little out of sorts at the moment and doesn't wish to exchange many pleasantries with our neighbours, I know not. It might be due to the soreness of his stitches he received because of those brutes on the street. But I get the feeling that's only part of the problem.

"So, you must be Lori Wolfe, yes? I've heard about you

from Lady Pomley. We will be sure not to tell any scary stories tonight; we wouldn't want to jostle you," a plump woman, Mrs Pembrook, whispers to me once I've taken my seat.

"Oh, no, ma'am, I'm Aspen, the older sister. My little sister, Lori, is over there on the other side of Mr Myrack," I correct her whilst pointing in Lori's direction. I hear a sharp inhale from Keagan when I called him Mr Myrack. He asked for it since he's been so informal as of late. Barely taking the time to speak to us.

I remember just last night I had to get some ice and salt from the kitchen for a terrible headache. When I passed through the dining room to the kitchen, I saw a figure in the dark with an empty bottle resting sideways on the table. It was Keagan in what appeared to be a drunken state resting in the faint light of the night from the window. As quietly as possible, I got the salt and ice in a cloth and tried to slip out the doors. Once I was in the dining room again, I saw he was still there. But this time turned towards me, eyes practically glowing in the dark. I felt the weight of his stare in the night.

I expected him to yell, throw the bottle, do anything outlandish a drunk would do. But he just stared, not in wrath, but in an almost pitious gaze. I guess that's why I wasn't afraid when I gave him my blanket. He may have gotten a cold anyway. *At least I'm trying to show some emotion and attempt to get along; he just bottles it up.*

"Oh, please forgive me, my dear, it's wonderful to finally meet you, though Lady Pomley has told me lovely things about you as well. You didn't seem to be scared at all by her ghost story though," Mrs Pembrook apologizes.

"I love hearing new ghost stories, and the ones I've heard about the town so far have been quite riveting. Do you handle ghost tales well also?" I ask, gesturing to the Flanigans who I know are listening in on our conversation.

"Oh, my dear, no, but my husband loves to tell them to our children at night, they eat them up," replies Mrs Flanigan.

"Oh, how lovely, and your husband, what does he do, may I ask?"

"Well, I'll let him tell you that; he can explain it much better than I," she says demurely. Whilst she tries to get her husband's attention, I take a quick breather and replay the conversation in hy head. I want to make sure I haven't said anything out of the ordinary or uncivil. I still feel so uncomfortable in these situations like Aunt Mae is ready to criticise me at any moment. *Breathe, Aspen, she's back home, kilometers away from here. She can't govern you any longer.*

"Hello, my dear, Miss Aspen Wolfe, isn't it?" Mr Flanigan calls over to me across the table, reviving me out of my trance.

"Yes, well, my wife tells me you are interested to know what I do? Well, I own an international jewel-exchange corporation, mainly working with precious gemstones."

I can feel my eyes twinkle when I hear this, and I try my best to keep my grin at a proper level.

"Really? So then you must know a lot about gems, am I correct?" I inquire as I fiddle with my cameo brooch recorder to switch it on for the conversation.

"Well, yes, very much so actually. Are you interested in jewels?"

"Oh, now what woman wouldn't be?" I say, laughing, looking around at everyone else in our conversation, causing them to join in light laughter before I continue.

"I was gifted a beautiful sapphire pendant by my uncle last year, and it is my favourite piece of jewelry. Are there any interesting things you can tell me about sapphires? I just love them," I lie with a coy smile.

"Well, they come in many colours other than blue. There are yellow, orange, green but the rarest is pink."

"Oh, a pink sapphire would just look smashing on my sister Lori, wouldn't you agree?"

"Indeed!" Mrs Pembrook agrees, smiling.

"Do go on," I say earnestly, with inquisitive eyes.

Keagan begins to raise his wine glass to his mouth. "Watch it," he warns me under his breath. But I ignore him as the conversation continues.

"All right, sapphires like rubies, are also quite popular for engagement rings today and are worn by royalty for being a regal gemstone. Oh, and this one is interesting if you happen to know of any inventors who like to work with electricity: Sapphires are an electrical insulator with high thermal conductivity, so in a simpler sense they can take on extreme temperatures of heat. They have also been rumoured to have supernatural-like abilities."

"Oh, now dear, quit playing, besides, I think she would rather hear about something else now," Mrs Flanigan suggests.

"Oh, no, ma'am, I love trivia facts. I find it strangely refreshing. And if I ever have the pleasure to meet an electrical inventor, I will be sure to tell him about the special qualities a sapphire possesses," I reassure the Flanigans.

"Wonderful, dear, you know, I have a cousin in London who is an electrical inventor and has the pleasure to work for the queen herself!" Mrs Pembrook states, lifting her head proudly as if it were her own son she was bragging about.

"Oh, what does he create for Her Majesty the queen?" I ask.

"Mainly inventing new weapons for Her Majesty's army and every now and then installing electricity into the palace. However, I recently received a letter from him mentioning how he will be working on an invention of high priority; none of the other inventors in the empire have successfully created what Queen Victoria and Parliament have been requesting."

"What might this special invention be, if you don't mind my asking?" Mr Flanigan asks.

"Now don't go spreading this around, but she has requested a flying machine."

"But that has already been created. There are flying train cars now," I say.

"Yes, that is true, but the queen requests something much larger, for far longer travel, something like... a war machine," Mrs Pembrook explains. Her crowd of listeners start to marvel at the idea of such a grand invention, and I find even myself thinking up ideas of designs for a titan of a machine that could soar through the clouds.

Just then, the dimies begin to serve dinner of stuffed quail, buttered bread, and boiled potatoes with mushroom sauce. The talking begins to erupt even more as we all mingle and eat. Throughout dinner, I pay attention to most everyone's behaviour and mannerisms towards each other. The only person who manages to disturb me is Keagan. He conversed with no one unless someone tried to include him, but then he quickly and efficiently transitioned the topic of attention to someone else. The only other time he opens his mouth is to eat. *We must have done a number on him.*

When it's time for the men and women to separate after dinner into the parlors for the evening chatter and gossip, I find myself glad I remembered to tag a fly on the wall to Keagan's suit. I'd at least have something interesting to listen to when I get back home. Male discussion seems so much more important than the usual gossip and talk of household fashion or decor that we poor females are attuned to discussing.

All we end up gabbing about is the newest chapeaux accessories or who will be attending what ball, and what scandal to gossip about next. I loathe shallow gossip, but I don't know exactly how to cleanly trail away from such topics like Lori has learned to. She knows exactly how to steer the conversation back to another meaningless topic.

I on the other hand am supposedly a great listener, at least that's what I've been told after picking up only bits and pieces of a conversation that's gone on for what seems like forever. But I must say, sometimes it's nice to have someone mindlessly drone on to you to get it out of their system, and as a plus I've concocted some of my best gadgets and schemes whilst someone else wags their chin. The only interesting gab I find useful is the talk of their dimies and how many each family has.

"Have you ladies noticed there's a surprising amount of homeless people in the city as of late? There hasn't been this many in years, certainly not in my day," Mme Thompson speculates whilst tightly gripping her cane, even though she's seated on the mint-green satin couch. I wonder if Cousin Harry is possibly in town. Sadly, I know that in the company of women like this it would be quite odd and scandalous to ask if anyone might have met or heard of my cousin.

Lori and I are already under enough scrutiny since we are orphaned and sent out of our home by our own family. But hopefully Keagan can contain any malicious banter about us from the men and say something along the lines of, *"They are simply traveling and seeing old friends like I did in my teens."* That is if he feels like sticking his neck out for us after all he has learned. I wouldn't blame him if he felt the need to add to the flames of rumors against us after deceiving him like we did.

"You know you're absolutely right. Why, whenever we stroll through town, at every stop we make there is one coming near our carriage, asking for shillings. Not to mention how cramped all the alleys are becoming because of them loitering around," a young lady in a copper gown across from me chimes in.

"Is there truly no more space in the mills for them to find work? Or perhaps they are just being lazy?"

"So many of them sure seem that way; desperate men and women who spend all their day on the streets doing heavens know what. And for what? To just spend all their night in the pubs and wrestling matches."

*Maybe if you realised the dimies are filling up nearly all their jobs, you'd see they were desperate, not lazy. Have your husbands visit them some time, of course, even if they do, it's not like they would have a conversation about the working class with you posh women anyhow.*

"Indeed, you know I heard from a reliable source that Lady Bloomberg's husband was seen gambling in the pubs near The Market again, this time they had to toss him out at three in the morning, drunk as a sailor. He returned home the next afternoon."

*Great more gossip.*

"Oh, how dreadful, I always warned her of marrying him, you know. But she was just so sure of his promises that he could get over his gambling behaviour. I pity her for the misfortune of such a mate," Mrs Flanigan sighs out.

"Well, I wish you could have warned me with my last gentleman caller," says a young-looking lady as she waves her hand with a large ruby ring at Mrs Flanigan.

"Keagan Myrack has always seemed to like the idea of short courtship engagements and long travels, hasn't he?" Mrs Flanigan adds, glancing in my direction.

"You know that's why he broke off their courtship; poor Rose was getting too close, and he couldn't handle it, just like the others," she adds, facing me now. The other women see this and turn towards me. I feel like I'm on a stage with a giant spotlight in my face.

"Miss Wolfe, you and your sister have been staying as company with Mr Myrack for a few weeks. Pray tell, is he truly as flirtatious and charming as he acts to the single women in town?" Mrs Flanigain asks.

"I would be lying if I said he wasn't flirtatious or charming at times; however, he is a kind host who knows when to act more civil and less playboy every now and then," I reply.

"Are you saying you defend his forward nature, after all the hearts he's broken, and just in this city alone? I can only imagine how many ladies' hearts he's hurt on his travels," the young lady from before accuses sceptically towards me with a raised eyebrow.

"You speak as if he has hurt you very cruelly. Pray, what is your name, Miss?" I ask as innocently as possible.

"Ruby Hughes, and Mrs Flanigan was referring to my sister-in-law, Rose Hughes. Oh, she wept for days after he left her, swore she would never love another. He claimed it was an emergency business trip, but we knew he was just trying to end the relationship with her," Ruby remarks.

"And how long did they court for, may I ask?"

"Oh, that's not as important as-"

"Now now, don't leave me in suspense. How long? She clearly seemed in distress when he left her. What was it? A couple of months?" I ask in earnest, sceptical that she is twisting facts to favour her sister-in-law. The very idea makes my temper rise, and I know she sees it in my gaze because she is frozen in place by the mere question.

"About three weeks," Mrs Flanigan pipes up, ignoring the tension between us.

"Three weeks! I know some couples get engaged within one week, but three is still a short amount of time for her to be so worked up as you described it. Did he promise her marriage and the world on a string?" I ask Ruby.

"Well... no, but the fact that he left her a letter instead of telling her outright. It's just so improper. It simply isn't done," Ruby adds, trying to get the women listening back on her side.

"Now that might not be true. I heard that they had an in-person talk about it, but when Rose refused to let him go without her, he left for business," another young lady adds before the whole group is putting in their two cents and debating facts. All the whilst Ruby is just trying to get the conversation back in order until she glares at me through the talking ladies. *Looks like I've angered the ring leader.*

I keep my gaze expressionless and level as I take a sip of tea. *I don't know if Keagan will support us in conversational gossip, but I can't help but feel the need to defend him.* He hasn't called the police and is even letting this take a toll on his mentality, the least I can do is protect his name. After all, I know enough of what it's like to be gossiped about.

I had just downed my third cup of tea when the clock struck ten thirty. A few minutes later, my conversation with the widow Bradford about her late husband in the war was interrupted. The men must have had their fill of gab, tobacco, and liquor for the night because they're knocking on the open parlor doors to collect their women. We turn to see a few men finishing off their cigars and glasses filled with scotch.

But Keagan, empty glass in hand, dark circles under his eyes, disheveled hair, has his collar undone as well as his bowtie. *He looks awful. What's more, he has a terrible energy emanating from him, though I can tell he's trying to hide it behind a faint smile.* The sight of his fatigued appearance causes me to stand up in the middle of the widow's conversation, making the talking slow to a halt at my sudden action.

*What did they do to him? What did they say to him? He didn't look that drained when we arrived; he was able to hide his feelings pretty well, but now I barely recognise him.* Keagan and many others in the room noticed my reaction and began to stare. To not make more of a scene, Keagan walks over to me whilst I quickly apologize to the widow Bradford for my sudden reaction, which interrupted her story.

"Ladies, are you ready to go home for the night?" Keagan smiles wanly as he extends his hand to me.

"Y-yes, we are ready, aren't we, Lori?" I say, taking his hand and tapping Lori on the shoulder.

"Pardon?" Lori blurts out as her conversation about shoes is interrupted with a woman who has gear-studded combs in her coiffure.

"It's time that we leave, Lori. It's getting quite late." As I say this, the rest of the men begin to join in more and collect their wife or date to leave shortly as well. Lori takes one look at Keagan and me with a blank expression and begins to rise.

"Ah yes, I believe I'm feeling quite tired myself, actually," she agrees then turns to thank the lady for a wonderful conversation.

We three make our way to Mr and Mrs Captain Reighleh and bid them thanks for their generosity and a good night.

"Oh, think nothing of it; we had such a splendid night with you three here. You know, Keagan, these young ladies are quite clever and observant for their age," Captain Reighleh's wife comments back.

"Oh, I know, they amaze me sometimes as well," Keagan remarks causing me to fan myself a little faster to ward off the embarrassing blush that's creeping up my neck. The dimie butlers aid us with our coats, despite our declined wishes, climb into the car and head for home.

"We remained on our best behaviour tonight," Lori points out like a good little school girl a few minutes into the ride.

"Yes, I noticed," Keagan replies emotionlessly. The rest of the ride is silent, and the air around us feels heavy. But I can't tell if it's the type of heaviness that will cause a fight, crying, or both, so I remain silent the rest of the ride and take note of the landscape around us instead.

When we finally arrive at the manor and enter through the front doors, Charles and Winona are there waiting for us, eager to hear how our first formal dinner went. But when they see our drained expressions, they stand like statues frozen with worried looks on their faces.

"What happened to make you look like this, my darlings?" Winona asks in a motherly tone. I sit down on a bench and lean back against the wall as my coat falls off my shoulders, collecting around my arms. Meanwhile, Winona is helping Lori take hers off before putting it up on the coat rack. I just glance at Keagan who is handing Charles his hat and cloak.

"The men and I had some very pressing topics to discuss tonight, and many of them were quite horrid to hear, to be honest," Keagan replies. He won't look at anyone, only the ground.

"Like what? Why was it so terrible?" I prod, even though I know better to stay silent. He raises his head to look at me, clenching his jaw. The seconds of silence feel like hours. I feel my chest rise and fall faster as my heart begins to race.

"Are you going to send us away?" I ask in a pathetic tone; I can't help it when I actually feel so pathetic. *What's one more family? What's yet another town? Maybe we are meant to become vagabonds.*

"What, no!" Winona asserts. "Keagan Theodore Myrack, you cannot just throw these young ladies out!"

Keagan gives Winona a pleading look and raises his hand to stop her from going on. Turning my way, he places his hands in his trouser pockets before addressing me.

"Why did you decide to do this; make that machine and save the dimies? What could make you break such dangerous laws that impose the death penalty? Why go to such great lengths?" he asks me from across the room. The look he's giving me makes me feel as if I'm on trial, kind of how the women talked to me tonight after dinner. I still recall the look Ruby gave me; I know she will have some things to say about me to her other acquaintances after our little debate tonight.

"They were our family when our own would ridicule and cast us out, they supported us, loved us, and even saved us when we couldn't save ourselves. And now that we have a chance, and the ability to free them, we will take it," I say as I feel my heart beat like a thundering storm. Keagan's gaze begins to soften as it lingers on me. The gossip from those ladies tonight swims in my head when he looks at me like that. I defended him without knowing any real facts about how he has been treating other women; I need to know what they are if I'm to trust him at all.

"I knew I had a good feeling about you girls, from the moment I met you! You're gonna free my people!" Winona says with tears in her eyes and both paws on her chest. *Winona's so motherly and kind; no wonder Keagan treats her so well.* I give her a warm smile before Keagan continues.

"You know that if anyone else were to find out, you both would be seen as extremists and most likely be executed for breaking not one but *three* laws. Are you really willing to stretch your necks out for the dimies, knowing what you could lose?" he says, nodding to my sister. My smile vanishes as I gaze at Lori and her at me. My sister means the world to me, but we both knew what we were getting into when we first began making the machine with Papa. I nod to Lori, and we both agree in unison.

"Yes."

Silence fills the air as the feeling of tension breaks at the sight of Keagan's smirk.

"Perfect, so when do we start?"

"Woah wait, you want to be a part of this now?" I question.

"Yes, I want to fight with you. I've been doing my father's dirty work in family business for years, going all around the world to find endorsers and make ties. I think I should do something that actually helps someone other than my family. That being said, I'm going to help you."

"Is that you or the scotch talking?" I question sarcastically.

"Hey, I can hold my own better than you think, and I'm perfectly serious. I want in."

"Not so fast. You have to be assessed first so we can figure out a good role for you."

"Role?"

"Yes, there are positions like philanthropist, fighter, mechanic, and gathering intel to name a few," Lori explains.

"Very well, when can we begin?" Keagan asks eagerly.

"Keagan...we realised what we were getting ourselves into when this began. Do you understand the sacrifices that you could and probably will make?" I remind him in a rather sceptical mood now.

"Well, besides the monetary sacrifices, and probable lack of sleep, I'd guess my reputation."

"And your families, your households, your very lives, and your mentality. This is not just some trip to Morocco or someplace where you win people over at a lounge with your words alone to help fund your cause and then celebrate the rest of the night. No, this is grueling hard work. We are on the run in the night swinging from buildings and fighting off rogues who attack dimies. Sometimes we even have to intervene between the dimies and their masters when we see that they are volatile. Yes, we get close to the elites and mill owners as best we can, but we are always wearing a mask of innocent curiosity when we speak with them, only to use their information against them later. There have been many injuries, broken bones, stabbing, the like, and we are almost always running from the law. But we always watch each other's backs, which is probably the only reason we are both alive right now," I elaborate with a deadpan expression on my face. Rising from my seat, I take a few steps forwards towards Keagan.

"So I will ask you again, are you sure that you want to fight with us? Fight for the dimies' sake, and not your own," I add.

Keagan's excited expression has long vanished. Kneeling to the ground and resting an arm on his knee, he keeps his head down as he speaks.

"It would be an honour to work alongside the both of you. I humbly ask to be a part of your cause, regardless of the dangers that are present."

I can't find any words to speak at this bold act of humility from such a seemingly proud person like Keagan. I just stand there a few feet away and look down at his back, remaining motionless, awaiting our response, I suppose.

"I say we begin your assessment in the morning so we all can begin fresh," Lori replies in a gentle tone. Keagan's head raises to meet my eyes and then Lori's, looking eager as ever.

"Agreed," I yawn out. *Tomorrow, Keagan Myrack, we will find your weaknesses and your limits and push you farther than you ever thought possible. Let's see how well you can truly hold your own.*

# A GAME OF CATCH

## LORI

The first training day was the worst for all of us in a way. Keagan managed to pin us to the ground a couple of times during sparring; but quit when he learnt it usually ended up with him getting flipped into the towel rack. I got elbowed hard in the ribs, which left a large bruise, and Aspen sprained her wrist after demonstrating a special landing that can save your life if needed.

He will have to learn a lot if he is going to make it through a run through the city with us. Knife fighting and blocking, how to shoot the grapple hook and swing from one building to the next, navigation from any building of any height and direction in the city. Not to mention we will be needing to prepare some black clothes for him – hopefully Winona could help us with that. Luckily he already knows how to fight and fence, if he really is up to snuff, then the first run at night shouldn't be too hard. Merely mapping out the city and looking for dimies to protect.

We took it easy the next day, using and demonstrating weapons and gadgets. Keagan had to try out a few including knife throwing, fencing, controlling a chain whip, and shooting the grappling hook. Although he nearly electrocuted himself twice with Aspen's bolt blaster 2.o, he fumbled with the grappling hook. The worst of all was when he set off a flash grenade in his hand, blinding all three of us for nearly five minutes when we tried to take it from him. It seems that at the rate we're going it will take weeks to get him completely ready.

Finally, after two and a half weeks of training and an assessment of Keagan's abilities, today is the big test. Aspen has been plotting and strategizing about this for two days. It was frightening sometimes when she was going over the plans, the way she giggled with that devilish smile of hers. And now that she has shown it to me, I know why.

Standing before Keagan in our night-running outfits, we prepare to begin the test, just as the waning light filters through the gym room windows. The warm room is filled with nervous electric energy that seems to come mainly from Keagan himself. He is decked out in his very own black cloth and leather running outfit and is equipped with the main gadgets like the grappling hook, stun gun, his special choice of a sword, and smoke bombs. We decided not to allow him to use flash grenades this time until he can use them properly.

"All right, now that you've had some substantial training, we have a test for you to see if you can truly handle a nightly round." Aspen begins nodding to me to finish it off.

"The entirety of the estate, every room, floor, and secret door may be of use in this game. Winona and Charles will act as officers, and if they catch or get their arms around you then you will be disqualified. And if you do not apprehend us in a matter of two hours; then we cannot accept you on the team for our rounds at night. You can still aid us, but just financially, as well as extracting needed information from elites and the like. Will you agree to these terms, Keagan Theodore Myrack?"

"I agree, Miss Aspen and Lori Wolfe," Keagan replies without hesitation, standing at attention like a soldier.

"Wonderful. Are there any questions to how the game is played?" Aspen asks.

"So to win the game I only have to catch one of you?"

"No. To win you have to catch both of us individually. If you catch us at the same time you get extra points," I clarify.

Keagan ponders this a second. He's seen us spar and train with him and each other in the gym, but he's never seen us on the run or fight with full force.

"All right, I accept. When do we start?" Keagan asks as Aspen grabs two bo staffs and hands me one with an eager smile.

"Now," she says, and we both thrust out our staffs to him, hitting him in the chest and stomach hard, sending him to the floor, gasping for breath, as we sprint out of the room. *We are gonna pay for that later, I just know it.*

Aspen and I split up immediately; she heads to the kitchen whilst I head to the end of the hallway near Keagan's room. Aspen and I have had plenty of time to search the house over for the secret doors, and one of them includes a false wall that allows you to sneak behind the rooms of the west wing. I push in the trick key moulding on the ground, causing the door to creak open. I hear footsteps coming this way and quickly jump behind the wall.

Shutting the door when I'm inside, I find the peepholes

that are actually covered in a thin film of see-through burgundy cloth. Not a moment later do I see Winona coming around the corner carrying a lantern. We wanted the house to be dark to give the feel of a normal nightly run. She ducks into Keagan's room and leaves the door open as it was. At least seventeen minutes go by, and I'm about to leave my hiding place when Keagan rounds the corner, he peeks into the study just for a minute before heading into his room.

All remains still for about twenty seconds until Charles comes into sight at the end of the hall. He is heading for the coat rack and seems to be fiddling with one of the jackets. I can't see what he's doing clearly, but he's probably just picking off some lint. We both freeze the moment we hear the loud commotion going on in Keagan's bedroom. Charles dashes towards the bedroom whilst Keagan is running out of it, yelling, "Sorry!" over his shoulder.

He fails to look where he is going and collides with Charles. The two bounce off each other and Charles quickly retaliates by going in for a rugby tackle. Keagan narrowly misses him. Once behind Charles, Keagan kicks him on the bum, causing him to fall head first onto a couch.

"I'm very sorry!" Keagan yells as he races down the hall.

When he is gone, I come out of the false wall and peek inside of Keagan's room. Winona is untangling herself from bed sheets on the floor, and when I turn my head towards the hall, I see Charles getting back up grumbling about his back.

"I'm too old for these shenanigans!"

I pass him by in the foyer and decide to wait in the next hall, maybe in the tea room this time. I watch Charles as he heads to the dining room and is out of sight in a second. Before I make it to the tea room I hear an outburst and thundering footfalls overhead on the second floor. I close the tea room doors and hide in some thick potted plants at the corner of the hall, in view of the stairwell. Keagan and Aspen are running at the top of the stairs towards the balcony before I'm even completely hidden.

*This looks dangerously familiar.* I think for a second as my memory takes me back in time to watching my sister and Keagan playing tag in this spot as kids. But back then they weren't careful enough. The fall, Aspen's arm, the screaming. They were playing on the staircase; that's where Aspen fell.

She broke her arm and was screaming and crying so hard as were Keagan and I, but he was begging for Aspen to forgive him. The next thing I remember is Papa leading us out the door whilst Mr Myrack scolds Keagan. The look in Keagan's eyes, I remember it as clear as day, was as if his very soul was being sucked out of him. *No, not again, not now! I won't let it happen again!*

"Aspen, look out!" I scream from the corner where I'm hiding, causing Aspen to turn abruptly in my direction. Keagan rushes at her, but before he can catch her, she jumps straight from the balcony and tumbles when she hits the ground, causing me to stifle a scream. *What is she trying to do, give me a heart attack?* Aspen starts running again but doesn't get very far before Keagan's on the ground as well and grabs hold of her. Wrapping his arms around her waist, he throws both himself and her on the ground, rolling on top of her.

"Caught you," Keagan purrs into Aspen's ear. She does not look amused as she is struggling underneath Keagan's weight and getting redder by the second. What a perfect game to put these two together. Now if I could just find a guy I could convince to play this game with *me.*

Aspen frees one arm and elbows Keagan hard in the face, catching him off guard momentarily, giving her the chance to turn around and vault him onto the steps with a strong push of her legs. My smile diminishes quickly; I don't wait for what happens next. Running my way into the next room to my right, I find myself in the study. Not one good place to hide in sight, I begin scanning and pulling random things off the shelves in hopes one could be a lever to a secret room. Aspen runs into the room giving me quite a fright since I thought it was Keagan at first.

However, by the sound of footfalls outside the door it doesn't seem like he's too far off. Aspen pulls out a large green book that opens a door in the bookshelf. We don't wait a second more as I pull Aspen and myself in, yanking the door behind us shut just as we hear the sound of Keagan flinging the door to the study open. There is a tiny peephole in the bookcase door where light is filtering through; it's the only light in this pitch-black space.

Suddenly very fearful for what may be lying in the dark, I fumble for my glow-in-the-dark baton. When mine is lit, I can see Aspen finding hers and lighting it. We can hear Keagan slowly looking around the room; Aspen nudges me towards the opposite end of the tunnel. We have to get moving before he finds us. This dirt tunnel must lead somewhere outside because we are dodging and stepping over hanging roots. I nearly scream my head off when I see a family of voles skittering away. It doesn't take too long for us to see a faint light as we continue down the tunnel.

"We must be nearing the opening," Aspen claims. Not a second after she says this we hear a door creak open, and with wide eyes, we turn in the direction we came from and listen. We wait in silence for a few heartbeats; the next thing I hear is the faint sound of quick footsteps turning into running. I grab

Aspen's arm and pull her to start running to the light ahead of us.

We burst through the root-covered opening, causing a rift of gold and blue snow to powder in the air. When the snow clears in the light of the setting sun, we look around and realise that this was the small tunnel we found the night we snuck out of the house. Aspen is the first one to focus back on the task at hand, pushing at my back to start running towards the trees across the road. We scramble to get our grappling hooks as we run, performing awkward jumps across the road. *Thank heavens no one was on the road to see that.*

The second we shoot out our lines I can hear Keagan running out of the rooted tunnel. We turn around just in time to see him sprinting and yelling at us. Much to his chagrin, however, we are shooting up to the high branches before he can get close to us. We are already swinging to the next tree when he gets his grappling gun out.

We seem to swing higher and higher as he chases us through the twilight-lit forest. Reaching a rather small meadow, we look around the open space and decide it's safe to swing out without being noticed. But as we swing towards the trees on the other side of the glen, I hear a terrible creaking sound before a crisp snap.

Right in front of me I watch Aspen fall in what seems like slow motion. I hear myself scream as I try to reach out to grab her. But she is too far away. I reach my tree and can only watch in suspense, praying Keagan catches my sister this time. He sees her as he is right behind us, almost brushing the snow off the ground, and grabs hold of her, catching her in mid-air. But the extra force of Aspen's sudden weight is too much for the small branch that Keagan is swinging on. They both fall to the ground.

"No!" I let out a scream again. I can't bear seeing Aspen fall, and yet I can't make myself turn away.

Too close to the ground now to shoot out another line, they hit the earth, tumbling in the snow until they roll into a snowbank under a tree. Their impact causes more white powder to fall on their already-frosted backs. He holds on to her the whole time. With his back to the tree, he slowly pulls her back a bit as he brushes her snow-dusted hair away. It looks like he's checking to make sure she's all right. I allow myself the breath again when I see that she is okay.

"Lo?" I hear Aspen call out.

"Yes? Are you all right?" I call back.

"I'm fine, but he caught me. So keep running!"

A big smile spreads across my face as I shoot another line out to the next pine tree. I guess I'll have to get the details of that little embrace later tonight.

Keagan chases me through the forest for about fifteen to twenty more minutes. We make a wide circle around the estate and end up on the back side, looking down towards the manor. Tired of swinging, I plop down on some rocks as I realise that my adrenaline is beginning to drop. Keagan reaches the rocks, and I push myself back up as I unsheath my sabre. I think a duel would be a nice way to end things. Though I know I'm not nearly as good as Aspen, I might be good enough to take on Keagan. As Keagan unsheathes his sword that's strapped to his back, I see Aspen trudging her way through the snow towards us.

"You have only twelve minutes left!" she calls out to us.

Winona and Charles must have heard her because they're

now turning the corner from the front of the house and running our way up the embankment. Before I can prepare to fight or even look Keagan in the eye, he hits my sword hard, sending me backwards. The duel has begun and Keagan is not holding back. Our swords clang together at a rapid rate, and it occurs to me that he was the one holding back during training. I push him away for a second to strategize, and I see that Winona and Charles are dangerously close now.

"Four minutes left!" Aspen exclaims as she looks anxiously from us to a pocketwatch and back to us. Keagan advances again before I can think of a new strategy; I can feel the beads of sweat running down my back. I see the sweat run down Keagan's determined face whilst we advance towards each other again. It's becoming harder to keep a grip on my sword; he's almost knocked it out of my hands three times now with his powerful blows. Winona has made it to the rocks and Charles is right behind her.

Seeing this, Keagan gives me a rough push, causing my arms to fly up as I stumble backwards. Whilst I'm falling back, he rips out my sword with his free hand. Winona is only about a metre away from him, arms outstretched ready to catch him. However, before she can take another step, Keagan wraps his arms around mine, pinning them around my torso as he plummets us both in the powdery snow nearby, trapping me underneath his body. I'm so exhausted I can barely struggle out of his grip, and his weight is too much for me to fight against right now. He just seems to hold on as tight as steel until I finally give up.

"You put up a good fight," he says in a ragged breath as he keeps his head face-down in the snow

"Yeah, but you still won," I breathe out.

"I had to."

The next thing I know, we are being lifted one at a time out of the small snow pit we made, brushed off, and carried away. Winona carries me cradle style since I feel as though I have been drained of every ounce of energy in my body. Keagan can walk but is still getting some help from Charles whilst Aspen walks between us as our group makes our way down the twilight-lit blue embankment.

"You ended with three minutes and six seconds left, by the way," Aspen says to Keagan who has the dopiest grin on his face when she announces this.

Once inside, Charles takes Keagan to his room, and Winona takes us to ours to be taken care of. Stripping out of our cold and sweaty clothes, Winona prepares a warm bath for us. Afterward, she helps us into some warm clothes and takes us to the living room, insisting that we sit near the fire before leaving to bring Keagan in for the same treatment.

"Thank you, Winona," we three say weakly as she goes the extra mile and swaddles all of us in blankets as we rest on the couch facing the roaring fire.

"Oh, tish tosh, I'll be right back with some hot soup. We need to get you three warmed up!" she announces as she heads back towards the kitchen. Charles must be helping her with the soup since he's nowhere to be seen. We sit for a few moments, letting the warmth seep into our cores before Aspen speaks.

"Congratulations, Keagan Myrack, you showed great endurance, resilience, and were quick to react. Especially when one of us was in trouble. You never gave up; even when faced with exhaustion you found a way to keep fighting and win, and under pressure as well. Welcome to the team," Aspen says extending a hand to him. Keagan gives it a quick shake but before releasing it, he kisses her hand and looks up at her.

"I hope to serve you well."

"Do get a room sometime, you two," I say snarkily.

"Lori," Aspen scolds as she takes her hand back and stares at me, flushed in the face now. Keagan and I get a good laugh as Aspen tries to regain her composure and sits even father back in the cushions of the couch. The rest of the night is spent by the fire, eating soup and sharing stories with Winona and Charles.

I recall when we were children how we got caught climbing things when playing hide and seek, sneaking cookies out of the cookie jar, or cutting each other's hair and clothes to make them more "fashionable". We always thought we were being super sneaky spies back then. Who knew that a few years later, and after weeks of training with Keagan, that we would be doing runs over the city for real mission and rescue work. We both finally feel comfortable with him coming along with us on a run.

I just pray that it ends well, and we don't get caught like when we were kids, with Aspen and me to blame. Whenever we would play with Keagan, he either had a hard time keeping up or would try to play the victim and say that it was our idea when we got in trouble. Let's hope he doesn't wish to repeat history, lest he wishes to dig his own grave.

# THE WAREHOUSE

## ASPEN

Keagan drives the three of us up and down the mountain slope to a small cliff overhang that looks out to the city. We park the car behind some snow-blanketed shrubs and thick fur trees.

"No one comes here at night, not even rogues or thieves. And especially not in this weather unless they want to kill themselves," Keagan tells us, reassuring us that the car and our location tonight would be completely secret.

"Why is it that no one comes here?" Lori asks curiously in a worried voice.

"Well, for two good reasons: it's private property, but my family is friends with the owner. The other is that there's a local superstition about this specific cliff, you've heard of it recently," Keagan explains as we climb the banks to the lookout point of the cliff.

"So this is Blu Man's Cliff?" Lori wonders aloud.

"That it is, and if you look higher on the slope you will find a marker in remembrance of Johnathan Blu; Lady Pomley mentioned it to me."

We look down at the low-lit city of Currlion just as its people begin to drift off to sleep or head to the local tavern. As I scope out the best anchor spot on the cliff for our wires to connect to, Keagan is still trying to secure all the gadgets and weapons we gave him for tonight.

"Hey Aspen?" he asks, tapping Lori on the arm.

"I'm Lori," Lori replies turning towards him with a questioning look in her eyes.

"Oh, my mistake, I just can't tell you two apart like this yet," Keagan apologizes awkwardly.

"That's the idea, and why we put these knife-proof plates on our chests; it takes away our feminine figure. Everyone thinks we are men," I explain.

"No one would expect a Lady to be able to do what we do," Lori adds.

"Which is why we use that to our advantage. Keeps the suspicion off us and makes for more fun in a real fight since they don't hold back," I say cheerily.

"Clever, but why so many gadgets... I mean, two grappling hooks?" he questions whilst holding them both up in each hand.

"We always carry an extra grapple shooter on us just in case of a malfunction with our main one," I state, walking over to him to help put them up on his sides.

"I see, this is ingeniously made, by the way, but the metal seems so strong; how did you acquire such materials?" Keagan questions whilst fondling the small gun-like device.

"Keagan, please, we still have our own dowry.... and we may or may not have taken a few candlesticks and some cutlery from our cousin's attic storage," Lori replies, causing Keagan to look back at me with a look of surprise. I just give him a smile that reaches my eyes and is teeming with mischief.

"You pretty little thieves," he says, amused, making us laugh a little.

"What else is there that I don't know about you?" he muses, leaning closer to my masked face.

"Quite a lot actually!" I reply, a little annoyed at his behaviour at such an important time as this. Pushing him back, I walk over to Lori who is surveying the area below us for people. No one around currently, it seems. I begin mapping out the distance to get out of the slum districts. It may take quite a while to get through the whole lot tonight, but luckily, the large majority of buildings in Currlion are two and three storeys with a few five-storey buildings every few hundred metres. These taller buildings will give us the leverage that we need to launch ourselves from one roof to the next.

"All right, masks up; we are gonna get flying soon. Keagan, you need to shoot right above the church steeple and then anchor your line in the ground like we do. Aim, shoot, pull, and anchor into the ground deep below the snow bank," I explain.

Keagan nods his head and does exactly as directed. Once we all successfully anchor our lines from the steeple to the cliff, Lori and I pull out one of my newest creations.

"The zip-line forward-and-reverse hanger has a wind-powered motor much like a large wind-up toy; it has a reverse gravity pull since a motor would be too large and loud," I explain as I place the hanger on the wire and Keagan follows in suit. Lori begins to jump in place whilst shaking out her hands as she prepares for the jump. *Poor thing. I know how much she hates the first jump of the night.*

"All right, n-now just jump off, holding tightly to the hanger," Lori says, doing just that, stifling a squeak. Once she is off I give wide-eyed Keagan a smile with my eyes and jump off the cliff myself, the crook of my arm tightly wrapped around the hook of the hanger. I look back to see how he is performing. He just jumped off, clinging tightly to the hanger, catching up in speed due to his weight difference.

We are off, soaring down our lines towards the chapel tower; Lori will be there to help us stop when we get close enough to it. I scan the ground as we pass over to see if there is anyone in need of immediate help. *Nothing yet. Maybe nothing will happen tonight but practice and mapping places out,* I think to myself as I near the tower. Lori pads my landing by catching me, and both of us quickly reach out to cushion Keagan's stop. We unhook the hangers and place them into the tower window in case we need to make a quick getaway.

"Won't someone notice the lines?" Keagan asks worriedly as we slide down the shingles of the church.

"Nope, I'll explain later," I say, raising my grapple shooter, aiming for the roof adjacent to us.

"Flip the switch with your thumb to pull up," Lori says, jumping gracefully like a bird off the roof as her line pulls back into the gun and tows her towards the next building. Keagan and I follow as he tries to jump out like Lori did. But sadly, her graceful style wasn't meant for him as he nearly body-slams into the brick wall – and he would have, too, if he hadn't caught himself by raising his knees. *That was painful just to watch,* I think as I jump out, legs to my chest, and spring them out before coming back into a ball when I meet the wall. I'm over the ledge first and after Lori comes, we help Keagan get over.

"Not so easy the first time as you thought, huh?" I say,

grinning like a snake behind my mask. Before he can give a snarky reply, we hear a scream coming from a short ways over.

"Break time's over. Let's go," Lori says.

"Oh no," Keagan says under his breath as he finds his footing on the rooftop. The thought of him already getting exhausted makes me all the merrier. We are able to jump and run over the next two buildings since they were close enough together in this poor cramped sector of the city. We look down the sides of the building the scream seemed to come from moments before, in time to see three dimies being harassed and cornered by metal men.

"Think those could be the metal men that Lady Pomley's dimies told her about?" Keagan whispers.

"They sure could be. I've heard many rumours about these *robots*. New oil- and steam-powered machines that detect, hunt, and attack dimies. But they are only seen at night for some reason," I say.

The dimies being cornered are being forced into the snow, held down against their will by the robots. The poor souls are trying to get out of their captor's grip in a hysterically feverish manner. One is even losing a few dark blue feathers out of fear.

"Down we go," I say, anchoring in my grapple to the railing and jumping clear off the roof, aiming for one of the robot's heads.

"Wait!" I hear Keagan object right before my foot collides straight on a bot's head, sending him into the snow and flailing around his arms in the process. As it falls, something long and sharp slices my left arm.

"Augh!" I cry out when I look to see what cut me. It was the bot's fingers; they are made of garishly long razor blades, and one is now painted red in blood. *That's unexpected.* The dimies that were held by the bot make a run for it, leaving one of their own held by the other metal man. Keagan and Lori make their way down towards me as I grip my bleeding arm. The bot that I sent flying is creaking back up onto his gyroscopic feet. *I guess we will have to get violent then.*

"Are you hurt?" Lori and Keagan call out as they slide down, causing the other bot's attention to them.

"Look out for the bot's hands!" I yell. Too late; one of the dimie bot's razor fingers lashes out again, and this time Lori gets hit. When the bot retracts its arm to attack again, Lori's mask gets caught with it and gets ripped in two, showing one side of her face. Before the robot can attack again, I jump and kick it square in the chest, sending it backward, releasing the dimie in the process. Before it can recalculate, I leap up onto its chestplate and cut out the main wiring on its neck. Oil spurts out the second I slash him, staining my clothes with its scent as we land on the ground with a slam.

Out of the corner of my eye, I see flashing bolts of electricity glaring near my face, but before it hits me, the man about to use it is knocked to the ground. It's Keagan who's on top of a new uniformed man, wrestling the electric stick out of his hand and putting the man in a choke hold. He isn't dressed like a policeman, but he's still a uniformed officer of some sort. I look to my left to see if the monkey-like dimie had a chance to run off with the others, but I see that she is under a weighted net now.

With her ears laid back she looks even more terrified than ever. I look back and see that Lori is trying to hide her face as best she can with one arm whilst dodging blows from two other dimie bots. That new bot and this man must have come because of the commotion caused. *There are probably more of them, and I bet they aren't far behind,* I realise as I launch myself off the dead robot I'm perched on and catch one of the arms from the robot about to attack Lori.

Using my momentum, and his spring-like arm as a swing, I swing from one side of the bot to behind it's back and grab a tight hold of the other arm.

"Slice it's neck now!" I call over its shoulder.

Lori jumps up to his neck and slits his wiring but keeps her head down in case he has some sort of facial documentation tech inside him. Grease and oil sputters out as the giant dimie bot sways and begins to tip back. I release its arms and shove the bot to its side, causing it to land in the snow with a thud. The already trampled dirty snow is turning black with oil as I head over to Lori, but her eyes are elsewhere.

I turn to where she was looking only to see another robot throwing his razor hands at us. Before we can flinch from the razors, Keagan jams the electric stick into the eye of the bot, sending its arms flying back out to its sides. Turning the stick on causes a large amount of electricity to fill the air around us. Jerking his hand away quickly and backing up towards us, he raises his arms to block us from what we all can sense is coming. The bot's head explodes as Keagan acts as a human shield by wrapping us up tightly in his cloak. I begin to feel my cheeks blush as this is the closest I think I've ever been next to him. *What am I doing? Now is not the time to dwell on things like this!*

When the debris has fallen, and Keagan slowly releases us, we can finally breathe out our ragged breaths. But our moment to breathe is halted by the sound of voices from more policemen coming. When he unwraps us from his embrace entirely, I shake my head and look over Keagan's shoulder for the dimie we were trying to save. The poor dear is still latched to the wall under the net and all of her yellow fur is standing on end as her clawed palms are gripping at the net.

"Are you glad I'm on the team now?" Keagan asks me cheekily, catching my attention. Without answering that stupid comment I grab hold of my grappling launcher, shoot to the roof, and put it in his hands, holding them together with mine. I'm about to pull the trigger when I give Lori the *following* sign.

"You are something else, you know that," I say to Keagan.

"Yes, thank yo-" I pull the trigger before he can finish, and up he goes along with that stupid face I know he's making before hitting the side of the wall with his shoulder. Keagan and Lori disappeared from the ground and over the rooftop in a matter of seconds as I cut the net holding down the dimie.

"Oh, thank you. Who are you?" she asks meekly, rising up, nearly grazing me with her pointy ears. I don't say a word, however, I just hand her an encrypted letter and push her to the alley opening. She begins to run, but not before looking back once more.

"Thank you," she says, and then she is gone.

"There is an officer coming your way," Keagan calls down in an urgent hoarse whisper. I immediately run over the fallen figures to the wall on my right and take out my spare grapple launcher, aiming it towards the roof moulding. But as I pull the trigger nothing happens. I can hear the man right around the corner now. I gave Keagan my first grapple, and there's no time to tinker with this one in time, so it's time to improvise.

Climbing onto a good-sized crate right next to the corner, I wait for the man to come. Before the constable can ask what was going on, I yank down hard on the handlebars of his long mustache and use his back as a springboard to reach the moulding of the second floor. Thus sending the policeman into the snow and rubbish bins with a great ruckus and giving me time to scale the rest of the way up to the roof. When I reach the top moulding, Keagan is there to pull me up the rest of the way. I would have protested since I've done this sort of thing countless times, but the gesture was kind and we had no time for argument at the moment.

Lori, during all of this, was on the opposite end of the roof, scanning the surrounding area. As we dash towards her, she turns to us, places four fingers up, and hits her other wrist three times. There are twelve constables and/or dimie bots in the general area. That's quite a lot but not the most we've been up against. We all hear the policeman I just knocked down call out for reinforcements with his whistle, six of them begin to run towards their comrade, whilst the others remain searching around and checking the alleys. I back away from the edge and look around, trying to find an escape route, when I see a ladder that leads to the adjacent building behind us. *The men on the ground will be up here sooner than we like,* I think to myself as I grab Lori's arm and usher us three towards the ladder.

When we get to the roof we hear the officers shouts getting louder and closer. They must have climbed to the top of the building by now; lucky for us we got a head start. Bolting and jumping from one roof ledge to the next, we find ourselves entering into the bay area where the old warehouses are; a handful look abandoned.

*We've outrun the police this time, but they may know what to look for now after I jumped that one officer. I just pray that no one besides maybe that dimie saw Lori's face, but even a dimie recognising us can be detrimental to our operation,* I say to myself as we catch our breath on one particularly old and rusty abandoned-looking warehouse close to the harbour.

I hang my feet over the edge of the rusty roof and gaze out at the cove, feeling a little light headed from the speedy run. I watch an air train glide off in the partially cloudy night as its multiple wings beat, catching glimmers of moonlight on their sleek surface.

Small circles of smoke puff out from its exhaust pipes as it trails away, higher and higher in the sky until it's beyond the clouds. Must be a special ride; there usually aren't that many air trains departing at three in the morning. It's nice up here with the cloudy night breaking for a moment, the moonlight bathing the rooftop we are on in a glow, and even that little light house on the cliffs that crests the bay's opening.

"I should come here again sometime," I say to myself out loud, smiling a little.

"If it makes you peaceful for once, you should come here daily!" Keagan blurts out in my ear teasingly.

"Ahh!" I let out a squeak of surprise that he gets a good chuckle from. *I can't believe that I didn't notice him till now! How does he always seem to sneak up on me and get my goat?*

"Sorry," he replies, sitting himself down next to me.

"You are not," I accuse.

"Maybe, but it's hard for me to be when I get a rise out of you and with such a view as this."

I pout behind my mask and open my mouth to comment back but he beats me to it. "My father and mother always loved that lighthouse, and for good reason."

Hearing the smile in his voice arouses my curiosity as I meet his gaze. "My father proposed to her up there, right at sunset." His gaze remains on the lighthouse; his expression portrays love for people that were once here. I feel my heart twisting painfully as he redirects his eyes at me.

"Your arm," Keagan whispers in alarm.

I look down at my left arm, and there's the blood-soaked gash from the bot's razor fingers. I'd forgotten about it with all the adrenaline I built up from the fight and run from the officers.

"Oh dear," I say, reaching into my hip satchel for a roll of gauze as I realise that the stinging pain is beginning to resurface. But before I can open my pouch, Keagan begins cleaning and wrapping up my arm himself.

"I'm sorry, I'm not the best doctor, but this should be fine till we get back home. Then Winona can take care of you," he assures me as he finishes tying the knot. I just stare at him; not many people have ever been this tender or close with Lori and me.

"Thank you," I mutter out, and Keagan gives me a smile with his eyes.

"Uh, guys, sorry to break up the moment, but you might want to check this out." Lori calls hoarsely over to us, breaking our trance in the process. Before we make a move, we hear the shouts of men in the distance. I scout out the ground and see a few large mangy stray dogs at the base of the building and nearby trash cans. If we step one foot on the ground, we will have those dogs on our heels and acting like sirens for the constables to find us. The only plausible way for us to turn is the way we came; which is where the voices are coming from.

"Come here quick and look inside," Lori urges, practically dragging us to the skylight windows. As we gaze inside, feeling the anxiety of what's coming our way, I quickly look over the building's interior. Perfectly empty of people, but then my eyes hit a strange large object in the centre of the warehouse. There's something off and erie about this building, but I can't place it.

"This is the building of the original slave-trade-portal generator," Keagan growls. *No wonder I got a terrible feeling from this place.* But that machine...the sheer size of the portal projector would allow crowds of fifty or more to be brought to our side in a matter of seconds. No wonder they got so many dimies to our world in a matter of minutes each day.

"Can we go in?" Lori asks as I begin to pry open one of the rusty window frames with my grappling-hook barb. The window gives with a rusty squeak as I prop it open.

"Well, it's been abandoned for about fourteen years when the trade ended, so..." Keagan responds but begins to trail off once I anchor my rope harness onto the now-open window ledge.

"We can't contemplate all night now, can we? You coming?" I ask. The sound of the men is coming frighteningly close, and with this, I begin to slide down my rope into the warehouse with Keagan and Lori calling out after me in a hoarse whisper.

"Aspen!" I look up to see Keagan frantically clipping himself onto the rope and sliding down after my feet hit the floor.

I run over to the moonlit machine and begin to examine it. I don't get very far before Keagan's in my ear again. I turn his way and notice instead that Lori closed the window as she slid down the rope. *That's my smart sis!* When she hits the ground and looks my way, I give her the whip signal. She promptly whips the rope hard, making the anchor come out of place and falls towards her. I turn back to Keagan who is whispering tensely to me, ready to pick a fight from the sounds of it, too.

"You can't just run into places like this."

"I can if it means a chance at freeing everyone at once. Besides, I scoped it out when you were talking up there. This place is empty," I hiss back, bringing my eyes right to the level of his mouth on my tip toes.

"Well, what is so important about this bloody rust bucket to come down here with what's going on out there anyway?" Lori chimes in, not bothering to whisper anymore, her anxiety bleeding through her words. I start scaling the massive machine before answering her. *I thought all of these old machines were destroyed in the explosions of 1872. I guess they couldn't move this to a museum for some reason. I bet the inner workings go through the floor.*

"Well, for one, we can hide here whilst it dies down a bit out there since we are trapped in practically all directions. And two, I've got a good hunch about this old rust bucket-" I pause, staring through the machine, and try to figure it out, whilst the gears in my own mind are grinding hard to concoct a new scheme.

"We can't just-"

"Shh, she's thinking," Lori whispers to Keagan as he tries to protest again. Keagan sighs grumpily and remains quiet, thankfully.

I move to the front of the machine where the portal lens is and genius hits me. "What if..." I start whilst crouching over the power lines.

"We connect our machine to this one as the portal door whilst still only needing to use the amount of power for ours!"

"Is that even possible?" asks Lori.

"It could be if we used the portal lens from this large one to simply project the doorway..." Keagan chirps up, surprising us.

"Yes, whilst Gear Heart does all the work!" I say, finishing his thoughts excitedly.

"Brilliant," Keagan praises, pulling down his mask, showing a bright smile.

"I hate to play devil's advocate, but when would you be able to connect them and possibly have time to tinker with this ancient and massive thing? I mean, it was shut down permanently because it was too dangerous to use anymore," Lori questions.

"There you go, thinking logically again," I reply cheekily, pulling down my own mask, still so excited about our find to be discouraged.

I start to take measurements of the portal lens and the attachment bindings but am soon interrupted by a rusty creaking sound. We all turn in the direction of the sound as a chill begins to creep up my spine. Keagan and I pull our masks back up and Lori shields her face with her arm. I see faint lantern lights coming from the far left side door. I can't see who it is over the old boxes and debris, but I've got a good hunch. Lori turns to me and that's when we hear them.

"Search the whole building; they might be here," yells a gruff voice.

"Over there! I think I saw something move!"

We don't wait a second longer and make a mad dash away from the men to the stairs on the left side of the building. When we head to the top, we can hear them gaining right on our tails.

"This way. I saw someone, I'm sure of it," the gruff voice orders.

We run through the closest doorway to our right and stop in our tracks. *This must've been the command room,* I think, seeing the cobweb-covered switches and levers. But there's no window to get outside the building from here. The men sound as if they are halfway up the flight of stairs, and there is no time to go to a different room. Lori heads for a hiding place in the debris. Before I can make a move, Keagan claps a hand around my mouth and tugs me so tightly to his body that we might as well be one. We dive below the command controls into a small nook where some drawers used to be that's just dark enough that we can remain undetected.

Fitting in tightly, my back to his chest, he wraps his cloak around us and lowers his hooded head, brushing up next to mine, causing heat to rise to my face quite quickly.

All performed in a matter of seconds and no time left before the guard stomps through the doorway and appears to be waving his lantern back and forth. His breathing is shallow and the lantern seems to be shaking a bit from what I can see, as the light dances on the ground.

I guess this place creeps out more people than just myself. Keagan's hot breath hits my neck, and I steel myself the best I can, gripping his arm that's snug around my waist. I can't see his face, but I can certainly sense the stupid smile on it right now, only causing me to burn up even more in embarrassment.

"Show yourself, c-coward!" the policeman calls out in a quavering voice. I turn my head carefully until my lips inadvertently hit Keagan's ear. I collect my wits and talk almost inaudibly: "If he gets too close or spots anyone, take him out."

Keagan agrees by drawing a check mark on my shoulder where his hand rests with the cloak wrapped in it. The shaky policeman moves around the room, sweeping the lantern light this way and that until it remains in one place as one of his comrades calls out down the hall.

"Did you find anyone?"

As he is replying back, I notice that the light is hitting a sawdust and glass-covered journal. It's strewn open to a page that shows words like: *New experiment fully functioning... when using...prec-stones.* My heart skips a beat, and my palms begin to sweat; something tells me I need that journal. Keagan still doesn't know about the sapphire we have or the little heist that Lori pulled off while we were at the dress shop. He can't read this book either, not yet at least. I feel strangely guilty for keeping so many secrets from him now that I realise how many there actually are. Except when I'm pressed up this close to him, it's really hard to keep any emotion secret, that's for sure.

The man leaves the room slowly, but I don't hear his footsteps; he's probably waiting outside for a partner or to listen if there really is someone here. We remain still like tombstones in a graveyard as we listen for anything.

"The boss wants us to check the next hall if this one is clear," another constable says. The man who was checking our room quickly agrees and follows his comrade to the next set of rooms; I know this because I can hear two sets of feet down the hall now. We wait a few seconds more until there is silence in our hallway. I peak out from behind where we are, and the room is empty.

"Now," I say, and Keagan rolls us out from under the desk; but we remain crouched down in case they might see us from the shattered glass outlook. Lori comes out of an old filing cabinet and needs help to come out quietly. Keagan heads over to her aid, giving me the chance to snatch the journal I found. As I pick it up from the filthy floor and quickly blow off the dust, I glance back to see if they were watching, before stuffing the book in my shirt between my stomach and the protective plate.

# BOTTOMS UP

## KEAGAN

Lori is back on her feet, and I turn to Aspen who's patting her chest and looking through the cracked window that overlooks the work floor below. Lori clicks her tongue twice, getting Aspen's attention. Once Aspen turns to us, Lori points to the doorway. Aspen places her fingers under both eyes then makes a sweeping motion on one hand with the other, they nod their heads in unison.

"Sweep the floor and find an escape," Lori whispers to me. Aspen carefully makes her way to the door frame on the opposite side of us and looks down the hall that's on our side whilst Lori does the same for the opposite side.

Aspen gives a thumbs up and so does Lori. Aspen sprints out of the door frame and down the hall with us tailing right behind her. We turn left and right through hallways away from the sound of the officers' voices until we finally see a small broken window that's slightly boarded up. With no time to spare, we pry off the boards as quietly as possible, but the worn wood has other ideas. An enormous groan is emitted from the final piece of wood that we detach; I wince at the sound as we remain silent to hear if the police noticed. That piece of wood did it for sure because there is a multitude of fast-paced footfalls coming our way.

Aspen anchors a grapple on the window pane, jumps, and slides down the rope quickly. Lori is right behind her whilst I throw the planks of wood into the closest room and rush back to the window, nearly hurling myself out of it. I never thought I'd be throwing myself out a window, but the fear of getting caught trumps the height of the five-storey building any day. I hit the ground running with the girls, and just as we round the corner of the block, I can hear the distant sounds of the confused men. We bolt through the snowy streets for what feels like an hour, down dark alleys and far away from the shouts of the police. Every now and then we have to duck behind crates and rubbish to hide from patrols and police carriages.

We run so hard I fear my legs will give out. Finally, we make our way back to the chapel and head to the side that is shrouded in shadows. The gothic architecture is detailed enough to allow us to scale up on our own; I'm still a little hesitant since it's my first church climbing. I'm going to feel so guilty come Sunday mass. As we glide through the cold night back up to the cliff overhang, I can feel the winter temperature beginning to catch up on my body.

I can barely feel my nose that must be running like a river by now. Or my hands or feet, though covered, they feel like stone about to crack. Once we climb up on the slope, I notice Aspen and Lori hunching over and wrapping their cloaks around their shaking bodies.

"C-c-come on, we haven't a m-moment to lose, we'll f-freeze if we stay out much longer," Aspen orders through chattering teeth. Before the words even leave her mouth, as a harsh gale rushes through the trees and down to us, bringing down snow with it. We bend over a bit more as we shudder from the cold and try to unhook our grapple ropes.

*Our job tonight is done, thank God,* I think to myself as we make our way up the mountain in my motorcar. I feel my body burning from pushing beyond fatigue and the cold; I just have to keep my eyes open a little while longer until we get home.

Winona ended up staying awake waiting for us whilst Charles went to bed early; he never was a night person it seemed.

"Charles promised to make breakfast in the morning if I stayed up for you three. I'm pleased that I did since I can hear everything! Now go and sit by the fire; I filled a basin with hot water for your poor feet. I'll go get the sherry, and when I come back, I want to hear everything!" Winona explains jubilantly whilst putting blankets around each of our shivering bodies.

"And that's when I look up and see Keagan jump out of the window head first. But he still manages to catch the rope and slide down in record time. It was incredible," Lori explained. She's taken it upon herself to describe in detail some of my more barmy moments to Winona. "Oh dear, I'm not sure I can take any more of these stories. My heart is racing! How did yours not burst from all you went though, Keagan?"

"It was probably because I saw Lori and Aspen perform each task first so I just had to follow them, and during the fights it was mainly a protective instinct, I guess," I say, giving Aspen a side glance. But she doesn't seem to notice since she's downing her second glass of sherry.

"Well, I for one am exhausted, and I know you three must be as well. So come now, it's time for bed."

"Oh please, Winona, we still need to talk about the night more and decompress a bit," Lori begs.

"I agree. Winona you needn't trouble yourself further with us tonight. We will get ourselves to bed soon," I say reassuringly. She doesn't seem to be very accepting of the idea though.

"I promise you, we will be just fine. You've been so helpful in making Keagan's outfit and taking care of us. You can rest easy for a little while, too," Aspen adds.

Winona exhales a heavy sigh as she nods her head in consent. "Oh, all right, but if I wake up to you three passed out throughout the house, you will have wished those guards had caught you," she says before coming behind me and ruffling up my sweaty hair. I can only imagine how many directions it's sticking up in now.

"So tell me, how is it we were able to leave our wires up? Wouldn't people see them?" I ask curiously whilst my cheeks burn from the sherry.

"Our uncle was a closet chemist and helped us create a thin but strong multi polymer wire that in a way cloaks the night sky. But sadly, on a full moon night, or if a bright lantern light hits the wire, then it can be detected."

"Wow, all right, then how about this one? How did you even know where to start with that machine of yours?" I ask, taking another sip.

"It was our papa who started to make the machine in

secret, actually. Aspen and I stumbled upon it one day in his study," Lori responds, yawning.

"Yeah, I got really curious about tinkering at t-the time and I noticed a few wires and cogs that were in the wrong places when I re-ref-referenced them to papa's sketches," Aspen adds, stumbling over her words.

"Our papa caught us working on it, but instead of blowing up at us, he saw that Aspen was doing a surprisingly good job for a beginner, and at thirteen, too. Ever since that day they worked on it together. I was in charge of the shape and design elements," Lori states, bragging on their work ethic.

"Thirteen! It's truly taken you five years to create such a small and powerful machine with the help of your father?" I ask, truly astounded.

"Yes," Aspen says plainly as she finishes off another glass of wine.

"You girls have quite a family. Your father taught you engineering, your cousins that used to be in the circus taught you acrobatics and dancing, and your old uncle taught you chemistry and fencing."

"Don't forget my favourite!" Lori blurts out, giggling.

"W-what's that one, sis?" Aspen asks cheerfully, her speech sounding a little funny.

"Poker!" she belts out, laughing, and it's so contagious that we all have to join in.

I take another shot of sherry before filling up everyone's glass again. This will be my sixth, or was it my eighth...oh well, I like it, it makes me feel all warm inside. I stifle a belch whilst laying on the floor, playing with an old spyglass.

"Hey Aspen?" I ask.

"Hmm?"

"What if you used this old telescope as your lens instead of that big one in the warehouse?"

"Shhh!" Aspen hushes me with a finger on her mouth. She looks so cute when she does that, it makes me chuckle again.

"Not so loud. That's a secret!" she whispers. "But if you must know, it would mean more w-work for me to use that le-l-lens than the one in the warehouse. I mean, I could; don't get me wrong-"

"Okay then, what if we use the light house instead? Ha! Could you see the look on the governor's face if we used it and projected the portal on the mountain... or city hall!" Lori interjects, making all of us laugh so hard we spill our sheri in the basin.

"You know we could use that, actually, if we really wanted to, but the light points to the horizon, not the ground, so we might have to break the light and lens to make it work...more sheri, please!" Aspen calls out. I reach for the last bottle from my special library stash, but when I try to pour our cups, nothing comes out.

"I must inform you ladies of a great tragedy...we are regrettably out of wine," I say.

"Aww... well, just the same, I think I hear my bed calling me. Goodnight, beautiful tricksters!" Lori calls out as loud as she can as she sways a little whilst walking out the door. There is now a lull in Aspen's and my conversation as we stare into the fire, but it doesn't last long.

"Hmmhmm," hums Aspen.

"What is it, love?" I ask her warmly, to which I hear a groan from her.

"Who were those men that attacked us tonight, the ones that came along with the robot and the tazing stick?" she asks.

"Funny you mention them, I had no idea who they were either. My friend Nicholas hasn't informed me of any additions in the yard; however, I did manage to take a good look at his name tag once he was unconscious. Dimie Watchman I think was the name of his division. I'll ask around about them later to my...oh friends," I say taking a long yawn.

"How odd. You know what else I've been thinking ab-about?"

"What's that?"

"We never saw where the tunnel led. Douse the fire, Keagan, so we can go and check out the secret passage now," Aspen orders me as she attempts to stand up.

The alcohol from the wine seems to lose all effects on me as I watch her getting up and stumbling towards the fireplace. I jump up and run to the front of her, grabbing her waist and begin to sloppily dance a very fast-paced waltz.

"N-No! I want to see the secret," she protests.

"And I want to dance; I told you I'd get that dance sometime."

"Keagan... you dance terribly. I mean.. *I* dance terribly," Aspen states out as we spin faster and faster away from the fire.

"We are a bit tipsy, love, and I'm trying my best," I say.

"I-I'm not!"

Before I know it, our feet get tied up and we tumble to the floor with Aspen landing on top of me. Safely far away from the fire now, I can see the faintest flames of light dancing off her loose wavy hair. Irresistible. I stroke her hair away from her face as her eyes flutter sleepily. When I move in closer to her, she opens her mouth like an invitation.

"You know, Keagan, you're not as terrible as the rumours said you were."

This reels me back momentarily. *How terrible do these rumours describe me?* "Gee, now that's a compliment I'll treasure."

"No I-hehe-I'm serious. You really pulled through tonight, and you looked great doing it. Oo-oops I shouldn't say that stuff. Your ego is b-big enough already," she says, eyes now closed as she slowly sinks down. All I can do is snicker as Aspen suddenly slumps against my chest, slowly falling asleep whilst mumbling unintelligibly. *What to do with the body?* I think, smiling as I stroke her back. If only she weren't so hard to open up like this; seems like wine works though.

Feeling her slumber peacefully, I watch the last of the dying embers flicker up into the chimney. I should feel excited after a night like tonight and to be close to such a woman. But I just can't shake the feeling that this is the calm before the storm. *I am on the rebel side now; no one said we would win or that this will be safe,* I think as I look down once more before scooping her up in my arms. I just wish that anxious feeling would go away.

As I carry Aspen down the hall, she busies herself by fumbling with my buttons and the collar of my black shirt. *Maybe I should let her drink wine more often. She seems much more open than usual.* When I give a slight knock on the door, Lori opens it, giggling in her night dress. I try my best to look anywhere other than at her as I hand over Aspen.

Seeing Lori in her nightdress was embarrassing enough; I'm just relieved that I didn't have to leave Aspen in her running attire for the night. *Hell will freeze over before I help Aspen undress whilst her little sister is still in the room,* I think to myself as I make my way to my own bed that's beckoning to me. *What new surprises are there to come for us?*

# PUZZLING PIECES

## LORI

I've never dealt with hangovers before in my life, but it appears that Keagan is immune to the effects of alcohol by the broad smile he gives us before going back to his morning paper.

"How many bottles of sherry did you three go through last night? I only gave you one bottle," Winona demands, drawing the curtains closed to keep the harsh light out.

"Ugh, we lost count," I groan as Aspen and I take our seats at the table.

"Winona, would you mind making them that special remedy you found last year?" Keagan asks her.

"Right away, and no more wine for you two until you can handle it properly," Winona declares, pointing at us sternly.

"Keagan, I thought you drank the most out of all of us; how are you all right?" sissy asks.

"Well, Aspen, to be perfectly honest, I've been drunk plenty of times before last night and have built up a tolerance since my first hangover. I now know how to fight a hangover the night of, and morning after, being drunk. One of those ways is this special concoction that Winona is mixing up for you right now."

When Winona brings out the drinks, it takes just one look at the two tall glasses of grayish green slush to feel even worse, knowing we have to drink it. When Winona puts the glasses in front of us we just stare at them. We look over at Keagan in disbelief, but he just shrugs his shoulders.

"Sorry, I didn't say that it would look or taste good, but it will help immensely within the hour."

"Bottoms up," Winona replies, looking expectantly at us, hands on her hips.

Reluctantly, I reach for my glass, and so does sissy. I try to drink as much as I can, but it tastes like I'm drinking hot tar. Aspen is quick to gulp down her entire glass and promptly a full cup of tea right after. I on the other hand feel even more dreadful than before by just looking at the glass. I can only drink a third of the liquid before my head spins and I have to push it away.

"Lori-" Keagan starts, but I raise a hand to stop him whilst I put a fist to my mouth. I simply must lay my head on the table. I feel my mouth begin to water, stomach turn, and a flash of heat comes over me. Without another word, I stand up quickly and run out of the room straight to the bedroom. I can hear my name being called and the sound of footsteps running after me, but if I stop now I won't make it to the loo.

After I have lost all of my terrible excuse for breakfast, I lay down whilst my stomach performs its own circus act of flips and turns. I somehow manage to doze off, and when I open my eyes again, our clock reads twelve forty-one. My head still aches, but at least I don't feel like I'll chunder a meal again. Slowly rising from the bed, I fix my hair at the vanity table, brush down my skirts, and make my way out of the room to find everyone.

Aspen, coming for me already in the hallway, catches me up on all that happened during my recovery. She and Keagan had discussed what we found last night in the warehouse but hadn't gotten very far in what they should do next. Taking me to the tea parlor, she shows me a few pages from a notebook she found last night, hoping it would be enough for her to figure out the inner workings of the old machine.

But it's lacking in many major areas as if it were written by a random bystander and not one of the engineers. There is something she shows me specifically in the time-worn pages. There's a page that explains the experimentation with precious gemstones. Apparently, they were mixed with a special chemical formula that allowed them to be the key to opening up the portal to the other dimension. Reading this page makes me feel better about accidentally pilfering that sapphire from the gear master.

"If only I had the blueprints for the original machine like the one in the warehouse, it could make things far quicker and safer for us. Besides, I'm pretty certain that building will be under watch for a while after last night," Aspen groans.

"Pray, where is Keagan?"

"Keagan is currently trying to think of anyone who might know or have any useful information about the old contraption," Aspen says whilst rubbing her temple.

We sip on our tea and finish the last of our sandwiches, all the while throwing out ideas that sound mildly too crazy to work. When Winona comes to clean up the remaining dishes, Keagan comes rushing into the tea parlor, where we are, with a large grin on his face.

"By George, I've got it. I have a friend who is an architectural engineer that's in league with the Governor," he exclaims.

"And how the hell does that exactly help us in this situation?" Aspen snaps back, slightly on edge because of her hangover; her drink obviously hasn't kicked in yet either.

"Because he is also a record keeper of blueprints, and his father was an engineer for the original Slave-Trade Organization. With his father's and Damon's connections, he's bound to have the blueprints."

"Do you really think there's a chance that he might have the blueprints for this machine?" I ponder.

"He's practically obsessed with schematics and building structures; if his father drew it there's a ninety-nine percent chance he will still have it in his house," Keagan reassures us.

"All right so how hard will it be to get the blueprints, and where does he reside?" Aspen asks.

"Let me handle that part; he's young money like me, and so is his new wife, Mary. I don't want to break into his home at night, and I don't want to steal from him. He is one of the few people I actually consider a true friend. Deal?" Keagan says, waiting for Aspen to agree.

"Deal, but we have to plan this out with you."

"Deal. And the same rules apply to you, too, Lori," he says.

"Okay, okay, deal," I say, waving him off.

At this, Keagan goes to the phone and rings up the operator.

"Hello operator, please get me 561 Wyvern Way Currlion."

After a few seconds of waiting for the connection, Keagan starts talking on the mouthpiece again.

"James, it's Keagan."

"Keagan, Old Boy!" erupts so loud from the phone's speaker he has to jerk it away from his ear.

"Hello James… yes it's good to hear from you, too. Say, old chap, I was wondering if I could bother Mary and you for a dinner party between our households. I wish to formally introduce you to the Wolfe sisters; they are friends of the family that are residing with me as of now. They're unfamiliar with many people here, and I thought that they would just get along swimmingly with Mary… Yes, I think so, too. Now I hate to ask this of you in such a way, James, but could we have dinner possibly at your house instead of mine? Why? Because we are redecorating our dining room. One of the Wolfe sisters has an eye for decor much like your wife."

"Well, if they have that in common, then by all means, come to our home. My Mary has been wishing to spruce up our tea room; maybe Miss Wolfe can inspire her whilst we catch up…," I overhear James calling out through the speaker.

"Mhm, yes, that time is perfect. Splendid. We will see you this Thursday night at six o'clock sharp. And when we get our dining room finished, we want you to be the first ones here to dine with us and enjoy it all the more." And with that he hung up the phone.

"All right, it's all set. In two days we will be at their house for dinner. Now what should we do in our spare time?" Keagan reassures us as he walks over to our seat.

"Now we plan, rehearse, and train," Aspen replies with a mischievous smile. I can tell she has already cooked up something in that mad-scientist mind of hers.

# BLUEPRINTS

## ASPEN

We rehearsed and went over the plan at least ten times. I just hope that Keagan doesn't get overly nervous and put the laxative formula in the wrong cup. If he spills it into his own or anyone else's but James'. I can't imagine how badly it would ruin our plans if one of us were to drink it on accident. He's set off enough flash grenades in his hands on accident to let himself drink a laxative as well. I certainly wouldn't put it past him.

I've been working and testing a mixture that should clean out a person's system in at most thirty minutes once it's activated, after about five to ten minutes of drinking. I still remember how peeved Charles was after Keagan explained to him that he tested our final mixture during lunch yesterday. The look on his pained and awkward face as he ran out of the dining room was priceless, however. But at least we know that we will have a time frame of thirty minutes to find and photograph the schematic before Mr Adlene should recover.

I decide to dress in my violet skirts tonight with my special cameo pin that Keagan gifted me. Lori is dressed in her teal dress that seems to complement the maroon embroidered vest and feathered top hat Keagan chose to wear tonight. We decided to take the carriage with Charles as the driver and Winona coming along as well so that she could spend some time with her fellow dimies. Winona does, however, have an extra job tonight in explaining our plan of freeing her people once I pass on the signal.

Keagan is beaming like a lantern the whole way to his friend's house. It's like watching a child about to open his first Christmas present. Before our carriage doors were even opened, Mr and Mrs Adlene come out the front doors in such jubilee it feels as if the world has grown a little brighter. Mr Adlene greets Keagan with open arms for a strong embrace as Mrs Adlene comes right up to us, introducing herself and her auburn-haired husband. "My goodness, Keagan, you best behave yourself with two such beautiful ladies in your home. Don't worry, we will have plenty of time for just the three of us ladies to become acquainted tonight," Mrs Adlene says reassuringly as she takes one of our hands in each of hers.

"Ha. I think we will be getting along swimmingly," Lori says, her energy rising.

Unorthodox, but just my style of formality, I'd say. Sweet as honey like the colour of her hair and buzzing around like a bee as well. Now I'm beginning to feel bad since we are planning to deceive them tonight. Perhaps we can still become friends in the future even if it's just a fraction of what Keagan's bond is with Mr Adlene.

Dinner is a delicious combination of leg of lamb roasted in rosemary and olive oil, green beans, and savoury buttered bread. During our meal, we get to know a lot more about Mrs Adlene, who seems to be the personification of a butterfly. Flying from one subject to the next whilst playing with Mr

Adlene, his hand always in hers. There were many surprises during that mouth-watering dinner, the biggest being Keagan; I've never seen him so happy and sociable without being a huge flirt.

I can tell that this visit wasn't just important for the mission, but for him personally as well. He and James have acted like two brothers being reunited ever since we stepped foot in the door. I'm relieved when the delicious dinner is through, however, that way we can get down to brass tacks.

Moving into the tea room for dessert and conversation, we enter into a quaint three-window parlor decorated in an older rococo-style theme of pastel colours and gilded moulding. Inside the gilded mouldings, on the mint walls, hang portraits of family and languid picnic scenes. The shelves on the left wall are filled with antiques, pictures of family and far-off places, and one large framed blueprint of the courthouse.

As James pulls out a seat for his wife, Keagan does the same for me with a warm smile, and then for Lori, but with his attention turned back to James and the empty seat next to him.

Once we are seated, Mary pulls the bell cord for the butlers to deliver the tea and cakes.

"So tell me, how do you know each other? Your fathers, I'm guessing?" I ask Mr Adlene.

"Keagan and I went to boarding school in London together; we were practically inseparable. Unless you count the times he was flirting with girls or trying to get out of trouble with teachers."

"Yes, or when you weren't poring over books in the library, failing at flirting with girls, or being a teacher's pet," Keagan debated.

"Well, if it wasn't for me, you would have served way more

detentions than you did. Plus, which one of us has a wife now?" James holds his wife's hand in his where the rings show. Looks like this is turning into a 'my horse is bigger than your horse' banter. Keagan, with a twisting smile on his face, looks like he is about to talk back again when the butler dimies come through the doors.

"Oh good, the cakes and tea are here. I told our chefs to make something special for the occasion: strawberry swirl cream cake!" Mary exclaims, my intuition tells me she wants to deter the men's little banter to a new topic as much as Lori and I. Lori had already finished two thirds of her cake, as was I with my cup of tea when everyone was finally served. *Why are we inhaling our food so quickly? Could Lori be as nervous as I for what's to come in the next few minutes? Maybe the cake really is that good; I haven't so much as looked at my own, so how would I know?* Lori finally slows down when a red bear-like butler is kind enough to refill my cup with his graceful clawed paws.

"Thank you," I say, looking up at him, he smiles and nods his head, showing curled ears like Winona's, but he doesn't meet my eyes. Seeing this, I can feel my smile beginning to fall. *It will be hard for us to gain his trust.* He and his fellow blue-bird-like butler pack up the cart after generously giving Lori another slice of cake and leave us to be with our hosts.

"Oh, I'm so glad you like the cake, Lori. We've been told our cooks are some of the best in town. We were very lucky when we chose them from the Market."

"Really? I've never seen anyone selling dimies in the market in town," I ponder.

"Oh no, it's the only place left in the city to buy dimie

slaves; it's called the Market, but it's mainly an orphanage-type holding facility for people to go and buy a slave or return the troublesome and old," Mary explains.

"I see. Um, do you know Lady Pomley?" I ask.

"Why yes. She was actually the one who told us to go to the Market instead of going to Brighton to get our slaves. Hers are quite skilled and obedient, much like ours. If you're looking to get a slave for yourself, the Market is the place to go," Mary says, smiling.

"Indeed. Thank you, I'll definitely keep that in mind," I say as my cup hides my mouth.

"You know, Aspen, I've been meaning to compliment you on your cameo pin. You've been palming it all night. Was it an heirloom?"

"Oh, no, actually, this was a gift from Keagan. He lost a bet."

Keagan shoots me a look at my last comment.

"Some things never change. He's always loved making bets, but certainly had his fair share of losses as well," James says.

"And fair share of wins. Speaking of wins, I noticed you still have my grandfather's old binoculars on the shelf over there," Keagan says, pointing to the shelf behind James, making him and Mary turn to glance for a second. Without missing a beat, Keagan swiftly pours the vial of laxatives into James' cup and quickly replaces it back in his coat pocket.

"I won those when we were trying to see who could ask out the prettiest girl in school for tea. Keagan was suave as he always was when he tried to ask her, but when I tried, I had tripped on a loose cobblestone and fell flat on my face. She laughed, helped me up, and said yes to me instead of Keagan. And the rest is history, I've been falling for her ever since,"

James says, looking at his beautiful wife fondly as she returns his gaze.

"You never told us that story, Keagan," Lori says with her classic daydream look in her eyes.

"Well, some stories are not mine to tell," he says, eyeing his friend. *I agree with that philosophy, some stories are to be told by certain people only.* James must be eating this moment up. He seems like the person who never got much of a chance when they were young to show up Keagan in front of women. Sounds like he always had two left feet. James reaches for his cup now, and I can't help but hold my breath as he takes a long sip of tea. And thus, the heist begins.

After eight minutes of talking, I nearly break Keagan's leg to get them to go into the room with the blueprints or any room other than this one.

"Hey! Uh, hey chap, I've been meaning to ask you about one of your antique rifles; I believe it belonged to your father," Keagan starts, nearly breaking character when I kick him.

"Oh, the old one hanging in the study or one of the mounted guns in the den?" James asks.

"The one in the study. I was wondering if I could look at it. There is a man in town who is trying to sell me a rifle in the same year and model, but before I add it to my family collection, I'd like to see what an authentic one includes and is made of--just to be sure that I won't get scammed."

"Certainly, Keagan," James agrees whilst washing down the last bite of cake with tea before getting up.

"Please excuse us, ladies, we will be back presently," James announces.

"No hurry, dear, I've been meaning to discuss the refurbishment of our tea room with these young ladies."

"I can feel my pockets burning now," James says with a smile.

"Oh, darling!" Mary chides as the men leave the room.

"Now I believe it was you, Lori, who is redesigning the Myrack dining room, correct?"

"Yes, ma'am, that's correct, and I daresay it's quite invigorating. It happens to be my greatest project yet."

"Well, no doubt, you must show quite a bit of talent seeing as how Mr Myrack is letting you do one of the first rooms ever built on the estate."

"Is that right? Well, he never mentioned that little tidbit. I feel even more honoured now."

"Indeed you should, ah, Aspen are you aiding your sister in her project as well?" Mary asks, turning to me.

"No, sadly, when talent for interior designing was given out, I was completely out of the room. My talents are more in jewelry and gadgetry accessories. That, like the new home furnishings, seems to be on the rise as of late in household and public interest. Take Lori's bracelet, I designed the bobble in the center to be a small powder compact," I explain as Lori flips open the centre fake jewel on her bracelet, showing a small mirror and powder pad resting inside.

"Bravo. Could you create one of those for me?" Mary replies, astonished. "I've always marveled at people who can think three-dimensionally like this."

"Thank you, perhaps you will receive one as a gift soon." I tease. I do believe it's better this way with our different interests so that we don't compete in what style of room or what candelabra goes where."

"Agreed, we can be quite competitive at times," Lori states.

"Well, that would be sisters for you, and thank you, Aspen, I'd be very grateful for one. Now, Lori, I'd like to see what you think I could do to this tea room we are in, it's just too drab for my taste anymore…"

Lori and Mary begin to ramble on about drapery and pillow fabric. I tune them out almost entirely as I watch the clock. Thirty seconds till the laxatives should strike.

"Excuse me, ladies I need to powder my nose," I announce, rising up.

"Oh, no trouble, dear, would you like me to ring for a maid to take you?"

"Oh, don't go to the trouble. Mr Myrack told us where the lavatory was before we came. Thank you though, Mary."

"You're welcome, dear."

And back to the rambling of wall colours and other tedious matters of home decor.

Once I exit the doors, I give a nod to the butler who stands by, whilst slipping him a piece of paper.

"Would you please give this to Winona for me?" I ask once the door is shut.

"Yes, madam," he says, dipping his head again, showing off his curled ears as before. Now as long as he gives it to Winona like it is, then it's up to her to explain their chance to go home.

I walk quietly towards the direction the men did earlier. As I listen closely towards the walls, I find the room where they are talking in and wait in a pastel blue satin chair nearby, fiddling with my boots in case someone sees me.

Five solid minutes have elapsed and two maids have already walked by with sewing kits, seeing if I need assistance. I hate lying to them, but it's the only way I can get where I need to be. Maybe his metabolism isn't fast enough for laxatives to work quickly like it did on Charles. However, I find it hard to believe that a middle-aged man with rheumatism would have a faster metabolic system than a healthy man in his early twenties.

I'm starting to lose hope as I change seats to the one on the wall of what I'm betting on is the study. It's a pretty good bet, too, seeing as how I'm listening through the wall, but I can barely make out what they are saying.

"Now during dinner ... mentioned something... new gadget you obtained... where again?"

"Oh, yes! When Mary and I ... Italy we found the most intriguing..."

"James... are you all right?"

"...Excuse me!"

The door swings open, and I watch James's lanky figure running pell-mell down the opposite end of the hall whilst hitting the wall as he tries to round the left corner. *So that's where the bathroom is.* I look both ways down the hallway to check to make sure no one is coming and quietly rush in the room just as James makes the turn.

I'm greeted by Keagan, closing the door behind me and taking my arm.

"Alone at last!" he says with a smile. I roll my eyes as he adds. "Our search starts here."

"You weren't exaggerating when you said that he was obsessed, were you?" I say as he leads me to the long wall of document-stuffed shelves.

"Not a bit," Keagan states, searching the labels on the right side of the wall. I begin to do the same on the left side. Each shelf seems to be filled with different types of prints; there's a shelf for houses' and estates' architecture dating back to 1780 to present, and others are simple things like hovering baby strollers and self-rocking cradles within this year's date.

"Keagan, did you ever ask your friend if he had the plans for your house?" I ask.

"I have many times throughout the years, and each time he has replied in vain. He says if he ever finds it, he will consider it a true jewel to his collection, and that I will be the first to see it."

"Well, I hope it can be found in our lifetime; I wish to see all the secret doors, too."

*I wish he had not used the word jewel since I still haven't told him about the sapphire that Lori accidentally acquired.* I try to forget these nervous thoughts by searching even deeper within the archives. I look all over, but there are so many sections and dates I can't seem to find anything and neither can Keagan. Taking a few steps back, I focus on the highest shelves. The one that catches my eye is the one that's labeled 'engines and gadgets 1800–1850'. *That's got to be where it is.*

"Keagan, over here! It's on the top shelf," I say.

Keagan responds by grabbing the shelf ladder and bringing it to the top shelf. "Ladies first," he says with a grin.

"Then what are you waiting for?" I say, pushing him towards the ladder as his smile flat-lines across his face.

"You know, in another life, you would have made an excellent spy."

"Yes, and you a great gentleman," I say without missing a beat.

Biting his lip, he ascends the ladder. As he searches, I run over to the door I came in and listen for anyone that might come our way.

The hallway stands in silence as I wait for him to find the documents. I can faintly hear the sound of moaning coming from the hall though; poor James, I hope I didn't give him anything too strong. *It's nothing personal, Mr Adlene, it's just business.* All I hear in the background is more shuffling of papers for at least two minutes and nothing from the hallway. I look back to see if he is actually looking, and he is, but now without his coat. Stretching farther out and across the shelf causes his shirt to tighten and form along his back each time he moves, and I can't help but find myself transfixed on him as he works.

"Found them!" Keagan announces, quickly reminding me what it is we are here for again. Walking towards James's desk, we unroll the document and pin it down with paperweights and stampers. There is an electric lamp on the desk – thank heaven. I take the shade off and turn it on as I hold it above the prints so I'll get a better shot in this drab-lit room.

As I'm bending down to look closer, Keagan is shuffling through the papers. I take my cameo pin off and pull the switch to use the camera; one of the pearls on the side that's slightly larger than the others moves, exposing a tiny camera lens. Seeing as there is no eye lens to see where I'm shooting, I raise the brooch high above the parchment and hope for the best picture. The shuffling stops.

"What are you doing?" Keagan asks, confused.

"Uhm, taking pictures."

"Wait that's the pin I bought for you, isn't it?"

"Um... yes."

"That man in the shop added on the camera, didn't he? That's why it was so much more than it should've been," Keagan pointed out accusingly.

"No... it was a camera and recorder double attachment," I say meekly.

"Ugh, Aspen!... Fine. Well, as you are using it, take a

picture of this, too," he says begrudgingly as he shoves the roll of paper on the desk. When I unroll it, I see that he found the parchment that specifically shows details of the power-source-to-lens-projection schematics.

"Thank you for showing me this; it's exactly what I need," I breathe out.

"You're welcome, but even so, I'm not sure how well the photos will even turn out. How on earth do you plan on actually seeing that picture when it must be microfilm? Emphasis on micro! You couldn't possibly see it well enough with a magnifying glass, and we don't have a microscope at the house."

"Tut tut, no need to worry. Simply see the picture, once it's developed, as a small projector slide. If you don't have a projector, then we just need a spare box, candle, large lens, and some mirrors," I reassure him as I roll up the blueprints. The moment I hand them back to him, we turn to stone at the sound of footsteps right outside the room. Frantically, he rushes to the storage shelves and replaces the blueprints whilst I duck underneath the desk at the sound of the door handle turning.

"Mr Myrack? Please excuse me, but have you happened to see Miss Aspen Wolfe? She seems to have disappeared and isn't where she said she was. Her ladyship has asked me to try and find her whereabouts in case she got lost in the house."

I can't place who it is, but it must be one of the butlers since they are looking around for me.

"Oh, I'm sorry, old boy, but I don't believe I've come across her since after dessert. I'd check the library if I were you, she might be there if not where she said she would be."

"Yes sir, thank you, sir."

"Oh, and have you heard anything from Mr Adlene? He

rushed out of the room with great haste. Is he all right?" Keagan asks, sounding genuinely concerned.

"Oh, sir, he seems to be out of sorts at the moment."

"Would you please take me to where he is? I don't want him to worry about his company whilst he feels ill," Keagan pleads.

"If that is what you wish, sir, then I will lead you to him."

I'm all alone in the room now once they leave. Crawling out from under the desk, I place the top back to what it was like before Keagan and I messed it up. Once it looks as untouched as possible, I head to the door and listen for anyone coming or going. Not a sound out in the hall. *It's now or never,* I say to myself as I turn the doorknob slowly to not make any sound.

Opening the door a crack, I spy out into the corridor. Taking my compact mirror bracelet, I check the other side of the hall. The coast is clear. I get out as fast and silently as possible and replace the door. Heading back down the hall towards the tea room, I can hear the butler and Keagan coming back.

I practically sprint towards the tea room; as I make the bend I stop on a dime just in time to meet the bear-like butler I gave the message to. He saw me the instant I rounded the corner, beckoning me to come closer. Handing me a new piece of paper, he looks me in the eye and extends his arm. I give him mine in a Roman handshake as he whispers to me, "Winona explained everything to us, and we all wish to be a part of it. We want to go back home."

"Is there anyone untrustworthy in the household that might turn on you? We can't take chances with this."

"None; I trust everyone here with my life. The Adlenes are nice people, but we were meant to be back home in our environment, living for ourselves, not in this cold climate and for someone else as a slave," he states.

"I couldn't agree more," I say with a warm smile, releasing our handshake.

With smiles on our faces, he opens doors for me, and I put my act back on.

"Aspen, where have you been?" Lori asks.

"I guess I didn't know where to go as well as I thought," I say with an embarrassed look on my face.

"I'd say not! Two of my maids told me that you were waiting in the hall for some time then just up and disappeared. I hope you actually found the powder room; did you, dear?" asked Mary.

"Yes, I did, but the room that I thought was the powder room actually wasn't; it was your husband's study, where they were conversing still. They showed me where the loo was just before Mr Adlene came out of sorts himself."

"What's this? Is he sick?" Mary asks, now truly worried.

"I can't say for sure, but he rushed in the lavatory quite quickly. As far as I know he could still be in there."

"Oh dear. Well, if he is not better in a little bit, I hope you will pardon me to go and check on him."

"We understand, Mary. It would be good to know that our host is all right," Lori reassures Mary with a gloved hand on her arm.

We go on with the discussion of redesigning Mary's tea parlor, now on the subject of curtains. *It seems though that we may have given too much laxative to poor James; it's been twenty-eight minutes and neither he nor Keagan have shown their faces. And none of the dimies have come back to let us know if he is feeling better. Mary* seems anxious after another fifteen minutes have passed, though she tries to hide it by talking about curtain patterns again. Mary is about to pull the bell cord for a dimie when Keagan comes back in the room with James who is looking quite tired and flustered.

James has the same look on his face as Charles had after we tested the mixture on him: awkwardly uncomfortable in appearance whilst failing to stand up straight. Seeing him in his condition, we decide to say goodnight so he can start to get better and rest. Winona and Charles come from the servants' quarters soon after we send for them; they say goodnight to the household and our hosts with a curtsey and a bow just before they leave to retrieve the coach.

"I hope you start feeling better by tomorrow, James," Keagan says, shaking hands with him at the door.

"You and I both! I'm sure it's just a stomach bug though. I hope my little spell will not deter you from accompanying us again some time," James says, leaning some of his weight onto Mary.

"Oh no, you need not worry, the night was splendid, and we cannot wait to be in your company again," Lori reassured James.

"I'm glad to hear it," James says, continuing to hold on to his wife for support. Keagan grabs my wrist as we bid our goodbyes, and he holds on to me tightly until we enter the carriage. Once the doors close the heated conversation begins.

"Well, I thought I gave him less than we gave to Charles. You gave me his weight estimation, but I guess we still gave him too much," I say, embarrassed.

"You've got that right! The bloke was in agony for almost an hour! Thirty minutes is more than enough time, but an hour? Next time, when we need something from a friend or family member of mine, we are using different tactics," Keagan orders.

"So laxatives for enemies only, huh?" Lori says, trying to suppress a smile.

"Correct!" Keagan says with a stern look.

"We need to take a trip to the Market very soon," I say after a tense silence.

"Aspen, I know you want to help them, but there's no way we can buy them all. There are limits to how many dimies you can have now based on the size of your estate. Besides, that would look very suspicious if we were to buy them all and then they mysteriously disappear," Keagan responds, looking dejected whilst rubbing his temple.

"I never said we would buy them," I say, my eyes are fixated on the floor.

"What are you getting at, Aspen?" Keagan is eyeing me now through his fingers.

"The dimies were stolen from their homes and kept in cells like animals. I say we steal them back to set them free."

"Aspen, are you saying you want us to go to the Market, free the dimies, and let them loose? They will just get captured again," Lori says.

"Which is why, with Keagan's permission of course, we can use the Myrack manor as the safe house until the machine is prepared to get everyone sent home."

"I don't think-" Keagan starts.

"It will save us a lot of trouble getting them out now instead of when everyone else leaves and they are left behind. The day we get everyone else in the city back home there will be no way for those locked up to leave their hold like the other dimies can. Everyone else can make an excuse to run errands or get food for dinner, or even simply sneak out, but the dimies at the market can't. It sounds like a very controlled environment where they are kept and watched until someone wants to buy them like a pet shop almost," I elaborate.

"Hmm," Keagan growls, looking out the window for a long time.

We pass through a small skirt of town where in a far intersection there sits a soup kitchen with a long train of poor and homeless people out the door. When I look away and back at Keagan across from me, I give a wan smile. He looks back out the window, but as we go through a darker area our reflections are all we can see on the glass.

Keagan jerks his gaze away from the window and looks at me once again, startled. *Is...is he afraid to look at his reflection? I thought what with all the flirting he always does he would spend hours in front of a mirror. However, it seems as if he couldn't handle two seconds of his own gaze. What's biting him?* I wonder to myself whilst he rubs his chin as he's bent over, elbows on his knees.

"Just promise us you will think about it. One way or another we will need to go there to get the dimies, otherwise they will just supply the town again with their children or die off. It's time for the growing population of poor humans to find work again. They definitely deserve a second chance," Lori says.

Another long silence follows until we are on the winding road to the Myrack estate.

"Well, if we do get them out and take them home, and I'm

not saying we will, but if we do, we will need to talk to Charles and Winona about it. They live at the manor, too, and if they come to the house, we will need to be prepared for it," Keagan says with a calculated expression. I can't help myself from grinning ear to ear. He is thinking seriously about this. Now the other obstacle at hand: developing and mapping out the microfilm.

# THE MARKET

## KEAGAN

Pins and needles are roving my skin as we lie in the snow. I can't believe I agreed to this. I really can't believe that Winona and especially Charles agreed to this. The ride back down the hill is an unsettling discussion in itself, every word showing me how much I underestimated these ladies.

"The Market treats the dimies like prisoners. The building is run by some of the lower-class people left in town from the plague. And because of this, they are eager to keep their jobs since the dimies have taken over so many of theirs. A place that needs human workers would be picked over in an instant, so these men are always attentive," Aspen explains.

"How do you know all this?" I ask.

"Deduction. I told you, I have a gift for listening in on conversations at parties," Aspen answers slyly.

"Yup, and mine is false virility; it fools men and women alike to trust me," Lori adds proudly.

"Damn. It's official, I will never play poker with either of you two; I'd prefer not to be robbed blind," I say, making the next turn.

We position ourselves on Blu Man's Cliff, right above The Market. Laying our stomachs on the fresh cold snow, we look over the foreboding building. We attempt to come up with a plan on how to get inside undetected, but it starts to take longer than we thought for a plan that would work for a facility such as this. After about fifteen minutes of drawing and redrawing out ideas in the snow, Lori seems to get antsy so she starts to walk around the cliff and all its tall slopes and boulders.

"There has to be a safer way than sliding down our ropes to get them one by one. There's no way it'll be that simple," Aspen states, sweeping away our latest plan idea with her gloved hand.

"Um, guys?" Lori whispers.

"We could set an alarm off and fill the place up with smoke grenades, then we can pull them over the wall," I say.

"Hey, lovebirds-" Lori says, which puts a smile on my face, but Aspen seems to ignore her even more for that. I know Aspen tries not to let her sister get under her skin, but I can distinctly see her furrowed brow as she draws out a new scheme.

"That won't work; the guards and dogs will be at our heels. It'd be too easy to-"

"Earth to barmies!" Lori almost shouts.

"Shhh, Lori, what is it?" Aspen spits back.

"Why not take this tunnel? It may take us to the ground," she states. Our attention fully on her now, she helps us get to her level of the cliff. Once there, we see the place is littered with old rotted barrels of rum, sugar, and other goods as well. What sticks out most is a tombstone with a large chip on its side near a small tunnel just large enough for a grown man to squeeze through. I stoop down to clear the snow off the tomb-stone, and it reads:

Jonathan Nathanial Blu

1691-1725

Fighter, friend, and lover

You will be avenged, dear friend

*So this is where they buried him.*

"How did you find that tunnel?" I ask, puzzled.

"It wasn't easy, but it was odd; it was like a voice was telling me to look under the old barrel," she explains.

"Maybe Johnathan is trying to tell us about the hole," I say jokingly.

"Well, then I agree with Mr Blu. I think this tunnel will take us to the base of the cliff. This looks like it was the way the thieves went in the story; sloping hills in the snow would have been too tiring to go up with their spoils, and they could have been caught easier. It looks like Blu found the thieves' secret, so they buried him here to mark it and keep people away from it with his story. That way a heist like the one in the story doesn't happen again," Aspen states.

"Clever deduction. I'm willing to get behind that," I agree.

"I guess it's not enough to scare us away then, huh?" Lori pushes me in front of her towards the old tunnel. When I turn back to object, the sisters both have the same expression. Big expectant smiles that I read as *'there's no way we are going down first.'*

"Ahh, all right, I'll go first down the creepy ghost hole," I groan, poking my head through the tunnel opening. Cold and foreboding, no wonder this hasn't been used in over a century; it's almost completely overgrown with roots.

"Ahh!" I yell, pointing at the hole, causing the girls to scream in fright as well.

"I can't believe you fell for that," I laugh out.

"This. Is. Not. The. Time. For. Jokes!" Aspen says in a heated manner, hitting my arm with her glove once for each word. I know she wants to be mad, but I can see the grin she is trying to hide.

I put my hands up and go into the tunnel for real this time; there better not be someone or something in there with us on the way down. However, I can't help but hear the faintest whisper that sounds like Lori's voice: "See? He's got a sense of humour as well."

Making me smile now that I have her to help play cupid for me and Aspen it seems.

"Okay, so watch the – ouch!" I say, hitting my head again on a low-hanging root, the glowing rods we use aren't bright enough, it seems.

"You okay?" Aspen asks from behind me.

"Perfect," I groan out, dodging the roots this time as the tunnel seems to flatten out now.

"All right, guys, the plan is that we are going to peek over the fence to see where the night guards are and then look for an opening. Once we find it, we go in carefully and quietly, making our way to where the dimies are kept," Aspen says, repeating the now set plan.

"And remember to keep your sleeping darts and smoke grenades in hand at all times," Lori adds as we hit a dead end.

It looks like an old extremely rusty sheet of metal; there are holes here and there where the bright snow peeks through. I look through one of the lower holes and see that the coast is clear of guards, dogs, and other barriers.

"What do you see?" Aspen asks.

"It's a straight shot to the wall; there is no spotlight on, but there is the barbed wire on top of the stone fence. The building looks to be two stories, like we expected, and the windows have bars on them. There's still that small hole on the top of the roof we saw on the lower half of the building that we could use, but it might be where the guards reside," I explain as best I can. "I say we stick with the plan and scope out an opening from the wall, and if we can't find a good one, we check out the hole in the roof."

"Deal," Lori and Aspen say.

The wall is no help at all since there is no opening in sight, but luckily, we have our back up plan that turns out to be the easiest course of action. Scaling to the top of the roof with our grappling hooks, and making our way across the roof to the man-size hole, we see that the room the hole belonged to appeared to be a part of the lavatory that was in great need of repair. *This place really does look like a jail, and a really shanty one at that,* I think to myself as we make our way down the hallway unseen. One unlucky guard on patrol for the second floor is immediately darted without being the wiser as he walks into the corridor.

After propping him up to the window, we take his keys and are able to scope out the rest of the floor to see if any more guards are on the night-patrol shift. We find only one other guard, but his lantern light is dimming, just like he is by the visible sag in his eyelids. Who could blame the poor bloke since it is at least four in the morning by now. The rest of the workers seem to be sound asleep themselves since I am the one who hears their snoring from the other side of their quarters. Just to be safe, however, we shoot the dozing man on watch with another sleeping dart, giving him sweet dreams for the next six to eight hours.

We decide to scope out the bottom floor to make sure there aren't any remaining guards on duty tonight. If there are, they would have to be neutralized so they won't become an interference when we plan to leave. Lined up at the bottom of the stairwell, I sneak a peek around the corner with a mirror. Looking into a hallway, I make out a gruff man with a double-barreled gun in front of a barred cell. Easy enough; just one sleeping dart should finish him off.

After he's darted and lands face first on the floor, we prop him up into a sitting position on the floor and take the liberty of emptying his gun of bullets. Peering through the cold wrought iron bars of the cell, we take note of all the cots filled with dimies in white sheets; many are shaking in their sleep whilst a handful have awoken from the sound of the guard falling. Helping ourselves to the sleeping guard's keys, we unlock the door and let ourselves in.

We decide to leave the door unlocked but make it appear closed so we can run out if the need should arise. Lori offers to act as the lookout by staying next to the doors and ready to take down anyone who may come by. What comes next are some very grumpy and scared dimies; I guess I would be, too, if three dark hooded figures broke into where I slept in the middle of the night.

"How can we trust you?" one of the large male bear-like dimies with ram horns calls out dangerously loudly, causing the small crowd to stir in whispers and doubt.

"Why else would we be risking our necks like this to break in here to free you?" Aspen asks.

"Massacre. None of us would really put it past your kind," the large dimie says, scoffing in Aspen's direction without looking directly at her. We've been trying to calm down and talk things through to the crowded room, but it's not so easy as it seems when they believe that all humans are the enemy. I can't blame them, from the looks of how they've been treated: shackled to their beds; rags for blankets that are too thin already. And the rank smell of rodents and mildew fills the room.

Aspen, taking a deep breath and staying silent after that harsh remark, begins to walk quietly over to his cot and hand him a parchment that I had Winona's help encrypting. He seems hesitant to take the paper, however, and squints at the form in the dark. Luckily, Winona has been able to practice and remember her native language over the years whenever she sees her fellow dimies. It has become quite handy since it could be the very key to gaining the dimies' trust.

Aspen pulls out a long match from a dry tinderbox. Thatcher must have caught sight of her dagger that sits next to the tinderbox on her hip when she lit the match. I know he must have because he gives it a long look before raising his squinting eyes in a death glare towards her. Ignoring his menacing stare, she extends the paper to him once more, and this time he takes it with a snatching motion.

"Hmm," he ponders. A few more minutes reading the full-length of the letter Winona wrote, and then I can see his eyes staring hard at the symbol on the bottom of the page. It was the symbol of Winona's tribe and it's chief before her village was overthrown by humans. An eye with four arms holding hands in the centre of the iris. He still refuses to look Aspen in the eyes. We have to connect to him if we are to succeed in their agreeing to come with us tonight. I think it's high time I play my hand in this deal; I've certainly had enough practice in this area.

"Just imagine it," I pipe up as I walk towards him as well.

"No more being chained to the bedpost at night. No more having to serve or answer to humans. Seeing your real home again." I stop at a tattered cot with a tiny bird-like dimie no more than four years old. "Free to live, to play, and grow up with each other for yourselves, not as slaves or servants," I say, looking around, causing their expressions to have a far-off look, probably imagining their lives without humans to rule over them.

"What say you, sir?" I ask now as I kneel next to Aspen so I'm looking up to the old dimie instead of down at him. His ears and face perk up when I use the word sir as he slowly turns his head towards mine. Seeing this, Aspen kneels down slowly as well, still holding up the long lit match. Finally, raising his eyes to mine in the wan light, I draw my mask partly so he can see my face better. Winona taught us that in her culture the eyes are the truth tellers; one can learn a million things by just looking people in the eyes.

That's why so many dimies often express similar emotional traits and behaviours as their masters; because they connect and communicate through eye contact. I try to let myself be as open and sincere as possible in the silence that is held between us as he is deciding if he can trust me or not.

"Not once have I met a human whom I felt I could trust or connect to. But you, boy, you just changed that. I believe you and have faith that you are trying to help us." The dimie rises out of his cot, chains clanking, and extends a hand to me. I take it without hesitation, in their fashion; much like a Roman handshake.

"They call me Thatcher," he says before turning to the room. "What say you? Are you willing to risk your life for your freedom like I am willing?" Thatcher asks the room.

Some of them stand up immediately. Many of the sleepy children are still not sure of the gravity of the matter since they never knew what freedom was and stand probably because others are. The few left sitting on their cots look scared and sceptical with their arms crossed.

"We are not going to force you to come with us; this is your choice. But remember, this will probably be your one and only chance for escape and the chance for a better life," Aspen says, lowering her mask to show her face better now as she looks at some of the sitting dimies. Not waiting long for a response, however, she turns to Thatcher.

"Thatcher, are there any more rooms that have dimies in them?"

"Yes, the floor above us has one large room, and there is another small one on the first floor."

"Will you please help us get the remaining dimies out of their cells whilst he stays here to release everyone in this room?" she asks, gesturing to me.

"My pleasure, but first, what should we call you three?"

"Till we get to a safe place, Kay," I reply as I replace my mask.

"Ren," says Aspen.

"Lo," Lori says before turning towards the cell door once again.

I take one of the keys from its ring as the ladies take the

other two for themselves, and the dimies that accompany them to free the remaining rooms. It doesn't take too long to unshackle everyone, including those who still sit down, scared to leave. When those that choose to leave begin to congregate towards the door, waiting for the two groups to come back, there seems to be a commotion coming from around the corner on our level. I shrug it off, however. *It's probably one of the teams coming our way.*

I hear the squeak of a rusty old cot and turn to see the remaining dimies coming to join us. One in particular, an old maroon bird dimie, gives me a nod and tight smile with her long cracked bill. She is scared, I can tell, but hope fills her eyes. Brave old girl; she's giving her last chance to us. I give them a nod before my attention turns back to Aspen coming down a flight of stairs towards us with a party of dimies in tow. Seeing this, I open the metal door and start to move dimies through the doorway. Almost everyone is out of the cell when Lori joins up with us as well with her rescued group.

"Now we take groups to the tun-" Aspen stops mid sentence as she looks past me towards the end of the hall. When I look to see what's caught her attention, I feel as though all my blood is leaving my body. A stunned guard is staring right at us. *He must have been the sound I heard in the hall earlier.* Next to me, Aspen raises her dart gun and shoots at the man, but misses by an inch when he runs back down the adjacent hall, yelling at the top of his lungs, "There's a break-in! Emergency! Wake up!"

"Thatcher?" asks Aspen, putting her gun back under her sleeve.

"Yes?"

"Where is the closest exit?"

"The main entrance around the corner to the right," he states.

"I guess we will just use the front door then," Aspen says, looking strangely eager despite the gravity of our situation.

"Please, tell me Ren is joking?" Thatcher asks me as we now rush towards the main hall where we passed the building's main entrance earlier.

"Hold it!" Aspen yells, pulling the pin out of a smoke grenade she rolls it towards the door before pushing us back towards the wall with her outstretched arms. A small but powerful explosion goes off, causing dust and splinters to fill the air.

"Now! Quickly!"

"Was that a real grenade?" I yell as we jump through what's left of the broken door.

"Of course it was!" she calls back as we lead the head of the group around the corner whilst Lori takes up the rear. Another explosion goes off in the building, and this time the doorway is plumed with smoke right before Lori rushes out with the last dimie by her side.

We charge towards the cliffs base when a small group of men with menacingly barking dogs appear in the trampled snow. They seem to be searching around the back of the grounds, cutting off our exit. Aspen and I put our arms out and skid to a halt, pushing everyone back momentarily.

"Well, change of plans: run to the city!" Aspen announces as she pushes everyone towards the dark town.

"Wait, you didn't plan for something like this to happen?" Thatcher huffs with a bewildered look.

"Not in the slightest. Kay, lead them on," Aspen orders.

"What about you?" I question.

"I'll stall them whilst you get a head start. Now go."

"Not this time-" My arguing hits a wall as Thatcher begins dragging me away as the group begins to run towards town like Aspen ordered.

I run ahead and guide everyone away from the building as fast as possible. I look back to see many of them having trouble keeping up whilst Lori aids the youth. Everyone helps each other to move faster, some even carrying the elderly or the young as they run. Through the dimies running, I see Aspen dashing away from the side of the building. She runs with one arm in front of her face before throwing something towards the hounds that are gaining on her.

I stop momentarily in fear, ready to run back for her at any moment. Instead I see a red mist envelop around the dogs, making them halt and cry out in pain as they paw at and run their faces through the snow. *She's safe, thank the Lord!* She is with us in a matter of seconds, and not a moment too late before shots begin to ring out in the night, zooming over our heads.

"What other secret weapons do I not know about yet, Ren?" I ask playfully, happy to see she is safe.

"Not the time, Kay!" she calls.

"Fine, then stop scaring me half to death tonight, all right?"

We reach the beginning of the city with the guardsmen hot on our tails. By the time we round the second corner, the sound of police sirens have filled the night air. *They are looking for us for sure, but with the sirens echoing off the buildings it sounds like they are coming from all directions.*

"Kay, you know the city better; lead us to a pathway home," Lori orders, pointing to the front of the group as she slows her pace to join the back of the pack.

Taking the lead, I have us round a few more dark streets

until I take us to our first alleyway, where I meet something hard head on before reeling back and halting the crowd again.

I look to see what I just hit whilst we take quick and ragged breaths. It's those goons that were harassing Jasper in the alley the day of the scuffle, except there are many more goons than I remember. The man I rammed into doesn't look too cheerful at me and neither do his mates when they see what looks like a trio of slave-nappers. They begin to creep towards us with murder in their eyes.

"Oi, where are you fellas goin with all that trash?" the same burly man that got away that day we saved Jasper, calls out to us.

"Yeah, how about we help you carry the load?" says another scrappy-looking character as he unsheathes a long knife from his metal leg.

We start to back away slowly, then turn to run like bats out of hell down the cobblestone street, only to hear the men behind us bellowing for our hides. When we turn the corner we see a few pubs are beginning to close up for the night whilst the gas lamps are still lit.

"We are too exposed here," Aspen states as we halt for a second to look around.

*I know this street; it's not too far away from Miss Masie's store.* "Quick, this way," I say as I lead the group towards the alleyway behind the shops now. These are definitely the shops close to Masie Lacy, and there's not a doubt in my mind that she will be willing to help us.

We run so hard from the crowd on our tail that we fail to watch where we are running. Before I can alert the group, almost all of us are slipping and sliding on black ice and right into a snowbank. I lie on the ground for a second and clutch the back of my head from the pain of that hard fall as it shoots through my tailbone to my skull. We can hear the men's, and now policemen's, shouts as they round the corner we just passed and catch sight of us.

"There they are! After them!" comes a shout in the distance.

Our breathing is quick and scarce as we three and the more agile of the dimies begin picking up the youth and elderly. Aspen manages to pull the pin on another grenade before tossing it over her shoulder. Not three seconds later, a cloud of smoke envelops half the alley.

"Quick, in here!" comes a voice farther down the alleyway

"Thomas?" Lori exclaims.

"You know this kid?" Aspen and I ask in unison as the boy comes running to us, taking a dimie's hand and leading them towards the back of the shop.

"No time for questions! Hurry!" Thomas whispers hoarsely.

The girls run inside without another word, but I stay outside to make sure no one gets captured or left behind in the confusion. The last dimie goes inside whilst the kid and I are right behind them. The child Lori called Thomas quickly bolts the door shut and turns off the gas lights. Everyone squats down on the floor, stays still and quiet. We hear the men shuffling through the snow as we watch their lantern lights flash across the dingy curtains as we hold our breath in anticipation. The men start to walk slowly through the alley, waving the lantern left and right when, from the stairs in the corner of the room, a light comes to life.

# THOMAS

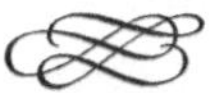

## LORI

"Thomas?" says the old shopkeeper in his night clothes. *Gerald!*

"Shh," we all shush him, silencing his questions quickly. The sound of men shuffling through the alley is beginning to die down. The blinds are drawn, but we can still see their light moving around until everything is dark and still once again. We wait for what seems like forever in silence to make sure they have all left. Gerald at this time begins to slowly work his way around the crouching dimies, until he comes to a short wooden table in the centre of the room. There he takes a seat on a worn wooden bench and sets the lamp down before speaking.

"Thomas, why is there a damn city's worth of slaves in my kitchen?" he asks Thomas.

"He helped us, sir. We would all be captured or dead by now if not for him," I reply before Thomas does.

"We would have what?" one of the young bird dimies exclaims before being hushed by Thatcher.

"Come closer, dear. Thomas, find some candles to light," Gerald orders as he beckons me to come near.

I stand up from my dark corner and walk around those on the floor until I reach the table. I stand before Gerald in silence as Thomas lights candles all around us in what must be their kitchen. Gerald stares at me harder with every candle that's lit. My face still has it's half mask on, but he is looking harshly at my eyes. Now that the room is lit better, Gerald's expression begins to change from confusion to recognition.

"This is the girl you sold the sapphire to!" Gerald exclaims, pointing at me whilst his attention is now directed on poor Thomas.

"The fake and the real were mixed up, and it wasn't my fault; it was the broken pipe," Thomas objects, lighting more candles.

"What Sapphire? When did you even come here?" Keagan asks Aspen, dumbfounded.

"Okay, this one was all her. You cannot blame me for this one," sissy snaps back.

"You sure? Because this sure sounds like something that would happen to you."

"And what is that supposed to-"

"It was my idea to buy the gems Keag-Kay not Ren," I stutter, almost giving away Keagan's name. "When Thomas rang me up, we got the two stones confused, and I ended up with a real sapphire, not the glass one I wanted to buy." I lower my mask to show my face, turning back to Gerald.

"A likely story; you obviously haven't tried to return the gem and now you want me to believe you whilst you're storing stolen slaves in my kitchen and shop! If you think that dimies will suffice as payment, I don't want them!" Gerald gripes.

"No, Grandfather, they help dimies, not hurt or steal them," Thomas pipes up, lighting the last candle. *I mean, we did technically steal them from the Market, but I think I should just keep that thought to myself.*

"Really, then what do you call this?" Gerald demands.

"Saving them," Thomas replies, candlelight burning brightly in his eyes like his untouched innocence..

"I like this boy," Aspen says.

"Me too," concurs Thatcher.

"I saw you one night, fighting those robots, and when your mask ripped I recognised you. I was about to call for the constables, but when I saw that you were protecting a slave from those metal men, I had second thoughts. Ever since that night, there have been newspaper headlines and rumours about a band of renegades roaming the streets at night, terrorizing the police, but I knew better. You were amazing fighters and you're kind to the dimies as well. So when I heard the commotion and saw you coming, I thought I could help out, too," Thomas explains. This makes me smile, but I still feel nervous knowing now that he saw us. *What was a little boy like him doing in that sector of the city at that time of night anyway?*

"I never liked the idea of bringing in slaves when humans can work much better and won't be beat as much or at all if they mess up. I raised Thomas to be against slavery as well for that reason. Besides, we are poor enough as it is; we would much rather the dimies go back to where they came from so more of the paupers in town can find work again," Gerald explains, ruffling Thomas's wiry hair, though Thomas doesn't seem to like it.

"Um, sir, I'm her sister. May I please have a word with you about that jewel?" Aspen says, shuffling towards us. Aspen leads him over towards the stairs and starts talking too quietly for me to listen in.

Whilst she seems to be persuading the gear master, I pull Thomas aside. "Thomas, have you told anyone that you know who we are or what happened that night you saw my mask torn? And I mean your friends as well," I ask gently whilst bending down to his level, my arms on both of his sides.

"Well… I did tell a few of my friends but-"

"But did you tell them that you saw a girl fighting? Did you tell them that you knew who it was?"

"I might have, I think I told two of my friends that are my age and that's it. But they just laughed at me."

"Did you tell them what I looked like? Do they have connections with anyone important in the middle or upper class?"

"My friends? Are you off your trolley, Miss? There's no way I could have friends that high up in society."

I mulled this statement over in my mind. Since he already knows what I look like, why not befriend him? If we are kind enough, maybe he will stay on our side.

"Would you like one?" I say, extending my hand.

"Really, Miss?"

"Mhmm, but you need to promise to keep our secret your secret. If people start finding out who we are, my family, Gerald, and you could be in grave danger. Do you understand?" I ask, giving his shoulders a light squeeze.

Thomas nods his head and takes my hand.

"I understand, Miss."

"Good, Thomas, you can call me Lo."

"Lo, that's a funny name for a lady." He chuckles with a questioning smile on his dirty face. His honesty makes me laugh, and I instantly like him even more now.

"Yes, I guess it is a funny name for a girl. But it's the name I can give you now. Once we get to know each other better, you can learn all our real names."

"Okay." Thomas nods with a wide grin on his face.

"Miss Lo, is it?" Gerald asks. "Walk with me, please," he adds, gesturing towards himself.

We stroll through a hallway that leads up to the front counter where we were first acquainted, he pulls out what must be the glass sapphire I was supposed to get and places it on the counter. The glass still looks identical to the real one at home, whether twinkling by the wan candlelight or in the sunlight, I would have still chosen the wrong one.

"Your sister told me that the special properties and size of the sapphire are exactly what you need for her machine to work properly," Gerald says.

"Yes, but it's my sister who is the inventor of the machine. She knows what it needs better than I do. However, I was being honest when Thomas and I said that it was an accident; I meant to buy the glass one, I promise," I say earnestly.

"I believe you... but I just lost a fortune in it. I'm afraid it will be best if you switch it out with the glass one you were trying to buy in the first place tomorrow. Or I will have to press charges, I simply can't afford to lose a gem that size."

"Oh, sir, please, there must be something else. If my sister said that we needed this for the machine then it is crucial for it to work. I can assure you," I plead as Gerald rests his thin elbow on the shop counter to rub his chin.

"I can promise you that my sister and I do not steal jewels or jewelry for that matter...just dimies," I say evenly with a smile at the end. That seemed to do something since he takes a great sigh before looking at me again.

"You people are in a dangerous sort of business; you know

you are dealing with the death penalty. And now with that crowd of desperate men looking for blood out there, you three are already worth a bounty. Pretty soon it'll start growing if you are not careful."

"You could have ratted us out, you know, and collected what reward they have for us, but you didn't. Why? If I may ask."

"You're right, I didn't. Maybe that's because even though I don't particularly like it when thieves store their spoils in my shop, I can tell when it's the wrong thing for the right reason," he concludes. I give him a weak smile since he is fully in the right to do anything at this time: call the police and collect a reward, or let us go and keep our secret. Or even wait until the reward gets bigger and expose us when he pleases.

"Well, I guess you can keep the sapphire, but only if you can do payment installments, and I want that in writing."

"It's a deal. You will get every shilling for your troubles as well."

"Hmph," he grunts, nodding his head. "Now, let's get the contract signed so you can be on your way with those dimies; they are bad for business if they stick around too long," Gerald huffs, trying to hide a smile.

"Thank you, Gerald," I say gratefully as he pulls out a parchment of paper that reads *Payment Contract*. *He's just an old softy under that gruff surface.* He chuffs as he readies his quill before gazing out the store windows. But his expression turns grim right before turning and shoving me back towards the doorway. My back hits the wall of the hallway, and when my eyes close on impact, I hear a loud shot followed by the sound of breaking glass.

When I reopen my eyes, I find Gerald on the ground,

clutching his chest that's turning a dark red in the candlelight. *Someone shot him.*

Sprinting down the hall, Thomas kneels before me and then turns to look into the shop only to see his grandfather wounded on the floor. Thomas accompanies his side in half a second, looking terrified with jittery hands, unsure of what to do. I pick myself up and glance over the counter top quickly to see who the shooter was, but what I see does not bode well for us.

"Lo! What is the meaning of this?" Aspen demands running around the corner with Keagan right behind her to see the men starting to aim again and throw rocks to break the glass.

"We've been found! Leave and make haste!" Aspen yells to the back room, causing a frenzy of shouts and shuffling to get out the door.

"Go with them. Go with them, Thomas!" Gerald yells.

Without a second thought I pry Thomas from Gerald's bleeding body and run to the back door.

"No, no, no!" Thomas screams as I carry him away.

As I run through the open doorway, I hear shouts coming from the other direction. I glance over my shoulder to see the police and their patrol bots running towards us from the end of the alley. Aspen sees them too and tosses two grenades towards them. The men skid to a halt, probably thinking it's a real bomb as the grenades fill the alley and roof tops with smoke and bright flashes of light, giving us the cover we need.

# THE GLOVE

## LORI

"Stop! We can't just leave him! We can fight and get the shop back," Thomas objects as we make a beeline for another alleyway.

"There was no way we could have done that, saved your grandfather, as well as ourselves in time. If we stay now and fight we could all be killed," Keagan puffs out as he carries two young otter dimies in his arms and one little bird dimie on his back.

"Well, then you should have left me; I could have done something," he objects again whilst clinging for dear life to my shoulders.

"Darling, if we left you there, they would have killed you, too, for helping us or for simply just being there. Those rogues are terrible men," I say as we finally make it to the tree-covered winding road that leads to the manor.

"They are after you, aren't they? Why would they break into the store like that then? And why did they have to shoot him? They didn't have to shoot him!"

"When tensions are high, and groups are gathered on

manhunts, riots can break out. When that happens, people seem to lose their sense of respect for others, and many can suffer in the turmoil," Aspen elaborates as she carries a fragile-looking otter dimie on her back. But Thomas remains silent instead of asking any other questions.

A little way's further, after we round the sloping bend twice, we start to slow down considerably now that no one seems to be following us.

"How much farther?" Thatcher asks as we trek further up the hill.

"Not much. We are almost at the safe point," Keagan grunts.

"Please, I must rest," one of the old dimies says, leaning over a walking stick he picked up.

"Me too, I'm tired," says a little bird girl who is starting to teeter.

Aspen walks back and scoops her up in her arms. She looks at me and then at everyone else. Our rescue group does look quite exhausted, and I can honestly say I'm tired as well. Sissy and I look around at the woodsy area and empty roads without a sign of life or a simple breeze anywhere. All is eerily quiet in the snow-painted landscape. It appears to be safe enough.

"All right, we can rest for a little bit, but we have to get home soon before someone else comes along," Aspen says, walking with the purple little bird girl to the snow. At this, everyone immediately plops their bums down on a rock, log, or bare ground with groans and sighs. The children come straight to us three and climb on top of our supine forms in a dog-pile fashion. They cuddle up tight as they shiver slightly through their torn clothes. I look over at Aspen and Keagan, and they are as covered as I am in children.

"You think we are covered enough?" Aspen jokes.

"You know there is always room for one more," Keagan says to Aspen with an outstretched arm.

"Oh boy!" a little red otter girl with curly horns on Aspen squeals, taking up the open space on Keagan. When Keagan looks towards the road again, I can tell he isn't as amused as Aspen or the little girl appear to be.

"We need a lookout," Aspen announces, starting to get back up and prying the objecting kids off.

"No, no, sit. I'll stick my neck out this time," Keagan says, pushing Aspen back down gently. Aspen must be tired because she didn't even protest. The children that were on him come to lay on our legs and atop each other or head to the adults for rest. Blindly, I watch Keagan walk towards the curve in the road with the little red otter girl tucked close to his neck. She doesn't want to let go. Resting against the trunk of a tree, he watches the road for passersby.

I realise that I haven't heard anything from Thomas in a while; I look down at my chest and see that under the fur of two blue and green monkey-like children with fanned tails, he has dozed off on my chest. Poor dear, though he sleeps soundly, there's grief painted over his dark wet cheeks and nose.

*This wasn't part of the plan, and we were never supposed to take in humans. What we'll do with Thomas is a mystery to me. Maybe after a household discussion we will come up with something. It was our fault that Gerald and his home were ransacked. Now to those policemen and goons, it looks like we've kidnapped Thomas. What am I thinking? We did kidnap him, just like the dimies. We ran away in the night with him.* I heave a great sigh and settle my head down on the trunk of a tree, and I hear a sigh in return.

"Lori, there was nothing more we could have done," Aspen whispers.

"I know, but Gerald and Thomas saved our lives, and we owe him a lot of money now. Gerald was writing up a payment plan for us before he got shot. What are we going to do? We practically kidnapped Thomas as well. We *did* kidnap him," I whisper hoarsely back as tears begin to sting my cold cheeks. *All this pressure tonight is beginning to break me.*

"Lori, we will figure this out; take a breather. What if we give the boy the money in installments like an inheritance? People will think it's from Gerald's or another family member's will."

"But what will we do with Thomas? It's too late to take him anywhere else tonight, and it's too dangerous to go back into town with that mob out looking for us."

"Well, he will obviously have to stay at the manor tonight whilst the household figures something out together. Now please, just rest for two seconds."

I try to lay my head down and think of something else, but it's impossible. Not a minute later, we hear a shrill whistle coming from Keagan's direction. We look his way, and he is sprinting towards us, pointing down the hill. *That can't be good.*

"Get up, get up, time to go now!" Aspen orders, picking drowsy children off her legs.

"What's going on?" Thomas moans sleepily, getting off of me.

"Someone is coming. We need to start hiking up the hill. Just follow me, all right?" I say, picking up the two young monkey dimies and following Aspen towards the patch of snow-covered pine trees down the road.

"Not just anyone, it looks like paddy wagons and constables on horseback, and they are coming fast," Keagan says, running by us, picking up an older green bear dimie with a hurt ankle whilst the little otter girl piggy backs him. Thomas does as he is told and stays by my side; he even holds a paw of one of the otter dimies as we rush to the snowy hill.

We make it to the snow bank and trek our way up to the tunnel that connects to the study. Holding up the thick tree roots, we usher everyone in as the sound of horses galloping come closer in each breath. The last few dimies are getting inside whilst I'm covering up the tracks with a branch, I can see the buggies coming down the road, their lanterns shining bright in the night and the faint sound of barking dogs coming from the inside of the paddy wagon. I start to move back up the hill where there are more bushes and coverage just as the last dimie makes their way up. Then, from the corner of my eye, I see the little red otter girl tumbling through the snow towards the road. *No!* I nearly yell out loud.

Rushing down the hill, my foot gets stuck in a rabbit hole halfway to her. When I look up, I see that the police lights have hit her petrified body staring back at them.

"Lo!" I hear Aspen and Thomas call to me through the barks of approaching dogs. I grab the nearest pine branch and pull myself out of the hole. Snow from a branch above me hits my back as I leave my caught glove behind on the pine needles. I rush down the bank, grab the girl and run off into the woods. I have to get us away from the rest of the group.

They are gaining on us; I can feel it. The sound of the dogs breathing and the thumping of the men's feet chasing me in the thick forest is all I can hear. The otter girl's grip tightens around my neck as she hides her face and whimpers. *That can't*

*be a good sign.* My lungs burn like hot coals whilst the air is so cold, both my eyes and nose sting as they run like rivers. Feeling my legs beginning to falter, I realise I can't keep running across this rough snowy terrain for much longer. I reach into my pocket for something, anything, that might help. I pull out three small balls, which must be the grenades.

I'm running over fallen trees and slick stones now as the sound of the policemen call out to keep up the search. For fear of tripping and the gnashing of those canines' teeth, I can't look to see which type of grenades they are or how close the dogs are to us. Clenching them in my hand just before sending out a silent prayer for help, I release them behind me. Pulling out my grapple, I shoot out to a far tree and swing near the top that is thick and dark with powdered branches. Covering the young dimie and myself with my cloak, we nearly become one with the tree pressing tightly to it. We wait and listen.

The dogs are whining. I never saw what went off, but there was no explosion and no bright lights. The tear gas bombs! God, was that a miracle. The men's voices below echo through the woods. I don't dare move or look their way. If any light catches my eye it'll shine out and we will be caught.

"Find them, men. We will be a laughing stock if we let them all get away."

*Too late for that.*

"And would someone get these damn dogs to quit whining and get back to work already? We are not here to take them on a nightly stroll!" the man's harsh deep voice booms out in the night.

"Fan out, this is a dead end." The men's voices get closer as they continue to search.

"Where could they have gone? Their foot-prints just stop,

and now the dogs can't even find a scent," a new voice says, much softer than the other man's.

"But they surely continue to whine," the mean-sounding man snaps. He is probably in charge since he can talk that way, or he's just grumpy since it's past five a.m. or something.

"Sir, we found this caught on a tree branch not far from where the figure made off with the slave."

"Was there anyone or anything else found nearby?" the nicer-sounding man asks.

"No, sir."

" Hmm, Officer Balt, give this to the trackers at once," the rough leader orders.

"Yes, sir."

A moment of silence ensues where the only sound includes the whining of dogs and the crunching of snow as the men walk around.

"Well, obviously something is wrong with them, even with the glove we found, they just act disoriented," says the softer voice.

"Some tracking dogs! Send them back to training if they can't find one measly thief and a slave, let alone an entire group of slaves on the run."

"We will never hear the end of this."

"You bet we won't, but we have caught those slaves that were loose in the street for questioning. Maybe we will get something from them instead," the leader's rough voice says, ringing in my ears. My heart begins to race again at the mention of this. *Did we lose people? And if so, how many?* My thoughts are interrupted by the sound of a terrible cry.

"Bloody hell, what now? Did they find something?" the leader asks.

"No, one of the dogs seems to have gotten their leg stuck

in a hunting trap. These must be the hunting grounds of the Flabisham's estate. We will have to talk to them in the morning."

"In case you had forgotten, it *is* morning! It is five-thirty in the bloody morning, and I for one am willing to put a close on this case until a more suitable hour," the rude leader yells.

"But we can't leave until the detectives come," the other man objects.

"Fine, you stay, and I'll go back to bed, besides-" The men's words begin to fade out as they walk off to where the dogs are. Now's my chance.

"Hold on tight, and don't utter a word," I whisper almost inaudibly to the little dimie that clutches onto me. I take a chance and look around through the branches to see what is happening on the ground. About eight men are on the ground in two groups of four, one clustered together tracking my foot-prints to where they ended. Whilst the few men left busy themselves with the now-shrieking tracking dog, I hop from one tree to the next until I'm far enough that they can't see me swing away. Seeing a large stone-crafted abode I realise we must be on the Flabisham estate as the men said. I rip off the sleeve of the little dimie's shirt and have her throw it on the ground. *That will keep them all busy. Now to get home.*

Rounding back all the way to the rear of the house, we run across an old slightly covered stone path in the garden that leads to the back door. After I stomp off the snow from my feet, I carry the otter girl to the study where everyone is supposed to be. Right as I open the door, I find myself looking down the sharp blade of a knife. Emitting an ear-piercing scream and falling back against the door, I expect to be gutted on the spot.

"Lori! Come here," Aspen says, pulling me into her arms

as she puts away her knife. Everyone's look of fear subsides as they see that it's me instead of a policeman at the door. Even Keagan was prepared with his sword at the ready. *They probably heard the door open and close whilst everyone was here and figured it was an intruder instead of me.*

"Careful, sis, you're showing a lot of emotion, they may mistake you for a French woman," I say, hugging sissy back.

"I don't care if they do, and I'm not ashamed to say that I was a bit worried," she says.

"A bit? You nearly broke my arm, you were clinging to me so tightly," Keagan says, interjecting.

"Is that so?" I ask curiously.

"I was terrified thinking they had caught you, and if they had Kay, I *would* have broken your arm."

"Would that be before or after you shook like a ragdoll and teared up on my shoulder?"

"I-I wasn't-"

I laugh at this, stifling whatever remark Aspen was about to let out. I explain dropping the sleeve on the neighboring estate and making my way back to the Myrack manor, taking nearly an hour getting here without touching the ground until I got to the clearing of the house.

"We waited painfully to hear if they had caught you or if you had lost them," Winona says, pouring the warm tea and bowls of steaming soup she and Charles prepared for everyone. What angels they are.

Ushering everyone inside, we do a headcount, but the others realise something seems to be amiss. *What those men said, could it be true? Could we have lost dimies tonight?*

"We must have miscounted," Aspen says, but when we check the second time after Keagan runs through the tunnel, we realise we didn't make it home with everyone. Though very few left behind, we didn't make it back with them all. I feel the men's words tearing a pit in my stomach as a wave of exhaustion washes over me. Aspen grips the couch for ease as I slide down the wall and curl up when I hit the ground... *We couldn't save them all.*

# REST AND GRIEF

## ASPEN

"Lori?"

She looks up, seeing it's Thomas. He pulls out a handkerchief for her, and she uses it liberally.

"Who's this young chap?" Winona asks us.

"This is Thomas. It seems that we have picked up more than just dimies that were in need of our help tonight," I say.

"Winona, please, we all must act fast. There are hounds near the estate. They found my glove and will be able to track me back to the mansion if we don't do something soon," Lori interjects, holding onto Winona's paw.

"Don't worry about that, Lori, it has already been taken care of," I say to her.

"What? What do you mean?"

"Right before you ran to get the little girl, Aspen doused you, that glove you lost, and the area around the tunnel with a liquid that kills a tracking dog's sense of smell for a couple of hours. And since your cloak and glove absorbed enough of that stuff, I think we can rest easy for the night," Keagan explains.

"I-I thought it was snow that hit me. I didn't smell a thing though."

"Of course you didn't, you were running away from it too quickly whilst high on adrenaline."

"But how did you…"

"I asked Winona about the Market and what she knew about it's finer details since her friends from other families are from there. That's how I knew about the dogs; they use canines to keep the dimies in line a lot of the time," I explain.

"And where was my bottle of this scent blocker?" Lori asks expectantly.

"On your hip, away from the grenades. I told you about it last night."

"Oh… really?"

"Yes, that's what you get for ignoring me," I snap back.

"Sorry," Lori mutters as she walks off to Winona with Thomas following her, which directs my attention back to our little predicament.

"Keagan?" I ask.

"Yes, dear?"

"Don't start with that again," I huff out. "What are we going to do about Thomas?"

"I don't know. Maybe he has other relatives in or out of town," Keagan suggests.

"Yes, but even if he does, people will ask questions about his disappearance last night."

"There will be questions no matter what we do now that he is here with us."

"I know, but those men that tore the shop apart are probably from that area. They would know Gerald housed Thomas and so would the police. What explanation would be reasonable or feasible for a boy of ten to be outside at three or four in the morning?"

"I'm thirteen, actually, I'm not that young," Thomas says proudly, interrupting our train of thought.

"What's all this then?" Winona asks coming our way, leaving Lori to pour the soup.

"We were discussing what to do about Thomas here," Keagan replies.

"Well, is there someone in town that can take care of you, darling?" she asks Thomas, bending down to his level.

"Well, I don't have any more family, but I do know Miss Masie," the boy answers.

"Yes, but since the shop was destroyed and you were absent during the attack, there will be questions of your whereabouts. Regardless they may even take you away since Miss Masie isn't your real next of kin," Keagan adds.

"Well, if he stays here he will be seen as kidnapped or dead since he lives in the shop that we ran out of. Those goons saw us running with him as well, I'm sure of it," I point out.

"Why don't we let Thomas decide?" Lori suggests to us.

I look at Winona, then to Keagan. Keagan shrugs his shoulders. We all look at Thomas for his answer.

"You said you needed the sapphire for an important machine."

"Yes," I agree.

"Could I see the machine? I could help. I'm good with my hands and have been learning how to repair gadgets." There is a sheen of desperation in his eyes that I cannot unsee. He has no family now and is in a strange place surrounded by unfamiliar faces. He wants to hold on to something that feels like home. I cannot deny him if this is his choice.

"Of course you can," I say, lowering my mask.

I take Thomas to see the machine, his teary eyes light up the instant he sees it.

"It's like nothing I've ever seen! How does the sapphire help the machine? Why is it in the shape of an egg? Does it run on gas or steam?" he asks curiously, looking at the two partial halves of Gear Heart and the chalk board with the designs and formulas scribbled over its dusty surface.

"Well, it's in this journal I found in an old warehouse. You remember that night you saw us defend that dimie?" I ask as I rummage through my stack of books and sketchbooks.

"Yes."

"Well, as we were running from the police after that incident, we hid and looked around an old warehouse by the harbour. Inside we found one of the original multi-dimensional machines. We figured we could try and use the lens from that one since it will make a larger portal. But other than this I found a journal," I explain, holding up the aged leather-bound book. Opening it up to my bookmarked page causes the old leather to crackle.

"This book has details of when certain precious gems, especially sapphires, are coated with the chemical compounds being pumped through the machine and then projected with light behind a lens. It allows there to be a 'rift' so to speak, and create a portal to connect our world to that of the dimies. See, look here." I point to the description I pored over countless times already in the old journal. The formula compound when shot through the lens reacts to the sapphire as it's charged by bolts of electricity, creating the window through a bridge of light almost. Connecting our world to theirs for just a few short moments.

"Bloody hell! And you're designing it in the shape of an egg, why is that?" Thomas marvels.

"Well, the last time this machine was completed, it did not have a protective cover and was destroyed. This time is different though. Lori gave me the idea for making it look like a giant Fabergé egg when she got the jewels from your shop. But I'm not sure that I can do all that ornamental designing on my own; it would take way too much time. You wouldn't happen to know anything about stone faceting, staining, or soldering metal, would you?" I ask coyly.

Suddenly, I'm back home with Lori in our papa's lab. The dispersed parts of Gear Heart lay before me on the worn wooden table. I was about to fiddle with the frayed wires that stuck out of the side of the piece I just put together. Then there's Papa next to the desk, looking down at my work with his discerning brown eyes. He had just found Lori and me tinkering on the machine, much to our surprise. He remained quiet for so long as he examined it with his work-magnifying goggles whilst we stood by waiting for our punishment. But when he turned to us, he extended his open hand to me, and with a smile under his clean mustache, he said, *"You're pretty good at this. Would you like to work on this project with me, little sapling?"*

"Sure I do, I'm still...was learning stone faceting from my grandfather but...not much anymore, I guess," he says sombrely.

A painful silence falls for a second. I remember where I am once again and that I'm talking to a child instead of my being one again myself next to my father. I lay a hand on his shoulder; the moment I touch him, he rushes at me and buries his face in my waist, unable to contain his pain any longer. I just hold onto him and let him cry for a bit before speaking.

"I'm sorry, Thomas. Truly, I am. Tonight didn't go as planned; we weren't even supposed to be anywhere near the shop or town," I apologize as he gives out a slight wail.

"Shh, I know the pain of losing those you love, Thomas. Lori and I are orphans now as well. I'd give anything to see my parents again even if it were just for a second. I still feel the pain, so cry all you like," I reassure him. He goes on mourning for a few more minutes until he begins to calm down and is breathing sharply as I hand him a clean rag. I release him and bend down to his face level whilst he wipes his nose.

"It's your choice if you want to stay here with us and be a part of this family. We would love to have you, but if you want to leave, we will understand."

He has a hard time looking me in the eye. Most boys don't like it when girls see them cry so it's understandable.

"You can decide later, but for now, let's get you some nice hot tea and a soft place to sleep." I wipe away his tears. I don't even try to put on a smile because what has happened tonight is nothing to be light-hearted about. Thomas nods and follows me out of my room to one of the guest rooms we prepared for the dimies.

Lori brings in a large tray of tea for those still awake and tucks Thomas in for the night as I help the other guests get comfortable. As I help lay down a sickly pale blue monkey dimie I can hear Keagan and Winona shuffling and situating our guests around in the room adjacent to us. All the while Charles picks up the bowls and cups from room to room on his rolling cart. I look over at Thomas and Lori and can't help but notice the way he stares at her. It reminds me of when Keagan saw me in the green dress for the first time, such a heartwarming sight after what tonight has dished out. Thomas doesn't last long after he finishes his tea and he soon drifts off into sleep, the last of his tears hitting his pillow.

*There's a lot to come, with the governor's ball two days away now, the blueprint pictures to look over with Thomas's help, and now taking care of the dimies and Thomas.* I make my way outside the room once the candles are all extinguished. Lori is already there sitting on a bench, taking off her boots and utility belt. I fall into an empty chair, close my eyes, and feel as if the weight of the world has just fallen on top of me. The sensation of fire courses from my eyes to my throbbing feet as they pulsate. *We have our work cut out for us for sure. If only tonight could have been different, all the dimies could be here, and a family would still be together.*

Feeling someone brushing my cheek, my eyes open lazily to see it's Keagan. There's a shine on his hand as he takes it away. That's when I realise I've been crying.

"Time for rest, it's after six a.m., and we've been up and fighting for too long."

"We messed-"

"Let's talk when we can actually think," he suggests as he cuts me off.

My gaze shifts to Lori, and I see she's nodding off as well. I reluctantly get out of my chair and collect my baby sister for bed.

"Nngh, Winona?" I can hear Keagan call.

"Please let the entire house sleep for however long they need; no wake up call, and that goes for yourself as well. Just leave that pot of soup out in the study with a few pitchers of water if anyone needs it, then treat yourself to bed...bed, my kingdom for my bed," Keagan grunts out. He's right, every-thing is a jumbled mess of emotions, memories, and thoughts. Tomorrow things will be clearer after rest.

# BALL OF SKINS

## LORI

From the time we left the house to present, Keagan can't seem to take his eyes off of Aspen. Although to be fair, she is wearing her jaw-dropping green dress with black lace detailing, so there's no wonder why. Winona helped prepare everything for her from her pin-up ringlet hairstyle with black lace and jeweled-cog hair combs, to the amethyst and onyx choker around her neck. Even the coat boy was gawking at her; he only stopped after the death glare that Keagan gave him.

This added attention and attraction can give me the chance to slip away and possibly find a gentleman for myself now. Aspen can't have all the fun all the time. Lucky for me, I've noticed that I already turned more than a few heads in my peach dress with roses on our way through the showy mansion. As we walk through the hallways of the governor's mansion, following the other dapper couples, I start to antici-pate the ballroom in excitement with each advancing step. Through the grand ballroom doors we stroll into the room where we find ourselves on a balcony staircase. One by one, the couples and parties of guests are being introduced to our host, Governor Damon. He is a man in his early sixties with a three-pointed peppered beard in an indigo suit and bowtie that consists of gears actually turning on their own.

"Governor Damon, I'm pleased to introduce to you my guests and close friends, the Wolfe sisters, Miss Aspen and Miss Lori," Keagan introduces us, and we curtsey at the mention of our names.

"Ah, so these are the young ladies you told me about. Well, I hope that you both live up to Keagan's description of your character. He's already right on one thing, you both are very lovely young ladies," he replies after a short bow.

"Thank you very much, Governor Damon," Aspen says whilst we curtsey once again just before Keagan leads us to the top of the stairs where we hand the announcer our invitations. After two other couples we are finally introduced to the room to join the rest of the applauding crowd on the dance floor.

I can't help but want this night to last forever. I want to take it in and experience it all. The size of the dance floor is immense, and the starry night shimmers just outside the huge windows. The elegant dancing, the smell of perfume, chocolate, fresh fruit and cheese is all so intoxicating. The party guests consist of the largest group of elites and exquisite couture I've ever been around. I never dreamt I'd be at such a momentous occasion. Now this is more of my scene, a place of laughter, waltzes, and handsome men for the picking. Aspen, on the other hand, looks like she is getting slightly strangled by her choker necklace as she smiles wanly whilst we are being introduced to the party.

I know she'd prefer a small gathering or dinner to this or, most preferably, a night running on the rooftops and inventing. Luckily for her, there is still work being done at the house; it's a good thing that Thomas prefers metalsmithing over dancing. He was so excited to start on the Fabergé' egg whilst the dimies held their own ball tonight, that sweet boy. Food, dancing, music; I hope we didn't forget anything for the dimie's little ball we prepared for them.

*This is still important, plus, whilst Aspen gets to have her fun most nights, now it's my turn to have a merry evening. At a normal fancy party and dancing the night away. Who says that renegades aren't allowed to have fun like this? After all, we work hard as well.*

"Oh, Lori, Aspen! I'm so glad that you could make it tonight," Mrs Adlene says, greeting us at the base of the stairs.

"Yes, I'm glad as well," I chuckle as we join hands in greeting.

"Keagan, I'm quite glad that you made it; now I'll have someone interesting to talk to," James says jokingly, making Keagan laugh as he claps a hand on his friend's shoulder.

"You will have to excuse us, gentlemen. I have a few people I'd like to introduce these ladies to," Mary announces, pulling Aspen and me away, arm in arm.

As we brush against the lords and ladies along the marble floor I can hear more people being announced. One in particular caught my ear.

"Master Peter Flemings."

And that was it, no lady or miss along with his name. I turn to look at the chap as he descends the stairs and see that he is most amiable. By the time Mary found the couple she wanted to introduce us to, four more men were called that were without a lady. I have a bountiful harvest ripe for the picking tonight.

After a bit of small talk with the Brandsons and Mary about interior decorating, and a jolly glass of punch, the music begins. Aspen begins to tarry with me as we sway to the tune. Not a minute later Keagan pops up out of nowhere.

"Excuse me, but I must steal away Miss Wolfe for the first dance," Keagan says, whisking away a dumbfounded Aspen. Now I feel a little bad, but not for long as I watch the scene in front of me. The crowd begins to disperse and make a grand opening for the dancers to begin. It was a simple dance, the newly introduced Chasse', but poor Aspen still looks nervous. She was never the best at ballroom dancing, always seemed to step on her partner's toes or her own.

"Oh dear, it appears that he has caught a new play toy."

"I wonder how long he plans to keep this one," I hear two women say right beside me.

"Oh, forgive me, Miss, but what is your name?" I ask, turning to the two gossipers.

"Miss Rose Hughes. This is Miss Minnie Price, and you are?" Rose says with a penetrating gaze. She is rather tall, but that would easily be overlooked with her flawless bronze skin.

"Miss Lori Wolfe. It's a pleasure to make your acquaintance. Now Miss Hughes, forgive me for saying so, but I find it hard to believe that Mr Myrack would act in such a cold manner as you were describing."

"Believe it, my dear, he did it to Rose, myself, and many others. We courted for four beautiful weeks. Then after months of not hearing from him, I come to find out that he is to go away for a year in Bohemia helping with his family business." She pauses to share a gaze with her friend as she snaps out her gilded fan. "What rubbish, I knew he was growing tired of me when he stopped buying me gifts and chocolates in the fourth week. But to just up and run away, without letting me come along after writing to him, is flat-out cowardice," Minnie says, a young lady with a thin frame and blonde bangs that almost cover a rather large mole near her sunken eyes. I glance down at my dress, then at Aspen's, as they turn once more. *He has been buying us special gifts. But he's also been giving up a lot for our cause and he's loyal to us, I know he is.*

"This wasn't the first time he has used his family business as a means of cutting romances with women either. That man did it to me two summers ago. As soon as business trouble comes up or a face prettier than your own, you are in the rubbish heap of broken hearts. Can you imagine such behaviour?" Rose sneers, leaning closer to me, tapping my arm with her gloved hand.

"I can, towards a few choice people," I mutter, taking a sip of pineapple punch. Keagan wouldn't just up and run away from us. Not after all that has happened now. It has already been a little more than a month since we arrived, and he has been nothing but faithful. *These women have a natural sense of rottenness about them anyway, I should take their words at face value.*

"Oh my, I believe that is Aspen Wolfe. My sister in law told me about her after a dinner party she spent with her a few weeks ago, pitiful thing she was. It appears that Mr Myrack has the unlucky pleasure of dancing with her." Rose giggles as she fans herself.

*Are you really going to talk about my sister like that in front of me?*

"Heavens, look, she has two left feet; she keeps botching the steps. They deserve each other, such bad taste," Minnie laughs, adding fire to the flame that's igniting inside of me.

"Well, I don't know, I've certainly met people much worse. Some are so rotten, that just being near them is sickening," I say, fanning myself whilst glancing at the swirling marble floor.

"Oh really? Pray tell, darling, who is it?" Minnie asks in earnest to obtain a new thread of rumours.

*It's you, you simp!* But I hold my tongue and just stare at her and Rose's expectant faces. I give a gentle curtsey and say, "Please excuse me, ladies, I believe I feel a bit too nauseous for conversation right now," I turn heel and leave before they can say another word. I can feel my nerves creeping along the back of my neck again. There's no doubt that those two ladies got inside my head and under my skin. Looking around for some type of distraction from the slanderous gossip, I spy one of the bachelors that was called out earlier just as the first dance ends. Everyone starts to find new partners for the next dance, and the handsome red-haired gentleman is making his way to me – I believe his name is Maxwell. I bat my eyes whilst fluttering my fan to cover half of my face. Such flirtation is crucial for the beginning of courting, in my opinion.

"May I have the next dance, Miss Wolfe?"

I look to my left and the gloved hand extended to me belongs to Governor Damon. I can't be rude and say no to the host. At least for one dance.

"You may." I smile, taking his large hand. He gives me a crooked smile, through his peppered mustache and beard as he leads me to the dance floor. I glance back to see the red-haired gent looking slightly defeated before he turns to lady Rose Hughes. *Of all the rotten luck.* The music begins, and it's the waltz, a classic. Towering a good foot and a half above me, the governor begins to lead the dance.

"Are you enjoying your stay here in Currlion?"

"Yes, it's quite a lovely town, but I must say that it's a bit scary as of late." I answer as we turn again.

"My word, in what way, my dear?"

"There is talk of hooded figures in the night. Crafty thieves I've been told."

"Ah, yes, you mean the renegades that have been running the rooftops at night. Well, fear not, dear, they do not seem to be running around the upper class estates. Our officers are far too quick for them anyhow; they will be caught soon, without a doubt."

"Yes, I suppose so," I muse. It seems that the police have not told the governor about my little run two nights ago. That or he is wishing to give out false hope to a seemingly innocent young lady.

"Besides, they seem to target slaves mainly, not lovely young ladies like yourself," he says with a raised eyebrow. I get a sickening feeling in my gut when he looks at me like I'm just about ripe for the picking. We continue in the dance quietly for some time until Damon speaks again.

"You know, I remember your father; he was always so kind, reserved, and yet brilliant."

"Oh, Papa; I miss him and my mother dearly."

"Ah, yes, your mother. She was one of the loveliest women I have ever met, and one of my late wife Octavia's best friends before the plague took them both. God rest their souls. You and your sister should feel pride for being her children. Hopefully, you both will make great choices in the future," he says gladly, but I can hear the double meaning in his words. We are the source of a lot of gossip as of late, considering we are residing in a house with a bachelor who has not had good standing with many of the ladies in town apparently. And that we have been kicked out of all of our family's homes in England before coming here.

"Well, our family wishes us to have a taste of life before

settling down, of course," I say, trying my best not to sound overly defensive.

"And taste it you shall," he wishes me as we take our final steps in the song. Whilst we applaud the musicians for the dance, Governor Damon leans down and whispers, "I hope you and your sister become great like your father. He was an exemplary man, but he could have been so much more."

"Wait, what do you mean he could have been so much more?" I ask, confused. *What more could he have done?*

"Well, didn't you know dear? He-"

"Louis old boy! Come, you must meet my brother, pardon me, m'lady," says a boisterous man in a gold-thread-embroidered vest with a bionic ear, interrupting us.

"Excuse me, dear, we will chat later," he apologizes before being swallowed up in the sea of elites.

I quickly find Aspen and Keagan in the crowd and get to hear how sissy nearly broke his foot when they danced.

"I tried to tell you I don't dance at balls," Aspen says defensively.

"Well, I see that now, but you could have told me why," Keagan rivals back whilst keeping one foot hovering off the floor.

"It's not like you gave me much of a chance."

"Is everything all right?" Miss Masie says coming up to us in a stunning mauve lace gown with jeweled combs in her towering hair.

"Everything is fine, but Keagan may need to sit out the next few dances. It seems he hurt his foot," I reply.

"Oh dear, well, don't ya worry, the night is young," Miss Masie assures us. Aspen doesn't look too certain though. From the corner of my eye, I see a grinning Japanese man with a feathered collar and bionic eye coming our way. "Keagan, I need to re-introduce you to one of our old classmates. He is in the middle of a new discovery in medicine," the man says, coming alongside Keagan. He points behind him, with his wine glass still in hand, at a large group of men who seem to be having a tight discussion amongst themselves.

"Really, might I join you? It sounds riveting," Aspen asks with a twinkle in her eye.

"I'm afraid it might bore you, my dear," the man says, in a scoffing manner.

"No, no, let her come along, Jin. She has quite the fascination for modern science," Keagan assures him before giving Aspen a wink. As they walk off, Miss Masie hooks her arm in mine and leads me to a new couple with her patented pearly smile.

"It's so nice to make your acquaintance, Miss Wolfe," Lord Godwin says, bowing to me, showing off his receding hairline.

"And it's a- oh!" I exclaim as I get elbowed hard in the back. What follows after is the loud sound of shattering glass from behind me. I turn around to see what happened as Aspen reaches my side in an instant, taking my arm protectively. There appears to be glass shards and red currant wine covering the ground. Many of the ladies and gentlemen around us begin to scatter from the mess in haste.

Some of the red wine has already begun to soak into the bottom of my dress, but my feet are bolted to the floor despite Aspen's light tugging on my arm. The dimie maid apologizes whilst beginning to pick up the broken glass on the tray she dropped.

"I'm so sorry, m'lady, please, forgive...me." In the middle of cleaning, she looks up, and there is a spark of recognition on her scared chimp-like face.

"It's you. You were the young lady that saved me." That's when I recognise her. *She was the dimie we saved from the bots our first patrol night with Keagan. My mask had gotten ripped to shreds that night; she must have seen my face pretty well, I guess. Thomas and now her, who else saw me that night?*

"Come again?" I respond trying to appear as if we've never met before now.

"You helped save me that night in the alley. Please, my master will electrocute me for this accident. You must take me from here, Miss, please," she pleads. Tossing aside the platter of collected glass, she grabs hold of the brim of my wine-stained dress with shaking hands. *The governor must be a truly cruel man to warrant this much fear. I thought I sensed something off about him.* Some of the dimie butlers begin to move through the crowd, that is intently watching the scene, to help their fellow worker. I glance around and notice none other than Rose Hughes and Minnie Price whispering behind their fans to other ladies around their age as they stare at the three of us across the floor.

"Gertrude, stop," a green-feathered butler orders, trying to pull her away from me.

"Leave off!" she exclaims, pushing his wings away with a flick of her strong flat tail.

"Please, I don't know what-"

"Your letter said you would save us...well, what about now? What about me right now?" she bellows hysterically as the wine soaks her maid's dress and apron. It appears as if she is sitting in a pool of blood and broken glass as the tears stream down her furry cheeks.

"You have us confused with someone else, please, control

yourself," I start as Gertrude's fellow dimies begin to collect her and drag her away from us, leaving a trail of blood-red wine following behind. My breath escapes me, and I feel my fear rising into my throat, threatening to make an entrance.

"I am *not* confused! You need to help me! You need to save us before it's too late!" Gertrude shouts as the doors close behind her, and the music starts up again as a different maid with brown fur and straight purple horns begins cleaning up the glass that her hysterical friend left behind.

"What do you suppose she meant by 'before it's too late'?" Aspen whispers in my ear. Before I can come up with an answer, a large-bellied, white-haired old man interrupts my thoughts.

"Are you ladies all right?"

"What was that all about anyway?" a younger gentleman queries us.

"How dreadful!"

"What a terrible display."

"Do you think they know something?"

We overhear the whispers and tattle going on around us, making it harder for me to think. *Everything is becoming so loud, I wish it would stop.* Aspen's grip on my shoulder tightens for a split second; she wants me to listen, and she will talk.

"We are fine, that poor maid must be terribly confused, however."

Aspen is often the better liar; she makes it seem so effort-less, I always hate fibbing, though. I can hardly bear to look at myself right now in the gilded mirror walls that line the ball-room. We, in our expensive ball gowns, at a party, rubbing elbows with the very people we are rebelling against.

And all the while one of the dimies we are trying to save is probably outside, or in the cellar or some dark cold place, getting a beating once again. This time leaving a real trail of blood in the wake. And for what? Asking for our help whilst we stand by and do nothing. I've never hated myself so much in my life, and I know Aspen must feel a similar pain as well behind that composed look of hers.

My thoughts of self-loathing are interrupted by another squeeze on my shoulder from Aspen, when I turn my head to see what it is this time, I notice the governor. Governor Damon has entered the throng of elites gossiping and conversing amongst themselves; but instead of returning small chat and introductions, Governor Damon is making his way towards us with an all-too-knowing smile that makes me feel even more uneasy. When he reaches us, we've recomposed ourselves and the men and women fretting over us become quiet as his presence in our small circle becomes known.

"Would you mind if I steal away these two young ladies for a few ticks?" he asks the group, but before they can agree or object, he adds, "I'd like to show you two my newly redecorated study, I've heard that you have a knack for interior design, Miss Lori Wolfe."

My heart begins to race a bit faster, but Aspen quickly replies with composure.

"Why, we would love to, Governor Damon. We are honored that you would be so considerate of our interest in home remodeling to show us."

I just nod my head and bid farewell to our little pity-party crowd before taking an outstretched arm of the governor. Aspen wraps her hand in the crook of the governor's opposite arm like mine, and we begin to walk towards the ground-floor hallway. Once we clear through the crowd, the governor starts a new conversation.

"There are some friends of yours waiting in my study. You see, there are more than just new paintings and tables that I'd like to show you two," Damon explains to us as we exit the ballroom and stroll down the low-lit corridor. My stomach begins to twist, and I can't seem to catch my breath; this does not bode well. We pass by a couple ogling each other as the man whispers sweet nothings into the lady's ear whilst she blushes behind a feathered fan. *That could be me right now if I were given just fifteen more minutes fishing in the crowd for a new gentleman caller.*

If only I had stepped two feet to the left when I was talking to Mr Godwin, I could be lavished over by a handsome young man right about now. Instead, I'm being escorted by the enemy to a private room whilst self-loathing myself for my actions due to a hysterical dimie. We turn down two more hallways until we arrive at what I'm guessing is his study, I brace myself for what I'm anticipating to come next. *He'll open that door and force us inside where Keagan and that dimie maid Gertrude are already in chains and the dimie bots have their razor fingers at their throats.*

But when Governor Damon opens the door, he gingerly welcomes us inside and the scene laid before us is not nearly as gruesome as what my overactive anxiety cooked up. Far from it, actually; Keagan is here, but instead of in chains, he's bantering with Lady Pomley on a couch. Whilst Mr Adlene is standing and conversing with a few other grey-haired lords and ladies that we have had yet to meet.

# THE UNVEILING

## KEAGAN

Everyone stands, which is customary; the ladies take a seat next to me on the chaise lounge as two men kindly give it up for them. However, I don't approve of the lingering stares from the gents as the sisters take their seats.

"I was explaining to everyone here just a second ago about the recent happenings that have been going on in the slave community and to our special police divisions as of late," says Captain Winston as he strokes his goatee.

"Yes, it seems that the bobbies have been attacked and stolen from right under their noses just these past few nights," says Lady McGreggor, pointing up her beak-like nose.

"Indeed, I've heard that the assailants can be seen some nights running from one rooftop to the next, then be across town in mere seconds like phantoms," adds an old bearded man I've yet to be acquainted with.

I try to hide a smile by itching my mouth. I take a glance at Aspen beside me who couldn't appear more unbeknownst of this information. *I bet she is eating this up right now.*

"Yes, yes, we know of the rumours; which is related to why you are here right now," Governor Damon concludes nervously, stealing glances at Lori.

"I am offering you all a proposition. You each have the chance to become great like your forefathers, and greater than in the days of our youth when the original multi-dimensional machine was still working," he adds.

"Is that so, what on earth have you uncovered, Louis?" Sir Gladstone, a greying man with a cane wrapped tightly in his metal hands, asks.

"By now you all have heard of the recent break in and slave napping that has occured at the Market, correct?" the governor goes on as everyone nods in agreement. *I can feel my heart rhythm falter a bit at the mention of that night.*

"Well, whoever stole them away was unable to keep track of them all. Those that were left behind, my commissioned officers, the Dimie Watchmen, found. After some hours of interrogation and questioning, we found out that these renegade phantoms are trying to get the slaves on their side so that they can revolt and cause an uprising by getting them back home. Meaning that somehow, there is another multi-dimensional portal machine being made or is already made. With this in mind, it is our job as the lords, ladies, and governor of this town to keep order, which is why seeing any suspicious activity, or hearing anything off, must be reported to me."

"Agreed, Louis, but what did you do with the slaves now that they have been interrogated? I mean, as you said, the Market holding facility had been breached,"

Captain Kipling asks.

Just hearing the word *interrogation* come from their mouths gives me a terrible image of torture for those poor souls. As well as a pain in my side from a memory I blocked out of my mind long ago. The sight of a whip flashes across my vision, causing my whole body to jolt.

"Are you all right, my boy?" Captain Kipling asks, letting out another puff of smoke from his pipe.

"I just caught a chill. Please, go on, Governor Damon," I reply gently.

"I'm glad you asked, captain," Louis Damon said, strolling over to his desk.

"You see, the dimies that were caught were quite old, and had been in that marketplace for many a year; that's when an idea came to me. We are wasting a resource right before our eyes, my friends," he says, picking up a large serving dish with its lid still atop it. I get the most uneasy of feelings in my stomach, and I can only anticipate the heads of those we lost on the platter until he lifts the lid.

It might as well have been their heads on the plate. But instead, it was their skins and feathers as hats, stoles, and gloves. I gasped along with everyone else when the lid lifted, but very few out of my own party appeared slightly repulsed. I recognise those maroon feathers that are wrapped into a hat; they are from that dimie that was reluctant to leave the Market at first. *But she trusted us anyway. They put the last of their hope in us, and now look at where they are.*

"As you see, we found a use for them, and soon for all others who die, are old, sick, or are troublesome. It'll be an excellent example to keep the others in line," Damon explains.

*This is madness!*

"Sadly, we didn't learn who was behind the escape, or who the mysterious figure running in the woods with a slave was either. Like you said, m'lady, they are almost phantoms."

"Is there anything we can do or should we just enjoy the furs and evening?" I ask, surprising myself that I was able to speak at all.

"Well, unless you can speak their language, or know a slave loyal enough to you to betray their own, then nothing for now. But otherwise, Mr Myrack, tonight just enjoy the ball and these special party favours. Here, I thought you might enjoy this hat; actually, it matches your vest embroidery," Damon says, extending the tophat of death to me with that crooked smile of his. I recall the stroke he had three years ago that disabled a few major muscles in his right cheek.

"Indeed, it looks divine with your outfit, the maroon embroidery will shine out now with a hat like that," agrees Lady Pomley with her already frivolously giant feathered hair.

I stare at the hat, looking at it this way and that in my hands, whilst the governor passes out more skins. But all I can think of is the body of that dimie that still has a look of freedom in their eyes. *All of it smashed to pieces in the form of a stupid hat!* I want to storm out, right out of this constricting place. However, my mind stops at a crossroads; I don't know what I should do next: tear the hat to shreds in rage or bury it for the ones we lost in sorrow. It feels as if the air is being sucked out of the room, and I need to loosen my collar. I do not dare, though, since the subject in our company is supposed to be one of surprise and giving, not nervousness.

"Thank you, Governor Damon. Never before have I seen such a lovely pair of gloves, and the faded mauve matches my ensemble perfectly tonight," Lady McGreggor muses.

"Indeed, who would have thought that our slaves could be useful to us even after they are gone?" Captain Winston muses.

"Yes, and I quite like the whole idea. Whenever I wear the

garments, I can remember the slave it came from and their qualities," adds Captain Kipling.

*How is everyone okay with this?* Maybe they are hiding their judgment in front of their host like the three of us. But as the governor brags about his murderous idea, I realise that everyone but us is fondling and looking at their gifts with greed in their eyes.

"Now I just wanted to have this quick discussion about this new plan of mine to start up a new business. Finding the phantom thieves, apprehending their machine, and starting up the Slave Trade Organization with a new aspect in mind to keep them in check. I will not make anything final or ask anyone to sign on at the moment since we are currently on a slave shortage and none have been reported to be with child in the past three months. So stand by until we can obtain more and let me know if there are any in your households that are reaching their age limits or acting troublesome. With that being said, if everyone is ready, let us rejoin the party and be merry," Damon says, beaming with enough self-pride to make me feel the need to bathe.

Everyone rises and mingles amongst one another as we stroll out of the study. I still have the hat in my hands, realising I will look rude or suspicious if I don't put it on. As I raise it to my head, someone wraps their arm in mine, catching me off guard and causing my arm to lower. It's Aspen, smiling at me like there isn't a thing wrong in the world. Leaning up to my ear, she whispers, "Yet another reason I can hate a ball… follow my lead."

I find myself smiling as we slow our pace whilst she takes the hat and looks it over like I had in the study. She then places her fur stole inside the hat she had received along with the gloves given to Lori. We separate from the group and stay behind in the hall, taking a seat on a cushioned bench in the corridor. I see Lori and Damon looking back at us before he takes her hand with a smile I don't completely trust. I'll probably have to rescue poor Lori from him soon.

"We shall bury them in honour of the fallen," Aspen whispers, fidgeting with the brim of the hat.

"I can't believe it's gone this far," I say.

"It could be worse still; there are rumours that in Paris, a few brothels hold the dimies for use there. At least England has enough class not to defile them in such a way. However, this is still a new level of madness," she states.

"I wish we could leave this minute, but it's far too early unless something at home needs our attention."

"We will pull through; we made it through that *lovely* presentation. The ball should be a breeze after all the chaos that has occurred thus far," she says; her voice is beginning to raise, and I can hear the tension in her words. She has yet to look up or down the hall or anywhere but the skins in between us. Cupping her chin, I raise it and see the beads of tears in her eyes fighting to spill over her rosy cheeks.

I know exactly how she feels for once; all the regret, fear, and pain that this job entails comes pouring out. You can bottle it up for only so long, I realise that now as if cracks are beginning to form on my very skin, threatening to let my frustration bleed out. Aspen takes a long breath to steady herself as the tears stop as quickly as they started.

"The road to home, that's where we can bury them with their own crosses. They deserve that," she says, beginning to collect herself.

"They deserved so much more, but we will give them

this," I agree as I remember that one poor old bird dimie. I wonder now if it would have been better for her to have just stayed at the Market.

# LOVE AND OBSESSION

## ASPEN

"NO, NO STOP!" I shriek out loud enough to wake me up. A gas lamp lights up from the other corner of the room. I turn, and through swollen eyes and strands of hair, I see Lori looking at me, concerned. A cold sweat is running down the length of my back and chest. With shaking hands, I pull back my wavy hair that was covering my eyes.

"Aunt Mae," is the only thing I say, and that is all she needs to hear to get on my bed and start comforting me.

"What happened this time?" sissy asks whilst stroking my back and putting her forehead on mine. I hate crying in front of anyone, but the tears piling up in my eyes just may betray my wishes for the second time this night. The dance and the skins were enough for one night I thought, but now I am handed this monstrous nightmare.

"This time w-was worse than the rest; it wasn't just Aunt Mae. Papa was with her. I was a mere child again, in the corner of my room, and I started hearing these voices. It was only Aunt Mae at first, like how she always began criticizing me when she first moved in. Bickering about my incorrect poise or lack of grace or manner, then Gear Heart appeared on the floor between me and Aunt Mae who was charging towards me with a hot poker, yelling at me. I tried to reach for the machine, but I could only claw my way on the floor unable to stand up or run; it stayed right out of reach. Until someone else picked it up; it was Papa, except his face was devoid of all his colour and warmth. The look he gave me was the scariest, most downcast look I have ever beheld.

'*Do you really think you will accomplish anything. With this?*' he glowered in a voice like ice, then he threw Gear Heart on the floor, smashing it into nothing but shards.

'*For that matter, do you really think you can do anything at all? For yourself...or them?*' he continued and gestured to behind him where the dimies, you, Keagan, and everyone else were in chains, being whipped and tortured! Aunt Mae was raising the hot poker above her head, about to strike me when I awoke." I sob out, unable to contain my pain any longer until I let out stricken breaths. Lowering my head to her tucked legs, I rest my head and let the tears fall. Lori, the kind thing she is, holds me tighter as she rubs my arms.

"Our father would never say that to you, or allow Aunt Mae to come near you in such a fashion if he were present. That's how you know for sure that it isn't feasible," she says in a soothing tone.

"What if... the dream was trying to tell me something?" I whisper. But she doesn't answer; maybe she didn't hear me. Or perhaps she always had a twinge of doubt in our cause and doesn't have the gall to admit it to me. Either way, I soon slip back into my subconscious, but not comfortably.

The dining room is filled to the brim with dimies of all ages, and to think, it only consists of half our party. The other half either remained in bed because of joint pain, or they ate their breakfast in the tea parlor since there was no more room with us in the dining room. We decided it would be best if the children were with us so they wouldn't get too out of control. I take the job of helping feed the youngest in the group, Lucy, for the morning whilst Keagan and Lori try to keep the rest of the kids eating and in their seats. We had to pull together nearly every spare chair and bench around the house for the dining areas, so the children sit around the lengthy table at varying heights.

Lucy is such a hungry little otter dimie, she's getting crumbs all over her clothes and red fur. Her webbed paws help her small hands grab onto large chunks of her scone. I often have to sneak food from one of her overfilled paws back into her bowl whilst she stuffs her face with her other. Her brother, Nox, and a few other young male dimies, are talking to Keagan about playing in the snow at night by the sounds of it. But he shakes his head no as he takes a sip of tea. It's still not safe for them to go outside yet, unless we take a group deep into the mountain at night, and that is strictly out of the question. I glance over beyond my untouched plate of food to Lori who is teaching a young group of girls how to braid their feathers and manes.

"All done, all done!" Lucy exclaims, raising her empty bowl to me.

"All done? Already?" I say in a playful tone as I wipe the crumbs from her face and paws. After she is a bit cleaner, I pick her up out of her seat and to the floor, she seems to like playing under the table after her meals without much fuss.

"No, up, up," she says with her arms and tiny wings

outstretched. Placing her in my lap, she immediately latches onto my white ruffled blouse in a tight hug. I decide that it's as good a time as any to eat breakfast then. I still can't seem to raise my eyelids the whole way, and even after my plate sits empty, I feel no energy coming back to me.

After our loud meal, we shuffle everyone except the elderly into the library for the daily lesson on reading and writing. Our lessons always begin the same, everyone takes twenty minutes practicing the alphabet in the English language – and their native language taught by Winona and Sonja, an older bird-like dimie with a mind as sharp as her horned beak. When one team is teaching, the other is grading penmanship and practice work.

Three fourths of the way through my lesson of verbs and adverbs, I decide through the fogginess in my head, to end the lesson a little earlier than usual. Most everyone makes their way out of the room, excited to play whilst a few stick around and pick out a book or two before leaving me at the couch by the fireplace. I work hard at my own research, but after an hour of compiling a rather large assortment of books, I find it almost impossible to read any of their fuzzy words. *I knew I had a terrible night, but I did not imagine to be this exhausted.* I begin to lay further and deeper into the chaise pillows until I cannot withhold it any longer. *I'll just rest my eyes for a short spell.*

Visions of precious jewels falling all around my person... Even though I am able to catch a few, they slip right out of my fingers like sand. The gem shower starts to move farther away. I begin to chase after it, but as I do, instead of jewels, it's rubbish and broken gears that rain on me. Running as fast as I can to the jewel shower, the rubbish begins to pile up around my feet. It grows taller and soon I am literally swimming in gunk and debris. Hands, paws, and wings begin to pop up from under the piles for help. As I reach out towards a hand to help, something grabs me first and pulls me under.

I wake with a start and find myself looking straight into a sea of blue. Keagan is gently caressing my face and looking at me with a strange expression that I cannot place.

"Bad dream? Why are you so obsessed with that machine? I mean, Lori tells me that you are staying up until all hours of the night; sometimes after missions as well. Darling, just look at yourself; you're burning the wick at both ends," Keagan goes on, cupping my sleepy face with his hand, a look of concern remains on his, though.

"You are exhausted. You can barely keep your eyes open, let alone read this bumf of books. Look Aspen, I'm sure that the dimies will understand if you take a rest day. This is all for them anyway."

"This isn't just about the dimies, it's about my papa, too!" I blurt out, feeling grouchy.

"I don't follow," he says, looking confused.

"It's a long story, just never mind, it's my business anyway." I wave off the idea with my hand. Keagan looks at my hand, pondering for a moment before responding.

"So, you're saying you are not willing to tell it? Or you are afraid to?" He keeps his eyes down whilst I give him a questioning glare.

"Are you willing to listen?" I question him, surprised.

"Of course, I've got time," he says tenderly with his signature grin. I let out a sigh, *what have I to lose? He will only bug me about it until I tell him anyway.*

"Well, this was back when our fathers were both alive. Lori

and I were still happy, eager little girls who loved nothing more than to spend time with our father. Papa and I had just finished the last pieces of Gear Heart and double checked its inner workings. Papa, Lori, and I were planning on going out into the woods one spring night to test our machine. We had to do it somewhere it wouldn't possibly blow up our house if something went wrong. Lori was going to act as a scribe, to jot down all the notes of what would happen, whilst papa and I would be the mechanics.

"We were almost ready to leave, but before we did, I placed the machine on a table in the foyer and then went to get the generator. At about that time, we received a visitor at our door. An elite, who was slobbering drunk. Supposedly, he came from a party and his car crashed into one of our trees. He was loud, stumbling, and angry from the moment he came through the door.

"I'd come back from the study with the generator by now and watched the terrible scene unfold. I saw the man become even angrier and volatile when he became confused as my papa tried to persuade him to take a guest room and lay down. He began shouting obscene words and knocking things over. Our butlers came in and tried to get control of him, but the drunk just shook them off like dust and grabbed the nearest thing he could get his hands on. Which, unfortunately, was our finished machine. He took it and threw it over our heads, missing us by mere inches. Our precious Gear Heart was smashed to bits on the wall behind us.

"I screamed and fell to the floor, grabbing pieces of the machine; Lori came rushing around the corner as she heard the commotion, ready with her pen and note paper. My father, unable to contain himself, pinned the drunk to the ground and began to beat the man. Father punched him till he was out cold. It took our butlers, a maid, and even one of our cooks to pull my papa off of him. When they finally managed to, he was weeping as well. For as long as I can remember my father, he always seemed to know what to do. But for the first time in my life, he just stood there, looking around, not knowing what to say, where to go, or even move.

"He looked at Lori and me, the broken pieces of Gear Heart on the floor, and the men carrying off the idiot who ruined everything. He stood there, motionless, as tears streamed down his worn red face. It took us two days to recover enough of the pieces and start figuring out what we could fix and what we had to start from scratch again. So much of it had been destroyed and bent beyond repair. My Papa died before he could see Gear Heart save the dimies. That's why I have to finish it before any more dimies die, or I'll die again as well."

Keagan was silent for a while before taking one of my hands in his.

"I'm sorry, Aspen. I know that all this means the world to you. It's your life and you feel that it's your purpose. I'm sorry that your father can't be here when it starts working," he responds genuinely. I feel the corners of my mouth itching to pull up in a smile.

"But that being said...Aspen, please, I can't just stand by and watch you hurt yourself like this, at-least let us-" he pleads with me but stops abruptly when he hears other voices in the room. I hear them, too, and it sounds quite like two dimies that we know well. We inch our heads over the wooden brim of the top of the couch and peek through the holes in its ornate design so we won't be seen completely. The first person I recognise is Winona; she is beaming with bashfulness as another dimie with brown fur holds her paw as he whispers to her. *It's Thatcher!* Keagan taps my shoulder, and we duck back down from the top of the couch.

"What do they think they're doing?" Keagan demands in a hoarse whisper.

"Haven't you even seen courting in play? You've certainly done it yourself many times," I answer.

"I know what they are doing; but why is he doing it with Winona?"

"Well, obviously he fancies her a lot."

"Not in my house and not with Winona!" Keagan states gruffly, beginning to stand up from our crouched position.

I begin to panic; he can't just interrupt them like this. *I have to stall him, but how?* I do the first thing that comes to mind: I grab him by the waist and pull him back onto the couch before he can make his presence known. However, he begins to struggle as he tries to pry my hands off. I fear that they will hear us if this goes on much longer. This is one of the few places in the house that is kept quiet, and Winona has been working non stop these past few days now that we have a full house to care for.

Many of the dimies close to my age and older have actually been helping out with the house work and caring for the young as well. But the work is never done, and Winona usually takes charge over most of it. *She deserves more than just a few precious moments alone with a great dimie like Thatcher, and I'm not about to let Keagan spoil it! What would Lori do? I don't have any more sleeping darts on me, so I guess I have to use my backup weapon, regrettably.* We continue to struggle until I'm partially in his lap; that's when I let him have it. I lean in close and kiss him on the cheek, which momentarily causes him to pause and avert his attention to me, wide eyed. I give him a pair of sad pleading eyes before enveloping him in a hug. I hold him in a way that covers his mouth up with my shoulder.

"Please, don't take this moment away from her; she deserves to be loved as much or even more than the rest of us. Especially with how hard she's been working as of late," I whisper into Keagan's ear as he slowly wraps his arms around my back. I can partially see through some carved holes of the couch's moulding. They continue to talk for what feels like forever, but is probably just a few seconds. Keagan's hug grows tighter, and I'm feeling more and more anxious and warm as time slips away. My heart is beating as hard as it was last night, but the feeling in my stomach isn't nausea this time. It feels like little sparks.

I'm usually calm under pressure, yet I can barely handle being held by him this time. Keagan holding me like this reminds me of when he hid us under the desk in the warehouse as the police searched for us. He cradled me so close and tightly to himself. I was nervous then, too, but that could have also been from the constable getting close to where we were hiding. But now we are hiding and there is no real danger; this is a real hug.

I watch Winona and Thatcher begin to slowly walk towards the doors, still conversing and gazing fondly at each other. I never see them leave the room, though; they are just gone all of a sudden. I didn't even realise they had left or how much time had passed. I do realise, though, that I'm still holding Keagan tightly. I begin to inch off of him whilst he slowly releases me. All of a sudden, he stops me by putting a firm hand on my waist and laces his hand in my hair.

"She's not the only one who deserves it, you know," Keagan whispers, staring at me intently as the firelight dances in the rays of his eyes. A strange feeling of guilt overcomes me, and I feel how tired I really am. I let my head drop a little as I lower my eyes. He tries to meet my gaze again before speaking.

"Aspen, just tell me what you need to find. I want you to go and rest whilst I do the research for you."

I feel the need to argue, but my sensation of exhaustion is stronger. I shift off of Keagan's lap and rummage through the large pile of notes and books. I pull out a small slip of paper that has a list of inventions, quantum theories, gemstones, physics, and electro mechanics written on it.

"Here," I mutter, handing him a slip of paper.

When he takes the paper, he also takes hold of my hand, rises from the couch, and pulls me up along with him. He quickly marches me to the library entrance, gives me a peck on the cheek, and sends me out. I turn back in time to see him tell me, "Don't worry about a thing. I'll get the information. You just go to bed. That's the deal, and no fake sleeping like the last time!"

And with that, he shuts the library door. *So forceful; that's different*, I ponder, smiling as I make my way to my room. I barely notice the young dimies running around my legs, playing tag, or the ones tossing jacks by the stairs whilst the elderly mend their clothes. I take in the scene, as if I were already dreaming, in a golden blur and slow motion whilst my hand lingers on the cheek he kissed. Before I realise it, I've changed out of my day clothes and don sleep wear. I fall asleep the moment my head hits my pillow. Finally at peace, knowing that I'm the one being taken care of now.

# THE SPECIAL MISSION

## KEAGAN

Two and a half weeks have passed since we got the dimies here, and Thomas as well. They're eating us out of house and home; but Winona and the girls have never seemed happier. *I'm pretty happy as well, I have to admit. What with such a full house, it's not so quiet and lonesome here anymore. I almost wish they never have to go, but it'd be selfish of me to wish for this plan to fail; everyone has put in their all to make this work. Myself included.*

*I wonder what the girls are scheming about for tonight's mission? I hope it's nothing like the past few weeks,* I think, groaning a little as I gently press my still-bruised side. Could be worse; I could have a cracked rib, or that dimie and Lori could have been killed. *Well, nothing a good stretch and workout can't help to prepare for tonight,* I remind myself, but when I get to the gym doors, I hear music and a loud banging noise. I crack the door open quietly an inch.

Lori is dancing ballet near the mirrors, Thomas practices shooting a grappling hook at the bars fixated on the ceiling, and Aspen is practicing her acrobatics on our cushioned mats.

Aspen's hair is piled up high in a tight bun, a wisp of dark brown hair falling around her face as she prepares to tumble again, knee-length flowy pants similar to our heist outfits. But her top, creamy, flowy, open slightly in the front, is wrapped tightly around her waist by a purple sash. *Beautiful.* Prepare, step, tumble, one flip then she catches the hanging rings and swings over three metres, releases, tumbles on the floor, and jumps up with a swinging kick whilst a knife appears in her hand. *Where did that knife come from? I didn't even see her reach for it.*

Thomas has put down the grapple shooter and tries to mimic the way Aspen is slashing the air with her knife. Seeing this, she sheaths her knife and adjusts his stance, slowly going through the motions of how to block attacks whilst she acts as the attacker.

"I think I'm going to go wash up and prepare for tonight," Lori calls over to her sister. *She already stopped dancing and even took off her dancing shoes whilst I was distracted? How long have I been spying?* Thomas turns to Aspen who gives him a gentle nod towards Lori who is turning towards the door, I scramble to the side that's in the opposite direction of their bedroom and lean against the wall.

But as Lori and Thomas exit, of course being an overly aware kind of lady who's been trained similarly like Aspen, she takes in her surroundings in front of and behind the door. She spots me easily, but before she or Thomas can speak or greet me, I put a finger to my lips and give them a wink. They stay silent as Lori closes the door with her own mischievous expression, she takes one look at the door that leads to her sister and gives me a wink in return. Then, taking Thomas's hand, just walks right off and doesn't look back. *Such a little cupid that girl.* Thomas looks back with a confused look in his eyes as I begin to open the door. I flashed him a smile just as music starts again. I turn my head and see that Aspen is beginning to dance ballet.

*I thought only Lori was the dancer? I knew Aspen could somewhat dance ballroom style, but I never dreamed ballet. However, after dancing with her at the ball a few weeks ago, I wouldn't call it dancing – more like foot stomping,* considering the pain in my feet and how many ice to heat compresses I went through to numb the pain. She pirouettes and chassés around the wooden floor. A crisp grande jeté through the air, her movements aren't like her sister's that are graceful and liquid. Aspen's are crisp and appear as if she is ready to fight with each movement. But as she tries to stick the landing, she falls to the floor with a thud. I rush in to help her to make sure she's okay when she bundles her legs to her chest.

Halfway through the doorway now, I watch silently as she rocks herself once and gets back up. She begins again to the music on the phonograph, and this time she doesn't fall but begins fouetté turns. I don't know how she does them, but they remind me of a ballerina I once pursued in Moscow. Brilliant dancer, but even she had trouble doing these turns. I recall her and her company telling me they are very taxing and very difficult to perform correctly. *And yet Aspen makes them look almost effortless.* Before I realise what I'm doing, I'm walking farther into the room towards her, eighteen turns in and each one makes her look more and more radiant. I see her face is laced with exhaustion and joy as she finishes her little performance.

"I didn't know you could dance like that."

Aspen takes a sharp inhale as she turns to face me. She stares dumbfounded at me for a few seconds.

"Don't tell Lori!" she says quickly, still panting.

Her words float in the air for a second as I think of how to answer. "On one condition. You save the next dance for me," I say, taking a ready fight position. "You know, you and Lori would have been wonderful ballerinas if given the chance."

"Tish tosh, we would cause too much trouble at the operas," she states, unlacing her shoes. The moment she prepares her ready stance, she advances with jabs and punches. I miss all but the last hook – straight to my ribs that are still bruised. I wince and retreat back in pain, holding my side. *I've got to shake her up somehow, or I'll be beaten before we even start.*

I advance back, but she follows, easily blocking my blows. Aspen suddenly knees me in the gut, causing me to double over, my hair tickling my forehead.

"Has anyone ever told you what an amazing figure you have?" I choke out, wrapping my right arm around her waist before jumping back, missing her next blow by a hair.

She stops mid jab. "Excuse me?"

Before she can react, I attempt to put her arm in a lock, but she slips out quickly. It looks like the compliments work, though.

"How you ever became so brilliant is beyond me, but what's more, it's only rivaled by your good looks," I pant out. This has to be my tenth compliment by now, and she has become quite peeved and distracted since the last time I tossed her on the mat.

"Grrr, enough!" she yells as she nearly roundhouses my head off.

"What's the matter? Never had a compliment before?"

"Augh" is the last thing I hear before being thrown on the floor with a hard thud. A second later, my arms are pinned down.

"Aspen, relax. I like stunning women to know that they are just that. You've been told that before, right?" I defend myself, trying to soften my voice, as I wait for an answer, but all is silent.

"Aspen-"

"Yes, I've been called pretty and the like, but only by older elites and rogues on the street it seems."

"But not beautiful, stunning, enticing?"

"...no," Aspen says as her grip loosens a tad. I use this and flip over, pinning Aspen to the mat where we are face to face. Through the hair that fell in front of my right eye, I see her exasperated expression.

"This isn't fair, I've been training for over an hour. You just came in," she rivals.

"You nearly flung me across the room! You have no excuse, Miss Hercules," I say, making a face. "So, Aspen, tell me, do you really think you have to become more like your sister, just for a guy to like you or think you're pretty?"

"W-well, I, uhm, it doesn't hurt to try, you know...and I never said I was doing it to impress men," she stammers out as a red hue begins to creep across her cheeks.

"You are one of the best liars I know when it comes to most people, but when you're talking to me..." I pause, inching closer to her lips that are parted, almost begging me to envelop them with my own.

"You're transparent as glass." I stare down into her deep forest eyes that I would be glad to get lost in. Before either of us make another move, I hear someone running down the hall to the door. Not a moment later does Lori bust through it.

"Mates, I just-" Lori's face is bright with excitement but stops short completely when she sees the scandalous position that we are currently in. I get off Aspen bitterly and help her up, both of us still a little flushed in the face as Lori tries to recompose herself and apologizes.

"I'm so sorry if I'm interrupting anything. I'll just leave."

Aspen stops her quickly by spitting out. "No, Lori, you're fine. We were just-"

"Sparring," I say, finishing her alibi.

"I'm sure you were," she replies sceptically with a smug face.

"What were you wanting to tell us, Lori?" Aspen demands, with an even redder blush than before, and her voice getting higher the more flustered she becomes.

"Hehe, right, umm, oh yes. Tonight is the night that we are celebrating. However, we aren't totally ready yet," Lori whispers with excitement so no one overhears too much.

"She's right, you know, we haven't prepared everything yet," Aspen says to me, beginning to calm down again.

"Well, then, let's crack on, shall we?" I reply.

By the time we all have changed for the night and finished the rest of the preparations for our special mission, we three have regrouped in the living room. I tend to the fire whilst Lori and Winona trim the tree. Aspen, at the tree's base, is packing in the last of the presents. The grandfather clock has just struck nine o'clock, shooting a bolt of excitement through my chest. Charles will be at the doors any second with the guests of honour. I dust off my hands and help Winona down the ladder after she lights the last candle. Turning to the doors, I see Lori and Aspen are already there waiting for Charles to give the knock to let everyone in. On the third knock, the girls open the doors, and the dimies that were behind them just stare at the scene in the room for a second, unsure of what to do it seems.

"Merry Christmas!" the four of us say whilst Charles, Lori, and Aspen take a dimie's paw (or wing), leading them to the tree.

"This is for us?" Lucy asks us as she plays with her wings.

"That's right," Lori replies.

"But isn't today the eighteenth of December? Isn't Christmas on the twenty-fifth?" Sonja questions.

"Yes, but this was the best way for us to surprise you since something even more spectacular might happen on the actual holiday," Aspen explains. *Okay, now I'm in the dark. What does she have planned for actual Christmas or Christmas Eve?*

Once everyone is closer to the tree, they begin to gaze all around the warm room. They now see all we had laid out: the holly that hangs on the mantel, the candlelit tree, the table of treats, and bowls of punch. Their eyes dance as if they are looking at the crown jewels.

I quickly pull up a chair and climb it to make the announcement. "Everyone, do you see those presents under the tree?" I ask.

Some nod their heads and others agree verbally.

"They are gifts for you. Find your name on your box, and that is the one for you. We will help as well," I announce.

The young dimies have already run to the tree before I even finished the sentence. We have been trying to teach the dimies proper English, writing, and reading whilst Winona and Sonja help teach the youth their native language. Their names were the first thing we taught them. It seems to be working since most of them are calling out another's name whilst holding their gift. What comes next is the tearing of paper and excited exclamations.

"It's a teddy bear!"

"A new coat!"

"A real necklace!"

We busy ourselves to help bring over mirrors from the corners for those with clothes and jewelry; each one of them appears as awestruck and grateful as the next. Living in the Market never gave them the chance to experience a real Christmas. I knew this from the start, but I never truly felt the weight of that until now as I notice their childlike joy even in the eldest of them.

As I help Eli put on his new vest and coat, I watch as he admires his green feathers next to the purple trimmings. Before I realise it, I'm looking at myself in the mirror as well, and I'm not afraid. Because it's myself that I see now, not my father, just me. I can look myself in the eye and see that I am my own person, not just a pawn that my father could use to do his bidding.

My trance is broken by the sound of a familiar voice. "Thank you, sir," Eli says, taking my hand and bending his forehead down to it.

"No one has ever given me new clothes before."

"Your welcome, Eli," I say, taking his wing in a Roman handshake. "It's going to be tough saying goodbye to you and everyone. You're the best poker buddy I've ever had, you know," I add as we release each other.

"Well, I should hope so. My last master was a gambler and was quite good with my help until he lost one night, that's how I ended up in the Market. He played against the warden."

"Very sorry to hear that, chap... but if he hadn't lost, you probably wouldn't be here now enjoying our celebration. Besides, you won't have to worry about the past for much longer."

"Quite right, quite right indeed," he says with a large smile across his long bill.

"A new pair of leather shoes...and they fit!" exclaims Thatcher from across the room, catching me off guard a bit. Winona is by his side with a great smile on her face. I know better than to stare, but I feel like a statue being chipped away for what comes next. He takes her paw, and with his other, rummages through the pocket of his patched coat. When he pulls it back out he is holding a flower made of paper, slightly crumpled, but in the shape of a lily. I know those to be Winona's favourite; they grow in the garden each spring just for her. What I don't know is what Winona will do next; however, I'm not going to wait to find out.

I rush to the refreshments table where many of the dimies have begun to congregate. Quickly grabbing a glass of punch, I head towards the fireplace in time to see Winona's paw on Thatcher's face. I feel the knot in my stomach tighten at the sight.

"Everyone... Ahem! Everyone, I'd like to propose a toast... Cheers to those we love, to those we have lost, and to those we will see again one day. We promise to everyone in this room, we will get you home or die trying!" I say, raising my glass as everyone's attention is on me.

"Here here!"

"Hurray!"

"Cheers!"

I look around for Aspen, but I don't see her. I take it upon myself to find her as I slip unnoticed out of the room whilst the celebration continues. *If she is tinkering again, I'm going to tie her down to a bed or couch or...something, I swear,* I fume as I make my way towards her and Lori's room. But when I charge into their room, prepared to see her working on Gear Heart, I see that it's empty and all the lights are off. I look around as I walk further in, past the bed, the bathroom, and see that the room is empty. Suddenly, something subconsciously pulls me out of their room and towards my own. I walk aimlessly there. Once I arrive, I take in my whole empty area, thinking myself foolish for even checking my own bedroom. I turn to leave, when out of the corner of my eye, I see a familiar dark green dress – not inside but out on the frosty balcony.

There she stands, resting against a dark wooden column dusted in snowflakes as she grips her shoulders tightly in the cold whilst gazing up at the painted sky. I take a spare blanket that rests on the couch and bring it outside with me. As I open the doors, Aspen turns immediately, looking slightly alarmed.

"I guess I've been found out, huh?" she smiles wanly as I put the blanket around her shoulders.

"You could say so. Getting some fresh air, are you?"

"Yes. We all needed a little celebration and a bit of rest," Aspen admits.

"You mean that you don't enjoy working yourself into the ground?"

"You mean just like how you get your bum handed to you everytime we spar? ...I'm sorry, I don't mean to banter right now. I came here to enjoy the silence for a moment, but your company is welcome, of course. I mean, this is part of your room anyway, and I was the one who came into your chambers so... mmm," I place my fingers on her soft lips to stop her from nervously babbling on.

"We can be quiet together; I don't mind either," I assure

her as I rest my elbows on the wood railing of the balcony and gaze out at the fading sky. We stand in silence together for a few peaceful moments, making me think back to the sight of the lighthouse. Aspen's arm finally healed from that razor cut she received a few weeks ago, thankfully.

"Do you miss the peace, Keagan?" Aspen asks out of the blue whilst playing shyly with the snow that rests on the railing.

"What?"

"The peace of a tranquil home to come to, without the worry of having to hide secrets. And getting to go places freely whenever you wish. Things are so much louder and some-times hectic in the house now... I guess I'm just wondering if you sometimes wish that the dimies never came here," she explains, her gaze transfixed to the snow she continues to draw shapes in.

"Aspen, I love the dimies being here; this is the happiest I think I've ever been in my life. Why would you think that I wouldn't want this?" I lean my head towards her, trying to reach her gaze. She doesn't answer right away, biting her bottom lip before continuing.

"When we first arrived, you just appeared to be in such good spirits, and you were able to see so many more of your friends outside of the house. I've never been so joyful myself, but I never really considered all that much on how you felt about the matter since it's your house and money that are at our disposal. I guess I was just afraid you'd rather have the household more like your father kept it," she says, still refusing to look at me and instead into the twilight sky. This seems to irritate me for a reason I can't pinpoint.

"Everyone always expects me to turn out like him, to take on his business and be a political elite figure just like he was.

But he's the last person I want to be like." I grimace, clenching my jaw as my mind flashes back to when I'd come home from school or a trip, always excluding me from the conversation, his gaze, and his love. As if I didn't exist. The only topics we would truly converse about were always on school, the political agenda, or who else I could try and manipulate into siding with the governor and father's business.

"But you and Lori gave me the chance to do something worthwhile with my life. I can choose to become my own person now," I state as I turn my head towards Aspen.

She just smirks and argues with, "Oh, tish tosh, with all the money you have at your disposal you could have become anyone you wanted, done anything you wished. Women seldom are allowed that choice no matter how much money they have to their name," Aspen's smile fades as she grows sombre again.

"You truly have no idea how far into depression I was until you two came to live here, do you?" I turn to her, now upright, flustered that she would think so little of me after everything we've been through thus far.

"I can't say that I do," Aspen replies worriedly in a quiet voice, facing me as well.

"Before you girls came, I tried to fill the empty pit inside of me with parties, traveling, drinking...women, but nothing worked. Nothing filled the void. Winona and Charles were the only ones able to keep me alive, but I was almost suicidal a few days before you came," I explain, leaning back on the beam. I am becoming overfilled with conflicting emotions of anger, frustration, and fear mixed with the eagerness to be open and vulnerable to her. I want her to know what was really going on.

"I had even wished that you two would decide not to come at all. But you did come, hair falling out of your bun and tired from a long trip, but your eyes were sparkling like the stars. From that moment, I could see that you both had a light shining in you, and I wanted to have any piece I could get of it so badly it ached. Every day with you girls was a surprise and a step out of my dark pit." I pause and catch Aspen looking dumbfounded for what's probably one of the few times in her life. I can feel my chest begin to shiver, I don't think it's from the cold though.

"But when I found out that you two snuck out of the house, I didn't want to believe it. I couldn't bear thinking that you were just out for my money whilst galavanting around at night with possibly other men. I wanted to stay angry with you until I began thinking logically again. And giving you both a second chance was the best decision of my life because now I have all of this. Partners in crime, a house full of rescued dimies who all love one another, myself included." I step closer and place a hand on her cheek as her skin burns with a blush, the other gripping the blanket around her shoulders.

"No amount of money can buy the feeling that I get when I'm around everyone here, Aspen. Especially when I'm around you. I finally feel whole again, and do you know who made that possible?"

Her eyes are searching mine as she gently shakes her head no.

"You did," I say, smiling, leaning in closer, and Aspen starts to close the gap between us.

"We found them, we found them!" hollered a group of little voices. We both jolt a bit and stare in the direction of the voices. Millie, Benny and Lucy are the excited culprits as they run to us. And thus our moment has ended, I guess there is a downside to having such a full house: almost no privacy at any time.

Aspen takes my hand that is by her cheek and gives it a squeeze before walking over to Lucy, picking her up whilst taking Millie's lavender wing. Aspen looks back at me, waiting to be accompanied, but instead I motion for them to get back to the expectant party, which is now eavesdropping at the door. When I'm truly alone once more, my mind slips back to how close I was to kissing her. Or rather how close she was to kissing me. I pound my fist on the railing in frustration, causing a pile of snow from the balcony roof to fall in front of me. That's when I remember the secret door in the fireplace. *I still haven't told them. I doubt if Aspen or Lori would even look at me again if they were to find what was in there on their own by now. I should tell them soon; not tonight though. Tonight is too good to spoil.*

# UNEXPECTED GUESTS

## ASPEN

"You know who you should have asked to come and help you pick out books, Aspen?" Lori begins as she starts climbing the ladder, pulling the books out from a tall shelf.

"Don't start, Lori," I warn.

"Keagan. I bet you would have enjoyed this view of him much more than of me and vice versa," Lori gabs on playfully.

"See, that's just the thing, Lori, despite what you think, I couldn't care less about such an idea. Besides, you're the one who's been wanting to climb and play around on these ladders," I answer back.

Lori replies dramatically, "Oh, Aspen, whatever shall you do when you realise you have feelings for him as well? I can just see it now: you're writhing under your sheets and calling out in the night from anguish, saying, 'What do these emotions mean? What are feelings? I do not understand!'" Lori calls down, playfully mocking me.

"Go ahead and gab, Lori, but no matter what you say or think, I have absolutely no ulterior motives when it comes to Keagan Myrack," I say evenly in a matter-of-fact tone.

"Is that so?" Lori says, drawing out each word slowly with her all-too-familiar smile of mischief.

"Lori, whatever you are scheming in that twisted little head of yours, I'm warning you now, *don't do it,*" I call up to her as she climbs higher.

"Yeah, yeah, which one was it again?" she replies, waving me off.

"It's called *the History and Almanac of Electro-Thermal Mechanics* and the other is *the Properties of-*"

"Oh hello, Keagan!" Lori calls out from the top of the ladder in such a sudden force that I turn to face the direction she was calling in, only to see that he is a little way's off, waving to us with a smirk on his face. But as I turn, I have let go of the ladder and accidentally bump it with my hip, causing it to come out from under Lori's feet, making her call out, "Woah, Aspen! EARTH TO ASPEN!" whilst dangling helplessly from the open top bookshelf door. It would be quite the sight if someone else were to see her dangling there whilst I frantically chase down the rolling ladder.

Keagan runs our way, unsure of who to help most whilst trying his best not to look up Lori's skirts out of decency. By the time I come back with the ladder, Lori can barely hold on any longer. Keagan is trying to steady the ladder with me whilst I can't help but start to feverishly laugh at the ridiculousness of the whole situation.

Whilst I cackle my head off, Keagan doesn't know how to react and looks genuinely concerned as a jabbering and flustered Lori makes her way down the ladder with a single book in her hand. Once on the ground, she thrusts the book hard onto my chest, nearly screaming, "Don't you ever ask me to pick out books for you again!"

I would have felt terrible and tried to apologize if I could, but I couldn't help myself from laughing even harder at this remark.

"D-don't be *hanging* this on me in the future, sissy, when it was your doing that startled me," I giggle back.

"AUGH!" she lets out, fully exasperated as she hops her way down the spiral stairs, obviously flustered by how I'm handling the situation.

"I wouldn't *dangle* this little matter over you if it had been me up there," I continue to jab at her, having a grand old time with myself since none of her schemes have backfired on her like this before.

"Oh, just shut up, will you?" Lori says, trying to be mad, but even from where I am, I can see her twisting face trying not to smile as she storms out of the library.

"Oh, come now, Lori, come on back up here and *hang* around with us!" Keagan adds. I am laughing so hard right now along with him that we soon hit the floor until we are out of breath and our stomachs hurt. "W-aha what was all that about?" he asks me.

"Oh, when Lori was trying to get a book for me, she startled me and... well, you saw what happened next," I giggled out as I rested my back on the book shelf. "What were you coming up here to see us for?" I question happily so he won't ask further about what it was that actually startled me.

"Oh, I just-"

"Master Keagan! The governor and a brigade of policemen are coming up the drive!" Charles practically yells through the servants' pipes that are in almost every room. I'm on my feet in a flash and sprinting as best I can down the stairs towards Lori and the dimies as Keagan talks back through the pipe to Charles.

"Thank you, don't let them in right away, climb up and

down the stairs before answering the door, buy us as much time as possible," he orders sternly.

The last thing I hear is Keagan running down the stairs himself whilst I dash out the door, only to see Lori bustle along a team of dimies near our age towards the small study with the secret passage. Down the hall, Winona pulls along a team up stairs. They must be splitting the dimies up to the best and quietest secret passages we know of in the house. *Good job, ladies, wait...the machine! I still need to hide it!*

Just then, little Lucy comes out of a guest room walking aimlessly around, rubbing her eyes. The tot's nap time had been interrupted. Charles has reached the last step of the stairs and is eyeing her and me nervously one after the other, unsure of how to act properly.

"I'll handle it. Walk slowly," I whisper hoarsely as I pass him, picking up Lucy in her white dress and rushing back to the study where Lori is now exiting the door.

There's a loud knock at the door followed by the chimes of the doorbell. I brush past Lori and stammer out, "Hide t-th-the machine."

She's gone as fast as my words came out and so am I. I flip the fake book latch, slide the bookcase open, and hand Lucy to the closest dimie there is to the door.

"Thank goodness," mutters her big brother Nox as he takes her in his midnight blue paws.

"All right, now no sounds, got it?" I rasp out, they nod their heads, and I shut the bookcase back into place and grab a book from another shelf. Brushing my skirts down, I walk as smoothly as I can out the door. The moment I step out the door, the governor catches sight of me.

"Why, Miss Aspen Wolfe! It is so good to see you again. How are you doing, my dear?" the governor bellows out from where he stands in the foyer with Keagan, looking as composed as ever whilst Charles hangs up the governor's frosted coat.

"Ah, Governor Damon," I say in a happily surprised tone as I stroll towards the men. "I do not believe we were expecting you or your men, but what a pleasant surprise to see you again, sir," I say with all the charm my body can muster in one lie as I offer my hand to the governor. As he leans down to kiss it, Keagan gives me one of his signature boyish smirks; I return it with a raise of my eyebrows and a slender smile.

"Well, haven't you heard, Miss Wolfe? Ever since the Market was broken into, and the slaves were stolen, it is now a regulation that all the homes and buildings in Currlion must go under a full sweep routinely until we find them all. Even our neighbouring cities are performing building checks to make sure the thieves aren't on the run with them. Besides, we can't afford to lose that many slaves without a fight to find the culprits. By the way, where might your younger sister be, Miss Wolfe?" the governor asks me as his uniformed dimie watchmen begin to pile in the house and check the staircases and foyer.

"Lori? Ah, I believe she is taking a nap right now. The poor thing was tired all day," I lie with ease. I hope Lori is able to sneak around the house fast enough and hide everything in the secret rooms. Just then, we all hear a loud thud coming from the second floor.

"I thought you said that Lori was resting?" he queries with a quizzical expression.

"Oh well, we thought that she was, but that was probably Winona or Charles cleaning up. They must have dropped something, I guess," Keagan replies for me as I feel my face begin to turn a little pink.

"Indeed; however, all the same, we will still need to check all the rooms Mr Myrack and Miss Wolfe. It's just protocol. Why don't we start with your room first then so we can let Miss Lori get back to sleep quickly, ehh?" Governor Damon says to us simply, but his eyes tell me he doesn't believe me one bit.

"Well, I hardly think it would be very couth to wake a sleeping young lady by a man about to search the room. At least let me arouse her so that she may become decent before you and your men search, ehh?" I reply, maybe a little too cheeky. The governor meets my gaze and ponders this request.

"Very well, Miss Wolfe. Lead the way."

I begin walking briskly to our room. I just pray that she has finished hiding everything in time. All the men pause outside our room as I open the door a crack and slide inside, closing the door behind myself. The moment the door shuts, I glance around. I see Lori popping her head out from the lavatory. Before she has a chance to speak, I put a finger to my lips and usher her back into the loo.

"The governor is outside of the room; we need to make you look like you just woke up from a nap. Did you have time to take care of everything?" I whisper in her ear.

"Yeah, they are actually under the tub, I found another secret door. Nearly broke my neck when I tripped on it, though." she answers as I help her ruffle up her hair a bit.

"Wonderful... Come on, you need to wake up and make yourself presentable, the governor has to search the room due to protocol," I call out loud in a normal tone in case the governor and his goons are eavesdropping. After Lori throws a shawl over her shoulders and sits back on her bed, putting on her best 'I just woke up' act, I invite the men in our room. Governor Damon comes into our room quite hastily actually where a tired-looking Lori just got off of her bed to put on her shawl.

"Please excuse us for disturbing your sleep, Miss Wolfe, but we must do a thorough routine check of all the homes and buildings in Currlion now since there is talk of rebellion, and the stolen slaves are still in hiding," the governor apologizes to her directly.

"Oh dear, then check all you like," Lori says sleepily. The men check the entire room and the bathroom as we wait outside the door. I can feel a shiver crawl up my spine as the men search near the bathtub. But the room is considered clear by the time the watchmen check my study where I used to work on Gear Heart. Whilst in there, one of the men picks up something from the floor and gives it to the governor.

"My dear lady, do you know what these are?" Damon says, walking towards me, holding up a good-size watch spring and a few washers.

"Certainly." I try to keep my voice even whilst my hands begin to tremble slightly.

"Uh, Aspen?" Keagan mutters with a furrowed brow.

"What? I know what it is," I say to him with a hurt and innocent look on my face; he still doesn't see my little act I'm pulling, judging by the confused expression on his face.

"That's a screw bolt sir, and little rings." I try to sound sure of myself as the governor gazes at me dead on and then at Keagan. I think that was enough for him to think me incompetent in the area of mechanics.

"Ahh, yes, well, I think this room is quite clean indeed. Ahem, we will be going to check the other rooms now. All clear men?" he replies with a smile.

"All clear, sir," a burly man says. Everyone leaves the room except Lori and me. The moment they shut the door, we both let out a breath of exasperation and fall into the cushioned chairs. I didn't realise how scared I was until they were out of sight, how afraid I still am by the sight of my shaking hands. I look at Lori who gives me a sideways glance before emitting a finite chuckle.

"I think I'm ready for that nap now," she says, making me laugh.

I hit her arm playfully and say, "They're just beginning. You're lucky though you get to sleep; I have to go back out there. I can't wait until they are gone. I was so scared."

"You, Aspen? Miss Robot-Killer and Slave-Rescuer, scared? Why, that's unheard of."

"Tish Tosh... now you on the other hand must feel normal, Miss Scaredy-" Lori cuts me off by playfully hitting my arm incessantly until I jump out of my chair.

I quickly head back out the door and see the men searching the rest of the rooms so I busy myself by heading upstairs to find Winona. I don't want Damon's dimie watchmen getting anywhere near her, and I know Keagan feels the same way. But I can't seem to find her, or Charles. I make it to the top-floor balcony window, where I see in the bright snow that Winona is picking mountain heather, and Charles is chopping firewood in the garden. *I should go down to help her. Who cares if the men think me unladylike to work in a garden? Upper-classwomen do it every now and then, I'm told.*

When I make my way to her, Winona greets me with a smile but keeps her head down mostly as we clip away at the flowers. Charles doesn't acknowledge me and continues building his small pile of firewood as if nothing were the matter. I crouch over the bush parallel to Winona. Glancing up at her face only for it to feel foreign to me since her smile is gone, and an intense line has replaced it as her jaw remains clenched. I can feel the waves of worry swirling around her. She seems to be the most terrified out of us all. Through the bush, I find her paw and give it a reassuring squeeze. A gasp escapes her mouth, causing me to feel so much for her at this moment. All of this, her people, Thatcher, us, her whole life, could be taken away if just one dimie is found. I never realised how much we shared in common until this moment. We both take a sharp inhale and let it out before releasing each other and resume picking flowers.

Whilst Charles places the chopped wood in the shed, Winona and I bring the bushels of flowers into the kitchen in silence and arrange flower pots to place throughout the house. As I make my way to the tea parlor, I give a quick curtsey to a pair of leaving officers; thank God I don't have to be in the same room with them. I feel nervous enough as it is without them watching my every move. The last thing I need is to drop this vase from nervousness and have them offer to help, thus prolonging their stay. After rearranging the flowers, I am content with its placement on the piano. I head to the parlor doors only to halt right at the edge of the opening as I hear, "Come on, boy, don't tell me you never get the urge to sneak into their room at night for a little slap and tickle with them," the voice of the governor says with lust fuming from his words like a dragon.

"What makes you think I don't? Of course I've wanted to, but above all of that I am still a gentleman," I hear coming from Keagan's voice, making my mind spin from what might have gone through his brain in the past.

"Yes, but even a gentleman needs to be satisfied. If I were you, I'd act fast and get my hands on one of them, or both, if you're feeling agile enough. If anything, keep Aspen and give *me* that little Lori Wolfe."

*The audacity of that man! How dare he say such things about Lori and me like we are just a slice of meat for one meal at dinner! I have half a mind to challenge him to a duel.*

"With all due respect to your position, sir, I will advise you to not speak ill or lustfully like so about those two young women in my presence. I am as of now their host and acting guardian anyway," I hear Keagan say authoritatively in a deep voice that demands to be heard.

"Well, it is not my doing that they have their rumours of traipsing around with multiple men in each town they stay in. Or for strange and unknown reasons, their own kin has practically forced them out of house and home to fend for themselves. It makes one think of what delicious secrets those women are holding. I'm surprised you aren't more curious to find out and tell. Or perhaps you are?" the governor says in a slimy manner. It sounds like he believes that Keagan knows our secret of why we are always moving, and wishes to find out. I find myself at a loss for breath as I wait for Keagan to betray us.

"I don't care what terrible gab some cowardly bloke or wench came up with, I will not hear another word of it about those two young ladies, are we clear?" Keagan says in a deep even voice that even I feel slightly threatened by.

"As a bell. Good day, Mr Myrack, and don't be late for the meeting. I'm expecting you to be there in a timely manner," the governor says evenly back to Keagan as the sound of feet die off and the resounding click of the door echoes through the halls. The realisation hits me that the men are out of the house, and yet I remain motionless at the tea parlor entrance. *He stuck up for us. Keagan truly tried to protect our reputation after he knew all the wrongs we have done.* When I finally realise that he is coming my way, I can tell he's already too close for me to make a clean escape down the long hall and decide to act as if I were coming towards him just now.

Turning into the hall towards his direction, I attempt to act nonchalant. However, I may have overplayed my part a bit since I practically ram myself into Keagan's chest like I'm in a deranged hurry to see if our guests have left.

"Oof, ah, Aspen, in a little rush, aren't we? How long have you been here?" Keagan huffs out, trying to regain the breath I just punched out of him as he holds me by the shoulders.

"N-not that long, I-I just came to see if our surprise guests have left yet," I lie.

"You know..." Keagan starts, rubbing my arms up and down, making it hard for me to think straight. "You really are not as good a liar as you think you are..." Keagan leans his head down so close to my ear that I can feel the heat of his face on mine. "You should work on that," he finishes.

My face is burning right now. I don't know what to do. I think about the advice the governor just gave him, which makes me feel even more nervous.

"W-well at least I know how to throw a punch correctly," I bite back with the lamest excuse for a comeback ever, making me wince. But it was still enough to cause Keagan to laugh full-heartedly, surprising me with the sudden change of behaviour.

"Is that a challenge?" Keagan says with a boyish grin and raised eyebrows.

"Maybe, but I simply thought we were just stating the obvious," I rival back with an equal girlish grin. His hands on my arms remain there a little bit longer before replying.

"Well, sadly we can't do any of that right now. I have to go pack soon; the elites and politicians of Currlion have been called to a meeting to discuss all the trouble that our trio have been making on our missions," Keagan groans out unenthusiastically before releasing my arms and coming to my side as we begin to walk down the hall.

"How long do you think it'll take?" I ask.

"Why? Are you afraid you'll miss me if I'm gone too long?"

"Hardly," I say, trying to stop him from flirting too boldly. I can't handle all the blushing this guy causes me. It's too embarrassing and too hard to hide.

"Honestly, it should take just a day; however, there was a time when my father was gone for one of these meetings for three whole days when I was a child. I remember the expression on his face when he came through the doors, he looked like he got hit by a cannonball."

I laugh at the image in my head of a flattened put-out face of Mr Myrack Senior. I feel bad for laughing but it's such a comical notion. I quickly regain my composure, however, as I catch Keagan stealing a look at me before quickly turning his attention forwards again whilst we walk back to the hidden rooms to let the dimies out. After we do, it's time for dinner with everyone. But Keagan soon excuses himself to pack for the elites council meeting.

I've lost track of how many days it's been since Keagan left. I can't seem to fall asleep without a terrible nightmare. My blame rests on the governor's proposal to kill and skin dimies who don't fall in line along with the looming anxiety of everyone we have already saved. Or I'm so restless that all I can do is think about Gear Heart and the original machine we've found in the warehouse. *How are we to combine them again? I think it's written on the chalkboard. We figured it out some*

*time ago, but Gear Heart is still incomplete. It must be ready in time, it must.*

So I continue to work tirelessly. I've tried to explain it to Lori a hundred times, but Mother Hen won't listen to me. She hasn't been the most cheerful companion either, going on and on about Keagan and the rumours about his recurring infidelity towards women. No doubt thanks to Her Royal Rottenness, Miss Rose Hughes. I've tried my best to block out those thoughts, but they keep coming back. *He has been gone a long while.* I still feel kind of bad for the whole sleeping-dart situation, but she's the one who tried to hit me with it, so she started that little war.

*At least Thomas has been of some real help since he finished the Fabergé egg frame a few hours ago... or was it last night?* I think to myself as I'm soldering two wires together. It feels like I'm trying to hold up two mountains the size of Everest on my eyelids and head. The wires are connected, and just as they are, all of the cogs, wires and colours before me begin to get even blurrier than they were a second ago. Everything on my work table is starting to fuse and morph together whilst my arms and body scream out for rest. I realise I'm going to pass out soon. Feeling it coming, I push away the machine and all the parts I possibly can, but only once since my head stays flat on the table at my first push.

# MOONLIT FEELINGS

## KEAGAN

I can't believe I just spent four days with those stuck up, pompous, insufferable... Argh, they don't listen to anyone but the governor and his psychotic ideas on how to take advantage of the dimies for capital. What's worse is the laws that he is proposing are going to make it much harder on Aspen, Lori, and me during our missions. Earlier curfew and official tagging of your dimie to identify against the stolen ones. Any dimie without proper identification from their master will be terminated and used for skinning.

I can believe, however, that he is offering up bounties for our heads, and encourages the common man to work with the dimie bots to catch us if needed. At least that sounds like a normal level of eccentric paranoia a powerful man would have. There are so many things that could go wrong now, but the worst is the surprise routine house checks, and it's all because of us. My blistering thoughts go sailing on like a ship caught in a storm, constantly being battered by black waves of hate, never getting a chance to prepare for the next swell. Lost in the recesses of my mind, I blindly drive myself through town, up the snow-covered roads noticing only one thing on the way: the three crosses we put up for the buried skins of lost dimies.

Finally arriving home again, my nightmarish mind is interrupted by thoughts of Aspen, Lori, Thomas, the dimies, and the machine. Thinking of them, and *her*, does make my anger subside. However, instead of peace, my anxiety grows for what could go wrong, what could be lost now more than ever.

*I wonder if Aspen has been making much progress on the machine since we had to move her 'lab' to my room?* I wonder to myself as I exit the motor car.

"Ugh, so glad to be home; after that four-day debate meeting, I feel like sleeping for four days," I mutter as I stroke Peaches's tawny mane, such a good horse. "That damn Damon and his policemen had to get smart and barge his way into my house! Aspen lost her workroom, and the dimies were almost enslaved all over again," I say to her. I never understood how talking to Peaches helped me clear my head, but it almost always did. I just wish this was one of those times. Giving her neck a pat as she snorts, I make my way up the walkway.

I grumble to myself as I burst through my front doors in a thoroughly put-out mood, with my eyes stinging from the bright lights. *Why in God's name are they still on at a time like this?* As if the clocks could hear my thoughts, they go off, giving two chimes as Charles hastily tries to take my hat and coat whilst I walk aimlessly in what I assume is the way to my bed.

"Let me take your hat and coat, sir!" Charles says rather eagerly for such a time of night. After I hand them over, Charles begins to catch me up on all that has been happening in the house during my absence.

"There are two new invitations for parties that are coming

up soon; the mayor and governor will also be attending both. Lori, Thomas, and Winona have been tending to the dimies with the occasional help of Aspen. Although Aspen..." the greying man pauses in a tone of dismay, causing me to slow to a halt so that my full attention is ready for what he is holding back.

"Miss Aspen has not emerged from your bedroom for almost three days. Only Miss Lori and Thomas have been allowed to visit her and bring her food or whatever else she might need to work. Lori says that she has been fixing the machine nonstop."

At this, my grumpy thoughts and emotions begin to morph into those of worry whilst my feet seem to be rooted to the ground.

"The clock rang when I came in, didn't it?" I ask, unable to remember what the grandfather clock chimes as questions swarm my tired brain.

"Yes, um, it is two o'clock in the morning, sir," Charles yawns out, I remain silent as I think about all the possibilities that she could have hurt herself unintentionally and become even more frustrated with each thought. *Why would she go to an extreme like this? How is it Lori couldn't convince her to rest or go to bed?*

"Where are Lori and Winona?" I ask Charles.

"They are in bed, sir. Thomas and the dimies are as well."

"Lori has of course tried to get Aspen to rest and go to sleep, correct?" I ask.

"She has tried a dozen times and failed just as many. Miss Lori even went inside with some type of sleeping-dart gun and ended up outside your room on the rug, stuck by a dart and asleep herself for six hours," Charles says, shaking his head.

"I must attend to her at once. I don't care how strapped we are for time right now with that machine," I growl as I storm away from Charles and blindly to my room. My thunderous mood is rising now more than in any of those meetings within the past four days. I bolt through my doors and march right in, sweeping the room for Aspen, but I don't see her at first. I head over to her desks in the right corner of the room farthest from the drawn curtains.

Walking amongst her lit workstation and her chalkboard that has readable and undefinable squiggles covering it, I notice that her lamplight is still on. As I stride back towards the work desk to turn it off, I glance at the work desk to see how truly cluttered it is. That's when I see her, starting with her brunette hair completely sprawled out over her head and the desk. Her outstretched arms poke out of the shining brown mound in the lamplight.

"Aspen," I breathe in as I cross over to her side of the work desk. All of my anger begins to fade away now that I see how exhausted she truly is and how hard she worked herself.

When I stroke her back gently and call her name it is apparent that she isn't wearing a corset or brazier under her loose baggy work shirt. This realization causes an immense heat to wash over my face, and I quickly jerk my hand away from her back. This rash movement causes her to stir.

Groaning, she raises her head off the table slowly, eyes still closed and face twisted in an expression of pain and fatigue. I stare at her pathetic position whilst picking gears and wire bits out of her hair and off her now red forehead.

"Aspen," I whisper again, deeply, to her as I pluck the last wire out of her hair then brush strands away from her face.

"Mmgh," she grunts as a reply.

"It's time to go to bed; you need to rest."

"No, rest...later...finish machine now...so close..." she replies almost unintelligibly.

*I'm done with this conversation.* "Sorry, Aspen, but this time you don't get a choice," I state decidedly as I lean her head to rest on my shoulder and pick her up out of the old wooden chair cradle style. As I do this, and begin to walk away from the work area, she keeps softly arguing.

"I can do it...have to....counting on me."

I carry her to my bed and lay her down on the down sheets that she immediately sinks into whilst I attempt to take her shoes off. But before I can even touch them, she tries to get back up off the bed. The only thing I can think of with my own tired brain is to pin her down. I catch her by the waist as she begins to slide off the bed and push her back down into the down comforter, pinning her there with me pressed on top of her. My hands linger where they are as I whisper, "Stay and sleep."

I find myself staring at her; it takes me a moment to fully realise just how close we actually are. I remain where I am though and patiently wait for her consent. Eyes still closed, but face no longer twisted in pain, the red mark on her forehead is beginning to fade away. Her hair looks like it was made to be splayed out on my sheets, laying there so long like stretching roots, pulling me closer to her... *She's never looked so tempting,* I think to myself disdained by my own thoughts.

"Ok," she replies breathlessly in such a canorous way that it takes the last remnants of my energy not to take advantage of the situation and her. I'm just thankful she is barely conscious at the moment or else she would see how red my face is right now, just inches from hers.

I finally have to remind myself that it's my job to help her right now, not hurt her even more. With this thought, I slowly lift myself off of the sleeping beauty, but keep my hands at her waist to lift her up onto the bed again. I unlace her boots and lay her gently under the now-warm covers. I gaze at her beautiful face as I move a few stray hairs from it; she's like a sharp note on a violin. Ringing in the recesses of my mind, aching to hold onto such a sweet thing and to remember the feeling that is emitted when it's present. Forever resonating.

My gaze eventually moves from her to her work table. Her lamp is still on. Like the undead, I slowly make my way to the table, but as I am about to turn the gas lamp off, I notice Gear Heart. It's outer shell has been completed; I don't dare touch it but I do bend down to its level. I marvel at it's Fabergé detailing and inlaid gems that are enveloped in swirls of bronzed leaf-like vines that creates a false feeling of delicacy. It's formed perfectly in the shape of an egg but the size of a large melon. *Brilliantly crafted. I wonder how much was Thomas's doing and how much Aspen helped.*

I pick up a magnifying glass on the adjacent worktable to get a closer look. That's when I notice something; the egg shell is cleverly made of two parts, but the edges of the two halves are so miniscule it's almost impossible to see without a magnifying glass. *The gaps between the bronze vines are filled in with pearlesque enamel, or perhaps it's stained glass?* And It appears that there is a gem missing, and a rather large one at that; the bezel is set for a heart-shaped stone and yet sits empty. I look around for a gem of that size but don't see anything glimmering like a jewel would, especially in all this creative mess. *However, there is that little black box next to an empty sack that has one small green glass stone laying on the cloth.*

"That box must have the missing gem," I say to myself as I begin to reach for it. But just as I'm about to grab the box, I hear the clock on my bedside gently chime three o'clock in the morning. It's too late for snooping like this, and especially with her being so close in proximity at the moment. I back away from the little black box and finally turn the lamp off, filling the entire room with darkness for a few seconds. But then clouds part in the sky, allowing the moon to illuminate half the room in a blue glow that hits the bed and the woman sleeping in it.

I've never been around a woman long enough to get so close to her as I'm becoming with Aspen. I've never really taken the chance to be open like we were on the terrace, or in the library. I'm only familiar with the average man's level of flirtatious courting and romance whether in bed or on the dance floor. However, this hits a whole new level of intimacy I was not prepared for. Under these circumstances, there are no set of common rules to follow or break, so we are on our own. It's never been easy or so black and white in my life; there's always been ulterior motives and another purpose for every person and event in my life, save Winona and Charles. Although Aspen and her sister lied to me, they were the first people who lied and used me for a cause that was actually worth it all and not for their own gain.

It could be so easy, *so* easy, to just slip under the covers and hold her in my embrace as we dream together under the moonlight. It could be so easy to press her unconscious body next to mine as I caress her soft skin. But... I know that as soon as I slide under the sheets, press her to my chest, and touch her soft skin, I wouldn't stop there; I couldn't. But I wouldn't dare hurt her like that, I'd sooner hang myself than hurt Aspen like that. I push off of the work desk and unconsciously move towards the couch. Feeling as if in a fuzzy dream, I strip down to just my undershirt and trousers and gather two blankets and a pillow to make my bed. I remember the last thing on my mind as I lay my head down, so exhausted my brain begins to slow to a halt. And then I take one last look at the moon-washed bed that now feels so far away...Aspen.

# WAKING DEMONS

## ASPEN

I should wake up soon. I know I need to do something important, but this bed is so soft and smells like vanilla I can't even remember what I'm supposed to do. I just want to drown all my thoughts out between two pairs of sheets in a heavy slumber. I take a long inhale; that scent is so familiar: vanilla. *I know someone who smells like that,* I think as I nuzzle my face deeper into the fluffy down comforter. Then it hits me like a bullet, causing me to sit straight up where I'm lying.

"Keagan," I say out loud before getting hit with a terrible pain in my head, making it throb for a few seconds. Hunching over, I apply pressure to my temple to reduce the pain. *What happened?*

Slowly, it begins calming down again, allowing me to think properly and open my eyes once more. I take in my surroundings: warm sunlight falls through the high windows. My workbench remains in the corner right where I left it. *I'm in Keagan's room...wait, I'm in Keagan's bed!* I think frantically to myself as I have an even more daunting realization: *there is no tight constriction around my abdomen. I'm not wearing a corset or brazier!* My face reddens as I look to my left, afraid to see Keagan in bed, but he isn't with me. I slip my hand under the cover next to where I was and move it up, down, and across the sheets where he would have lain, but there is no heat or imprint in the sheets his body would have left behind. *It doesn't look as if he's slept there at least for a few nights. If I slept here then where did-* my thoughts skid to a halt as I look at the strewn blankets and pillows on the couch that faces the end of the bed. Then I catch a shocking sight in the mirror that is across the room. *Me.* I pat down my hair and look at my clothing. *My God, I look as horrid as my head feels. How long have I been asleep?*

All my questions come to a stop at the sound of the bedroom doors opening. I meet Keagan's eyes where he stands in the doorway, unmoving. I remain seated in bed. I have no words to say when I take in his appearance. His hair is in disarray, clothing is minimal: just pants, suspenders, and his undershirt that's slightly unbuttoned, exposing skin. I find myself unable to take my eyes off him. I must look frightened because he just remains in the doorway, eyes bolted to mine. He finally makes the first move, walking briskly towards me whilst I stay still partly under the covers. He stops right at the bed's edge, putting his hands on the down comforter whilst speaking gingerly: "I hope you're feeling refreshed; you certainly were out long enough."

"How long was I asleep?" I ask.

Keagan looks off towards the top right window with a calculating expression, and in doing so, I see how tired and ragged he truly looks from the sight of his scruffy face and worn eyes. *He probably feels even worse than he looks, the poor bloke.*

"About seventeen hours," Keagan answers calmly with a smirk.

"What?" I exclaim.

I begin to scramble and shuffle the sheets off of me, causing me to nearly tumble out of the bed. My mind spins as I walk aimlessly around the room, trying to recall what happened the past few days and what to do next. Keagan tries to call me to his attention, but I don't listen; I'm too frantic.

I feel a tug on my arms. Keagan grabs me by my shoulders as he looks straight at me and talks in his soft voice. "Aspen... you need to calm down. Take a deep breath. The house isn't burning down. We are fine."

"What happened, Keagan? What happened last night is still fuzzy. I can't remember a thing." I implore him to tell me as I rest my hands on his chest. I need stabilization and he is the closest thing for that at the moment.

"When I returned home last night, I saw you hadn't slept or rested practically since the day I left. Charles also told me that Lori and Thomas were the only ones allowed to see and feed you. You wouldn't rest even when Lori begged you. When I came into the room last night I was scared and furious, but so was everyone else." He pauses, and my gaze adjusts to the sight of the floor as my memory rushes back to me from last night. I feel my face turning red from heat. I remember the pain in my head and Keagan's voice, him carrying me and laying me down... *His body and he's so close to me on that soft bed... "Stay and sleep."* I turn my eyes back to his, which are staring worriedly straight at my face that is currently burning hot.

"I remember now," I say, taking my hands off his chest.

"Come here, darling, you need to sit down."

We sit in an uncomfortable silence as Keagan pours me a cup of tea and hands it to me. Warm and inviting, he calls it a Moroccan tea blend. Something he brought back with him from one of his adventures, no doubt. After a few sips to calm my nerves, the past few days begin to sink in. I've made much progress on the machine.

"Everyone has been asking about you; if you're all right, if you're sick, if they can help, and even if you've abandoned them," Keagan explains with signs of worry on his face.

"Oh dear, well, please, tell them I'm right as rain and that there is nothing to worry about; Gear Heart is almost finished."

"I think it would be better if they see and hear it from you… you know, when you join us for dinner tonight."

"Oh, that won't be-"

"Necessary? I think it is, Aspen. You're doing it again. You're disregarding your health, and now the feelings of those around you, for that precious machine of yours."

"I'm doing this for *them*, and if I need my seclusion to get the job done then so be it."

"Well, in that case, if I have to tie you to the bed frame just to get you to go to sleep every night then so be it."

I look at him like he's gone mad. *What an idea!* "You wouldn't dare!"

"Try me," he says, leaning closer.

My mind is still spinning, trying to put everything into perspective. "I guess I did cross a line this time. I've never worked that continuously without sleep. I didn't scare anyone too much, did I?"

Keagan just stares at me with raised eyebrows and an expression that says it all: *What do you think?*

"I know what keeps you up at night, Aspen: that machine of yours." He nods in the direction of where Gear Heart sits on my work desk. "And yet I wonder," Keagan ponders, scooting closer to me with a determined look in his eyes, giving me that stupid nervous feeling in my stomach again.

"I've heard a scream once or twice from your room, though I bet there have been more. Someone calling out in your room in the early morning and late night. Take last evening for example," he goes on, making gestures with his hands with each theory whilst his body is now lying back onto the couch cushions.

"So either you are torturing people in my house at night, your sister and you fight more than you lead on, or you are having severe nightmares." With that last theory, he stares at me dead in the eyes. I quickly avert my gaze back into my now empty teacup.

"They're just bad dreams," I reply flatly.

"Who are you trying to fool? Just bad dreams don't make you scream out in the night. Personally, I don't think a woman should have bad dreams. I think there should only be one reason a woman should call out in the night when in bed."

At his last comment, I stare back outside and thank God the light is a warm hue so he can't see me blush.

"Aspen, I'm not trying to scare you or make you feel uncomfortable, at least not this time," he goes on whilst resting his left hand on my knee. "I'm just worried what those nightmares might be about, if I could help you and... if I am possibly responsible for hurting you in those dreams," he finishes, and I turn directly to him only to see the young boy from long ago who did hurt me once, and the look on his face is there again.

Fear, regret, and anguish; from that expression it seems as

if the last thing he ever wanted to happen was to relive the past and cause me grief and pain again. I feel my heart swelling in my chest as I catch a lump in my throat. *Maybe it's time to open up more, to be vulnerable. He was vulnerable towards you at the Christmas celebration. Be brave like him. You can do this.* I give a painful smile whilst resting a few fingers on his hand that remains on my knee just before I set the teacup down on its saucer.

"In my dreams, I'm the one trying to save you and everyone else, but each time I fail and get nowhere. I have to watch everybody physically suffer for what I couldn't fix. No matter what I do, everything just gets worse and more painful and terrifying to watch," I say, heaving a sigh before I continue. *Come on, put on your trousers and be strong. You can be vulnerable.* "Lori and I have a very cruel aunt that stayed with us as our guardian when our father died; she tried to make us the perfect proper ladies our father would be proud of at least that's how she put it. She is in my dreams a lot, acting as an abusive demon it seems now that I look back on them." I make a face before continuing. "Well, Lori seemed fine most of the time, but I was barely ever good enough. At first, she corrected us with harsh words, but when papa died they morphed into more of a beating than mere correction," I continue with tears beginning to well up in my eyes.

"Needless to say, she used my 'not being a proper lady' as her excuse to send us away and out of our house to one of our many cousins' homes so that we may 'get more acquainted with societal norms' as she put it. She took almost everything from us, and would have taken the rest if it were not for the will." My cheeks feel wet now; I know I shouldn't talk so much, but I can't stop it now. The truth must come out.

"Aspen," Keagan says in a quiet tone that could break a heart, but I don't stop.

"Because...as she put it, I was far beyond repair and would surely find my place one day as a fisherman's wife if I were even that lucky. I just hope a fisherman can handle seeing a woman... w-with a few s-scars." My tears and emotions are running like a waterfall. All the pain and the memories of my demons come at me at once. I take a sharp inhale as I cover it up with my hands. Everything she did to me, to Lori, to the household. Some things just can't be forgotten. I don't realise it immediately, but Keagan is brushing away my tears and tilting my chin up for me to look at him. I open my eyes just a crack and see the pain on his face like mine. Trying to muster a smile in a low voice, he coaxes me, "Shhh...you're safe now, Aspen. I promise I won't ever let her or anyone hurt you or get away with treating you in such a way ever again. Do you know why I won't let that happen, Aspen?"

I'm at a loss for words so I just shake my head as more tears drop from my chin. As he draws closer to me, I can feel my pain slip away like silk. He tries to comfort me as I'm held in a strong embrace from the side, rocking back and forth slowly. But the tears run on, and it takes every ounce of willpower I have not to cry out loud anymore from all the abuse I've hidden away.

"You are one of the most precious and exquisite things to ever come into my life, and I can't bear to see, let alone hear, that you've been hurt in such a way," he whispers in my ear and then does something that surprises me: he kisses my forehead, then my nose, where the tears were running rivers down my cheeks.

I feel him trying to kiss the tears away, and I let him, as he traces along my face and jawline with a heat I never knew before. He pulls away for a moment long enough for me to open my eyes and see him looking at me in the waning light of day, like I'm the only thing that keeps him sane in this world.

I reach for him and rest my fingertips on his jawline, then return his kiss, this time on his lips. One sweet simple kiss, but what follows is his own passionate one. I've never acted this way before with sincerity; I can't even get a grip on what's happening. I hold on to him now for dear life as he drowns out my sorrows in his tender embrace. I could stay forever in his arms; it's so warm with him that I can't catch my breath. Our kisses deepen, and with each one he leans me farther back into the soft cushions. I feel the lightning coming from his fingertips that caress the length of my waist and back whilst mine are tousling through his soft hair.

Our breathing becomes more ragged as our kisses become more incessant. Keagan pulls away, but only for a second, and finds my neck. I'm unprepared for the feeling that ripples down my spine as his lips nearly brand my skin with the heat of their mark. Never have I wanted anything more than a feeling like this; I never even knew that I wanted it so much until this moment.

Keagan's embrace becomes so passionate, feels so much like home, a place where I belong, as I myself almost forget how to breathe. I can't even recall how we ended up here and what started this. All I know and want is him. A moan escapes my lips, causing Keagan to bring himself back to my mouth once more before pulling away gasping for breath. He stares down at me with an intensity similar to the time he caught Lori and me sneaking in from our first mission, but this time there's no anger or annoyance. All I see is something compassionate, yearning, and... loving.

"Aspen," he murmurs, brushing away a loose strand of hair.

I feel the urge to tell him how I feel but can't find the words to say. Instead I pull him to me in an embrace and rest my chin on his shoulder. All I want is to stay here with him. I want to know the man I cannot hide these feelings for anymore.

"What you have done to me was something I promised myself could never be possible. I didn't want it to be," I whisper.

Keagan pulls away to look me in the eyes. "I don't understand, do you not want me like this?" he asks with fear in his eyes.

"No, that's not what I mean. I just never wanted to be another girl you fancied for a week or two and then dropped out of nowhere. I've heard the rumours, and so has Lori. I was so caught up in trying to make you the toy and be the one pulling the strings that I didn't see how you were also pulling *my* strings. And seeing that happening, I became scared to show all of myself to you."

"Aspen, are you admitting you actually care about me?" he questions with all his boyish demeanor returning to his gaze.

"Um, well, I..." I mutter, flustered by his sudden attitude.

"You care about me! You, o' high and mighty, care about me!" he calls out as he rests his forehead against mine.

"Oh, shut up," I say, trying to sound nonchalant, but I can hear my own smile when I utter the words. I rest my hand on his chest and feel his heartbeat: strong and rhythmic. I can hear my own in my ears as well as they soon follow in rhythm together. I open my eyes a crack to find Keagan gawking at my face.

"As much as I want to keep you to myself, I know there are a lot of people out there who want to see you, too."

"Right now?" I ask, surprised he'd let me go that easily.

"Hmmm, no, how about at dinner? What's a few more minutes?" He smirks before burying his face in my hair and neck.

*What's a few more minutes, indeed?*

# A HAPPY REUNION

## LORI

"Lucy, please stop squirming, tonight is an important night. Remember that Keagan said there would be a surprise at dinner," I say as Charles catches the dash of red running around the table for the third time tonight, nearly toppling over the main course dish that Winona is bringing out.

"That's why I'm so excited! The first surprise we had I got Pamela. I can't wait to see what happens this next time." Lucy climbs back into her seat and holds on tightly to her Christmas doll Pamela. Charles doesn't look amused, I bet he was happy when Keagan grew out of that clumsy phase.

Once Lucy is seated, her big brother Nox grabs her webbed paw. "Please, Lucy, be a little more patient, I'm sure it won't be much-" Nox stops short as he looks beyond me, speechless. I notice the rest of the room has grown silent and begins to stand up as well. I turn to see what's the matter and stand up out of my seat immediately, causing the chair to topple to the floor.

"Aspen! You gave me such a fright, I hope you know, along

with everyone else!" I exclaim, marching straight to her and Keagan. She looks nothing like she had the nights I came to help her. Her hair is pulled back, half up, half down, her attire is no longer loose and scandalous but neat and proper in a ruched skirt and dinner frock. And there isn't a bag to be found under her now-bright eyes.

"Nice to see you, too, Lori. By the way, how does your leg feel after that long nap you had the other day?" She smirks.

"Now, now, girls, this is not the time or place for a quarrel. You both can kiss and make up during dinner," Winona orders, pushing us towards our seats. On our way to our chairs, I notice Keagan whispering something to Aspen, making her giggle. *Now I know I'm missing something big. What happened last night? Should I have tried to intervene? What kept her in his room until dinner even after he checked on her two hours ago? And how did he manage to get her to rest for so long? Did he tie her down or hold her the whole night through?* When we saw him this morning, he did look quite tired and bedraggled without his usual day-collar shirt, vest, and coat. Perhaps he did have to wrestle her a bit to make her compliant. *If he hurt her in any way, I swear-*

"Lori! pass the potatoes, please!" rings in my ears, snapping me back into reality now that I see Winona is calling expectantly across the table whilst Aspen is waiting to hand me the full plate to share and pass on.

"Sorry," I say, taking one and passing it to Nox and Lucy. *Aspen's just got to open up.*

"I hope that you were able to get a lot of work done," I tell her.

"Oh, definitely, I think we have made some great progress," Aspen says with a smile.

"We?" I reiterate as everyone begins to mingle about.

"Oh, um, Thomas and I on the machine; we should be able to finish it tonight," Aspen blurts out, her smile now gone.

*What are you hiding, sissy?*

I feel like a child again when father was around and he and Aspen would spend hours each day working and testing parts for the machine. I remember trying everything and anything to get the amount of attention that he gave Aspen. The dance and baking lessons. I know he loved me just as much as her, but I still wish I could have played a larger part in something so important.

"Mhm. So tell me, how did Keagan manage to get you to go to sleep?"

"Oh, it wasn't that hard. I was so exhausted when he found me he just tucked me under the covers."

"Horse pucky. I don't believe that for one second, now tell me what really happened," I demand.

"Not now, Lori." Aspen gives me a sideways look that makes me realise I've been slightly insensitive about her finally being amongst the living again for her hard work.

"I'm relieved to see that you've received the rest you deserve; everyone is. I'm thrilled you've gotten so far on finishing Gear Heart. Papa would be proud, you know."

"Thank you. Truth be told, I missed being around everyone here, even you."

I look at her and see the playful smirk on her face. I almost felt insulted for a second. After a few bites of shepherd's pie I can't help but ask her, "Could I see it? The machine after dinner? That way we can catch up as well," I ask timidly. I realise now how much I've missed her company, and now that she is here, it feels as if I've been on withdrawals since I last saw her.

"Oh, may I see it as well?" Thatcher asks.

"Yeah, me too!"

"I want to see the machine as well," Nox says.

It seems that we have been overheard, and now the whole dining room erupts in curious banter.

"How about it, Aspen? May we see the machine that will bring them home?" Charles asks.

"Yes, we all can see the machine perform a test run tonight outside, but I warn you, it might be late at night, so kids, tonight you may stay up past bedtime."

"Yay!" the young dimies exclaim, followed by the adults. There is so much hope in their eyes that I can't help but cheer along with them. I raise a glass in a toast.

"To Aspen and Thomas, where would we be without your brilliance?"

"Here here! To Aspen and Thomas!" Thatcher adds enthusiastically as he pats Thomas on the back. "

"To Keagan! Where would we be without your home and generosity?" Eli raises another toast. Winona and Thomas smile bashfully to the cheering crowd and my heart warms at the sweet sight.

After dinner, Keagan wanted to spend some quality time with everyone else whilst Aspen could finish the machine and we could catch up alone. Sissy isn't usually one to give great detail for subjects of romance; however, for once, my ears were burning by the things she explained to me.

"I cannot believe you of all people let him hold you down like that," I say, wrapping my coat over my shoulders."

"I can hardly believe it myself. Just please, don't make a big deal out of it. You freak me out when you do that," Aspen replies, lowering the machine's inner workings into the Fabergé outer shell.

"Got it. Mum's the word... but still, you have a beau now!"

"Lori!"

"Sorry!"

Satisfied with our little sister's talk, Aspen calls Thomas into the room so they have a chance to test the lid and lens mobility to make sure they are fluid enough. Wouldn't want the parts to get stuck halfway during the first test run. I gaze at the beautiful shell that Thomas made and see that he has a true talent as an artisan metalworker. *I wonder if Aspen had time to teach him anything about the engineering side of Gear Heart. He's such a bright boy, I just hope we can find a good home for him, and give him a bright future. We are renegades anyway, what good influence could we be to him?*

"Lori?" Thomas asks, staring back at me. *I'm just spacing out too much today.*

"I'm sorry, dear, please, go put your coat on; it's extra cold out there tonight," I say, and he is off.

"You don't need to worry about him that much, you know."

"Worrying, who said I was worrying?" I ask defensively.

"Lori, I know you. You're a cute little bundle of worries. Plus, when you stare at someone for that long, I can tell something is troubling you deeply. Thomas is a wonderful and brilliant boy; we will find a good and proper home for him. I just know it," Aspen says reassuringly.

"You really think so?

"Of course. Now please, go get Keagan, Charles, and Thatcher to come here so we can bring this outside. It's time for a test run."

# TEST RUN

KEAGAN

After Thatcher, Charles, and I bring the generator and Gear Heart to the back door, we round up all the blankets and coats we can find for everyone in the house. Charles helps me in preparing the older dimies whilst Aspen aids Lori in getting the youth bundled up, which was fine by me since they were still jumping and running around. It's quite fun watching them try to wrangle the children long enough to wrap them up.

Getting Gear Heart outside and up to the rocks on the snow slope isn't too difficult, it's actually quite lightweight. But waiting in the cold with everyone whilst Aspen and Thomas rev up the generator: not pleasant. It's past midnight now; so we know that no one in their right mind will be around so deep in the forest at this hour, or at least I hope not . There is no moon out tonight and even the stars are covered by dark clouds. It really is the perfect night for a test like this; perhaps that's another reason why Aspen was in such a rush to finish it.

"Everyone, we need you to stand back behind the trees. If there is a blast we want you out of harm's way," Aspen orders, and we all do as she says.

"Will you be all right?" I ask.

"Don't worry, I have a long cord for the switch. Thomas and I will be behind the rocks, watching," Aspen assures me, securing her goggles over her eyes. "Also, it might be best if everyone didn't watch me turn it on, it could be very bright for a second," she adds before heading to the rocks.

Lori, everyone else, and I hide behind the trees and brush, covering our faces for what might come. My curiosity is too great, and I sneak a peek at the Fabergé egg on the rocks as steam begins to puff out of its sides. Just then, a fox comes in the clearing, looking and sniffing around the egg. *That little guy better get going soon.* The machine starts to sputter and come alive. The fox's fur stands on end whilst he bares his teeth, and yet he still doesn't run off.

The machine begins to move and grow; parts are twisting this way and that as the eggshell lid rises, exposing the machine's vast inner-workings. The lens that rests inside of the lid stretches outward from the machine with a large blue stone transitioning from in front to behind the lens. Copper pipes rise from the inside of the bottom shell as they spray out some type of chemical onto the gem and lens. This continues as a low hum resonates across the ground, then a bright blast of light bolts through the night.

It only lasts for a second, but it's enough to make me see spots. I hear a thump on the tree I'm next to, and when my vision clears, I see that the fox has run right into that tree and begins to shake its head. He stumbles a few steps back before dashing off into the forest. When I look back to Gear Heart, I see something miraculous; it's projecting a small portal on the rocks. *They made it possible to go through the rift again.*

"Everyone, come and see!" Thomas calls, running out behind their safe zone and looking up at the portal. We all trudge back through the snow and crowd around the small window. There we see tall trees of multiple colours and deep purple sky.

"That's it! That's home! That's our home!" Thatcher cries to Aspen as he takes her hand and shakes it vigorously. Everyone comes to look on the sides of the portal.

"I recognise this place; this isn't too far from my village where I lived when I was a child!" Lila, an older bird dimie says, leaning on her cane.

"You're right," Sonja agrees. "I can taste the ruslea berries now," she adds, wiping away tears with her feathers.

I rush to Aspen and pick her up in a tight hug, spinning all around. *My brilliant, radiant Aspen made this possible. Everything: my new purpose in life, the dimies' freedom, and perhaps one day a future together if she will have me.*

"I love you, Aspen," I say in her ear as I put her down.

She opens her mouth to speak but is immediately interrupted.

"Bravo, Aspen, Lori, Keagan, and Thomas. You have given us the greatest chance of a lifetime, and you were honest through and through," Nox says next to us with his fist in the air.

A cheer rings out, and we were soon enveloped in a hoard of *thank yous* and embraces. I guess I'll catch her again sometime later tonight or in the morning. Everyone looks so happy and is either dancing or conversing rapidly about home. Then I see it: Thatcher planting a kiss on Winona's cheek.

"Oi, Keagan, what's wrong? You look a little down," Lori asks me, breaking my attention away from them. She looks in the direction of the happy couple, and a wide smile instantly spreads across her face at the sight of them together; which only adds to my nerves.

"Aww, look at that, Winona has a special someone, too," Lori whispers in a high-pitched voice, tugging on my coat sleeve.

"Yeah, how sweet," I reply, trying to sound nonchalant but it comes out rather gruff instead.

"Keagan, aren't you happy for Winona and Thatcher since they have each other now, thanks to our help?" Aspen teases, but I don't appreciate it when it's about this topic.

"Can we please talk about anything but this?" I whisper back.

"Keagan, doesn't like the idea of Winona courting because he's too protective of her," Aspen mocks, batting her long lashes at the word courting.

"I have a right to be protective of her; she is family. Just like I have a right to be protective of you two mischief makers," I state.

"Aww, hear that, sissy? Keagan loves us," Lori gushes before they both are suddenly hit with snowballs. Dashing off behind me, they attack their assailants with handfuls of powdery snow as the rest of the dimies join in the battle. Someone stuffs a handful of snow down the back of my shirt, causing me to jump and call out a bit. When I turn to see who it is, I find Nox carrying away his little sister Lucy with powdery paws.

Most everyone begins with small teams and partners like Eli, Charles, and me. However, the strategy of teams quickly disintegrates, and it becomes a free-for-all until every last one of us is lying in the snow, laughing and covered in snowflakes. I sit up and look around at everyone and see many of the children, and a few of the adults, are mimicking Lori and Aspen as they make snow angels. In the other direction, Charles is leaning up against an old pine tree, smoking a pipe, appearing quite content with the smile that rests on his face.

I stand up and pat off some of the snow sticking to my bum and legs. Looking back up, I turn to look at the portal again, which is still glowing bright, but see that it has other admirers as well. Winona and Thatcher hold one another in an embrace as they gaze inside the dinner-plate-sized portal.

I don't dislike Thatcher, but I can't say that I am too keen on the idea that they are courting. Maybe it's just my own selfishness wanting her to remain here as a part of *my* family. If she were to choose to go with Thatcher, I'd probably never see her again unless it's through the skin of the rift when we send more dimies home. I can't remember a time when Winona wasn't a part of my life or household; even on my long trips we would write to each other. Aspen was right when she said that she deserves this as much or more than the rest of us. But I still can't help but want her to stay. *I have no right to make her remain here whilst others leave. What will I do if she chooses to go?*

# THE FIREPLACE

## ASPEN

"That's the last one; they are finally asleep. How do you suppose Keagan and Charles are faring putting the toddlers to bed?" Lori asks as we close the door to the last of the adult dimies' bedrooms.

"Get off that this instant!" Charles calls out from the room down the hall.

"Jimmy, stop stealing Lucy's doll!" Keagan grunts as if he is in a struggle from the same nursery.

"Does that answer your question?" I say with a smirk.

"We should probably go help...actually I'll help, you go to bed. You've worked harder than everyone combined," Lori orders.

Trying to be more compliant and listen more to my body, I turn to our room when a tiny thought comes into my head. *Whatever became of that secret room in the fireplace? You never did go to explore it.*

"Lori, hold on a moment. Remember that secret room I told you about in the library; the one under the fireplace that Keagan said we could explore later?"

"Yes, I remember; the one where he saved you from the rising torrents of fire."

I just stare at her, take a deep breath and sigh. "You are so dramatic. anyway, why don't we check it out now? We've been too busy getting sidetracked by our work to explore the house as much as we wanted to."

"Didn't Keagan say it was just a drafty spider hovel, though?" Lori reminds me worriedly.

"He did, but I have a strange feeling that he was lying. What do you say we go and search it for ourselves? I'll leave a note on the nursery door, and Keagan can come and join us once he's done with the toddlers."

"Mmm, fine, but if I get bit by a spider you're in trouble; you know I hate spiders."

"Life as we knew it, far and deep, prickles and burns on angels' feet." I quote Keagan's clue he gave as I press the moon on the map with the tiny "M" initial on it. Both of us have a lantern, dust rag, and a cane for cobwebs.

"Ready?" I ask.

"Let's get this over with," Lori moans nervously.

"Hey, we may find a long-lost family treasure. Keagan didn't even know about this secret door when I found it, so who knows."

"You're sure cheerful for someone about to walk into a slew of spider nests," Lori points out as I take the first step into the tunnel.

Damp stone steps run down to a dark and low-hanging ceiling room from the fireplace opening. Halfway down, I say, "Well, I only see a few webs here and there, but nothing major; it just looks like a lot of boxes, a workbench, and old covered objects. Probably furniture."

I make my way to the workbench, shining my light over the desk, pictures, and sketches of an engine of sorts, pinned on the wall. Resting my lantern on the table, I brush my fingers over the run of books that have dates on their spines from 1845 to 1884. Taking a random one out I hold open the first page to the light and read the words:

This Journal Belongs To :
Baltus Myrack
Year : 1878

*This is Keagan's father's journal. Would it be right to look into it without him?* After all, this is his family's secret room and information, not Lori's and mine. I gaze up at the pictures on the wall as I hold the book in my hands and notice that the engine looks strikingly familiar to...

"Aspen, come here!" Lori orders. I turn and see that Lori has uncovered a mass from under one of the tarps. I walk over, leaving my lantern on the desk and see under her light that she found a pile of old rusty machine parts and magnifying lenses of various sizes.

"These are the same parts that were used in the blueprints for the original portal machine," I say, crouching down to examine them closer.

"Then...then what are they doing here?" Lori asks meekly.

*I have a hunch,* is what I wished to say, but I'd hate to even entertain the idea. I uncover a wooden crate next to us as Lori holds the light overhead, exposing a pile of newspapers. After an insect or two scatters away, I can make out the headline that catches my eye.

August 25, 1872

**Slave trade ends in disaster after machine meltdown explosion!**

"I remember hearing about this," I say before reading aloud the article. "'The majority of the machines used for the portal transporter that creates a 'window' between our dimension and the slaves became so overused and overheated that the engine parts melted together or broke whilst the machines were in use. The outcome was a deadly blast. There were 1,578 in counting casualties and injuries of the workers in the company. This number does not include the average 2,100 men that were abandoned on the other side of the portal because of the sudden explosion that closed the gates.'"

I look at the paper under the one I picked up and see that its article reads: 'due to the heavy number of workers lost, and the machines being so highly damaged, the Slave Trade Organization was officially terminated by Parliament within a week of the explosive disaster... Search parties fail at returning the lost workers with the limited and restricted use of the remaining machines.' *Why would Mr Myrack keep these things in a secret bunker?* I feel as if the answer is right in front of me, but I wish to ignore it like it couldn't be feasible.

I walk back to the workbench, scrutinizing the sketches pinned on the wall in the dim light. I can hear Lori shuffling through papers and pulling off more tarps behind me as I try to read the Sanskrit-like text on the sketches. Unable to decipher anything, my gut decides for me that I should look further into the journal. Flipping through the pages as if someone else has possessed my body, I skim each page until I find one with a letter stuck in it. It's addressed to Mr Myrack from my papa. I open the letter without a second thought and read out:

Dear Balt,

I understand the slave trade business has been outlawed for some time, but your ideas of beginning again seem almost too far fetched. Parlament ended the organization because of the dangers that the machine would inflict on those around it and the massive amounts of energy it consumed. There was barely enough energy being made for the machines whilst they were in use to begin with. But for you I will take a look at the blueprints from Mr Adlene. Surely with his help, and our old notes from the original machine, we can figure something out.

Your Friend,
Asher Wolfe

Stumbling backwards, the note drops from my hand and hits the floor. My breathing is in tatters; I cannot believe what I just read. I grab the note and place it in the light, reading it over again carefully. This letter makes it sound as if Papa wanted to help Mr Myrack recreate the machine for the Slave Trade Organization instead of going against it like he told us. We were always taught to help and respect others, especially the dimies. *Maybe he was just using it as a ruse to actually make the machine to help the dimies instead?* I think nervously to myself. Grabbing hold of more journals from years after 1878, I shake them out over the table. Letters begin to fall from each one, creating a small pile on the table.

"Aspen, you need to see this," Lori states worriedly as she nears me.

"What's wrong?" I ask with searching eyes.

"Read this and you'll see why. Why are you so frantic?" She hands me an old book open to pages filled with numbers and accounts. I hand her the first letter I found in return.

"Read this yourself as well," I reply.

"This is Father's writing."

"It is indeed," I reply, looking through the book closely.

On the left side page I see accounts of taxes and dues for the land of the Myrack estate, bills for food, medicine, and other expenses. Nothing out of the ordinary, so I look to the right-side page and notice they are accounts of income and profit. But I can't make out from where they came from. I hold the book closer to the light, and in the section of supplier the scrawled letters come into focus: Slave Trade Organization.

I reread the letters again, and again, but they have not changed at all. I look at the other rows and see that they are almost all filled with income supplied by the Slave Trade Organization. *Now there is something that wasn't framed on the manor walls.* I flip the pages until I reach the end of the writing, and on the last entry page, I see that there are still pensions coming to the Myrack bank account as of four months ago from the organization. That was around the time Keagan's father became ill. The Myracks have been making money off of the slave trade even after Parliament stopped the collection and trafficking of the dimies. *How could we not have known? How could Father have wanted to help-*

My attention is brought back to the letters and their secrets. I quickly find one in the pile dated 1881, *the year father and I started working on Gear Heart together.* With shaky hands, I empty the envelope and read the letter. Lori's now by my side, reading it along with me.


Dear Balt,

I've stumbled upon a new prodigy inventor in my own household. My eldest daughter, Aspen, was caught red-handed fixing that damn tubing that I've been telling you about for months. My Aspen fixed it in under ten minutes, whereas I couldn't in three months.

I wish to make her my assistant permanently; however, she loves the slaves too dearly to hear that we are making this machine to bring in more. But I don't think I will finish this machine any time soon without her help. What do you propose I do, Baltus?

> Your friend,
> Asher Wolfe


*Didn't you ever wonder where your father knew how to create the machine out of thin air, and an even more advanced and safer version from the notes he had? No, you just went along with it and helped him make it because you were his stupid brilliant girl. You were so caught up in helping the dimies and spending time with Papa that you didn't see a thing, you blind fool!* I wince at the thoughts storming my mind. I can't breathe. This damn corset is too tight, this room is too dark and cramped. This is a nightmare. It has to be.

I tear through letter after letter, handing my discarded ones to Lori. Each one I read makes me want to destroy everything in this godforsaken bunker the further I read. Every word makes the pit I'm in deeper and deeper.

Aspen's working for us now, I told her it's to free the slaves. Even little Lori is wanting to help "save them". 1882

Just a few more months till the machine is ready. Start planning to talk with Parliament. 1883

She's a great asset, maybe we can convince her to make more machines after parliament gives us clearance. I'm sure She will be more willing once she sees the profit the business creates. 1884

The words begin to blur in my frenzy until I stumble upon a photograph that must have been in one of the journals as well. From the back, it reads, *Opening of Slave Trade Organization-1849*. There are names listed in order from left to right; I only recognise four, however: Louis Damon, Gregory Adlene, Baltus Myrack, and Asher Wolfe.

Turning over the picture, I see the words weren't lying either; Father and the men are holding the certificate to the organization whilst in front of a giant portal machine along with a few other men.

"Lori?" I mutter almost unintelligibly. I get the sudden

feeling that I am the only person in this dungeon of a room, and that the doors are about to be locked for good.

I turn to her, but there is only a pile of letters where I was handing them to her. I turn to see her rocking herself in place as her hands are wrapped around her head.

"Oh Lord, this can't be true. This just can't be!" Lori cries.

I can feel her anxiety that envelopes her as it begins to grab tight claws around my own lungs. Her hands rubbing her face, head, arms. She's about to have an attack. Taking a journal and stuffing it full of letters and the photograph, I turn, grabbing hold of Lori's hand and rush us back up the steps. Halfway up the stairs, we stop short as someone fills the bright opening of the exit.

Keagan holds a lantern under his face as he gazes down at us with a stricken expression. The glow that's emitted from the lantern illuminates his face in a ghastly way. Almost twisting it into that of a demon looking down upon us as our prison keeper. Maybe that's what he has always been. Maybe that's always what he's looked like, but I've been too blind and stupid to figure it out as well.

# UNMASKING

## LORI

"You knew. You knew about this the whole time, didn't you?" Aspen screams, pulling me up the steps as her voice echoes across the chamber walls.

"Yes, I knew. I admit that I knew, but I was going to tell you-"

"Was this before or after my sister lay in your bed!" I snap out suddenly, feeling fear and fury at once, interrupting Keagan.

"What else were you planning on lying about? Maybe that all the money your family earns and spends is still coming from the Slave Trade Organizations?" Aspen accuses Keagan as we back him up to the end of a couch.

Looking rather scared, he puts down the lantern and raises his hands up.

"Yes, but-"

"But what? What, were you planning on using Lori and me? And once everything is together, you'll just turn us in to the governor and police?" Aspen erupts back, throwing letters and a journal at Keagan's chest.

"No, Aspen, Lori, you know I wouldn't do that," Keagan replies pleadingly, not bothering with the damning evidence flying around him.

"Do we?" I snap as tears spill out of my eyes, I cover my mouth with a shaky hand to stifle myself.

"Keagan, we thought we knew you, but now we find you've been keeping this a secret this whole time. How long have you known?" Aspen asks. His short nervous breaths can be heard as Aspen and I wait expectantly.

"I've known where the income of the household comes from for five years, but I only found out about the fireplace bunker when Aspen stumbled upon it--I swear on my life," he replies evenly.

"Oh, I wouldn't put your life on the line right now if I were you. How could you keep it from us? It's bad enough our fathers did, and now you!" Aspen growls.

As mad as I am, I feel fearful of even sissy right now, never have I seen such anger seethe from her.


"I did it because I was afraid! I was afraid that if you knew, you may have stopped your work or chosen to leave and that you would have resented me and my family!" Keagan says, beginning to raise his voice.

"This is about both our families! Not just you and yours!" Aspen yells and silence follows suit. The ringing of nothing-ness is maddening as the air is thick with malice. Then the sound of ragged breathing catches my ears; it's Aspen. I expected pillars of fire and smoke to be coming from her mouth, but instead she's at a loss of breath. I find myself beginning to breathe again as I crouch down on the floor.

"Your father sent you to all those foreign countries not to

study abroad, but for the sake of creating allies and partners for what was left of the organization, didn't he? Not his family political business campaigns for his mill. So how can we believe that you are against it now when you've built it up so much?" Aspen goes on.

"Because it was my father who wanted it! I was a mere boy, with barely a real family and a broken home, getting sent around the world to do my father's dirty bidding!" Keagan yelled out just as loud as Aspen now. I cover my ears, but all I hear in my head is the continuation of the information and the fight. Dropping my hands from my ears and wrapping them around my sides, I hear them continue.

"He used me, just like your father used you. He exploited my ability for charm, youth, and persuasion all for his gain whilst your father used your brilliance and innocent mind just the same, *for his gain!*" Keagan yells. Pausing for a second, he walks closer to Aspen's shaking body.

"You'd put your father on a throne if you could. You loved him so much and thought the world of him. I couldn't help but feel responsible if I told you something that made you view him anything less...darling," Keagan reaches his arms out to her; the look of desperation in his eyes makes the knife in my heart plunge only deeper. Aspen quickly backs away, however, leaving Keagan at a safe distance from her.

"You both must believe me, please. I'm sorry I hid this from you. I lied, yes, but what about-"

"But what? Y-you think you can just say sorry and it'll be forgiven in an instant? The conspiracy we believed all through our years comes crashing down for us to see the wrenching lies from men we've always looked up to! You have tried to cover this up, and you think you can say sorry and expect us to just crack on?" I call out, scaring even myself from the screech in my voice. Aspen sees my distraught position and keeps her eyes on me as she speaks again.

"But what indeed? The dimies won't trust any of us if they hear about this, and Lori and I surely-"

"No, Aspen, I mean, what about you and me?" Keagan cuts her off, taking Aspen by the shoulders as he almost chokes on his words.

Aspen looks at him straight in the eye as she gives him her cold reply.

"What *about* us? You need to get it in your head that getting them home, and the machine, everything we are doing, means the world to us. When Lori and I first set our minds to do this job, we knew the costs. We knew that we could lose each other in the process, and we are all the other has now for kin as we see it. So whatever you and I had between us needs to be put aside for the sake of the mission, understand?" She brushes his hands off her shoulders in a jerking motion. By the expression of despair on his face, I can only relate to the pain he feels at that statement from the truth we found tonight.

"You took an oath. The question is, are you still with us? Are you still willing to keep that binding promise?" I manage to choke out, because it appears that Aspen is at a loss for words.

Keagan looks as if he is slowly becoming a ghost himself. "Of-of course I am," he stutters out.

"Then prove it by continuing with the plan. In a few short days New Year's Eve will be here, and that is when we send everyone back home. Prove to us you are with us by helping get everyone through safely," Aspen orders.

"I won't let you down, I-"

"*But*, if I see any signs of infidelity – if I find even a hint of loyalty to the watchmen or governor – I will personally make sure that you never get the chance to double cross us again," Aspen states in a tone that could bring a pot to boil.

Keagan goes from looking shattered to completely empty as he stands before Aspen with a sombre look on his handsome face.

"I will not fail you," he answers like a soldier about to meet his fate. He turns his fixed grim expression from Aspen to me. "Goodnight Wolfe sisters." He grumbles nodding his head as he leaves us whilst he exits the library.

I just stare at the scene before me; it feels like a splintering nightmare that has stopped to a halt. Aspen, still standing, is breathing sharply as she continues to quiver. *What did we just do? What kind of rift did that secret room just put in the plan? Is it our team? Why do I have to care at all? Why do I have to care about everything so damn much?*

"He feels really terrible." I state the obvious.

"Good," Aspen snaps.

"What if he feels betrayed?"

"Fine. Now we feel the same kind of pain for once!" she says, beginning to sway and shake harder with each step she takes as she paces, slowly.

"How do you feel then?" I ask, not even sensing the words coming from my mouth; I feel almost completely absent inside.

"Great, just great. I knew I should never have trusted him. The moment I let my guard down and allowed him to creep into my head, he turned on not only me, but you as well," she huffs out as she attempts to pick up the letters strewn across the ground. "I'm fine. This is fine...this is terrible," Aspen says as she hits her knees on the floor suddenly, tears falling from her eyes whilst she hunches over. I just watch on as if through fogged glass, seeing her pouring her heart out on the floor.

I feel as if I am living out the nightmares that still haunt us as we sleep, where neither of us can reach the other as they are being tormented in pain. Now, as my body feels paralyzed, I live out every nightmare I've had this past year. Aspen is in unquestionable anguish just out of reach, and all I can do is sit, watching through drunk eyes whilst the demons in my head make the world too loud yet again.

# NEW PLAN

## KEAGAN

"Where is Charles?"

"He fell asleep an hour ago, I found him wrapped around an empty bottle of sherry. I swear, I am tempted to ban that wine from this house if we can't behave with it!" Winona exclaims.

Thatcher chuckles at this, which brings a smile to Winona's face and a headache to my cranium. It's bad enough that the homecoming plan is a day away, but now there is an emergency change of plans tonight at the witching hour.

"We can do this without him; we will be fine. There isn't anything important that he will need to know about this change anyhow," Aspen decides.

"So besides Charles, are we all here?" Lori asks. We look around the room as Lori calls names. Thomas, Aspen, Winona, Thatcher, Lori herself, and me. We are all here.

"Good. Tomorrow, Thatcher and Winona, can you please relay this new plan to the rest of the dimies?" Aspen asks.

"We would be delighted," Thatcher says.

Aspen nods her head in satisfaction before continuing.

"Now at first, as you know, we were going to have two teams of dimies and humans sneak to the warehouse in different intervals. But now we found out the governor is hosting the New Year's Eve festival and giving a speech before midnight. Hence, the guards will be sparse throughout the town and placed thickly in the crowd and near the governor for said festival, which will take place here at the city capitol," Aspen explains, pointing to the location of City Hall Square on the map we've laid on the table.

"But to keep an eye on the governor and keep track of the amount of bots or policemen that are present, our group will be split up into two teams. One will take the dimies to the warehouse and home whilst the other acts as lookouts," Lori adds.

"Thomas and Lori will now be our lookouts. You two will have the radio communicators that Thomas and I have recently perfected. He can show you how they work, Lori. We need you to tell us if the governor leaves, if there's any suspicious activity, or if any constables are coming our way. You two should be positioned...here, as best you can," Aspen explains, circling an area of flats near City Hall Square.

"And where shall I be?" I ask, trying to sound innocent.

"You will be with me and act as the doorkeeper to make sure the dimies who aren't a part of the group at the house can go home as well," Aspen responds curtly, not even looking up from the map. Now I'm very annoyed, I won't take this sitting down.

"Well, I can tell you don't trust me now, so why not make me look out for the governor? I'll be out of your hair and out of your way then," I say, beginning to sound peeved.

"If there is anyone that I don't trust in our group, I want

them by my side so I can snuff them out if needed. That is why you will be with me, whilst Lori and Thomas will be the governor's lookouts," Aspen says flatly.

She has been keeping me at arm's length ever since the fireplace-room visit. Our conversations have been short and to the very jagged point. Not to mention she has completely moved her workspace back into her room. Even during our run last night, she kept Lori and herself a few feet away as often as she could, but at least we got the flyers for the home-coming day out for the dimies.

*There's no way that it will be kept a secret amongst the dimies now after our little swing through the entire city*, I think back to when we ziplined through each sector of town that one night, drop-ping papers everywhere. "All right now, we have already sent out the message of homecoming to the dimies in the city - thank you, Thatcher and Winona, for coding them," Aspen says with a pause for recognition.

"Since most everyone will be distracted by the festivities of the celebration in the town square, the dimies will get the chance to escape from their masters' homes and help each other get to the rendezvous point here." Aspen points to the warehouses next to the bay.

"What if someone sees us and follows?" Thomas asks.

"We've thought of that, for example...the papers tell about the general location that the dimies should go, whilst Thatcher and a few other dimies will be posted on the edges of the buildings in a square near the warehouse. They have proven that they know a majority of the dimies in the city, which is why they are the designated guides. They weed out the ones we can't trust by directing them the wrong way, in case they have a tail trailing them, whilst the ones who aren't being followed and the ones who would truly wish to go home are sent to the warehouse," Winona explains.

"Everyone here, even you, will be equipped with the necessities: sleeping darts, smoke and flash grenades, and a brass-knuckle electrocutor for a last resort," Lori explains, laying each weapon down on the table.

"Now team A, that's Keagan's and my team, will be arriving at the warehouse pretty late since the fireworks go off at midnight and the governor's speech will commence around eleven forty-five. That gives us a fifteen-minute gap in time to get from the Blu Man's Cliff tunnel and all the way down to the wharf. Lori and Thomas will split up from us after Blu Man's tunnel and contact us before the speech begins, if they are in a safe enough location," Aspen explains.

"And once we give team A at the warehouse the clearance that everything is fine, we will let you know when the fireworks begin. Then it's bon voyage and welcome home for the dimies," Lori adds.

Everyone agrees that the plan is sound enough, and we end the meeting for the night. As everyone leaves for bed, I stay behind to help Aspen clean up. I start taking the paper weights off the map and roll the paper up. Turning off the lamp, I turn to hand the map to her. When she sees this, she quickly snatches it without even a glance in my direction. I can still feel her anger even when she looks anywhere but at me.

"Aspen, please, don't act this way. I know I messed up terribly, but what happens after all of this, anyway? What will it take for you to forgive me?" I ask, half angry, half pleadingly.

"After *all this*, Lori and I will be taking our leave to London or Wales. You can live out the rest of your days doing what you do best: running alone," she says with a voice like frost itself.

"You don't wish me to come along then?"

"No, I think it'd be best if you didn't come with us. Besides, if you come with us what would the town think? What would the governor think right after the dimies leave then see that you and the entire household does as well?" Though there is truth in her answer, I can tell that it's mainly because she still doesn't trust me.

"You know, you could improve in candour as well, love," I say accusingly, walking to face her. "The sapphire that Lori accidentally stole, that we now have to pay an orphan for, the little secret that you both carry weapons on you even during a leisurely walk and know damn well how to use them, the fact that you set up an unauthorized trip-alarm system for your room." I fire at her, causing her eyebrows to raise high at the last secret of hers. "Didn't think I knew about that one, did you? And how about the juiciest one of all? The fact that you and your sister are renegades stealing away dimies in the night to bring back home with an illegally made machine," I say, feeling the heat on my own face increase a bit.

"Yes, I'm not the most honest person, believe me, I know. But what about the fact that you hid a secret not only concerning your deceased father, but mine as well? Everything we were raised to believe were lies themselves. Both of us and everyone else under this roof are living off an inheritance gained from what we are rebelling against. We are hypocrites on our own part, and you lied about that. Yet the worst part was that you knew! You knew the entire time and never told us, whilst allowing me to get close to you!" she accuses me, raising her voice as she counts on her fingers the crimes committed against her.

"At least my sister's and my wrongdoings were for a noble purpose. You seemed to hide this from us so we would still like you. You were selfish since you wanted us to stay for your benefit rather than enlighten us of the situation. So what, now you want me to say that we are even or something?" she asks with a flip of her hand.

"I want us to forgive each other and put the past behind us, Aspen. I don't want to be mad at you, and I can't stand for you to be mad at me for this long. I forgave you when I found out about all your secrets and kept moving forward. I wish you'd do the same," I plead.

"Well, excuse me for not being quick to forgive about this bomb of a secret. And by the way, if I were truly mad at you, and completely distrusted you, I wouldn't let you be a part of the homecoming mission. I would have tied you up in a secret passage instead." She points her finger at my chest angrily before taking a long sigh.

"Lori's and my faith in you is minimal after it was shattered that night. It'll be a long time or take something huge to make us rely on you as we once did. So just drop the whole thing; it won't matter for much longer anyhow." She then hastily grabs the remainder of her supplies and promptly leaves the room.

I watch her leave and can't help but feel even worse than before. I really ruined everything that we had with just one secret. One huge, damn, crushing secret that I failed to tell them when I had the chance. *What could have changed if I did tell them? Would they have trusted me more? Would they have even wanted to stay if they knew? Dammit!* I think, pacing to the roaring fire.

*Probably not, I wish I had burned every last shred of parchment in that bunker when I found it, then things would still be together. And I* could still be on good terms as we were. If only you could throw a piece of our life to the flames and rewrite it ourself, but humans are not so lucky or powerful as that. Not even a machine like Gear Heart could change the past once it is written. Now I must live with mine and what I have done to it, despite how much I regret it.

# PIECES COMING TOGETHER

## LORI

After our final celebratory dinner of being all together for one last time, we prepare for our homecoming mission. Once we do a headcount for the whole house, we get everyone together and sweep the manor from top to bottom to make sure nothing of theirs was left behind. At ten o'clock that evening we are ready to go. Practically everyone in town will be in the main City Square for the New Year's Eve celebration.

"Is everyone ready?" I ask from halfway up the stairs to gain a better look at everyone.

"Yes!" our large group of guests replies.

"Do we have Gear Heart, my toolbox, and the generator?" Aspen asks.

"Yes, and before you ask again, yes, we have the radio communicators," I respond.

"See?" Thomas talks into the microphone, making his voice echo out of the one Keagan is carrying on his back. Keagan chuckles, and I glare at him until he becomes silent again.

"All right, everyone, here's what's going to happen. We will take the secret tunnels in the woods to get into town, and from there, we will head to the rendezvous point as quickly and quietly as possible. Help each other, but don't be seen; keep your eyes out for the police and dimie bots as well as your fellow dimies. We are going into enemy territory, and it will be dangerous. Everyone has to work together for this to go smoothly. Remember that tonight is for you. I would also like to apologize for the delay. This night was originally supposed to be your Christmas Eve surprise; however, here we are now. What better way to begin a new year than back home and unrestrained." Aspen explains, stopping for a moment as her expression goes from serious to one of sympathy and longing.

"New Year's Eve will mark the beginning of your freedom, and that is why today is so important. I think I speak for everyone living here when I say that...we love you, respect you, and wish you the best in life. And well...we hope you will remember that not all humans were horrible people," Aspen adds. And if I'm not mistaken, I catch sight of a tear fighting to escape her eyes as she looks out at the crowd.

*This isn't for Papa anymore; this isn't even for us. It's for them. Maybe it always has been. Maybe we were always selfish and foolish in our minds to want this because we believed it's what our papa would have wanted.* I look around at their faces: Sonja, Lilith, Lucy and her brother Nox, Thatcher, Winona, and every dimie we've helped pull free... they look touched but still a little scared. I feel the same way.

Before I get too emotional, I pull up my mask as Aspen begins the way to the study to the secret bookcase tunnel. Charles opens the bookcase and ushers us in with a rather eager look on his face. I have a feeling that he's more excited to get the dimies out of the house than to be sending them home. I guess he has gotten a little sick of tending to such a large household after years of caring for a small quiet one.

I can tell Aspen is experiencing that chronic pain in her arm as she rubs it on our descent to the end of the tunnel. Once we make it to the end, we split up into teams of three as planned. After making quick dashes from thickets to thick snow-covered trees, I send out a prayer of thanks for the foggy night in the hills. The thin crescent moon rests low on the horizon in the rich colours of fire as we make it to Blu Man's Cliff. We climb the rocks leading to the old mine shafts that take us straight down to the poor districts below and the now-abandoned Market. Once we are at the edge of town, Thomas and I separate from team A, and head off to find a good perch near the courthouse square. I wave to Aspen and the rest of our family as we turn a corner. Sissy and a handful of dimies wave back before we lose sight of each other. I'm a bundle of nerves, I feel the urge to stay by Aspen's side growing the farther away we run from her.

The city is illuminated like the stars themselves tonight: bright, abundant, and full of life. *I'm glad that my part of the mission is close to the excitement of the party. I bet Thomas and I will even see the fireworks go off,* I think to myself, trying to put my mind to happier matters. As we near the first building, we get our grappling hooks ready. We shoot out just as a pair of people round the corner, two armed policemen who see us swinging head-on above them. Planting my feet firmly on the wall, I shoot two darts just in time to catch the men raising their pistols to us. The men drop like flies a second after the darts penetrate their skin.

"Nice shot," Thomas says as we climb over to the rooftop.

"Thanks," I say, ruffling his head and messing up his cap.

"Hey!" he whines, readjusting his hat back.

"C'mon, let's get going. We have to beat team A by getting to our point first," I say, bouncing off a bit until he runs along with me. Thank the Lord we taught him how to shoot and use the grappling hook, because there is no time to waste now.

As we fly from one building to the next, we watch the party below right in the thick of it. The farther we go into the city, the greater the crowds of people become – some dancing, others drinking with a pal and a pint. Everyone seems to be singing and cheering no matter where we go. As much as I'd love to be noticed and invited in for the celebration, I'm relieved that they are too consumed in themselves to notice the two dark figures bounding across the buildings above.

The clock atop the tall domed city hall reads eleven thirty-five as we arrive at the roof of a four-storey hotel. *This should serve us nicely as a lookout point.* Hidden away by plenty of chimney spires and close enough to other buildings of similar height, we can stay safely hidden up here. I look out to the party below and witness the most tightly packed dance area I have ever seen. Whilst the City Square is packed to the brim with dancing couples, the sides are filled with policemen and common folk eating and drinking together in the pubs and restaurants. If they aren't drinking or dancing they are playing a game of cards, whilst the children run and dance or play vanishing jacks.

My mind goes back to the days Aspen and I used to play games like that as Thomas and I get situated on our perch. Sissy and I loved vanishing jacks – it was so stressful at times though. I remember how frustrated I got when my little hands couldn't pick up all the jacks before the bouncy ball hit the ground again, activating the disappearing mechanism in the jacks. I recall the day the jacks weren't able to reappear again after I stomped angrily on the ball. I can still recall the cry of pain as our papa found the last jack we couldn't find, with his bare foot. *Ah, memories.*

I remember how sissy and I used to try our best to stay up late on New Year's Eve. We never could make it to midnight until we were teenagers. It's hard to imagine how many nights we stay up now, and so far past midnight at that. *Who would have guessed?* I think as I move the dial to tune into team A's communicator. With no luck, I shift it back to Thomas who tunes in with Keagan's radio in half a second; the light turns from red to blue, showing that we are connected. Picking up the microphone attachment, I clear my voice and prepare to speak upon seeing the light turn green.

"Hello down there. Can anyone hear me?"

"Aye, Lori, we hear you clear as a bell," I hear Winona's voice speak through the headset attachment. Thomas was so smart to think of that attachment since we want to avoid people hearing us as much as possible. Sadly for Keagan though, he will be needing a new telephone in the tea room since we had to use parts from it for the headset.

I give the thumbs-up to Thomas, handing him the microphone whilst putting the headset between our ears.

"How are things down there?" Thomas asks, as the roar of the festivities continues on.

"Everything is going smoothly on our side. You should see how many of my people are here – they even helped each other break out of chains just to get here. It looks like the entire city's worth of dimies managed to come. How are things on your side?" Winona exclaims over the sound of a large crowd around her.

"We have the perfect view of the podium where the governor will be speaking in a few minutes. Nothing is out of the ordinary and we are safely hidden," Thomas replies.

"Wonderful. We are standing by if something changes," Winona replies.

"You'll be the first to know," I say before placing the mic piece back in its slot on the side of the radio box. The light-bulb turns from green to blue as the connection clicks off.

We decide to make ourselves comfortable by resting our backs on a chimney spire, I busy myself looking through the crowd with the adjusting binocular goggles. How I wish I could be dancing the night away with a gentleman, having my first pint, maybe stealing a kiss or two in the heat of the crowd. Perhaps at another ball or New Year's Eve, someday. I take my goggles off; I don't want to depress or distract myself with daydreams when today is too important to lose sight of our target. I turn to Thomas, who is looking out curiously around one of the chimneys, appearing to enjoy the festivities from a distance as well.

"Hey Thomas?"

"Yes, Lori?" he replies, facing me again.

"What was New Year's Eve like for you? You know, before we came along?"

Thomas sits down in the rough gravel of the roof, thinking hard. "They were always a surprise."

"How so?" I press on. That's not usually the response you get from people about a holiday they know is coming.

"Well, my grandpa always made them feel special, like a surprise. He was interested in pyrotechnics and combining them with gadgets. He always made something special each year for the whole street to enjoy during the celebration. Each time we would be gobsmacked," he explains enthusiastically with stars in his eyes.

Turning to me, he gestures with his hands as he describes every detail. There is so much happy energy pouring out of him I almost forget why we are up here on this drafty roof.

"I remember one year when he invented these wind-up fairies and dragons that could actually fly with their beating wings and shoot out tiny sparks until they fluttered to the ground. Every shop owner on the street was given a toy. We all headed to the snow banks at the edge of town so we didn't catch any buildings on fire. We waited until the city fireworks went off. Then we wound them up until they were all flying with sparks coming from everywhere. That's one of my favourite memories; I've even been able to keep both toys. The other years grandpa always had the toys explode as part of the show."

"That sounds absolutely amazing... Wait, you mean you still have yours with you even now?" I ask, confused at what he means.

"I do actually. A wing had fallen off the fairy and I didnt want Grandpa to see it broken. So late one night, as I was finishing fixing it, that's when I heard you and the others in the alleyway. I had it in my pocket when you rushed me out of the shop. I'll show it to you when we get home."

I just stare at this boy with a smile before speaking again.

"Oh, Thomas, I know Gerald would've been proud of how you are spending this New Year's Eve. I could never imagine something like you described. It takes a real genius to create something like that," I say, meaning every word of it.

Thomas turns to me with the biggest smile I think I have ever seen on a child.

"He's here! Quiet! The governor is here!" someone in the crowd calls out just before an applause erupts. Our attention is turned back to the real reason we came here. I scramble to put on my goggles again whilst Thomas mans the radio. I look to find where the podium is, and I find Governor Damon walking with his guards' backs to us. He turns towards the crowd, and that's when I see his face. It looks like him, but something doesn't seem right. Waving to the crowd, he gives a big smile. There's something odd about that smile. I adjust the lens to zoom in closer on the governor and notice that it's a full smile. Not slanted like I saw during our dance in the ballroom, and the hairs on his head are almost all grey and slightly balding in the back of his skull. He had a full head of evenly peppered hair the night of the dance.

When he opens his mouth to speak, I hear there is a different tone in his voice; it's much higher than it should be. *That is not the governor. From far away, he could easily pass off for Louis Damon, but close up, with my binocular goggles, I can tell it's an imposter. Something is up I can tell, and it does not sit well with me.*

Frantically taking the mic and headset from Thomas, I hand him the goggles whilst he looks at me worriedly as I try to contact Aspen.

"Aspen, Winona, anybody listening? Something is wrong, the governor has a decoy. I repeat, there is someone taking his place."

"Some of the guards are beginning to leave, too, towards the docks," Thomas whispers hoarsely.

"And there are guards coming your way, Aspen-" I'm cut off by the sounds of screaming.

"You've betrayed us! It's a trap!" I can faintly hear coming from the speaker.

"Aspen, what's going on?" I demand, my voice returning to

a normal volume; I don't care if anyone hears us up here now--this is a life-or-death situation.

"Listen!" I hear my sister scream. I do listen, but what I hear makes me feel like I'm made of brittle twigs about to snap.

# THE REAL COWARDS

## ASPEN

"All right, everyone, get in quickly and head to the centre!" Keagan says, standing watch outside the warehouse with the sleeping-dart gun at the ready. I herd everyone into the centre of the room. Once I get there myself, I climb on top of the original machine and put down the radio communicator. Pulling out my pocket watch, I see that it's eleven thirty-eight; we are right on time, and now I can quickly disassemble the large lens to work for mine.

"A little help," Winona calls up.

I turn and see her green outstretched paw reaching for a hand and she tries to climb atop the machine. As I'm pulling her up onto the massive portal generator, I look around and see that there are hundreds of dimies that have come here today for the homecoming; all of them pooling into the warehouse with eager and scared expressions of what awaits them.

It's good Winona is by my side, so everyone will feel a little more at ease knowing one of their kind supports this plan and helped make it happen. I work fast, knowing that the festivities at the courthouse square will begin soon, or maybe they already have. All that noise will serve us as the perfect cover to allow the dimies to escape without detection.

"Lori and Thomas should have made it to a lookout point by now. Winona, can you try to call them to make sure everything on their side is fine?" I ask Winona, still holding her paw as I pass the radio communicator to her.

"Aye aye, Captain," Winona says with a determined look in her eye as she takes it.

"Lori, Thomas, can you hear me?" she says, powering and tuning the radio just like I showed her this morning. I get back to detaching the lens and its overly rusty bolts. *Stubborn things, I'll have to oil them. I hope I remembered to bring a can in my bag.*

"Hello down there. Can anyone hear me?" I hear Lori through the speaker. I take a sigh of relief at the sound of my sister's voice. *Everything is running smoothly, though I can't say the same for these bolts.* Fed up with them, I take a mallet out of my toolbox and secure the wrench tightly on the tough bolt before giving it a powerful whack. A sharp screech rings out, but the bolt is loose and the others are soon undone with a little oil. It takes twenty more minutes to situate the lens perfectly along with Gear Heart and the connector I created to attach the lenses so the machines stick together despite the vibrations emitted.

I glance over and watch Keagan keep an eye out the doors when Thatcher, Sonja, Eli, and Jasper make their way in after ten more minutes. He's being generous today, giving the dimies a chance to make the meeting after the cut-off time for departure.

After waiting a few more minutes, he closes and locks the doors and makes his way through the crowd to meet Winona and me up on the old portal machine. Once Keagan's on the platform, I give him the thumbs up to gather everyone's attention for the safety procedures before the send-off. Keagan faces the crowd and cups his hands, but the voice that comes out is not his own.

"Hello-"

All of a sudden, I hear a few dimies begin to scream, causing many others to follow, pointing upward. When the three of us on the platform look up to see what the trouble is, I immediately feel a large cracking sensation in my chest followed by the sinking of my heart.

"Hello Mr Myrack, Miss Wolfe, and fellow rebel slaves."

We stare in horror at Governor Damon accompanied by his dimie Gertrude that we saved in the alley and our own Charles. They stare down at us like cats stalking cornered mice.

"So glad you could stop by," Charles says with a wickedly curled smile, exposing a few of his blackened dead teeth.

"It's a trap!" a dimie yells out.

"You lied to us," another accuses us.

"You lured us to our doom!"

"No!" I scream out, trying to gain them back to our side. We could still fight them off and make it out of this with our numbers. But my efforts and thoughts get blown away by the sound of clicking triggers on guns. The governor's policemen and robots begin to come out of the woodwork as they appear on the over-rail bridges, the floor, in the old wooden crates, with all gun barrels pointing to us and the dimies.

"One wrong move and it'll be a massacre. Now you wouldn't want that, would you, Miss Ringleader," Charles calls down mockingly to me. I see red as I turn to tear Keagan apart. He looks my way as I pull out my knife. I begin to raise my arm when one of the officers decks his jaw whilst another plunges an electric stick in his side, causing him to cry out in agony. My eyes widen in shock at the scene before me. In a matter of seconds, I'm on the ground, enveloped in volts of pain unlike any I've felt before, causing me to scream my head off.

"Aspen, what's going on?" I can hear Lori's voice call out through our radio when the torture stops momentarily and the men begin to pick us up. *Please, God, don't let them hear her!*

"Listen!" I scream out. I glance in Keagan's and the radio's direction to see the radio has been turned on its side from the scuffle, but the microphone is out of its slot and the light glows green. *They can hear us!*

The men don't stop working or talking, but Lori does; I know she and Thomas can hear everything that's going on. A robot comes to hold my wrists in handcuffs with one arm whilst his other projects out razor-blade fingers near my throat.

"You say that you'll slaughter us, but would you truly waste the only dimies left in the city like that?" I rally.

"Well, if your machine that you so kindly brought out for us really does work as I've been told, then what do they matter? They can be used as our first shipment of pelts," the governor points out smugly. *Dammit, he knows! Hang it all!*

"You know, as of a few days ago, I would have never guessed that you were the phantoms at night sending out those obscene coded papers," Damon announces before gesturing to Gertrude and Charles.

"We only decided to tell the governor about the plan three days ago. Gertrude and I had been sending letters to each other through your clothes and pockets. They were intercepted in the street, parties, and face to face. You never suspected a thing," Charles explains.

"Gertrude, you can't be serious?" Winona questions, looking straight at the yellow monkey-like dimie with her toothy smile.

"You know, I never much cared for you, Winona. you were always too close to the Myracks. Almost like they were your family," Gertrude sneers at Winona instead of answering the question.

"They *are* my family!" Winona cries back proudly before a guard slaps her to silence.

"HEY!" Keagan and Thatcher shout in unison, and the governor raises a hand.

"Let them speak freely; they won't have many chances after this anyhow," Damon announces.

"No, no, Winona. They stole you and me, as well as the rest of us, away from our real families! And if being here makes you finally see that, then I'm in the perfect position to watch you figure it out," Gertrude snaps, slamming her yellow paws on the metal railing.

"So what's in it for you then?" I question her.

"Why, I thought you were smart enough to piece that one together by now. Power, of course. You didn't save me the night I spilled the tray of wine, so I'm saving myself. You never took me to live at the Myrack manor like the rest of these sorry slaves. However, now that I've proven my loyalty to my master, he treats me kindly, never could have done it without all your work, though," Gertrude explains smugly.

"And you're actually willing to sacrifice your own people for this? You said it yourself that humans aren't your family," Keagan counters back.

"Why would you side with Damon? Don't you want to go home?" I add indignantly, to which the trio of scum above us begins to laugh heartily.

"You-you really think that just sending them back would be the best course of action?" Charles chuckles out as Governor Damon makes his way down the stairs and walks towards us.

"He's right, you know, there is no place these slaves can hide where I will not find them again," Damon gloats as he climbs atop the machine he originally helped make decades ago. Strolling nonchalantly over to me, he cups my chin in a grip so tight I fear it'll bruise me.

"You know perfectly well what the penalty is for stealing slaves, and at this scale, it's not going to be pretty for you or your group. But don't lose heart, you won't die just yet. Not before you watch a special show on our ship to London tonight," he says with a gamey half smile. "Now hold on, I just realised we are missing someone. Where's your lovely little sister, Miss Wolfe?" The governor smiles curiously, putting the image of a snake in my mind as he releases my chin.

"Sir, the younger Miss Wolfe was not found throughout the building or its perimetre," a watchman on the ground says, saluting Damon. I remember then that Charles didn't find out the change of plans last night. Originally, Lori was supposed to be here with me today instead of the courthouse square; I have to make it so they still believe that.

"What?" I breathe out, trying my best to sound shocked.

Damon slowly turns back to me with a look of loss in his eyes. "Looks like your sister was wise enough to get out when she could. It's quite apparent now that your plan was doomed to fail from the beginning, eh?" Charles says, making his way down the ladder with Gertrude behind him.

"Captain, go ready the freight ship for departure. We will be sailing for London as planned. I have a meeting with the queen and Parliament for the showing of a new and improved multi-dimensional transporter machine. And you Miss Aspen Wolfe will help in showing Her Majesty," Damon orders out in a gloating manner.

"May we have a last request?" I plead through my watery eyes.

"Depends, what is it?" Damon asks flatly as I see the dimies being shackled right behind him all with mixed emotion on their faces. Fear, anxiety, hatred, mostly directed at me and my group.

"Please, as our last wish, let us gaze at the lighthouse one last time as we sail away. It has special significance to us," I plead. *If Lori doesn't get that hint, I'll haunt her as a ghost forever, I swear!*

"Oh, of course I can allow that." He smiles before continuing. "Now's my turn to take back what I've lost." Damon's half smile diminishes and a small twitch creeps along his mouth. Where loss shone once before is now replaced by a dark madness in his grey eyes.

# TO THE SHIPS

## KEAGAN

The fireworks have begun as we are taken to the freight ship the governor was talking about. Each time an explosion goes off, it illuminates the ship, showing the cargo and supplies already on its deck being taken below. Damon truly was ready for us, and Aspen's machine. I remember how my blood boiled as they frisked Aspen, Winona, and me for weapons. As we pass the end of the warehouse, we see the men putting Aspen's Gear Heart, tools, weapons, radio, and even her father's journal into a trunk for the journey.

As we walk in the back of the group, we see the long line of shackled dimies lined up to the freight ship. I remember the constable's orders on how we were to be kept separated from the dimies so no one does anything rash whilst we all walk in our chains to the ship. However, we are still close enough to see their woebegone faces as the colours dance off them from the fireworks. What a turn of events for such a celebratory day to now become one of sorrows. I know this isn't the first time some of the dimies have been carried off in chains; many are used to it by now living in strict households. It still repulses me each time I see it though.

"What a glorious new year this will be; if only my Octavia could be here to enjoy this," Damon says, watching the fireworks as we are led across the deck to the galley, deeper into the ship.

"Keagan, what happened to the governor's wife?" Aspen whispers to me as we walk past the thick-barred cages that they prepared for the dimies.

"Lady Octavia? I believe she died during childbirth. The babe didn't make it either. My mother was a good friend of hers; yours, too, apparently. It was about fourteen years ago, I think, a few years before our mothers passed away," I say, just before we are shoved into our individual barred cages that are far away from the dimies as well as each other.

"So I take it that Sir Damon doesn't like to fail then, after losing everything but his title?" Aspen deduces as the guards lock our cages.

"That's an understatement, and he nearly did lose his title after losing everything else."

"Now he is obsessed with success. Look at that, I can relate to him," Aspen muses sombrely.

"Oi, enough chattering for the both of ya!" a watchman guard yells at us after banging his baton against our cell bars.

We remain silent for a long while as the guards fill the remaining cages with the other dimies. From where my cage is, I can just make out where Winona and Thatcher are. Her head rests on his shoulder as he rubs her arm in an embrace. For the first time, I don't mind Thatcher showing her affection. I'm glad she has someone like him to be there for her when I can't be.

Every now and then, I catch a glimpse of Aspen gripping and rubbing her hands along her legs and arms, whether she's trying to find a leftover weapon or skeleton key, or she is nervous, I know not. I ease my way down to the ground like Aspen already has, though I still feel the burning sensation in my side from that lightning stick. I can't even touch it without searing pain coursing up my spine. Finally leaving it be, I rest my back on the cold bars so I can watch when the guards come and go, until I see a familiar figure coming towards us. Much to my chagrin it's not someone I wish to be near without a sword or gun in my hand.

"What a show you all offered today! Truly, it was quite entertaining," Charles says as he chews on a bite of a pear he's holding.

"You know, Aspen, you and little Lori would always go on about how saving the slaves and returning them home was your wish. To me it seems like the only reason you wanted to free them was to appease your dear papa's dying wish. It's almost a shame you didn't know that his dying wish was to actually get more of them into our world for the slave trade. You still made it possible; you both should be so proud," he sneers at us with a condescending tone.

Aspen just sits in her cage with her fists clenched, head down, refusing to look at Charles.

"Bug off," I say, unamused.

"Hmph, you know, maybe it wasn't for your father after all. Could it be that the both of you wished to feel as if your family were less broken?" he goes on, ignoring me.

"I said shut up, you clod," I snap as I force myself up and shake the bars.

"Less torn."

My knuckles are white now as I grip the metal so tight I feel I could bend the bars apart.

"Less of a disgrace from how I've daily witnessed the way you women compose yourselves. Hardly fit to be real ladies."

"That's enough!" I yell, not able to contain my anger any longer.

Charles looks at me stupidly, opening his mouth to speak, but instead we hear a laugh, and a loud one at that, coming from Aspen. A ferocious smile paints her face as she snaps back at Charles, which wipes that smug idiotic grin of his away.

"You're right. You're right, okay! We are broken, and uncouth, and come from an upside down family. But I'm proud of it! I'm proud to be unruly and upside down, wishing for the freedom of others and myself." She begins to rise again, coming to meet his face at the bars. "I'd much rather be this way; otherwise, I'd be just like you: spineless, lacking empathy, and full of so much greed and hate that you can't see how blind you really are!" she bellows out accusingly.

Charles just stares at her in shock at her audacity, as do I. I notice the upcurve of Charles's mouth before Aspen does.

"Aspen-" I try to warn her, but I'm too late.

He spits his mouthful of pear in her face, making her reel back and frantically wipe it off. A low growl emits from my throat at this action.

Charles throws his head back, laughing, backing away from her cage towards mine whilst his attention is on Aspen as he points at her.

*Just close enough.* I reach through the bars and manage to grab hold of the snake by his lapel and pull him right into the metal with a bang. Once he's there, I wind back my arm and nail my fist into that shocked face of his. He goes spiraling to the ground, clutching his nose and mouth that are soon dripping blood. He takes one look at me to see me glaring back at him through the bars.

I hear the guards yell out as their footfalls approach the scene. When they get close enough, I realise that I recognise a policeman all too well. Nickolas Finley, traitorous so-called friend that was part of the police force the day we aided the dimie Jasper in the alley. He stares straight at me through the bars, with a poker face.

"You should know better than to pull a stunt like that," Nickolas says to me grimly.

I just glare back at him.

"I could say the same about you," I murmur dejectedly.

The ship begins to rock up and down more than earlier; we must be getting near the middle of the harbour.

"Finley, subdue Myrack. We have to help Mr Morris here get to the deck," Nick's captain orders as they carry away the piece of rubbish.

"Don't worry about that," he replies, plunging an electric shock stick through the bars right next to my face, missing me by inches. Once turned on, it emits the loud sparking sounds of electrical currents. I figure out his ploy, and I begin to scream in pain to play along. He takes a quick look around, as if my cries were too loud, and throws something into my cage in the blink of an eye. He turns the electric rod off and pulls it out of the cell. I fall to the ground towards what he threw in and see that it's a small key. I look back to catch him giving me a quick nod before walking off to the other cages. Looks like he remained a friend after all, even if it might be for the last time.

I quickly hide the key on me and turn back to Aspen who sits in the centre of her cage, hunched over, taking her hands away from her ears, appearing completely despondent.

"Aspen."

"Please" she sniffed "No more talking," Aspen murmurs, her voice breaking with each word. *If only I could reach you, I'd hold you tight, do anything to make you feel the slightest bit better.* I stare at the ground through the bars that separate us; it's as filthy as all get out. I run a finger through the grime, and it leaves a clean line.

"All right, no talking, but please look over here, just for a second. Please, Aspen." I say as I write out the word towards her. Slowly, she turns her head and stares at where my hand points on the ground. K.E.Y.

She looks up at me now with questioning eyes, I point to my chest and her eyes widen in a small flicker of joy. It doesn't last long, however, as we both hear the sound of boots stomping our way. I smudge away the word quickly and wait where I sit for them to pass by as they have been doing for the past hour. However, two sets of four policemen stop at our cages and begin to unlock them.

"What's this?" I groan curiously, pretending I'm still in pain.

"Governor wants you on the main deck; say's it's your last request," a policeman says, coming in and pulling me up forcefully by the chained shackles around my wrists.

Once on the main deck, we see everything is illuminated brightly by gas lamps and spotlights. Walking farther across the planks, we soon find the governor sitting near the railing, on a bench, staring off into the horizon that mixes with the indigo sea. I look in the same direction but fail to see what he is watching due to a pile of crates.

"Sir, we brought the prisoners as you requested," the leading guard that brought us announces, gaining Damon's attention.

"Splendid, thank you, Officers. Now, my honoured guests, if you two will take your seats, we can begin the show," Governor Damon chirps as he rises and gestures to the bench he was resting on.

"What's this show about exactly?" Aspen asks sceptically as we are pushed forward to the bench.

"Look there." He points to the right in the distance. The lighthouse. It's lit with its spinning spotlights for passing ships.

"Now you two can watch your friends die as we sail past your precious lighthouse. If only your fathers could be here to see all you have done to make our job easier." Damon smiles before walking off to the line of officers manning their guns.

# THE LIGHTHOUSE

## LORI

Dashing over rooftops as fast as our legs can go, we make our way to the warehouse. *I just hope we aren't too late. I wonder if we made a mistake by leaving the radio communicator back three blocks? It doesn't matter right now though; it was only slowing us down anyhow.*

I recognize this area from the first time I was here the night of Keagan's first run with us. If Aspen wants us to do what I think she was trying to tell us on the radio, then our only chance of success is by getting Gear Heart back somehow.

"Thomas, wait, the warehouse is to the right. Hurry!" Jumping to the next rooftop, I make a quick turn around the corner of a chimney and nearly push two armed policemen off the roof. I turn in a flash, catching Thomas, and quickly covering his mouth, I pull the both of us back behind the chimney corner we just rounded. I back us away one more chimney's length from the men and sit us down out of their line of sight. Breathing heavily, I watch the steam billow out of my mouth as I try to think fast. I peek around the corner using my compact mirror and see that there are gunmen on our roof and atop the warehouses. *They must be there to take out anyone who may try to run off.* Peering farther off beyond the gunmen, I can make out a long line of something on the ground. It's dimies walking in chains around the warehouse corner to the docks.

*What would Aspen do in a situation like this? Probably just knock them out; but there are too many guards on the ground. They would no doubt see or hear the struggle since we are right above them.* I fumble through my pockets for what weapons I might have, and out of the corner of my eye, I see Thomas doing the same. We dump out our pockets in a small pile of snow so we won't make a sound. Six sleeping darts, two brass-knuckle electrocutors, three grappling hooks, twelve grenades (four of each type), and my compact that contains pins for opening locks. I think hard at what possibilities we might have and Thomas writes out options on his notepad. After a few minutes of comparing ideas, the craziest one yet pops into my mind.

After running it by Thomas, he agrees that it sounds like it may actually work. There are no other feasible plans I can think of clearly since we are losing valuable time. Every second we don't act means my sister and everyone else we care about is being taken away or worse. I take a deep breath, and as I exhale, I aim and shoot the four men on the warehouse roof; at the same time, Thomas knocks out the remaining two on our roof, all with sleeping darts. Jumping to our feet to catch their guns and limp bodies, Thomas lays one down as best he can, and I take the other behind the chimney wall. Thomas strips the man of his coat and trousers as I look away in modesty. I couldn't bear to strip an unconscious man even with our stakes as high as they are. As I don the officer's clothes and pistol, Thomas takes the other officer's coat and puts it on the now-trouserless officer.

"Lori, I see where they were putting Gear Heart," Thomas says, running around the corner.

"Pray, tell me!" I say, following him to the edge of the roof.

"The trunk; look, those two guards are locking it up." Thomas points to the two men on the ground near a large black travelling trunk with chains wrapped around it. The chains are secured by a single sturdy-appearing padlock that a third guard is currently locking.

"Do I look convincing?" I ask, stuffing my pockets full with my portion of the weapons.

"Almost," he says, climbing up to the chimney and rubbing his hands along its inner walls. Climbing back down with a black hand, he liberally rubs them together and then along my cheeks, chin, and under my nose. I really wish I could have thought of a different plan now as my mind runs on about how terrible this must be for my skin. *This better wash off when we are safe or I'm going to go mad.*

"Okay, now you're ready," he says with a grin. I don't wait another second as I jump to the next roof that the men on the ground can't see and use the grappling hook to get to their level. *The sooner we get that case, the sooner I can get this soot off.* I hold the gun like the other policemen have been, on my hip, as I walk around the corner and towards the two men just beginning to lift the trunk.

"Oi, blokes, the captain sent a carriage for the trunk; it's coming around the corner any second. Hop to it!" I say, in the gruffest voice I can muster.

"We have orders to take it to the ship ourselves," one of the men replies.

"Now do you really think the governor would want you to

walk it there when it's more valuable than all three of you combined? And in a way that you could easily drop it? No, the carriage is coming around soon, now come on. Unless you want to explain to the governor and the captain why the precious cargo was the cause for their delay to see Her Majesty?" I say, turning away to the alley I just slipped out from.

"All right, all right, we be coming," I hear one of the men say before muttering something under his breath. I let out a slow breath as I wait for them to get closer. The doors to the warehouse are still wide open as the men inside are sweeping the place out for anyone or anything valuable that could be hidden. All the working lights are turned on, painting the building in a faint grey-blue haze. I keep my hat down low as we turn the corner of the building and head into the alley.

"You can put the cargo down since the carriage isn't here yet," I say, turning towards them. Once they do, I rest my stolen gun on the trunk, which is the signal for Thomas to do his part. I walk away a little from the corner as I see a small sphere sailing into the open warehouse doorway followed by another. When the first grenade goes off, enveloping the building in a blinding flash of light, I act as shaken as the other men. One officer takes the gun I laid down and immediately rounds the corner.

"You three, stay here and guard the box!" he says, popping his head back around the corner just before the second grenade goes off. I can see the red mist of tear gas float in the lamplight just outside the doors. Now it's my turn. I reach up my coat, where it looks like I have an itchy back, and put my weapon to my side. The officers on the opposite sides of the trunk look antsy to see what's happening as they hear their coworkers cry out from whatever they think the explosions were. I walk back to the front of the trunk where the lock is and look at one man, then the next. *Breathe in... breathe out.*

"Sorry, mates," I say, aiming the grappling hook at the officer chin who is furthest in the alley whilst plunging the tasing side of my brass knuckles in the other officer's neck. The first officer's eyes grow wide half a second before I pull the trigger.

I hastily pick the locks with my compact pins, and after a minute, Thomas is at my side, watching the corner in case anyone else comes upon us. I hear more men than just the ones crying out now, reinforcements have probably arrived to see what the explosions were about. Just then I hear the melodious click as all the tumblers mesh together, unlocking the lock. Taking off the lock and nearly tearing the lid off, I reach inside and grab the Fabergé egg whilst Thomas grabs the generator.

With what we came for in our hands, we book it to the lighthouse. As we run away, I catch a glimpse of the officer I shot with my hook and see how bloody and bruised his chin is as it begins to stain the snow. We run hard, not stopping for anything else left in the box; not when we hear shouts behind us, and not when I turn to see that we are being followed.

"This way!" Thomas calls, making a fast turn down a completely dark street. *Everyone really did try to attend the celebra-*

*tion in town, didn't they?* I haven't seen a soul except for the occasional homeless bum here and there since we began running. I can still hear the men at our heels though. No matter how many turns we make, they are still frighteningly close behind us. My lungs burn as hot as embers when I desperately reach to my back for my grappling hook but fail to find it. I suddenly think back to when I shot the policeman with my grappling hook; I dropped it in the snow to pick the lock on the trunk. And of course, I thought I'd remember to retrieve it before we left. I can't believe I left my extra grapple back at the house today.

"Thomas, do you have your grapple still?" I ask in huffs as we run.

"I can't remember; I think so." He's trying to keep up as we both carry the generator. I hastily reach into my hip pouch for something – anything – and grab hold of a grenade. Giving it a good-luck kiss, I pull the pin and drop it to the ground. *Please, God, let it be tear gas or something helpful.*

A bright bolt of light shines out behind us for several seconds. At first I think lightning has struck behind us, until I realise it was but a flash grenade. It did seem to help since we've been in the dark for so long; even the firework lights don't reach us very well. *A flash grenade would easily blind anyone in this darkness who's running straight at it. It should delay them long enough for them to lose our trail. I hope.*

Running through the dark streets of the outer district that's the farthest from the city makes me feel as if we are playing a part in that ghost story of Johnathan Blu--being tracked and hunted down by the angry villagers in the cold dark night. The sad part is that in our situation, we would probably have been seen as the band of thieves that run off in the night with stolen goods. Maybe that's why it feels like in every dark window we pass, there is someone inside aiming a gun or waiting for us to run by to attack us. We are seen as the bad guys for doing what we believe is right. *Maybe that's what the gypsy who stole Jonathan's fiancée felt as well: "She was my woman first,"* I think, sending a shiver down my spine.

The top of the lighthouse grows larger and larger as we near the end of the sea-washed side of town. I can hear the faint voices and footsteps of people behind us. I knew it was too good to be true to think we were in the clear. We make it to the lighthouse out of breath and out of sorts, crouching down to the ground at the lighthouse's base. And I attempt to regain my bearings, I start to survey the area. In the distance, at the bottom of the hill from where we are, where the town ends, I can see a small group of men and a dimie bot looking around--probably for us. I gaze out into the harbour to see a freight ship in its centre, travelling quickly to its opening where we are. *Aspen, and everyone else, is on that ship, I just know it.*

"Go, go up now! I'll stay down here to guard the door," I order Thomas.

"I can't just leave you here!" Thomas argues.

"Well, you are going to. You will be able to figure out how to use the lighthouse lens for the machine, I'm sure of it. I'll just slow you down. Now go quickly," I command, shoving him in the door as I notice the group coming towards us.

"Fine then, take this!" he shouts back, handing me a pistol; he must have taken it from one of the guards we knocked out. I watch him climb the stairs in haste. The moment I close the door behind him, the world around me seems to fall silent. I hear nothing the entire time the men come, not when we fight, or when the lighthouse spotlight fixates on the water. Only when I fire two warning shots do I finally hear again. But once I shoot, I hear more gunshots following mine in the distance.

# HELP, DEAR MOTHER

## ASPEN

*Even if we were to free ourselves we wouldn't get far,* I think to myself as I glance from left to right and see the guards fully armed with a gun in hand, hip knife, and baton stick in each of their belts. We sit and watch a line of dimies being brought out under the bright gas lamps. Governor Damon takes his time to look them over, picking out the sickly and ones with imperfections in their pelts from the group.

"Forward march!" he orders out.

A line of constables walk out, electric-blast shotguns in hand. Those guns are said to be as powerful as a bolt of lightning.

"Stop! Don't shoot, stop it!" I yell.

"Damon, stop this, you don't have to do this!" Keagan calls out.

"Silence, you thieves!" a guard barks at me, pointing a Tesla pistol straight at my face. Those pistols are just as powerful as the electric shotguns; however, it is even harder to control the flow of electricity. I give him a face just as their cries ring out before a line of shocks silences their screams.

My head turns back in time to watch the row of dimies fall limp on the wooden planks of the deck. A blood-freezing scream rings in the air, and it takes me a second to realise it belongs to my own tortured lungs. *My nightmares are becoming a reality.*

It takes a while for the dimie robots to collect the bodies and take them back below deck. Keagan nudges my head, and I look him in the eye to see he needs solace as much as I. I rest my forehead next to his, and to my amazement, our guards allow it. The governor decides to bring out the remaining dimies to watch the massacre as well.

"Since you know what will become of those with the best pelts, you can start saying your goodbyes now and give your final prayers. Think of this as my parting gift to you. But remember to thank who was responsible for bringing you here today: your glorious liberators, Keagan Myrack and Aspen Wolfe," the governor says in front of everyone with a flourish in his hand in our direction.

"Get ready," Keagan whispers to me as I watch Governor Damon talk privately to the captain of the guards. When he reaches the base of the staircase that leads to the upper deck, he waves goodbye to us, I just stare back, throwing knives at him in my head. As Damon walks up the metal staircase, a new line of dimies are brought out and chosen from again. Damon must be going to sleep in the captain's quarters. It is past midnight, and he will want to look presentable by the time the ship makes it to London.

Once he is out of sight, the captain of the guards will select the extensive row of dimies to dispose of. In the long line of dimies, I see two familiar faces: Nox and-

"Winona," Keagan says, seeing her in the firing group. He

acts as if he's frozen, unable to do anything as the men prepare their guns.

But before anyone can make another move, a glaring light illuminates all of us. Everyone looks away till the light jerkily moves down and into the water near the ship. There is something strange going on with the lighthouse's beam. I glance back and see the gunmen rubbing their eyes and looking out at the water where the light is resting some ways off. Confused, we all watch and wait a few seconds. The captain marches to the edge of the railing to see better, creating a momentary ceasefire as we wait.

I watch, along with everyone else, and see that there is a flickering image showing up through the light projection. Then, in a flash from the lighthouse's spotlight, the projection becomes a portal to the dimie's dimension. *Thomas and Lori got the message and pulled through after all!*

I lightly kick Keagan's leg, and he instantly snaps back to life, unlocking his shackles and passing me the key; I free myself in a second. Grabbing hold of his hand, and giving it a momentary squeeze, we hop into action. Keagan promptly attacks the guard on his right whilst I follow in suit. As I struggle to knock my keeper unconscious in a choke hold, I hear a thunderous explosion followed by broken glass and screams. I turn to prepare for the worst when I see that Keagan has destroyed many of the shotguns' glass containers that generate electricity inside the Tesla pistol.

I've heard the horror stories about the poor dimies who had to be the test subjects when shooting the broken guns. They were fried from the inside out when using a blaster with a shattered container. If those men shoot one with broken glass now, it would mean certain death for them and to those around. Unfortunately, two of the guards don't realise that important piece of information as they try to fire back at Keagan. Half the guards see this and attempt to run. The bolts of electricity shoot out in jagged live wires not from the barrel of the gun, but from the open electrical generator. The volts of energy wrap themselves around four men and a dimie nearby in a frenzy of light. After three seconds of continuous volts, the gun the man was firing explodes, throwing the bodies haphazardly around the deck.

Keagan jumps over the fallen, firing at the other men as he chases them. I turn my attention to the captain whose gun is already following Keagan's direction. Without a second to waste, I aim and fire the Tesla pistol in my hands. I miss him by an inch, but in the process I hit the pile of crates behind him, causing a domino effect of cargo crashing to the floor and piling on top of him. The captain loses his gun over the edge of the railing in the process as he tries to free himself.

I turn back to the bench we sat on and try to find the key. Finding it under the seat, I jump atop the boxes of fallen cargo for an announcement.

"There's your escape for home; now fight for it! Take it for your own tonight! And let no human stand in your way ever again!" I yell out to the crowd of dimies as I point to the portal projected on the water. As they cheer back, I bound down the crates and rush towards them to begin unlocking their shackles.

Only five are unlocked and wringing their wrists when Keagan reappears around the corner calling out, "Aspen! Bots and watchmen coming in fast!"

Before he even finishes his sentence, I hear the roar of a small army coming our way. And not a second after, the ship's alarm goes off, turning the bright lights flashing red. I hand the key to Winona, and she works fast to free her people. In the corner of my eye, I see a few dimies running off, probably to jump ship. Others, however, stand ready, picking up fallen pistols, wooden planks, anything they can get their hands on to fight a gang of bots and men coming our way. I turn and see Thatcher standing next to me with a broken metal pole raised and ready.

As the enemy turns the corner, we immediately rush back at them, roaring at the top of our lungs. Even dimies that are still chained up rush at the men, pounding at them with their fists and wrapping their chains around a few men's arms and necks.

Shots ring out in the night as the men slowly push their way through us. I see bots slicing dimies apart and wounding their own policemen by accident in the process, as well as dimies beating robots and men senseless with whatever they can. The fight breaks out in madness as I aim for another dimie bot about to slash three cornered dimies. As I fire my gun, an explosion erupts barely an inch from my eyes, sending me flying along with a few others around me. I land in a rough position against an unconscious policeman. Or perhaps he's already dead. Regardless, I feel a shooting pain trailing from my legs to the back of my skull.

Opening my eyes slowly, I see that I'm looking up the barrel of a shotgun to the dimie watchman taking aim. Out of the corner of my eye, I see another row boat full of dimies lowering themselves into the sea to go home. *At least they will be safe now.*

My assailant wears a grin on his face as he lowers the gun from my eyes to my chest. Fumbling my hand around the floor behind my back, I find something in the hand of the unconscious policeman I fell on. Hearing the gun click as a bullet enters the chamber, I whip out the object, hitting the barrel hard, and jump in the opposite direction before punching the man in the back of the head as hard as I can muster. Staggering a little, I look in my hand and see a long sharp knife with a metal handle. Giving the dazed man another hit on his head with the handle knocks him out cold instantly.

The ground is covered with fallen dimies, men, and torn pieces of robots. Yet, surrounded by it all, I feel nothing; as if my ability to feel is locked away, unaware of what's really happening. Behind an obstruction of cargo, I hear more fighting and gunshots. Grabbing the closest pistol I can find and tightening my grip on the knife, I make my way around the obstruction. This reminds me of the stories we would hear about the sea wars between Blackbeard's pirates and the queen's navy. Gunpowder, smoke, and the sharp scent of iron from blood fills the air. *I never envisioned it like this. The wars were always described to be so much more glorious, whilst this is so... gory,* I think to myself as I step over a pile of men lying in a pool of their own blood.

I turn the corner to see a few dimies still fighting off two more guards, whilst another group of dimies pile in the last rowboat. A few others still jump over the railing into the water to swim their way home. I notice then that I haven't seen Keagan for some time throughout the fighting. My heart races in the fear of the state I might find him in. I run out into the fighting, shooting down another robot before looking all around at the bodies on the ground and the men the dimies are still fighting. Then I see it...

The sound of metal clatters to the ground as I drop my knife and pistol and run my hands through my raggedy pinned up hair. My entire being is shaking and comes closer to the ground as I stare at the wooden planks below my feet, splattered in blood and oil. *This can't happen this way; it just can't! This wasn't supposed to happen like this. I could have prevented this, made things different in some way.* My mind screams at myself as I stare at my red and black hands.

Someone or something trips over my crouched form and falls flat on the floor, unmoving. This causes me to look back up, and I see that what I had hoped was just imaginary, was in fact true. Against the railing I watch Keagan slowly rocking back and forth on the ground, holding Winona tightly in his arms as she lies limp. The last bot on deck falls in front of me before a monkey dimie rips out its wiring on its neck. Running over the busted robot, I hear more splashes from the water below as more dimies escape. But the sound of sirens grows louder now. I turn my head in time to see another slew of guards and robots coming from the opposite side of the ship. I try to collect myself enough to speak the words *we need to leave now!*

Reaching Keagan, I get a better look at Winona; she looks almost peaceful as he hugs her tightly. Another form approaches us from my left: Thatcher. Before he even gets near Winona, he falls to his knees, reaching out to her with tears in his eyes.

"We were going to leave together, start a new life together. Now it's-it's all gone," he moans, finally reaching her. He just stares, appearing too afraid to touch her to make her death real. I hear the men closing in on us.

"Keagan…I know I'm asking the world of you right now, but we have to leave now, there are-"

"I won't! I can't! Aspen, help her, we can still save her life. We have to try!" Keagan shakes his disheveled grease-splattered head and turns to me in a state of desperation. I place two fingers on her neck and feel no life inside her. I notice the blood dripping from the back of her head and know all too well there is nothing anyone can do right now.

"She is with her kind again. She's gone. Now I'm sorry, but we can't wait any longer. We must jump now!" I say nervously, looking back at the men and robots climbing their way over the massacred bodies towards us.

"No, I-"

"Please!" I cry out, grabbing both of their attention as the sound of the men are yards away now.

"Please, I can't bear to lose you, too! I've made a mess of everything! Don't let me mess up this life with you as well!" I cry out, tears streaming down my face.

Keagan glances back at the men running towards us and extends his hand to me. I take it and turn to Thatcher, but he is not by Winona now.

"Ahh!" Thatcher roars out, running head on into the crowd of men with two pieces of wood.

"Thatcher!" Keagan calls out, holding on to me now.

"Go, go now!" he yells back, knocking out a guard with a plank. Seeing a trio of robots speeding towards us, we make a beeline for the railing.

Just as we make it over the edge, I feel a searing pain ripping through my back and shoulders. I cry out before we hit the skin of the water. Feeling the suffocating shock of its icy depth, I see bullets whizzing by in the water around us. *We need air!* Breaking the surface for a quick gasp of breath, once the air enters my lungs, I cry out from the fire that is emitting from my back. The bullets come dangerously close to us now as Keagan tries to pull us away amongst the few bodies that are floating around us.

As we try to swim away, however, we are abruptly pulled

back under the black water by some unseen force. In a panic I begin to thrash around. *We've come too far to be eaten by a sea monster!* But instead of toothy jaws, a soft paw quickly grabs my wrist. I open my eyes and make out an otter-like face just before being taken deep below the surface and pulled fast in the direction of the lighthouse. Keagan, alongside me, is being pulled by one as well. Every now and then we rise to the surface for air. Once we are close to the shore, we rise to the surface again.

"Thank you for everything," and "Yes, yet again," say two voices that I recognise.

"You're welcome, Jasper and Eli," Keagan says whilst I try to keep myself above the water. Keagan and I watch them swim off back to the portal for a moment. Then the shock of the cold water returns to my head, and we begin swimming towards the shore. Halfway there, Keagan has to pull me along. I can't help it though, there are stars dancing in front of my eyes and my vision begins to blur more and more the closer we get to land.

The moment we are able to stand in the water to walk to shore, I tumble over in the surf. Keagan has to help me the entire way to the beach. Trying my best to walk once we are on the sand, I can't seem to see straight and end up stumbling once more as the world spins. Just as my legs give out, Keagan catches me before I face-plant on the ground. As he grabs my upper back, I let out a scream from the sensation under my shoulder blades. *Did he just slice me or something?*

Jerking his hand away, he quickly lays me down on my stomach and touches my shoulders gently. I couldn't even fight him off if he had slashed me; I've never felt such exhaustion or pain. Everything hurts twice as bad as the night we stole the dimies from the Market.

"You're bleeding! One of the bots' hands must have cut you," I can hear him say.

"Mngh," is all I can make out as my mind and senses begin to slip away into a fuzzy darkness.

"Aspen! Keagan!" I hear a girl call out somewhere far away. *Wait, it's my baby sister, Lori. I want to see my pretty Lori bird.* I try to pick myself up but find my body on the sand once more. I seem to lack the strength to do anything but listen to my name being called. *I'm too cold to fall asleep in the sand,* I think as my body quivers like a baby's rattle. *Lori and I are supposed to go to London when the dimies are sent home. I'll fall asleep in London then, but we will be late for the train if we don't leave now.*

"London...train," I say as I feel three pairs of hands on my numbing body; one holding my hand, one on my shoulders, and the last brushing some grit off my face.

"Aspen, you must stay awake. Please, don't leave us!" I hear a man's voice call out in the distance as the faint shaking in my shoulders feels almost forced now. Then they all disappear along with the coldness of my body and the rough sand on the shore.

I find myself staring up from under the Aspen trees on our estate back home. Lori is a child again as she and Papa are running around chasing one another in the tall grass. Her light hair gleams in the warm sun as she runs as fast as her little legs can from Papa just before he catches her and begins to tickle her in the wildflowers.

"My little sapling," I hear my mother's voice say near me. I turn and see that I lay next to her as we swing in our favourite hammock. She begins to hum a lullaby as she holds me close.

I'm a child again, like Lori, as I see how the world looks so much larger than I remember. My mum begins to stroke my wavy hair as the lullaby ends on a soft note. I no longer feel exhaustion or pain. I don't even recall what happened before I came here.

"Can I stay here with you, Mum? It's nice and I feel happy here," I ask in a higher pitched voice than I'm used to.

"I'm happy here with you, too, my love. But you can only stay to rest for a spell. There are many still who need you, like your sister, that little boy, and the young man you care for so much."

"But...what about you?" I yawn out. My mother looks me in the eye dearly before she kisses my forehead.

"My little sapling, you needn't worry about me. I'm already safe and sound. But there are many who are not; there are dimies and humans alike who need someone like you. This is only the beginning, Aspen. But fear not, I will see you again," Mum says meaningfully with a voice as lovely as a song-bird...Just how she used to sound. As her image fades away in a bright light, I'm enveloped in a new warmth that cradles me to a dreamless sleep. My last thoughts of my mother resonate in my head just before I completely drift off into my dark subconscious.

*This is only the beginning.*

**For Reading My Book!**

I really appreciate hearing all of your feedback.

I need your input to make the next version of this book and my future books better. Every review matters, and it matters a *lot!*

Please take a minute to leave me an honest review on Amazon or wherever you purchased this book letting me know what you think of the book.

Or click this link for more exclusive book content such as:

- New secrets and stories
- Official art of the characters, maps and cities
- Aspen's inventions

Thanks so much!

Michelle R Young

ACKNOWLEDGEMENTS

Gear Heart started out as a dream I had in my high school senior year. I kept re-dreaming it and expanding the story's possibilities in my head for a year. It wasn't until I was on a trip in the Philippines that I realized "I've got to write this down!" Despite my disabilities I hand wrote the ten pages of content while I was there that turned into the first three chapters of the book.

Now flashback to when I was a kid, I was diagnosed with two learning disabilities that hindered my writing: dysgraphia and ADHD. I grew up hating to write anything for school or anything in general due to my disabilities. I was always thinking up poems and story ideas in my head, but never truly writing them down unless it was an assignment. Then Gear Heart came along.

I'd like to thank my parents for all the late nights of helping me write when I was a kid, and my friends who first looked at my scribbles for Gear Heart and encouraged me that it had potential. My first readers and beta readers: Katie Potter, Hannah Stanley, Abigail Meredith, Cassidy Tinsley, and

Katelynn Pizzio-- you women are incredible and are loved so much! I'm grateful for my wonderful family, for believing in me and supporting me during the whole process.

I cannot thank my wonderful launch team enough. I would not be where I am today without your awesome support: Valerie Trevino, Lauren Olvera, Sydney Symes, Kayla Painter, Ranee Mourlam, Alex Hudson, Jet Parker, Amanda Figueroa, Andrew Hudson, A.J. Hutchinson, Kat Lapatovich Healy, Lena Vorobets, Samantha Peacock, Jared Chapman, Kathleen Hudson, Cidell Rosipal, Brittany Parsons, Victoria Kamilar, Theresa Bello, Rachel Knowlton, Coral James, Shayla Alexander, Lauren Mayfeild, Rae Mojica, Beth Culpepper, Claire Randal, Savannah Rene, Chelsea Pigao, Rene Vrhovec, Deirdre Stokes, Tricia Toole, Tricia Griffin, Hannah Miner, Gracie Lopez, Julia Dragolich, Erin Gilliatte, Michael Collum, Faith Upton, Lauren Reed, Hannah Diaz, Emily Brand, Chase Brand, Darby Woods, Rhonda Grosser, Mackenzie Luttrell, Carter Hannah, Mike Bessette, Lance Martin, Andrea Bessette, Preston Young, Dalene Young, Pierce Young, Malley Nelson, Leslie Wilson, Regina Cummings, Kara Burton Barr, Sam Rice, Stephanie Van Den Heuvel, Isabella Venegoni, Amber Wagshal, Chris Erler, Alli Hydeman, Gwen Murphy, Cassie Larsen, Jim Lewis, Jayme Deville, Jessica Cosgrove, Alexis Besch, Sara Hinkle-Morrison, Kerri Klentzman, Victoria Wykoff, Adrian Murphy, Raini Polk, Kayley Ryan, Tiara Koren, Margaret Whitaker, Chuy, Rachel Hugo, Anissa Howell, Rachel Connor, Deja Terry

# ABOUT THE AUTHOR

Michelle Young is an artist, writer and social media specialist that helps businesses with their networks. When she isn't writing, she can be found painting, hanging out with her friends, or simply marveling at nature. Texas born and bred, she has a positive outlook on life and where God has planned for her next. You can see more of her creations and stay tuned for her next book by visiting her and our heroes at www.Mypureart.com/

facebook.com/Mypureartshop

twitter.com/MichelleRYoung2

instagram.com/michelleryoung_author

amazon.com/author/michelleryoung

pinterest.com/michelley0961

tiktok.com/@michelleryoung1

patreon.com/mypureart

# DISCLAIMER

*Disclaimer: Gear Heart is a work of fiction. Names, characters, businesses, places, events, locales, and incidents are either the products of the author's imagination or used in a fictitious manner. Any resemblance to actual persons, living or dead, or actual events is purely coincidental or twisted for the purpose of the different fictitious world the characters live in.

SELF- PUBLISHING SCHOOL

NOW IT'S YOUR TURN
Discover the **EXACT 3-step blueprint you need to become
a bestselling author in as little as 3 months.**

Self-Publishing School helped me, and now I want them
to help
you with this FREE resource to begin outlining your book!

Even if you're busy, bad at writing, or don't know where to
start,
you CAN write a bestseller and build your best life.

With tools and experience across a variety of niches and
professions,
Self-Publishing School is the only resource you need to
take your book to the finish line!
Say "YES" to becoming a bestseller:

https://self-publishingschool.com/friend/

Follow the steps on the page to get a FREE resource to get started on your book and unlock a discount to get started with Self-Publishing School

www.ingramcontent.com/pod-product-compliance
Lightning Source LLC
Chambersburg PA
CBHW030829110726
47900CB00006B/1814